Painting

a novel by
Tom Gillespie

"I could not stop reading. With a fascinating subject matter and a surprising journey, Painting by Numbers is a stunningly clever and mesmerising read that will keep you enthralled to the very last page."
Alison Wells, author

"[Gillespie]... is the new Dan Brown with a splash of John Grisham. I couldn't put it down." 10/10
Minxemoo Reviews

"An absolutely thrilling thriller. When they coined the phrase 'This book is a real page turner', they were talking about 'Painting By Numbers' "
S & J Book Shelf Reviews

"a story that had me thinking. Even after I'd finished it, I had to go back and read parts of it again. I was completely fascinated... "
The eBook Review

Discover us online:
www.crookedcatpublishing.com

Join us on facebook:
www.facebook.com/crookedcatpublishing

To Jeni

The Author

Tom Gillespie was born and grew up in a small town just outside Glasgow. After completing a Masters in English at Glasgow University, he spent the next ten years pursuing a musical career as a singer/songwriter, playing, recording and touring the UK and Europe with his band. He now lives in Bath with his wife, daughter and hyper-neurotic cat, where he works at the University as an academic English lecturer.

Tom writes long and short fiction. A number of his stories are published by www.eastoftheweb.com. He is also a regular contributor to fridayflash.org.

Tom's writing has been described as terse, minimalist, hyper-realistic and ambiguous, where layers of meaning are conveyed using a concise and economical style. He enjoys dark, edgy psychological dramas that explore the trials of modern life, and the often surreal complexities of the human mind.

Painting by Numbers is his first novel. He is currently working on his second, along with a collection of short stories.

Acknowledgement

My thanks to

Patrick Ismond
Priscilla Morris
Dr. Fynn Scheben
Tim and Trina Ratcliffe
Maureen Vincent-Northam
Helen Howell and
Laurence and Steph at Crooked Cat Publishing

for their support, encouragement and unflinching honesty

Love and gratitude to you all

Tom Gillespie
Bath, October 2012

Painting By Numbers

In the dark, the painting remains motionless, silent, expectant. But when the morning sun glistens through the skylight windows of the gallery, the surface begins to move, slowly at first, but then with increasing purpose and urgency. The minutiae of the moment gather together and spill out across the canvas. The colours assimilate and align. The geometry calibrates to exact specifications. Objects and players assemble at their marked positions. Every motif and emblem returns to its designated space within the frame. The gilded wooden border creaks as the flow of paint pushes against the joints. Then the cracks and blemishes of age race across the reformed arena, and like the memory of water, the network of predetermined patterns follow hidden and mysterious pathways, scattering, dividing and multiplying as they rush to complete their journey. At last, the painting is one. It sinks back into the wall and settles on the three brass hooks that hold it in place. Soon the attendants will arrive to take up their daylight vigil. The doors will swing open, the ambient air temperature will be checked and regulated, and he will come to sit and look and wonder.

PART I

The Loss of Innocence

Jacob inserted the key in the narrow socket and turned it anti-clockwise until the pendulum started to swing. He carefully reset the hands to exactly twenty-three minutes to nine and when he was sure that the mechanism was willing to maintain its own momentum, he closed the glass casement, buttoned up his coat and left the flat. He caught the number six to Argyle Street and then the underground to Kelvinbank. From there it was a short walk across the river to the city gallery. As he approached the entrance, a uniformed attendant was removing the steel security bar from the front door. He held it open and Jacob squeezed through. Inside, he passed his coat and bag to the cloakroom assistant. She studied his expression.

"Are you all right, Jacob? You don't look well today."

"I'm fine."

She handed him a ticket and he ascended the grand staircase directly opposite. On the second floor, he entered the Baroque Room. He walked to the end and sat down facing the painting. The lights on the ceiling were too bright. They produced an artificial glare and the resultant surface sheen obscured some of the detail. But Jacob had found the perfect spot, exactly three inches from the end of the bench, to sit and contemplate the vast mystery of the canvas. He took out his notebook and flicked the page corners until he located the last entry. He glanced around to see if anyone else had come in but the room was still vacant. He liked this time in the morning. It never lasted very long, but for a brief, tantalizing moment, he was alone with his painting, with no distractions, no other eyes or minds removing ideas from the great work that loomed over him. He fumbled in his shirt pocket for a pencil, licked the end and wrote down the date at the top of a fresh page. Now he was ready to look.

The painting was large, twelve feet by eight, and was hung in a vulgarly elaborate gold frame. An adolescent girl was standing on the left hand side of a mahogany panelled room. She was in formal dress. Cream and gold flowing garments covered pale skin. The cloth was heavily embroidered in an ornate pattern of floral swirls and loops, her face pallid with a slight hint of crimson around the cheek bones. She was leaning against a full-length mirror with a similarly ornate border, the back of her head revealed in the reflection. In her left hand, she was holding what appeared to be a leather-bound book, with the words Poemas de M– inscribed on the cover, her fingers obscuring the rest of the title. There was a small table to her immediate right with a wineglass balanced on the edge. Her right arm was extended and her forefinger was touching the rim. On the far left, a panelled door was slightly ajar. A hand gripped the edge and an indistinct shadowy figure was peering through the gap directly at the girl, the eyeballs painted in an intense brilliant white that stood out against an impenetrable black background. Reflected in the mirror and on the right, a courtier was kneeling on the floor. He was also in formal attire, a crimson sleeveless tunic over a white flannel shirt, puffed up three quarter length breeches and mud-splattered boots. Against the rear wall, a blazing fire illuminated the room. There appeared to be papers burning amongst the flames. The entire scene was shrouded in a creamy yellow haze that gave it a dreamlike quality.

For the last three days Jacob had been working on the area between and immediately surrounding two letters, D and V which were just visible on the neck of a dead pheasant laid out next to the girl's feet. He drew a line with his eye from the top right hand corner of the letter V to the leg of the table. He then measured the actual distance with a small reel of thread, carefully avoiding any contact with the surface. He calculated a relative distance of three feet, twenty-one point three inches. This matched an earlier reading he had taken from the knuckle of the courtier's left hand to the outside edge of the girl's dress. It also corresponded to the distance from the tip of the girl's extended right index finger to the floor. He entered the data and returned his attention to the small space between the two letters. He was about to extend the spool again when he noticed a tiny blemish on the down stroke of the V. Part of it was missing, as though it had faded or flaked off. He scribbled the observation in his pad and put it down on the bench. By now a few people had come in and were shuffling around. He stretched and looked at his watch; twenty to twelve. Over three hours had passed. He put the cotton reel and ruler in his bag and went downstairs to the café.

***

He pointed at the counter and the girl picked out a plate of sandwiches.

"Did you say tuna?" the girl asked.

"Mm."

She handed him four triangles of soft white bread, crusts removed, neatly stacked together, with a thin layer of fish paste, barely visible between the slices.

"Drink?"

"Coffee. Black, one sugar."

While she prepared it, he opened up each sandwich and picked the cucumber out. "What shall I do with this?"

The girl turned and looked at his outstretched hand. She shook her head and collected the gluey mass from his palm. He wiped the residue on his trousers and waited by the till.

"I don't like them either. It's an overrated vegetable, don't you think?" she said, placing the cup and saucer in front of him.

He handed her a ten-pound note and the till drawer sprung open.

"Trouble is they're in everything aren't they?"

"What?"

"Cucumber – sandwiches, salads – what's that Greek thing?"

"Tsatsiki?"

"That's it. Tsatsiki's loaded with the stuff. Disgusting. They are strange though, you know what I mean? Are they a vegetable or are they a fruit?" She picked at the slimy residue on her fingers. "Look, seeds. That means they must be a fruit, but they aren't, are they?"

"Can I have my change?"

"Oh sorry. Why are we so obsessed with them? Is it the weather?"

He placed the cup and plate on a tray and found a table in the corner. Opening his notebook, he examined some of his most recent entries. He flicked back four or five pages and scanned previous calculations and deductions, following a logical path to the last result. Although he had unravelled and unpicked a sizable portion of the work, he was far from finished. The damaged letter puzzled him. The missing fragments had created yet another complex set of variables that he couldn't explain. Perhaps it was the result of its age or some form of camouflage that the painter had employed to confuse and mystify. Or it could be that the letter was still intact, but he just couldn't see it. He turned to an empty page and in the top left corner he wrote,

Poemas De M– Who?

"Hello."

He looked up. It was one of the gallery attendants.

"My boss Bob says I should say hello." The attendant looked fresh-faced and a little flustered. He was trying to squint at the pad.

"Hello," said Jacob. "Why do you have to say hello to me?"

"Bob says you're in here that often you might as well be one of us, so – oh, my name's Ian, by the way."

"Hello Ian. Are you new?"

"Yes, I started yesterday. Are you an art teacher or something?" He squinted at Jacob's notebook. "Is that your er… lecture notes or–?" He glanced up to his left. There was a security camera pointing directly down at them from the ceiling.

"See for yourself." Jacob handed him the book.

"What's this? What are all these numbers?"

"They are to do with one of the paintings upstairs."

"The one that you're studying?"

"That's right."

"So the numbers are like some kind of calculations?"

"Yes."

"How?"

"How what?"

"How do they–? What are you calculating?"

"Well, these here, for example, relate to three different types of pigment."

The attendant looked at him, his mouth hanging open.

"Colours."

"Huh?"

"Well, 38 represents taupe."

"Top?"

"Taupe, light brown."

"Oh right." His mouth started to pull down at the edges. "So it's a bit like painting by numbers?"

"Something like that, I suppose."

"And what about this long list down here? What's all that about then?" His eyes flicked back to the camera.

"Look, Ian, what's going on?"

The attendant turned back.

"Nothing, nothing's going on. I'm just curious, you know?"

"Curious."

"We're all interested."

"Who is 'all'?"

"All of the lads here. We're all interested. You know?"

"Really?"

"Oh yes."

Jacob dropped the coffee cup down on the saucer. The clatter resounded around the café and a few of the patrons glanced up from their newspapers and cream teas. He stood up and the attendant shifted his footing. There was a long pause while the boy tried to decipher Jacob's body language. Finally Jacob broke the silence.

"You know what, Ian," he said, leaning into the attendant's face, "tell your pals up there," he pointed at the ceiling, "curiosity killed the cat." The attendant grimaced and returned the notebook.

"Sorry. I didn't mean to offend."

Jacob gathered up his things and pushed past him. As he left the cafeteria he looked back and saw the assistant pick up his empty cup and put the rim to his nose. Back at the painting, Jacob tried to gather his thoughts and find the spot he had left. But the assistant's behaviour had unsettled him and he scratched his head in frustration. It was no use. He'd have to start again tomorrow.

When he got home, the flat was empty. He found a small handwritten note on the kitchen table.

Got tired of waiting
Out with Rhona
Dinner in oven
Don't choke on it
Don't wait up
E

He pulled the lukewarm casserole out of the oven and sat down to eat. As he picked at the dehydrated remains, the cat appeared and rubbed itself against his leg. He bent down to stroke its back, pulling at its tail gently. It purred and went over to its bowl by the fridge. He got up and searched the cupboards for food, but he couldn't find any so he scooped out a portion of dried remains from his plate and dropped it into the cat's bowl. The cat sniffed at it for a few seconds, turned up its nose and began to whine.

"I don't have anything else," he said, pulling its tail again. "It's your mother's fault." The cat complained again and jumped up on to the worktop. He opened the window and it disappeared out onto the roof terrace. A cool breeze blew in. Jacob stretched and searching for his cigarettes, he unlocked the terrace door. The cat had now climbed up onto the roof and was making its way towards its favourite chimney stack about three doors down. Jacob sat on the step and lit a cigarette. His hand shook as he blew out the match. It had been over six months now and, although he felt he was close to the breakthrough he was looking for, the intensity of his research was taking its toll. From the beginning, his department had been dismissive and the Dean had categorically refused to grant him a sabbatical. He felt alone and isolated, grappling with something unsupported, just out of his reach. He inhaled the smoke deep into his lungs, held it there for a few seconds and then blew the thick cloud high into the air. He watched the cat as it scurried round the chimney pot, sat down on top of the apex of the roof and studied the street scene below. He finished his cigarette and went back into the flat.

In his study, he booted up the computer and started to transfer the day's findings to his documents file. When he was almost complete, he clicked on the sub-folder marked history, and re-examined his notes.

In the course of his investigations, Jacob had uncovered a multitude of theories and suppositions about the painting. It was an enigma that had baffled art historians for many years. It was thought to be Spanish, completed some time between 1631 and 1642, and indeed x-ray and carbon dating confirmed this to be the case. But no tangible evidence of its existence emerged until the latter part of the 19th Century when it was recovered, smoke damaged but intact, from a house fire in Nimbes, a small village in the Languedoc region of Southern France. Town Hall records revealed that it had been owned by a Monsieur Heddon, a local magistrate, but that he had inexplicably refused to reclaim it. The local council took possession and after almost ten years of languishing in a basement storeroom, it was finally auctioned off to a private collector from Paris. It was during this period, that it most likely acquired the title La Perde de L'Innocence – The Loss of Innocence. It was bought and sold a further three times until finally, in 1923, a mystery benefactor donated it to the City Art Gallery.

The artist was unknown, although following further restorative work, the initials D and V were revealed on the neck of the dead pheasant, elegantly laid out by the girl's feet. This discovery prompted historians to speculate that it was the work of Diego Velázquez, Spain's most celebrated Baroque artist. He was certainly a possible candidate, a theory that the gallery was keen to promote. The colours, the use of light and shadow, the realistic setting and the strange manipulation of perspective seemed consistent with his style and approach. But Jacob wasn't convinced. Velázquez was renowned for allegorical painting, work that was highly complex and layered with hidden meaning. To simply paint his initials on the side of a dead bird was somewhat implausible. Also, little was known about Velázquez's personal life beyond 1630, so it was very difficult to substantiate or refute any of the prevalent theories. And it didn't explain its discovery in France. Jacob believed it was more likely that it was the work of an almost unknown artist called Manuel Piñero. Records suggest that Piñero had been a student and understudy of Velázquez, and for a short period had assisted him on a number of commissions, but biographical details of the man were hard to come by and a great deal of fog surrounded his life. In fact, some critics had even questioned his relationship with Velázquez at all. Jacob's research, however, had uncovered a number of consistencies in style between the Glasgow painting and two or three other compositions attributed to Piñero.

The characters in the scene had also generated a great deal of controversy and possible further links to Velázquez. Some scholars believed that the girl belonged to an ancient aristocratic dynasty from northern Italy, and that the painting contained hidden references to a number of Renaissance paintings. It was true that Velázquez had travelled extensively, visiting both Belgium and Italy, and that a vast spectrum of historic and contemporary allegorical artists had influenced his work. However, the link was tenuous. Another theory was that the girl was, in fact, his niece. Velázquez would frequently use his own family and friends as models, and a girl, allegedly his niece, appears in his most famous work, 'Las Meninas'. But Jacob couldn't see the resemblance. He therefore believed that the girl was a fiction, an imagined beauty. As for the courtier, he was also highly problematic and again may have been a deliberate fabrication, devised by the artist to draw the viewer in: to speculate and mythologize the apparent profundity of the work.

Rubbing his eyes, he closed the documents file and opened his email. He scrolled down though pages of unread messages, mostly from his department secretary, until he spotted an email from a gallery in Seville. He opened it up and scanned the message, translating and skipping over unfamiliar lexis:

Dr Boyce,
Thank you for your enquiry. We have one small lithograph by the artist Manuel Piñero... The work is untitled but is believed to date from between 1628 and 1632 and forms part of a collection of sketches and outlines

*made by the artist in preparation for a larger composition
that was allegedly destroyed by the artist on completion... A
second related sketch is currently in storage at El Prado,
Madrid... I have attached a jpeg image of the work I hope
you find this information helpful.*

Kind regards,
Dr. Maria Agustina Sarmiento
Curator
Museo de Antiguedades y Arte
Sevilla

He clicked on the attachment and the image filled the
screen. The drawing was of a young woman holding what
appeared to be a partially opened fan. Though she looked a little
older than the central figure in The Loss of Innocence, her
features were very similar. Using the mouse, he zoomed in on
her face but the image became over pixelated and lost definition.
He saved it to his research file and shut down his computer.
Opening the top drawer of his desk, he fumbled around until he
found a postcard print of the painting. He liked to keep notes
on cards as well as on disks as it helped him store the
information systematically and logically in his head. He copied
the figures and calculations onto the back of the card, careful to
cite readings accurately. He turned it over and looked at the
painting again. It was a study of the left hand portion of the
work. The courtier was missing from the scene and the girl's
glance towards him now seemed different. Her emotional state
was altered in some way. The look of fear had transformed into
one of vague indignation or disgust. He shook his head, put the
card in the drawer and went to bed.

***

He heard her come in around one, keys rattling in the lock
followed moments later by a loud clatter as she knocked

something over in the kitchen. She pushed open the bedroom door and it hit the wall with a loud thud. He lay still and listened to her grunts as she grappled with the complexity of undressing in the dark. Finally, she slumped down with a sigh on her side of the bed.

"Did you have a good night?" he asked.

"Did you enjoy your meal?" she slurred.

It was too late for an argument. He touched her back as she dropped her nightgown over her shoulders. She slid in next to him, rested her head on his arm and mumbled something.

"What was that?" He nudged her. But she was already asleep, her throat vibrating gently. He turned on his side to escape the smell of alcohol and cigarette smoke and concentrated on his own breathing.

When he woke, she had already left for work. In the kitchen, he poured a coffee and lit up a cigarette. She hated him smoking in the flat but she'd gone so what the hell, he thought. He searched for an ashtray and on the worktop, he discovered a small scrap of paper with the date 23rd September written neatly in the centre. It wasn't in her handwriting. He glanced over at the calendar on the wall. September 23rd. He stared at the numbers, hoping something would pop into his head.

After a while, he put the paper back where he'd found it and poured himself another coffee.

Jacob shifted position on the bench. He was too far right. He moved three quarters of an inch to his left and found his line. He took out his pad and began working again. The letter V, although apparently incomplete, appeared to sit at an angle that drew the eye towards the girl's right hand.

The hand was the first element of the mystery he had worked on, gathering notes and investigating a variety of scholarly theories and arguments. It was held at an unusual angle with the small finger tucked under the palm, the two middle fingers tight together and the forefinger pointing down to the floor. Allegorical artists had often used hands to convey secret messages and hidden truths. The folded finger could indicate a religious reference or a coded signal to another artist, and the two together may allude to the holy trinity, the crucifixion or piety of God. But it was the forefinger, twisted to a near impossible angle that seemed to point directly towards the letter.

He got up and measured the distance. As he approached the surface, a left handed triangle began to appear, from the fingertip to the letter, up to the left eye of the dark intruder peering through the door, and finally back to the girl's hand. He grabbed his bag and rummaged around until he found a blank postcard. He plotted the three lines of the triangle. Then from the corners he drew another line to the middle of each side. Where the lines intersected in the centre, they crossed directly over a silver candlestick on the floor by the fireplace.

Jacob stood back to take in the whole painting. The triangle now seemed an obvious and deliberate design choice. As he moved slowly back towards the surface, the holder remained lifelike and remarkably accurate. The flames of the fire glistened on the silver surface and crimson coloured wax had formed a solid puddle around the base. He could just make out a tiny thread of grey smoke swirling from the top of the wick. And there was something else, on the base, inside the sheen of the metal, a reflection. He couldn't be sure without a magnifying glass, but it looked like a face, blurred and indistinct. He screwed up his eyes to see if any familiar shape or feature would form but the reflection remained undefined. He pulled his head back and the image seemed to fade and blend with the surface of the holder. Tone and colour shifted slightly as he moved away. He glanced up at the gallery lights. Perhaps they were causing a distortion, an optical illusion.

He returned to the bench. A girl was sitting on the other side, with her back to him. He turned his head slightly and he could just see her shoulder, pale and delicate skin, partially covered by a loose fitting strapped top. Her breathing was laboured, her small frame moving gently up and down. He

18

opened his notepad but he could hear her throat click as she inhaled. Every few seconds she sniffed and wiped her nose with the end of her finger. Jacob fumbled in his coat for a handkerchief but his pockets were empty.

She stood up and disappeared behind him. He wanted to turn but knew that the movement would draw attention to him so he waited to see if she would move back into view. A few seconds passed. She reappeared to his left. She was kneeling down by the side of the painting opposite, examining some detail in the bottom corner. She was in her mid twenties, looking to him to be a bit frail and unkempt. Her hair was dark, tied back in a ponytail but a few strands had escaped and curled up around her ears. He noticed a small bald patch, a triangular area of bare skin, to the left of her crown. Its smooth whiteness stood out against the black of her hair.

She had a canvas bag over her shoulder that was adorned with a collection of badges of various shapes and sizes. He leaned over to try and read the words on a small triangular-shaped plate that glistened under the gallery lights, but he was too far away. She sat back on her knees and sighed. Jacob looked away, afraid that she might spot him leering. He waited a moment and looked again, but she had gone. He glanced around the gallery. A few people were milling about, gazing vacantly at the artwork. His notebook fell on the floor and as he reached down to pick it up, something flickered across his face. In the painting, the surface of the candleholder stood out, bright and gleaming against the deep set black of the mahogany panelling. He licked the end of his pencil and continued his work.

The Glasgow Hum

The flat was cold and dark when he got home. He hung up his coat and bag and checked the clock. As the pendulum swung backwards and forwards, the mechanism echoed reassuringly down the hall. He looked into the bedroom and he could just make out Ella's shape under the eiderdown. He peered at the swollen mound for a few seconds and when he was sure that it was gently rising and falling, he carried on to the kitchen. He opened the fridge and checked the contents. There was still nothing to eat but he spotted a half empty pack of beers lying in the bottom drawer. He pulled out a bottle and popped the top. Sitting down at the kitchen table, he sipped the beer slowly and closed his eyes. A scratching noise at the window made him turn. The cat was outside, pawing at the glass. He pulled at the heavy sash and it hopped in.

"Let's see if we have anything for you this evening," he said, pulling its tail affectionately. In the cupboard, he found an opened foil of food. He scooped out the remaining portion into the cat's bowl and it gulped at the contents, purring contentedly. He opened the door of the terrace and sat down on the step with his beer.

The hum had returned. It was a low pitched indistinct drone that seemed to begin around midnight and go on until just before dawn. For months, residents in the East End had been complaining about it, saying that it was causing all sorts of medical and psychological disturbances. The council received a number of angry letters, and the story had even made the papers and the local TV news. Noise abatement officers had been out a few times to the area with measuring devices, but they had failed to locate the source, as the hum seemed to elude measurement or electronic detection. The other strange thing about the phenomenon was that not everyone could hear it. The pitch was such that, ironically, only people with poor hearing could pick up the subsonic rhythmical vibrations the hum generated in the atmosphere.

But despite the local hostility to the drone, Jacob liked it. He found it soothing and reassuring. When he focused on the ebb and flow of its gentle reverberations, it slowed his heart rate and calmed the galloping thoughts in his head. Tonight, it seemed slightly louder with an additional melodious tone buried somewhere within the heart of the sound. He hummed along quietly, trying to match the pitch and after a moment, the cat brushed against his leg and joined in, whining along in disharmony. He smiled and sipped his beer.

"You're a good singer," he said, flicking at its ears with his finger. The cat swiped its paw at him playfully, then leaping onto the wall, clambered over the roof until it reached its usual position perched on top of the apex of number 23. A sound behind him made him turn.

"Are you coming to bed?" Ella was standing over him in the doorway, her face crumpled with sleep.

He stood up and leaned over to kiss her but she turned away and disappeared into the toilet. He finished his beer, locked the roof terrace door and switched everything off. When he got to the bedroom, she was back under the eiderdown. He removed his clothes, put on his pyjamas and slid in next to her.

"You're freezing," she said, inching away from him.

He lay on his back and focused on the hum. He imagined the sound vibrating the oxygen molecules inside the room, each atomic particle spinning gently and knocking into its nearest neighbour; a great underground machine generating thousands of tiny resonating spheres spilling out from a fissure in the

Earth's surface and combining to form a grand unified symphony of harmonious movement. He closed his eyes and dropped instantly into a deep, restless sleep.

***

He was running through the oil thick darkness of night, skimming the surface of the Earth with his toes, careering over wasted ground and dereliction. He stumbled and then, regaining his momentum, he raced onwards, the ground sucking at his legs, trying to slow him down. A half moon appeared, and ahead of him he could see the tall spikes of a large wrought iron gate. He accelerated forward and threw his body at the frame. The ancient hinges screeched as the gate flew open. The hum was deafening now, a deep thunderous roar accompanied by an ear splitting scream like the hysterical wails of a child. He held his hands to his ears as he ran but the hum was inside his head, vibrating the plates of his skull and rattling his teeth together. Fumbling and falling again, he reached a point he thought must be the epicentre. The rubble and mess cleared and a space opened up ahead of him.

As he approached, he could see a large spherical hole, its widening circumference disappearing into the darkness beyond. He stopped, and the soles of his feet touched down onto the dirt. He moved towards the edge and peered into the blackness. He inched closer and his left foot slipped over. Pulling back from the brink, his heel dislodged a protruding rock and it fell into the void. As it disappeared, the pulsating throb of the hum paused for a fraction of a second, but then resumed its relentless, demented mantra. As he turned to look for another projectile, he felt something grip his left ankle. Instinctively, he pulled back but the object tightened and began dragging him towards the hole. He grasped at it and tried to pull it off, but it coiled tighter still, cutting off the flow of blood to his foot. He sat down on the edge of the precipice and fumbled around for something to dislodge it.

Just under the surface of the dirt, his fingers located something hard and sharp. He prized a thin metal blade out of the ground and raising it above his head he thrust it with force into the invisible object beneath him. But as the point of the blade penetrated the thick leathery membrane of the sentient manacle, he was wrenched violently towards the waiting chasm. He snatched at the parched desiccated earth as his body was dragged over the side. First his legs, up to his waist, and then finally his whole body tumbled over.

He was falling now, backwards and head first, spinning uncontrollably into the darkness. The faint light on the surface quickly receded and within seconds it had vanished. He felt a sharp piercing pain in his spine between his shoulder blades. There was something alive, flapping wildly behind his head. The screaming had now reached a crescendo of disharmony. His body began to spasm and a searing heat raced up through his legs, into his chest and around his skull. His body twisted and contorted in agony as jet-black flames began to consume his skin and flesh. He prayed for the end to come but still his body continued to fall.

Soon, his existence was all but obliterated and nothing remained of him but a lifeless, blackened carcass tumbling forever downwards into the infinite abyss.

Verlaine & Rimbaud

He woke up disorientated, his pyjamas drenched in sweat. He reached over for Ella but she wasn't there. It was light. He looked at the clock. 7.43 am. Stumbling out of bed, he went to look for her. She was in the kitchen, getting ready for work. She was frantically moving from one side of the room to the other, taking a bite of toast while inserting, removing and then re-inserting papers into her briefcase.

"I'm late," she said, gulping on a mug of coffee. She picked up her keys and pushed past him. Fumbling for a moment with the door lock, she stopped and turned to him.

"You're going in today, aren't you?" she said.

"Yes," he replied, through a prolonged yawn.

"Promise me, Jacob." She frowned at him.

"I will."

He went to give her a farewell kiss but she was out the door before he could reach her. He returned to the kitchen and looked for his cigarettes.

When he arrived at the museum, he found the doors bolted shut. A small handwritten note attached to the inside of the glass read,

Closed for staff training. Open at 1.00 p.m.

He'd forgotten it was Friday. He turned around and looked back down the steps into the world. It was raining and the streets beyond were deserted. He followed the path around the side of the building and left the grounds by the rear gate. He found himself at one end of an elegant tree-lined avenue. He hadn't been this way in years and even in the rain the simplicity of its design had a surprising clarity about it. The leaves were beginning to change colour and some lay scattered on the grass. He started walking and stopped by an old fountain on a grass verge. It was one of those municipal indulgences installed in the Victorian era and was rather worse for wear. On top was a broken statuette of a girl holding an urn and presumably water once poured out of its spout. One of her arms was missing and her face had lost a few features. The pool below was full of wet decomposing leaves and mould. Yet, despite all of its flaws, Jacob found it quite beautiful. On the side, there was a small inscription in Latin.

In vita nos peto tripudium verum.

He carried on towards the river. The rain was getting heavier but he was too preoccupied to notice. When he reached the bridge he stretched over the side and looked down into the murky water. The Clyde was flowing fast, and appeared almost glutinous. Various bits of debris and rubbish floated past, an old tree stump, plastic shopping bags and polystyrene packaging. The traffic behind him had come to a standstill. From a van opposite, a man shouted to him.

"Yer no plannin oan jumpin in, ur ye?"

Jacob turned round and waved reassuringly, but then returned his attention to the mass of water flowing beneath him. He watched its progress as it cut through the city and disappeared behind a group of factory buildings. Crossing the bridge, he continued walking until he reached a few shops. There was a delicatessen full of Italian delights, a pokey little haberdashery, an off licence, and beneath that, in the basement, a second hand bookshop. He walked past, but then changed his mind. He descended the stairs and tried the door. It was locked, but there was a small bell to the right of the handle. He pulled the knob and a distant tinkling sounded somewhere at the back of the shop. He waited but no one came. He rang the bell again. Still no one. He was about to return to the street when the door suddenly opened. An old man stood in the doorway. He was holding a sandwich with crumbs clinging to his unshaven chin, and he had what looked like a long dribble of egg yolk on his cardigan.

"Sorry about the door, I'm having an early lunch. I don't usually lock it. It's just that we had some trouble last week with the off licence. It's not ideal."

He ushered Jacob in. The shop was gloomy and warm. There were books everywhere spilling out of shelves, onto tables and gathering in great mounds on the floor. Each bookcase was labelled with titles such as Fiction, Philosophy, Military History and Existentialism, but a great many had escaped their categorical prison camps and invaded the territory of neighbouring genres. It was clear that at one time the shop had catered for the nearby university but it was highly unlikely that any student today would know of its existence. Jacob took off his coat and shook it gently. The man approached.

"Would you like me to take that? I'll hang it up for you."

Jacob handed him his sodden coat and suddenly felt as though he was in someone's private living space.

"Do you want something to dry yourself with?" the man asked.

"No, I'll be fine." Jacob wiped his face dry with the back of his hand.

The man disappeared and Jacob picked up a book from a pile immediately to his right. *The Secret Lives of Robert Burns*. He looked up to see if it corresponded with the category on the nearest shelf, *Human Biology*. Near enough, he thought. He put it down and moved on. Negotiating his way between teetering columns of moth-eaten literature, he picked up another and then another. Then he came to *Art History*. The makeshift paper label had curled at one edge, as though attempting to disengage and flee from the oak frame. It read *Art Hi*. Scanning the shelves for anything of interest, he was about to pick out a book when the man returned.

"Are you looking for anything in particular?"

"Do you have any books on the Baroque period?" Jacob said, unsure if he wanted the man to know what he was doing.

"I have a number of excellent titles concerning the Baroque period. Which school are you interested in?" 'the man continued.

Jacob looked at him. "Spanish."

"Ah, I see you are a man with discerning tastes. In my mind, the Spanish School is perhaps the most, how shall I put it," he paused for a moment to consider his words, "exemplary of the entire period. I'm sure there are a few reference books buried away somewhere." He glanced around his shop. "Someday I'll have time to sort everything out. But there is one book that I think you may be interested in." He went into a small room at the rear of the shop. Jacob could hear him rummaging around and muttering to himself. Finally, he reappeared clutching a small paperback.

"In my view, this is *the* definitive critique of Spanish Baroque painting. Jacob took the book and 'glanced down at the faded cover.

"*El Arte de la Alegoría,* 1426 - 1640. By P. Manuelo, I can't say I've heard of him."

But the bookkeeper wasn't listening; he was preoccupied with the front of his cardigan. He'd spotted the egg stain and was busy trying to pick the remains of the yolk out of one of the button holes.

"Oh dear, what a disaster I am today." He flicked the dislodged crumbs onto the floor. "Manuelo was one of the foremost art historians of the 19th Century. I tell you what, why don't you take the book anyway. I'm sure you'll find it invaluable." Turning the book over, Jacob scanned through the blurb on the back. There were a number of recommendations from other critics and a quote, presumably from the writer. It read,

It is now clear to me that the intention of all allegorical artists is to mislead, manipulate and deceive.

"Definitive, you say?" Jacob said.

"Yes, at one time, but what with modern investigative techniques, x-ray and the like, and the dreaded P.M."

"P.M.?"

He pursed his lips and whispered: "Post-Modernism. Some of his theories have been disproved, and of course, historians love to create jobs for themselves so they have a tendency to – how shall I put it?"

"Re-write history?"

"Exactly. No, I think you will find that the core of his work remains an indispensable research aid. Are you a student or—"

"Well, yes, kind of."

"We offer a ten percent discount on all books purchased. And for University staff members."

"How did you know that I worked at the University?"

"Well, I've been running this bookshop for forty-three years. You get to know people a bit. You start to develop a sixth sense about these things. And you are wearing academic's shoes," he added.

Jacob studied his loafers for a second. "Really? Are we that predictable?"

"I'm afraid so."

Jacob turned the book over again. "I was actually looking for something by the art critic Zillinger. I'm doing some research on allegorical art."

"Well, Zillinger is of course an undergraduate favourite but you strike me as someone who has moved onto a higher level of study." He leaned in closer to Jacob and lowered his voice again. "Students these days, they steal absolutely everything, like magpies they are. I'm not a betting man but if I were I'd lay my

28

life savings on the certainty that the entire works of Zillinger have been plagiarised time and again in thousands of lifeless regurgitated essays and assignments.

"No, Manuelo is the one for you, a forgotten genius, the one who made it possible for the likes of Zillinger to flourish." He took the book from Jacob. "You see, Manuelo was an exponent of the law of empirical wisdom. He was the one who rediscovered the map, laid the signposts, showed all future scholars the way. I am sure you will find this book in-dis-pens-able." He tapped out the syllables on the cover.

Jacob was beginning to feel uneasy. In the months he'd been working on the painting, he'd never come across a P. Manuelo or a law of empirical wisdom.

"It's very strange," Jacob said, "I'm not acquainted with either of them. What was it about?"

"Well, I'm no art scholar but it's something to do with observational truth, the relationship between what can be seen and the actualities of reality. Manuelo believed that by looking at and observing a represented object or person, it becomes real, and in a painting, both the artist and the viewer instil some form of truth in these represented objects. Or is it the other way round? I'm sorry, it has been quite some time since I read it, so my précis may be a little confused. I think, basically it's about the marriage of two belief systems, mathematical truth and spiritual belief, or to put it another way, a marriage of order and organised chaos, if you like." He smiled.

Jacob flicked through the book and when he reached the glossary, he ran his finger down the list until he came to the entry for empirical wisdom. Strangely, the definition had been heavily crossed out and, underneath the blackened section, there was what appeared to be a short mathematical equation handwritten in small neat letters.

$V = mP^3$

Jacob closed the book. "So when did Manuelo come up with this theory of Empirical–?"

But the man was at the counter and was ringing it up on an old mechanical till. Jacob handed him the book and he dropped it into a small paper bag.

"That'll be £6.39 which includes your ten percent discount plus a little more for wear and tear."

It seemed a little expensive considering the state it was in but Jacob felt too embarrassed to refuse. Perhaps it would be a useful addition to his research. Or the man was simply a crafty salesman, a highly unlikely deduction considering the surroundings and his appearance. The man helped Jacob back into his coat.

"I hope you find what you're looking for."

"Thank you," said Jacob, unsure what he was thanking the man for. As he was leaving the shop, the man called out, "Don't forget," and tapped his waistcoat. Back on the street, Jacob could feel the book in his coat. It fitted snugly into the contours of his breast pocket. He looked at his watch. It was a quarter to twelve.

***

Mrs Skinner jumped up from behind her desk as Jacob walked through the reception.

"Oh, Dr. Boyce."

Jacob ignored her and carried on down the corridor towards his office. She caught up with him as he reached his door.

"Dr. Boyce. It's good to see you. Is everything OK?"

"Fine."

"It's just that Professor Colby would like to talk to you and there's quite a bit of mail waiting for you in your pigeonhole."

Jacob turned to her.

"Oh," she said, stepping back from him slightly.

"What sort of mail?"

"Well, there's quite a bit, and your assignments that need to be marked." Jacob fumbled with his keys.

"The deadline was some time ago," she added.

He unlocked the door, stepped in and closed it quickly behind him. He could hear her muttering something on the other side and then she said loudly,

"Shall I tell the Professor that you'll pop by to see him later then?"

After a few moments more, he could hear her retreating back up the corridor, her heels clacking on the hard stone floor. He glanced round his office. The room was in chaos. Papers were strewn all over the carpet, cabinet drawers were half open with debris spewing out, and his desk was stacked with piles of assignments, overdue library books and the mouldy remains of a lunch. Negotiating the debris, he opened a window to let out the reek of stale smoke and rotting food.

He sat down and unpicked the half-eaten sandwich from the surface of his desk and dropped it in the overflowing bin next to his foot. He pulled at one of the drawers under the desk but it was jammed. Levering it backwards and forwards, it finally gave and flew open, sending more papers and postcards cascading down into his lap. He searched around until he located the university staff contact book and flicked through until he reached the mathematics department. Running his finger down the list he stopped at a name he recognised. 'Prof. J. Napier. West 4.21.' The Professor was renowned for his ground breaking work in the 70s on optical geometry but was also apparently somewhat of an authority on the history and development of mathematics. So he might be able to shed some light on the law of empirical wisdom. He was about to pick up the phone to call the switchboard when it started ringing. He hesitated for a moment, fearing a long tedious conversation with his Dean. But after a few more rings he changed his mind.

"Hello?" he said.

There was no response.

"Hello?" he repeated.

There was a faint click and the line went dead. He put it down and it rang once more.

"Hello!"

Again, there was no reply but this time he thought he could hear someone breathing on the other end.

"Who is this?"

The breathing paused for a second and then continued again.

"Is there anyone there?" He pressed the phone to his ear and he could just make out a faint wheeze or rasp in the breath.

"I'm going to hang up if you don't speak."

Suddenly, the line screeched and Jacob pulled the handset away from his ear, but when he listened again, the line was dead. He slammed the phone down in anger, quickly scribbled a note of the Professor's number and left his office.

Napier's Bones

"He may be at lunch; shall I ring through for you?" the departmental receptionist said, picking up the phone on her desk.

"No, that's OK, I'll check myself."

She pointed down the hall and told him to take the lift to the fourth floor. Professor Napier's office was tucked away at the end of a long dreary corridor. Jacob tapped the door gently but there was no reply. He tried again, this time with a little more force.

"Come in," a voice replied from the other side.

Jacob opened the door slowly and peered inside. In complete contrast to the apocalyptic horror of his own office, Napier's was Spartan and immaculately clean. There was a large antique mahogany bureau by the window, a couple of overfull boxes on the floor alongside a large anglepoise lamp. The Professor was kneeling down, rifling through the contents of one of the boxes. When he saw Jacob, he stood up. He was exceptionally tall with flame-red hair and matching beard, and was wearing a 50's style tweed suit complete with a bright green tartan bow tie.

"Excuse me, Professor Napier, I'm Dr. Boyce from Earth Sciences. I was wondering if I could have a word."

"It'll have to be only one, I'm afraid." The Professor spoke with a strong Morningside brogue. "As you can see I'm on the move."

"Where are you going?"

"Home. It's the first day of the rest of my life. I'm now

officially retired."

"Oh. Congratulations."

"That's not a word I would use to describe it."

"Right," Jacob said, awkwardly.

"Beheaded."

"Sorry?"

"Surplus to departmental requirements and all that," the Professor continued. "What did you say you are studying?"

"No, sorry, I'm not a student. I teach Earth Science over in West building."

"Ah, a rare pleasure, it's not often we see you guys over here." He approached Jacob and shook his hand. "Aren't you all supposed to be rather," he paused to consider his choice of words, "phobic when it comes to mathematics?"

"Not quite."

"So, bearing in mind that I am waiting for my wife to come to take me away, so to speak, how can I help you?"

"I wonder if you knew anything about a mathematical theory or principle called the Law of Empirical Wisdom?"

The Professor stared at him for a moment and then smiled.

"If you pardon the expression, but why on earth are you interested in such an obscure mathematical theory?"

"It's just part of a research paper I am working on."

"What field of Earth Science are you in, Dr. Boyce?"

"Plate tectonics and seismology. I'm involved in a project to improve prediction rates for plate movements around the world."

"And your enquiry relates how?"

"My research is a little more tangential." Jacob was beginning to feel a little irritated. He wanted a straight answer but the Professor seemed reluctant to elucidate.

"Clearly," the Professor said. "Could you explain a little more?"

"Well, I've been studying a painting that I believe may contain or demonstrate a unique mathematical formula."

"Hold on, you said a painting?" the Professor interrupted.

"Yes."

"Aha, now I see the link."

"The link?"

"Please do continue," the Professor said, ignoring Jacob's question.

"—some kind of configuration that may help to predict apparent random movements in plate alignments and the subsequent earthquakes and seismic activity that follow." It wasn't entirely true but he thought it best to keep it simple.

"A painting indeed, fascinating." Jacob wasn't sure if the Professor was being sarcastic. "Which one?"

"It's a Baroque composition in the City Art Gallery down the road."

"What a fabulous premise. So you think this painting has hidden treasures waiting to be discovered?"

"Something like that."

"Well, the 17th Century, and of course, the Renaissance as a whole was a magnificent era for science, creative arts and invention," the Professor continued, "but mathematics in particular, was going through some of its own remarkable and revolutionary transformations. Radical theories and pioneering mathematical concepts were springing up all over Europe. There were so many important figures during that time – Wallis and his work on integral calculus and the infinite series, the modern binary system established by Leibnitz, Fermat's research into analytical geometry and the founding of probability theory. Not forgetting Descartes, Bernoulli and Newton. And if all that concentrated genius wasn't enough, there was also a whole gamut of groundbreaking and important inventions that would throw open the doors of mathematical possibility."

"Such as?" Jacob asked, interrupting the Professor's impromptu lecture.

"Well, a good example is Napier's Bones, which could be described as one of the world's first complex multiplication

35

devices."

"Any relation?" Jacob interrupted again.

"Indeed." The Professor nodded. "I believe I'm a cousin nine times removed, or something like that. Napier came up with a clever device where numbers were engraved on animal bone or some other suitable material, and by placing them in a specific order, elaborate and surprisingly accurate multiplication became possible. In effect, he invented the first semi-portable calculator, though perhaps a little more gruesome."

"And Empirical Wisdom?" Jacob shifted his weight from one foot to the other.

"The Law of Empirical Wisdom is a rather obscure and strange theorem that first appeared in the 12th Century but didn't find certain popularity until the Renaissance period."

"Why was that?"

"I think it was because it draws on ideas that were fashionable at the time, metaphysics, ontology, cosmology, optical geometrics and even a little bit of creationism. It results in something that's a bit of a mess and a little odd to say the least."

"What do you mean?"

"Well, it got bogged down in rather too much hokum involving astrological mysticism, universal design and, frankly, ridiculous claims about predetermination and fate. The law was inspired in many ways by Fibonacci's pioneering work on number sequencing and of course, Pacioli's definition of The Golden Ratio. But it was an obscure 17th Century Italian mathematician and philosopher called Celino Celini who masterminded the formulation of a more mature and all-encompassing version of the theory. Have you come across him?"

"No." Jacob replied.

"I'm not surprised. His life and work are one of the great neglected riddles of science. Celini came up with something called Codex Umbino."

"What?"

"The name is a nod to Da Vinci's great treatise on painting, Codex Urbinas."

Jacob shook his head.

"Let me show you." The Professor went over to a blackboard that stretched across the entire width of the rear wall and retrieved a small stick of chalk from the tray below. He scribbled out a long formula, commenting as he wrote. He stopped once or twice and made some alterations and corrections to the sequence. "I think this is it. This is the bare bone structure of Codex Umbino," he said, his hand hovering over the last section.

Jacob followed the sequence as it weaved across the wall. "But that looks more like particle physics than mathematics."

"I suppose Codex Umbino could be described as a first stab at a theory of everything," the Professor replied.

"You mean Quantum Electron Dynamics, but that's ridiculous."

"Why?"

"Oh, come on, Professor. Celini lived at least 350 years before the discovery of the atom. How could he possibly have known about the existence of atomic particles?"

"Of course you are right, and indeed your disbelief is understandable, but despite the obvious technological limitations, Celini had what you might call an obsessive interest in the microscopic details of life and the spaces in between things, as it were. So in a philosophical and a mathematical sense at least, his mind was working at a molecular level."

"But I still don't understand how he could." Jacob shook his head again.

"Celini spent most of his adult life dissecting animals, birds mainly, measuring and recording wingspans and the constituent parts of feathers and quills." The Professor pulled at the bristles of his beard, picking and twisting individual hairs as he spoke. "Over the years, he systematically analysed and catalogued the dimensions and geometric calibrations of thousands of wings. He studied their shape, the intricacies of feather design, geometrical relationships, even their colours and optical properties. And from his lists, he applied Fibonaccian logic and came up with an elaborate mathematical formula that he thought not only explained why birds fly but also provided what he believed to be proof of a universal order or the blueprint, as it were."

"Angel's wings."

"Exactly, but he wasn't satisfied with the Fibonacci solution."

"Why was that?"

"Some of his measurements and calculations didn't quite fit the golden number theory. There were tiny inexplicable imperfections in the formula that he couldn't explain. He believed that there was some other missing force or measurement involved in the design of the feathers and their interaction during the process of flight. He became fixated on the areas around and between the quills and the minutiae of tissue structure. Over the years, he carried on modifying, adding to and adapting his theory until finally he formulated The Law of Empirical Wisdom."

"So how do we get to quantum mechanics?" Jacob asked.

"I suppose this is the strangest part of the story and perhaps the most relevant to you," the Professor said. "As his obsession deepened, he began to create what he believed were visual representations of his law in painting and drawing. He produced vast canvases of bizarre human-bird like hybrids along with complex diagrams that he claimed encapsulated the law. Every element of his bizarre creations he considered intrinsic and vital, from the consistency and chemical composition of paint, the choice of pigments, the type of fabric used in the canvas, geometrical relationships and perspective, the interplay of light and shade, even the brush strokes and hand movements of the artist and the emotional response of the observer—"

"What?" Jacob interrupted.

"Well, yes." The Professor nodded. "He believed that the act of observation generated what he described as a newly created and interdependent life force that contributed to the formulation of the universal order."

"The observer effect?"

"Or the uncertainty principle, depending on how you look at it." The Professor smiled at his unintentional joke. Celini believed that the act of observation and the subsequent response could generate a type of energy, and when this combined with each of the other key elements in the codex, the collective life force could literally inhabit solid objects, vibrate their essence and render them alive or, as Celini defined it, architecturally divine.

"You mean, his paintings could move?"

"That is what he believed. For whatever reason, perhaps by accident, Celini had somehow stumbled on the rudiments of atomic and quantum dynamic theory, a recognition of the interactive relationships of matter, light, space and time."

"I don't get it," Jacob said. "Why would someone with such groundbreaking ideas—"

"Be forgotten?" the Professor interrupted.

"It doesn't make any sense."

"I think his absence from the mathematical timelines may be the consequence of what happened to him."

"What do you mean?"

"The further Celini pursued his ideas, the more he seemed to antagonise the Church."

"But why, surely he was trying to prove the existence of God?"

"You might think that but The Vatican in the 17th Century was not entirely keen on science or any of its practitioners attempting to unpick the mysteries of God's great master plan. No, they viewed Celini's work as a profanation and a threat to the established religious order."

"Not much changed there then?" Jacob quipped.

39

"Alongside that, according to Vatican records, he was also involved in strange goings on."

"Like what?"

"All that was recorded was the phrase 'dark activity' but there are no records of what that actually means."

"So what happened to him?"

"Eventually the Church got its way and he was tried for heresy and sentenced to death."

"Jesus." Jacob shook his head.

"I don't think Jesus had anything to do with it," the Professor said. "Much of his life work was destroyed, his reputation was deliberately and systematically undermined, and the Law of Empirical Wisdom conveniently faded into almost complete obscurity.

"So how do you know so much about him then?"

"Well," the Professor smiled, "I suppose I'm what you'd call a champion of lost causes." He paused for a moment and added, "I've always been fascinated by the neglected and the condemned martyrs of science. I think there's still a tremendous amount we can learn from their tireless, some might even say demented, pursuit of," he paused for a moment, "not so much the truth, but an understanding of the unexplained. Celini may have been as mad as a March hare but he still made, what I believe to be, a significant contribution to the field of mathematics, and trailblazers like him should always be remembered and celebrated."

"Absolutely." Jacob nodded.

"There's something else though that might account for his relative obscurity," the Professor said, glancing back at the blackboard.

"What's that?"

"Look at the formula again. Can you see anything unusual about it?"

"You mean apart from the fact that it looks like 20th Century quantum mechanics?"

40

"The last sequence in particular," the Professor added.

Jacob followed the flow of numbers and symbols across the board again, but when he reached the solution, he began to sense that the sequence wasn't quite working logically. "Is there a part missing?" he asked.

"Removed," the Professor said. "There is a significant link in the chain that clearly must have been removed after the formula had been devised.

"But how do you know something's been taken out rather than simply not worked through properly?"

"It would have been impossible to construct the formula beyond the missing section, here and here." The Professor circled two parts of the formula. "And then within the solution, here, there just has to be some additional part, otherwise it doesn't make any sense. The two terms have to occupy the same space but they don't. There is no symmetry. Do you understand that?"

"I think so. You mean the formula has been tampered with."

"Or vandalised."

"Do you think it was the Church?"

"No one is quite sure. Some of Celini's notebooks were discovered at the end of the 19th Century, in Madrid of all places."

"But why there, when he lived and worked in Rome?" Jacob interrupted.

"Perhaps they were stolen or smuggled out of Italy to avoid falling into the hands of the Vatican. But a number of pages containing significant calculations and footnotes were either defaced or torn out of the books. So to this day the complete formula remains a tantalizingly unresolved puzzle."

"Have you tried to solve it?"

"Many have tried, myself included," the Professor smiled, "but it is a frustratingly difficult and complex conundrum." He turned to Jacob and added, "but how all of that relates to your painting and plate tectonics, I'm really not sure. I hope I haven't

41

confused you."

"No not at all. You've been extremely helpful."

"Who is the artist?" the Professor asked, returning to his box on the floor.

"You mean of The Loss of Innocence?"

"Is that what your painting is called?"

Jacob nodded.

"Interesting."

"Why?"

"Celini believed that his law would enable man to finally see the world through God's eyes, rather than those of a child. And the artist?" he asked again.

"Unknown, though some critics believe that it could be a Velázquez. But my money's on a lesser-known Spanish artist called Manuel Piñero."

"Aha, a Spanish connection. The plot thickens."

"So do you think there's a possibility that Celini's theories could have influenced the Spanish School?"

"I've no idea, I'm afraid, but I would say one thing though."

"What's that?"

"Although the codex is obviously incomplete, one characteristic is quite simple to identify, in his paintings at least. In the few that survived the Vatican's vandalism, Celini's use of three dimensional geometrics is quite unique."

"In what way?"

"Well, superficially his use of vanishing points doesn't make mathematical sense."

"I don't get you."

"Look, I'll show you." The Professor knelt down by one of the boxes and after a moment of searching, removed a small notepad. Setting it down on his desk, he flicked through until he found a blank page. He then checked his pockets for a pen. "Ok," he said, staring at the paper, and then he continued, "If you examine the orthogonal lines that he used to create the perspective within his compositions, they don't quite converge at the designated horizon points that he has set." He drew two elongated arches across the page and Jacob leaned over to the desk to get a better look. "There is always at least one stray orthogonal that appears to bend outwards and continue into its own separate vanishing point, like so." He repeated the same design beneath, but this time inverting the curve to try and illustrate his explanation.

"You mean a curvilinear line?" Jacob said, following the Professor's hand as he completed his rough sketch.

"It's similar, but unlike a curvilinear line, it is the painting that seems to bend rather than the line itself, and this clever optical trickery can generate a slightly disorientating sensation for the observer, when the eye shifts from one orthogonal or transversal line to the other."

"You mean the Mona Lisa effect?"

"Precisely. A mathematically generated illusion that hoodwinks the eye into believing that a portion of an image has shifted or moved." He turned back to Jacob. "So if your Spanish painting exhibits this peculiar characteristic, then there is a possibility of a link with Celini's law."

"Are you familiar with the equation $V = mP^3$?" Jacob asked.

The Professor thought for a moment and then said, "I can't say I am. Where did you come across that?"

"I have a book," Jacob said, searching his pockets. But before he could remove it, there was a knock at the door.

"That'll be my wife," the Professor said. "Come in."

A grey haired woman popped her head round the door.

"Are you ready?" she said, impatiently. "I've been waiting downstairs for over twenty minutes. The car is on a double yellow line." Then she spotted Jacob. "Oh, sorry, I didn't see you there."

"Muriel, this is Dr. Boyce. It is entirely his fault that I am late," the Professor said, winking at Jacob.

"Yes," Jacob responded. "I'm so sorry."

"Not at all, Dr. Boyce," she said, stepping into the room. She

43

had a metal calliper strapped to her left leg and was leaning heavily on a walking stick.

"Can I help you carry anything down to your car, Professor?" Jacob offered, now feeling rather guilty.

"No, that won't be necessary," the Professor smiled.

"John, let the Doctor help you. I can't carry anything."

"It's no trouble," Jacob said.

"Well, if you have time and you don't mind. Could you take the one over there." He pointed at the largest box.

Jacob bent down and attempted to lift it up but it wouldn't move.

"Don't worry," the Professor said, "you take the other one."

"Lead the way," Jacob said, following the Professor and his wife out the door. On the way down to the car, Jacob glanced inside the box. It contained a number of books and papers, and a few items of stationery. On top, there was a black and white photograph of a group of formally dressed men outside the entrance to an equally formal building. It must have been taken in the 1950s but Jacob realised that the Professor's attire hadn't changed much.

"It was my first day," the Professor said. "See if you can spot me."

Jacob scanned the line of faces until he came to a young bearded man in the back row wearing a bow tie and grinning broadly.

"Is that you up there?" He pointed with his nose.

"A picture of innocence," the Professor said, smiling to himself.

When they reached the car, Jacob deposited the box on the back seat and the Professor's wife got into the driving seat.

"I'll just pop up for the remainder, dear," the Professor said to his wife.

"Well, hurry, otherwise we'll get a ticket," she replied, adding, "I forgot my disabled badge."

"I'm sure they'd let you off," Jacob said, trying to reassure her.

Before he left, the Professor turned to Jacob. "Well, good luck with your research, Dr. Boyce. I hope you find what you are looking for."

"And good luck to you too," Jacob said, shaking his hand.

"Goodbye, Jacob," he said, holding on to Jacob's hand a moment longer. Then as he walked back towards the department entrance, he stopped in the doorway and shouted, "Lost causes, remember!"

Jacob waved and the Professor disappeared into the building. He said his farewells to the Professor's wife and looked at his watch. It was just past lunchtime. He made his way through the campus and as he cut across the West Quadrangle, he noticed a girl on the far side. She was walking quickly with her bag tucked tightly under her arm. She seemed to be hugging the side of the building, following the edge of the narrow pathway along the wall. When she reached the end of the Quad, she made a sudden and unnatural 90 degree turn and carried on along the outer perimeter. As she neared him, Jacob realised it was the girl from the gallery. She continued past him and made a second right-angled turn at the next corner. Finally, at the end of her great loop around the square, she stopped opposite the history building, and then, after lingering in the doorway for a moment or two, she stepped inside. Jacob carried on across the quadrangle and out into the noise and bustle of the West End.

Café Berolli

He found a seat in the corner of the café and hung his coat on the chair. After a few moments, the waitress approached and he ordered a large coffee. Removing his notebook, he began to annotate some of the figures he had scribbled down earlier. When the waitress returned with his drink, he sipped it slowly and flicked the pages backwards and forwards, looking for any indications of Celini's law. On a fresh page, he copied down a series of equations and formulae and was about to rework them when a voice interrupted him.

"Hello stranger."

Jacob looked up. It was Martin Griffiths, one of his colleagues from the department.

"Shit," Jacob muttered under his breath. "Hi Martin," he said. "How are you?"

"How are you, more like? Where the hell have you been?" his colleague asked, moving towards the vacant chair on the other side of the table.

"Researching," Jacob said abruptly.

"You're not still working on that painting of yours, are you?"

"Mm." Jacob sipped his coffee.

"Christ, man. Colby thinks you're taking the piss."

"Colby can think what he likes."

"Have you seen him recently?"

"No."

"Jesus, Jacob," Martin said, leaning in closer, "he's fucking pissed off with you. He's threatening all sorts. You need to go and talk to him. Calm him down."

"I've got nothing to say to him."

"He's furious though, Jacob. He could sack you."

"It's his loss." Jacob was beginning to get agitated. "Look, Martin, I'm kind of busy at the moment."

"He's serious, Jacob. He could have you out in a week."

"As I say," Jacob repeated.

"How's Ella?" Martin persisted.

Jacob looked up. "Fine, why?"

"It must have been a terrible thing to deal with?"

"It was, but now she's doing OK."

Martin paused for a moment. "She called me, you know."

"When?"

"A couple of weeks ago, maybe three."

"Why, what for, what did she say?" Jacob asked.

"She said that she was worrying about you and if I knew anything she didn't?"

"Like what?"

"You know."

"I don't know."

"If—" He paused again.

"Oh come on, spit it out."

"If you were seeing anyone."

"Oh, for fuck's sake." Jacob sneered and dropped his coffee cup down with a clatter.

"I wouldn't have told her anyway, but are you?"

"Do you honestly think I'd tell the most indiscrete man in Glasgow if I were having an affair? So who the hell does she think it is this time?"

"I don't know. She didn't say, but you can't really blame her. She said that she never sees you and there was that time before."

"That was years ago and, anyway, I never had an affair. I didn't even touch the girl, for fuck's sake."

"You thought about it though, didn't you?"

"I can't believe she would call you before talking to me,"

Jacob said, ignoring Martin's question.

"We're friends, Jacob. We've known each other a long time. We were in Chile together, remember?"

"How could I forget. A love that daren't speak its name."

"Oh don't be stupid."

"You have always had a thing about Ella," Jacob said. "You've been after her for years."

"Look, I'm sorry I told you. She didn't mean anything by talking to me. She is worrying about you. We all are. We can't afford to lose your expertise." Martin put his hand down on the table in front of Jacob. "Please, Jacob, stop this nonsense with the painting and come back to work. Our research has stalled and we desperately need your input."

Jacob sat back in his chair and took another sip of coffee.

"Well, don't say I didn't warn you. I hope you find what you're looking for, Jacob, I really do." He stood up. "I must say your efforts are admirable, I'll give you that – insane maybe but admirable."

Jacob stared into his empty cup, willing him to leave.

"Speak to Ella, OK?"

"I thought that was your role," Jacob snapped back.

Martin shook his head and picked up his bag.

"She's been through enough, Jacob. Don't make it worse for her." When Jacob was sure that he'd gone, he called over the waitress and ordered another coffee.

***

It was after four when he finally made it to the museum. The cloakroom attendant smiled as he deposited his coat.

"Late today, Jacob?"

"Things to do," he replied.

Upstairs, the gallery was busy. A group of kids from one of the local primary schools were visiting. They were running around laughing and shouting, excited to be out of the classroom. A few were in the corner rummaging through large tea chests stuffed full of period costumes. The teacher was doing her best to control them as they tried on various items of clothing. On the other side, a row of tables had been set up with paper, sketchpads and crayons, and a couple of kids were quietly drawing and colouring in. Jacob sat down on his bench and shuffled left and right until he thought he'd found the correct position. He opened his bag and removed his notebook and reel of thread. Focusing on the triangle he had discovered yesterday, he allowed the lines to re-emerge and the image to settle in his mind's eye. But before he could begin his work, a boy sat down next to him.

"I'm drawing your picture," the boy said.

"What?" Jacob looked down at the boy who was wearing a sea green waistcoat and matching three quarter length breeches, his long dark hair curling down over his face, obscuring most of his features.

"It's a competition. Do you want to see?" The boy held up an A3 sheet of paper. It was a rough, simplistic interpretation of the scene, but the boy had managed to capture the essence of the shapes and colours. Jacob thought it was rather good and it reminded him of a Picasso.

"Why is the girl sad?" Jacob asked.

"She's not sad, she's angry."

"She's doesn't look angry in the painting."

"Yes, she is." The boy shook his head.

The boy's version of the side table next to the girl was significantly larger than the original, covering nearly a quarter of the entire composition. The glass was falling, with cartoon streaks to indicate rapid movement.

"What's that there?" Jacob asked, pointing at a crudely drawn object resting on the table top.

"The murder weapon!" The boy sneered, and raising a clenched fist, he jabbed himself in the neck three times and then toppled to the floor, writhing and hollering, feigning a fatal

49

blow. His teacher dropped what she was doing and ran over.

"What have you done to him?" She scowled at Jacob.

"I haven't done anything," Jacob protested.

The boy screamed louder and clutched at his throat. The teacher knelt down to attend to him, but after a moment or two, she realised what was going on and bundled the boy briskly to his feet. Continuing his pantomime performance, he staggered over to his classmates and they all huddled together giggling and nudging each other. The teacher roared at them and then turned back to apologise to Jacob.

"They've such vivid imaginations at this age," she said, trying to play down her error.

"Long may it continue," he said, smiling at her. She picked up the boy's artwork and returned to her class. As she told them off again and shouted out a few more instructions, the boy turned back to Jacob, drew his finger across his throat and then followed his teacher and classmates into the next gallery.

The room fell silent and Jacob tried to refocus on the painting again but the incident had unsettled his thoughts. He got up and approached the painting to examine the side table in more detail. He scanned the configuration of pigments and brush strokes of its surface, but apart from the goblet resting precariously on the edge, the table top was bare. He returned to the bench and waited for his concentration to return.

After some minutes, the isosceles triangle finally reappeared, diagonal lines once again criss-crossing the centre of the candleholder and the distinct outline of the face re-emerging out of the reflected sheen on the base. The hardened wax obscured a section of the image, but there was enough for Jacob to make out the faint pink and white of a cheek and the dark of an eye socket.

From his bag he removed a small protractor, and measured the angle of intersection of lines at the centre of the candleholder base. He then checked the angles around the edge of the triangle and both sets were identical, 71° by 31° by 31°.

Each measurement was exactly 1° short of a Fibonaccian triangle. He stepped back to double check, and as he pulled away, a second, a third and then a fourth triangle appeared within the first. Within seconds, more triangles began to emerge from the surrounding area, lines traversing and crisscrossing until finally overwhelming the canvas in a complex mosaic of geometric shapes and patterns. As Jacob rubbed his eyes, the yellow sheen on the surface of the candleholder suddenly erupted, sending rays of white light out across the gallery. He looked up at the skylight window but it was still a rain-smeared dreary day outside. A single beam shot straight from the centre of the base into his left eye, searing through the iris and exploding on the back of his retina. Jacob snapped his eyes shut, but the light continued to flare inside his head. He stumbled backwards onto the bench and, grasping frantically at the leather surface, tried to steady himself, but his body continued to sway uncontrollably. The muscles around his stomach began to spasm and he held his hand up to his mouth to try and quell an increasing urge to vomit. He felt someone grab his arm and he opened his eyes.

"Are you all right, Jacob?" An attendant was leaning over him, steadying his rocking body.

"I'm not sure," Jacob said grimacing.

"You look as though you need to go home."

"I think you might be right," Jacob said, attempting to stand.

"Hold on." The attendant pushed him back down. "You need to give yourself a couple of minutes."

"I'll be fine. I just need something to eat."

The attendant looked at him for a moment and said, "A couple of minutes, OK?"

The attendant returned to his seat by the entrance, glancing back a couple of time to check that Jacob was all right.

Jacob straightened himself on the bench and glanced round the gallery. A couple of visitors were staring at him but when

51

they saw him looking, each returned to their prospective art works. Jacob wiped a line of sweat from his forehead and pulled his jacket straight. When he felt suitably recovered, he collected up his belongings which lay scattered around the bench and moved towards the exit. The attendant smiled at him.

"Are you OK now, Jacob?"

"I'll be fine, nothing a beer wouldn't cure."

As he left the gallery, Jacob looked back at the painting. The patterns had vanished and the candlestick holder had returned to its normal hue. But from the doorway, the reflected face in the base now appeared to be smiling.

Ella's Dream

When he got home, he could hear Ella moving around in the kitchen. She had spread out piles of photographs and cards on the table and was flicking through them as though she was looking for something.

"What are you doing?" Jacob asked, removing his coat.

"God, are you OK?" Ella said, turning to him.

"I'm fine."

"You don't look fine."

"It's just a bit of a whisky rush. I stopped at the pub on the way home."

"Jesus," she said and turned back to the photos on the table. "I thought it was time to put some of these in albums. I bought a couple today, but I think I might need a few more."

Jacob glanced down at the montage of muddled and overlapping images.

"Look at this," she said, picking one up. It was a picture of her when she was a girl, around eight or nine. She was on a beach with her mother.

"Sylvia was very beautiful, wasn't she?" Jacob said.

"Why are you so surprised?" Ella smirked, digging him in the ribs. "I hope you're not planning on an elopement?"

She picked up another. "That looks like Chile." She squinted at the image for a moment and handed it to Jacob.

"Venezuela. Remember we went to the rainforest for a week. You hated it."

"I did not," she said.

"All those spiders and creepy crawlies." He started playing with her hair and she stepped back from him.

"You were the one scared of the spiders," she said, flicking his hand away.

"I spoke to Martin today," Jacob continued.

"You went in to work, then?"

"Yes."

"And you saw Professor Colby?"

"Yes," he lied, "he said that you rang him."

"Who?" Ella asked.

"Martin."

"Big mouth strikes again." She dropped a handful of photos down on the table. "What did he say?"

"That you were concerned about me."

"Understatement."

"You don't think I'm having an affair, do you?" Jacob said suddenly.

"Did Martin say that?"

"Well, he implied that you had said that."

"Oh he is such a shit stirrer. I should have known better. I didn't say that at all. I'm worrying about you, Jacob, because of this obsession with your research and the fact that we never see each other." She stopped and looked at him.

"Oh Christ, Ella!" Jacob exclaimed." When are we ever going to get over this?"

She didn't respond.

"Ella."

"I just need to know."

"Need to know what?"

"I need you to say it."

"I don't know how to respond to that?"

"A simple yes or no would be fine."

"I barely have the energy to get home every night. I don't know when you think this clandestine liaison takes place. Bloody hell, Ella."

She picked up a few more photos and shuffled them around the table. Jacob put his hands on her shoulder.

"No. OK?"

"OK," she said finally. He attempted to hold her, but she pulled away and continued to scrutinise the images.

"And anyway," he said, "it's not an obsession."

"So what would you call it?" she snapped back.

"It's part of my work. It's difficult and time consuming but it's not an obsession."

"So you could stop at any time, no problem?"

"God you make it sound as though I'm a junkie."

"Well, could you?"

"Of course I could, it's important to me but not that important."

"I don't believe you."

"Look, Ella, don't make me stop now. I will, if that's what you want but I am very close to a breakthrough and all this hard work and sweat would be all for nothing if I were to just give it up."

"*I* give up," she said, putting some of the photos into neat piles.

After a moment's silence, Jacob tried to change the subject.

"Martin said that you talked to him about your dad."

"I love this picture," she said, holding up a large colour print.

"Did you hear me?" Jacob repeated.

"I don't feel like talking about it."

"So you can talk to your bosom buddy Martin but not to me." Jacob's words spluttered out before he could stop them.

"Jacob," she said, turning to him. "Martin is a prick. You don't need to be jealous of him."

"I'm not jealous. It's just that sometimes I feel a little cut out of your world."

"You feel cut out? I never see you. I have no idea what's going on in yours," she said.

Just then the cat came in through the kitchen window. It jumped up on top of the photos on the table and pushed itself under Ella's arm.

"Naughty cat," she said, dropping it onto the floor. It licked at its paw nervously then rubbed against Jacob's leg.

"Have you fed her?" Jacob asked.

"No, could you?"

Jacob found a tin of cat food in the cupboard and emptied the contents into her bowl. The cat ignored it and jumped back through the window and out into the night.

"Suit yourself," he said.

Ella sat down at the table. She picked up an old black and white photo and Jacob squinted at it over her shoulder. It was a shot of her father in his late twenties or early thirties. He was standing outside the entrance to a building. In his arms, he was holding a baby. His left foot was resting on the bumper of an old Morris Oxford car.

"That's me," she said touching the image of the baby. "Dad always held me that way. Mum hated it."

"What do you mean?"

"Like this," she said, demonstrating her father's technique, "balanced on one arm. Mum thought he'd drop me, but he never did."

She pushed the photo under a pile on the side.

"I don't mind talking about him, if you want to," Jacob said.

"I'll finish this in the morning," she said, ignoring his offer. "Do you want a drink before we go to bed?"

"OK, what is there?"

"Brandy?"

"Fine."

She disappeared into the living room and Jacob picked up the photo again. Her father was outside his department building. It may have been his first day. The building's facade hadn't changed much, though the University had since renumbered everything, so the large 23 beneath the Maths department plaque had now gone. He looked at Ella in her father's arms. She was tiny, yet appeared joyously contented.

He pushed it back under a pile and, rustling through a few more, located the photo that she had been admiring when he came in. It was a shot of Ella in her early twenties, standing assuredly on top of a mountain ridge. Her arms were outstretched and she had her back to what appeared to be the edge of a cliff. The view beyond was spectacular with snow capped mountain peaks framed in a clear turquoise blue sky. Jacob had taken the photograph during an extended field trip to Chile. Ella had joined him for a holiday and they had taken time out to visit the Andes. The precipice at Ella's feet was part of a major fault line that ran through the mountain region. He remembered that she'd complained that even on holiday, they couldn't escape his work. The sun was glistening in her eyes and she was smiling openly, with the same euphoric life-affirming expression. He could see why she liked it so much and why he fell instantly for her when they first met. He put it back down on the table as Ella returned from the living room with two glasses.

"Shall we?" she said, gesturing towards the roof terrace. Jacob unbolted the door and she followed him out. She put the glasses down on the wall, and leaned over the side.

"Careful," Jacob said. He sat down on the door step and lit a cigarette. Ella turned.

"Do you have to?" she said, pulling a face.

"Sorry. I think I do." He puffed heavily on the end and blew the smoke high above their heads. She handed him his drink and turned back to look out across the rooftops. She spotted the cat moving around behind a chimney stack at the end of the row and watched it for a moment before speaking, almost to herself.

"What do you think she does over there all night?"

"She's the keeper of the hum," Jacob said, smiling.

"What?"

"You know, the guardian."

"I know what you said, I just don't understand it."

"She's over there waiting for the hum to begin and when it does she looks after it."

"You really are a strange man, aren't you?" she said, sipping her brandy.

"It's probably a bird's nest or a rat run or something," he said.

"Maybe it's the neighbourhood cats that produce the hum," Ella added, now enjoying Jacob's idea. "You know, they all get together at night when we go to bed, and they sit on the rooftops and wail in unison."

"Now who's weird?" Jacob replied, smiling

She sat down next to him on the step and sipped her drink.

"It's cold," she said, drawing her elbows into her sides.

He put his arm around her but she pulled away.

He finished his cigarette and flicked the dying stub over the side of the terrace.

"I'm going to bed, are you coming?" he asked.

"In a minute," she said, staring at the cat who was now positioned in her favourite spot on the apex of the roof.

Jacob went back into the kitchen and as he rinsed his glass under the tap, he watched Ella through the window. She was rocking backwards and forwards and seemed to be muttering something under her breath. He turned off the tap and leaned in closer to the open window but he couldn't make out what she was saying. He put the glass on the draining board and went to bed.

***

He woke from a restless sleep, and after a few seconds of transitory fog, realised that Ella was sitting up in bed. He turned over and squinted at her through one sleepy eye. Both her hands were upturned and resting on top of the quilt. She was crying, her body rocking gently backwards and forwards in time with her laboured breathing. He turned onto his back and sighed.

"What's the matter?"

She didn't respond.

"Tell me love, what is it?"

"It's nothing, go back to sleep."

"Please, Ella."

"Why did he do it?" she said at last.

Jacob put his arm around her and she pushed her face into his chest.

"It wasn't your fault," he replied, "your father was ill. He just couldn't take it any more. He wasn't thinking straight. He didn't mean to hurt anyone, least of all you and your sister. He just needed to go. He'd had enough."

"You know, he still wakes me up," she said, pressing her hands into the quilt.

"It will get better." He picked up her hand and squeezed it gently.

"I just feel so terribly lost." I don't know who I am anymore."

"Love," he said, kissing her forehead.

"But I get this overwhelming sense of loss and I feel so terribly alone, like Dad's just died again."

"You're not alone," he said. "I know it's horrible right now but it will pass. It just takes time."

"Christ, Jacob, next you'll be saying time is a great healer," she snapped.

"What I mean is the chaos you are feeling now will eventually subside. You are grieving and it just takes time."

She got out of bed and put on her dressing gown.

"Where are you going?" he asked, sitting up.

"I need a drink, do you want anything?"

"Yeah, whatever you're having."

When she'd gone he slid back down under the quilt and stared at the ceiling. He traced the fragmented line of a plaster crack from the top left hand corner of the room to the central cornice. He stretched and extended his leg into her space of the bed. It was cool and relaxing. He began to drift back to sleep.

"Do you still want this?"

He opened his eyes. She was holding a glass above his head.

"Thanks." He took it from her and propped himself up on his pillow again. She removed her dressing gown and climbed back into bed, pushing his leg back over to his side.

"I don't know why I couldn't cry at his funeral," she said after a couple of sips of her brandy. "It seemed like I had betrayed him. It was like admitting that he'd gone and if I let go I would be in some way forgiving him for what he did to us." She started to cry again.

"Come on, love, this was not your fault."

"But what if I do the same? Am I capable of it, too? What if I'm part of that legacy and I can't stop it from happening? I feel sometimes that he has a sort of control over me. It fills me with such dread. Oh God, why do things have to change so much?" She dropped her head and sobbed freely, her body bouncing gently up and down on the mattress. He took her arm and tried to calm her, but she pulled away. "I don't know who I am any more."

"I'm here, love. I'll help you. I'll get you through this. I always do, don't I?" His words felt hollow and, feeling a sudden rush of guilt, he held her tighter.

"I am so angry with him and what he did to us," she said.

"You have every right to be angry."

"He didn't—" She stopped to swallow another swell of emotion. "He didn't even leave a note. How is that for selfishness?"

"He was so depressed he was probably incapable of writing one."

"Oh, come on, my dad? This is the man who wrote articles and academic papers and book after bloody book. He was an eloquent writer."

"But he was clinically distressed, you know. The illness had affected his brain, the tumour, I mean."

She put the glass to her lips, and tried to take a sip but her hands were shaking too much. He held it for her and she gulped down two large mouthfuls. The hit of alcohol seemed to help her a little and she stopped sobbing.

"Maybe he did leave a note," she said, taking the glass from him again.

"What?"

"Mum might have found one."

"I don't think so. Anyway, if she had, why wouldn't she have shown you it?"

"I don't know, maybe he'd written something terrible about us?"

"Ella," Jacob interrupted, "Your dad loved you. He loved you all. He wouldn't do that. This was about him and the pain he was experiencing."

"So why would she hide the note then?"

"She didn't. There wasn't a note. Even your mum wouldn't be that callous."

Ella finished her drink, put the glass on the bedside cabinet and slid back down under the cover. He followed her and pushed against the warmth of her side. She shifted away from him and he rolled onto his back again.

"I'm going to ask her," she said.

"Don't Ella, please. You're all very fragile. It'll only upset her."

"But if she did find one, I need to know."

"She didn't, honestly. It's just the mess and madness of grief making you think like this."

She didn't respond but he could tell she was still mulling it over in her head. He held his breath for a moment and tried to locate the hum. He couldn't distinguish it from the electrostatic roar of her silence. After a while, he gave up and tried to think of a way to relieve the heaviness of the darkness surrounding them both.

"Ella?" he asked, his voice momentarily dissipating the pressure. "You know I love you, don't you?"

She didn't respond. Instead, she took his hand and held it against her cheek. He stroked the skin gently with his fingertips, backwards and forwards, until finally he was sure she was asleep.

***

The next morning, he went to his study and continued the process of transferring his latest findings onto the computer. Afterwards, he plotted a scaled down version of the triangle in red ink on a large poster representation of the painting, which he had blu-tacked to the back wall of his office. The print was now covered in a mosaic of scribbled calculations, observations, lines, shapes and mathematical formulae. From the exact centre of the candleholder he drew a vertical axis through the triangle to the top of the poster, and then repeated the same procedure with a horizontal line. It was now clear that the candleholder was acting as some kind of visual prompt and a bridge between two major sections in the painting.

Returning to his computer, he noted down a few more observations and then, opening up the internet, he ran a search for more information on the Law of Empirical Wisdom. Before the search was complete the connection went down. He tried again, but it would probably be offline now for the rest of the day. He shut it down and searched the desk drawer for a small pair of scissors and a protractor. He dropped them into his bag and got ready to leave.

On his way to the museum he called into the University library. On the History floor he looked for a subject librarian but there was no one at the desk. He logged onto the catalogue system and ran a keyword search for empirical wisdom. Hundreds of entries came back. He tried again, this time including Celini's name and it produced only one result:

Divina Mathematicas: Art, Mythology and Scientific Discovery in the Renaissance.

He noted down the shelf number and went to locate it. As he passed through the gloomy rows of book shelves, the automated lighting flicked on and off. When he reached the relevant section, he scanned the books from top to bottom, and then from left to right but he couldn't find it. He glanced back towards the entrance and spotted a librarian stacking shelves.

"Excuse me," he said, approaching her.

"Shh. This is a silent floor," the librarian hissed.

"Sorry," Jacob said, lowering his voice. "I wonder if you can help me?"

"Come to the subject enquiries desk in five minutes," the librarian said and then carried on filling the shelves.

He returned to the bookshelf and continued his search. After a few more minutes, he gave up. As he was making his way back to the front desk, he saw the girl from the gallery sitting in one of the study booths by a window. She was leaning over a large book, the sides of which protruded over the edge of the table. She seemed to be scanning the pages frantically, her finger running left to right, chasing the lines of the text. From time to time, she would stop and scribble down some notes in a small pad of paper. And then her manic search would resume. Jacob picked a book randomly from the shelf and inched closer to her, and when he was within a few feet, he glanced up again. She was wet with rain. Her hair was tied back but a few strands hung down around her face with droplets of water dripping from the ends onto the table. Every couple of seconds she sniffed and wiped the end of her nose with the back of her hand. He moved in closer still to try and make out what she was reading. Her finger stopped moving. Jacob thought she might have sensed him staring at her, so he retreated back into the gloom of the row and replaced the book on the shelf. When he finally thought it safe enough to look back, she'd gone.

The librarian located the book within a few moments of searching. She withdrew it from the bookcase and thrust it into his arms. It was unexpectedly heavy and Jacob almost dropped it. He silently mouthed the words 'Thank you', and the librarian shuffled back to her desk. Holding it up to the light, he examined the front cover. Beneath the bold crimson title was a detailed section of a self portrait by Diego Velázquez. The image was cropped and the eyes, nose and mouth were highlighted, dissected and framed by a number of geometrical shapes. Jacob returned to the desk where the girl had been sitting. As he put the book down, he noticed a tiny droplet of water on the surface. He reached over and touched it. It was warm.

"What am I doing?" he muttered under his breath. He sat down and, brushing the splashes of rain from the desk, he opened up the book and scanned the contents page. But finding nothing that seemed particularly relevant, he turned to the index. Under theories, theorems and laws, he ran his finger down the list until he found a single entry for empirical wisdom. He flicked back through the book but the relevant page was missing. It had been torn out and only the ragged edge remained along the central spine. He searched around and under the desk to check that the page hadn't fallen out. To the left of his foot he spotted a small white triangle of paper. As he leaned down to pick it up, a light spluttered on in the aisle opposite his desk. He glanced down the row but there was no one there, and after a few seconds the light flicked off again. Returning to the scrap of paper, he turned it over in his hand. One side was completely blank, but on the other the equation $V = mP^3$ had been neatly written across the width of the triangle. He placed the fragment down on the table and fumbled in his coat pocket for his recently purchased book. He studied the cover notes again.

"An indispensable read," said one critic. "Manuelo has achieved in one book what others can only dream of in a lifetime", read another. He flicked forward to the glossary and relocated the formula written under the defaced paragraph on empirical wisdom. The calligraphic style was identical. He stared at the equation for a moment, trying to work out what scientific label each letter might represent, but he couldn't make any sense of it. Turning back to the contents page, he found only one relevant section in Chapter 4 entitled, Celini's Law and The Calculated Deceit. He flicked forward and scanned the content. Much of Manuelo's analysis seemed to confirm the Professor's precise of Celini's Law, but also he asserted that his theory had a lasting influence on 17th Century allegorical artists and their work. Manuelo's main argument however, was that empirical wisdom was a calculated and deliberate deception, and the alignment of all the players and elements in the composition generated a clever illusion that the painting was moving; a trick of light and design rather than a scientific fact.

When Jacob reached page 239, it was covered in handwritten notes, in a language he didn't recognise. Some key words and phrases had been circled and underlined, with arrows linking sections together and one paragraph in particular had been heavily underscored. Jacob scanned through its content:

"Objects such as rose petals, scarlet ribbons, silver jewellery, were often employed to denote an act of betrayal or deceit. In "La Mano Chastite", (Manuel Piñero (1637), Galeria Regional de Català, Barcelona), an infidelity is symbolised by the inclusion of the blood stained letter opener, half concealed in the right hand of the jilted lover. In this example, the moment of duplicity is qualified by an unseen act of violent revenge. For Piñero, vengeance was the sweet challis, the preordained consequence of a scorned and battered heart."

He felt his chest tighten as he read the artist's name. In the course of his research, he had managed to uncover only three academic references to Piñero, but the information provided had been threadbare to say the least. He turned to the bibliography and was about to look for more information on the artist when a noise made him look up. Someone was moving around close to his desk. He leaned over and peered down through the gloomy row opposite. At the far end, an indistinct figure was just visible. It was swaying gently from side to side and seemed to be moving in and out of the bookshelf, its form appearing and then melting back into the shadows. The movement should have activated the light sensors but the area remained dark. He stood up and stepped into the aisle, and as the fluorescent tubes clicked and stuttered on, and the stark white light streamed down into the row, the figure disappeared. When he reached the end of the aisle, he looked down the next and the one after that but there was no one there. The floor was completely deserted. Returning to his desk, he had a feeling that his things had been disturbed. He grabbed his bag and searched the contents for his notebook. It was still there, tucked into a side pocket. He picked up the fragment of paper, slipped it into page 239 of his book and hurriedly left the library.

***

When he reached the museum, he ordered a drink in the café and sat down at his usual table in the corner. He found his cigarettes and, fumbling for a match, finally managed to get one lit. He drew heavily on the end and then took two or three sips of his coffee. After a couple of minutes he began to feel a little better. He glanced around the room. It was deserted. The waitress was busy on the far side clearing a table. He called her over.

"Do you have an ashtray?"

"You can't smoke in here," the waitress replied.

"Since when?"

"Yesterday," she said. "We have a new manager. He's a non-smoker," she added, smiling at him.

Jacob took another puff and nipped the end between his

fingers.

"Sorry, not my rule," the waitress said, returning to a pile of plates waiting on the other side of the room.

Jacob gulped at his coffee and then opened his notebook. He retraced the thought-prints of his research, reviewing measurements, checking and cross-referencing calculations, and examined the formulae and equations used to identify relationships between hue, pigment and geometric patterns. He re-examined the collected data on the painting's three identified vanishing points; the slightly ajar door on the left, a window above the girl's head and a small painting in the far right corner of the room. He tore out a page from the back of the notebook and copied down relevant numbers and calibrations. Next, he focused on the six or seven pages of thoughts he'd compiled on the girl and the courtier. Finally, he reviewed the complex observations he had noted regarding the two letters on the neck of the dead pheasant and the candleholder nearby and their link to the teetering cup on the table. Despite the thoroughness of his review, he still couldn't find any tangible evidence or influence of the law of empirical wisdom within the elaborate design of the painting. He searched his coat for the book and, scanning down the list of bibliographical summaries, he read through the entry for Manuel Piñero:

PIÑERO, Manuel Francisco (b. 1609, Barcelona, d. unknown)

The lesser-known baroque artist was the youngest of six children. Both his parents were peasants. Between 1632 and 1639 the young Piñero worked as an apprentice and understudy to Diego Velázquez. During this time, Piñero absorbed many of the skills and contemporaneous styles of his teacher and produced two paintings of notable quality: La Perde D'Innocence (1636) and The Chaliced Hand (1637).

In 1638, however, Piñero abandoned his studies and,

following a series of high profile society scandals and heinous crimes, fled Madrid as the prime suspect. In his lifetime, Piñero's work was ridiculed and renounced as inferior pastiche. As a result, he may have destroyed many of his paintings and sketches. However, it is now widely believed that he was responsible for a number of highly credible forgeries previously attributed to Velázquez. The date and circumstances of his death remain a mystery.

He removed the fragment of paper from page 239 and, studying the equation again, he tried to reason a connection between his own calculations and the mysterious formula in front of him. He turned the book around in his hand and examined the notes written in the margins and in the spaces between sections, but all he could understand was one word written down the length of the outside edge of the page. *Aqui.* The calligraphy resembled the same precise style as the equation on the scrap of paper. Scrutinising the cover again and the tired, wrinkled spine, he wondered how many people had owned it and what would be the probability of the girl being one of them? He folded his summary sheet, closed the book, and finished his now cold drink.

He manoeuvred himself along the bench until he found his line, and focusing on the isosceles triangle he had discovered yesterday, waited for the lines and angles to re-emerge and the image to settle in his mind's eye. When he had located the shape, he searched around in his bag until he found the protractor. He stood up and re-measured the three angles; 71, 31, 31 degrees. He measured them again and scribbled the numbers at the bottom of his summary sheet. He looked down at the candlestick. It seemed different today, the sheen on the silver surface was distinctly duller and less translucent, and the shadowy reflected face on the surface had also faded slightly. He scrutinised the features again and he began to consider the possibility that the face could be an optical illusion, a calculated deceit, as Manuelo described it, rather than an actual reflection. He returned to his bag and, removing the reel of thread and scissors, he measured out a precise length of thread and laid it down on the floor in front of the painting. With frequent reference to his notes he repeated the procedure over and over, until the gossamer-thin lines of cotton criss-crossed a vast area of the floor. Some passed under his bench while others stretched out beyond the middle of the room.

After about fifteen minutes he had produced what he believed to be a two dimensional representation of the perspective depicted in the painting, complete with outlines of key objects, orthogonal and transversal lines, and vanishing points carefully plotted and marked. Working on the last few threads, he ran a line from the relative position of the goblet to its target vanishing point on the horizon line, marked by a criss-crossing network of threads at the rear of the plan. As the line approached point zero, it seemed to narrowly miss its target by a fraction of an inch. Jacob reeled out more thread and he continued the line beyond the boundaries of the plan, across the room, stopping finally at the skirting board on the far side of the gallery. He tried another, this time running the thread from the position of the candleholder base to a second vanishing point. Again, the thread almost playfully veered off to the left and would have reached the opposite side of the room if his reel hadn't run out of thread. He checked and rechecked his calculations, but his measurements appeared to be accurate. He picked up his notebook and at the top of a fresh page he wrote four words.

Evidence of Celini's Law.

He began measuring the relative distance between each of the vanishing points and their errant orthogonal lines when two attendants appeared in the entrance along with an elderly man. As Jacob looked up, the man pointed at him and the attendants approached.

"What are you doing?" the first attendant asked.

"I'm just trying to work something out," Jacob said, briskly.

"Jacob, it's Ian," the second attendant said. "We met before? I was asking about your work, do you remember?"

"Oh yes," Jacob said. "The curious cat."

"Look, I think you'd better do as John says and clear these up," Ian continued. "It's just that they are causing an obstruction and, well you know, E.U. health and safety and all that."

"I just need five minutes and I'll be done."

"Now please," the first attendant said, kicking at the threads with the toe of his boot.

"Don't do that," Jacob said.

"Please," the second attendant urged.

"Fuck!" Jacob exclaimed, his voice reverberating around the gallery.

He knelt down and, picking up a thread, he began rolling it carefully round his finger.

"More quickly please if you don't mind," the first attendant snapped.

"All right!" Jacob gathered up the threads into small bundles and stuffed them into his bag. When he was done, the attendants returned to their chairs by the entrance and after a few moments, one of them let out a loud guffaw.

"Something funny?" Jacob called back to them, but they got up and disappeared into the next gallery. Jacob returned to the safety of his bench and, looking back at the painting, his eyes flitted from one vanishing point to the other as he tried to visualise the anomaly he had just discovered. In his periphery, the face in the candleholder sharpened and shifted slightly. He looked directly at it and the features froze. He repeated the circular movement again, switching his focal length from one section to the other, and once again, the reflected face turned, stared straight at him and smiled. Perhaps, this was evidence of the illusional or misleading optical characteristics of the law. He stood up and stretched his legs. Two hours had passed and the P.A. system whistled and then announced that the Museum would be closing in 5 minutes. After scribbling down a few more hurried notes, he made his way back downstairs through the foyer and out into the darkening skies of the early evening.

***

Ella was in the living room. The lights were out, and the flames of the fire illuminated her frame as she huddled close to the grate. She was stabbing at the coal with a poker.

"Jesus, Ella, it's like an oven in here," Jacob said, unbuttoning his coat.

"I had Professor Colby on the phone this afternoon," she said without looking at him. "He wanted to know why you've been avoiding him." A piece of coal rolled out onto the hearth and she pushed it under the grate.

"I haven't been avoiding him," Jacob said.

"For God's sake, Jacob." She put the poker back on its stand. "You told me yesterday that you'd been to see him."

"I tried but he wasn't in his office," Jacob said, unconvincingly.

"Bloody hell." She shook her head.

He looked down at her. She had been crying. Her eyes were swollen and her cheeks flushed. She was rocking backwards and forwards slowly in her chair, picking at an imaginary stray thread in her dressing gown.

He pulled up a chair next to her and sat down.

"What's the matter, love?"

"I can't do this any more," she said.

He tried to reach for her hand but she stood up.

"What's it about?" she asked. "Are you not happy with me? Have I done something wrong?"

"Of course you haven't . It's just something I need to do. I've

71

told you all this before. Let's not row tonight, please."

"I'm not having a row, I just want you to explain to me why you are so determined to fuck everything up." She leaned against the fireplace and reached inside her dressing gown pocket for her cigarettes. She lit one and drew heavily on the end.

"I didn't know you'd started again," he said.

"There's quite a few things you don't know about me," she replied. "Add it to the list."

"Oh Ella, come on. In a few days I'll be finished. I'm really close. Please don't ask me to stop now."

"You carry on," she said dismissively, flicking her ash into the fire.

"It's just that this is really important to me."

"Am I not important to you?"

"Don't be daft. I only need a bit more time, a week at the most and then I'll go back to work. I promise."

"You promised yesterday and the day before that and the weeks and months." She paused for a moment to catch her breath and then continued, "You know that they are going to suspend you, don't you?"

"What?"

"A number of students have been complaining about missed tutorials and unmarked dissertations. Colby's been to HR."

"Ah, for fuck's sake," Jacob said. "What a prick."

"It's your own stupid bloody fault. He's only doing his job. He doesn't have any other choice if you refuse to go and see him and sort it out. He was actually quite sympathetic. He's worrying about you. The whole department is concerned."

"Are they hell, otherwise they would have given me the sabbatical I'd asked for."

"But your research is insane, Jacob." She puffed again on her cigarette.

"Look, I'll go and see him tomorrow and sort it out," he said.

"You've been saying that for months, Jacob," she interrupted, "but it never happens. You just go on and on and it gets steadily worse. I've been really patient with you. I've been a bloody saint about it, to be honest. But I've had enough now. It's killing me, Jacob. I want you to put an end to it right now before—"

"Before what?" he jumped in.

"I'll go back." She hesitated for a second. "I'll leave, Jacob. I mean it." She took another drag from her cigarette, inhaling deeply and blowing the smoke high into the room.

He remained silent and continued to stare into the flames, the agitation building in his chest.

"OK, why don't you do that. You go back to your mother," he snapped.. "if you think it's so bloody awful living here with me. She'll help you. She's always been good at highlighting my fucking faults, confirming all your darkest suspicions about me. How did she describe me?"

"Oh don't go there again, Jacob." Ella interrupted.

"No, wait," he continued, "I'm a cheating, drunken, selfish nutcase and – oh yes, best of all – a bloody misogynist. I tell you if anyone—"

He stopped. A small yellow flame had appeared behind her, creeping up from the hem and around the side of her dressing gown.

"Fuck, you're on fire!"

He jumped out of his chair and grabbed at her lapels, pulling her one way and then the other. She looked down and started hopping around him. He yanked at a sleeve and tried to force an arm out. He twisted her elbow back, almost pulling the shoulder out of its socket until finally her arm was free. The gown was ablaze now. He could feel the heat on his hands and face as he worked to release her.

Her left wrist remained caught, wrapped around the remainder of the gown. He wrenched at the sleeve until the stitching began to give and with one final jerk, the fabric ripped apart and the blazing gown dropped to the floor. He grabbed the tongs and snatched at the bundle until he had a sufficient grip, then thrust it into the fireplace. As he did so, large pieces of burning cloth fell onto the carpet. He stamped on the flames and kicked them into the hearth. He then ran to the kitchen and filled a basin with water, returned and threw it over the fire. A plume of smoke belched out of the fireplace, and the charred remains hissed and sizzled in the grate. He leaned against the wall and tried to get his breath back. She was standing by the door. The torn sleeve of her dressing gown was still dangling from her wrist, inside out. He spluttered and tried to speak to her, but the words wouldn't form. He cleared his throat and tried again.

"Are you all right?"

She was making a low-pitched whine. He thought she might be hurt but then he realised she was laughing. She started snorting. It was infectious and soon he was laughing too. He put his arms around her and they both stood there for a few moments shaking up and down as they enjoyed the euphoric after-effects of shock.

Suddenly, she kissed him, a hard passionate embrace. Her tongue flittered in and out of his mouth as his hands slid down the length of her back. But as he started to ease the strap of her nightdress from her shoulder, she broke off in another fit of giggles.

The Narcissism of Small Differences

The following morning, as Ella was leaving for work, Jacob repeated his promise to her that he would deal with Colby, but the threat of losing his job now made the need to complete his research even more pressing. He dressed quickly and left for the gallery.

He deposited his coat with the cloakroom assistant and returned to the painting. The room was busy with wet bedraggled souls in from the rain trying to warm up. He scanned the floor for the girl but she wasn't there. He sat down, adjusted his position and waited. Quite soon, the triangle reappeared and lines criss-crossed over the candleholder. He focused on the face reflected in the base. The hardened wax obscured a section of the image, but there was enough for Jacob to make out the faint pink and white of a cheek and the dark of an eye socket. This was clearly no optical illusion as he had previously considered. From his pocket he removed a small magnifying glass and held it up close to the detail. The image expanded inside the glass. He twisted his wrist and the image followed the movement of the lens as it turned. When he pulled back, the image blurred, and when he held it near, the face seemed to focus and define itself again. The pupil was small and blue, with a deep shadow under the lower lid. It was staring straight out of the painting, directly at him. This was impossible. The candleholder was on the floor. The angle of reflection was too flat. For anyone to get their head that straight they'd have to twist their neck sideways. It had to be something deliberately imposed upon the image, a calculated insertion.

He stopped abruptly, and turned. The girl was standing in the entrance, staring at him. He was aware of how odd he must have looked, hunched over, peering at the painting through a magnifying glass. He sat down and pretended to write something in his notebook. She approached and stood behind him. He could hear her breathing; the same click and wheeze as she inhaled. The hairs on his neck started to rise. She walked around, slowly, her body shifting sideways towards the bench. Now she was directly in front of him, blocking his view. She inched closer, to within two feet. He looked up. She was staring over his shoulder at the painting opposite. Closer still. He could smell the rain on her clothes. He attempted to speak but his mouth was dry. He tried again.

"Excuse me, miss, but I'm trying to..." He pointed, narrowly missing her leg. She looked down at him and smiled.

"I'm sorry, am I in your way?"

"Well, eh... yes, sorry." She stepped to one side, but remained too close. "I've got a thing about this painting," she said.

Jacob turned round.

"Oh, the Rubens. Yes, that one is beautiful."

She sat down on the bench facing in the opposite direction. "Wouldn't it be great..." she paused.

"Sorry?"

"Wouldn't it be fine just to hang in a moment like that, to lock yourself into the frame?" He glanced at her and felt the longing return. He looked away.

"And no one would ever know," she suggested, "never really know what you'd done before and what you were about to do?"

"Well I hadn't—"

"You come in here a lot, don't you? I see you," she interrupted.

"Yes, I suppose I do," Jacob smiled. "But I can't remember seeing you in here before," he lied.

"Oh, I'm here." She wiped a droplet of water from her cheek. "I'm always here, too, except you are there and I am here." She nodded at her own canvas and then turned to him. "Tell me, why do you like your picture so much?"

"It's difficult to say."

"I'll tell you why I like mine, if you like." She smiled.

"Yes well, if you want to, I mean, if you can."

"Stillness," she said, pausing as though to demonstrate the meaning. "I like it when nothing moves, when everything is suspended and held in one perfect, significant moment. Out here there's too much movement, not enough certainty. The painting helps me deal with that. I don't know if that makes any sense."

"Oh yes." He shifted his weight onto his left side and twisted discreetly so that he could look at her more completely. Her hand dropped onto her knee, the palm upturned and open. The pulse twitched in her little finger, up and down in a slow relaxed rhythm. She breathed in and continued.

"I come in here and hope that one day it will happen. If I look at the picture long enough, if I focus my mind on the whole and on the detail, I'll find it, you know, the stillness." She looked at him. "Sorry, that might sound a bit weird."

"No no, quite the contrary."

"For me," she continued, "it's a bit like your glass on the edge of the table."

Jacob turned back to his painting.

"We don't know why it's there or who put it there or what's in it. We can only guess. And we also know that sooner or later someone or something will knock it over and it'll smash into pieces on the floor. There's a kind of inevitability about it. That's its destiny. But inside that moment up there, we know the glass can never fall. It will always remain, locked inside its own space. And yet we continue to watch and wait. Maybe it will, maybe it won't. We don't really know." She turned her hand over and gripped her knee. "Out here in the real world, the glass would probably fall and we would feel some initial relief, some deep felt satisfaction hearing it shatter. We would nod our heads and say, 'Told you so. That's fate.' But our conceit always turns to feelings of failure, even resentment that the girl let it fall because we let it fall." She paused and breathed in again. Jacob watched the whites of her knuckles pulse as she tightened her grip. "And in the end, all that is left is movement and the chaos of a shattered glass. Our belief in fate is just an excuse to avoid the sheer terror of chaos and our inability to control it."

"But if you believe in fate," Jacob said, "then surely there's nothing we can do to stop it."

"Who said I believed in fate?"

"Well, I thought—"

"Oh no, that's the beauty of it," she interrupted. "You don't have to believe in it. It just happens. Belief is irrelevant. We intervene and it's fate, we do nothing and it's fate, too. Fate makes us think that our options are limited while at the same time providing us with infinite possibility. You see, the stillness up there removes fate. It removes the chaos of possibility and all of those things we believe govern our lives." She paused again and looked at her painting.

"But isn't that the exciting thing about life?" Jacob said. "You never know where you are going or what will happen next? Surely free will is by definition chaotic. It gives us the freedom to choose our own pathways and our own infinite possibilities."

"You think so? You think that you have free will?"

"Yes, I do."

"That you can control chaos?"

"I'm a scientist, I suppose I hope that I will be able to explain it and understand it at least."

"You're wrong," she said. "Free will is just an illusion, a con trick, cooked up by fate."

"What do you mean?"

"Fate dangles free will in front of our faces like a carrot that we pursue but never quite reach. It's like when you go to the supermarket and you stare at the shelves stocked with endless varieties of breakfast cereals. We sweat over which one to choose, which one is the tastiest, the healthiest, the best. But in the end it doesn't really matter because they all taste and look and cost the same. Yet every week we pace up and down the aisles searching for something different, something special to brighten up our mornings, change our lives, expand our healthy lifestyle options. You see the great possibility of fate leaves us restless, neurotic and exhausted, it lets us believe that we have the free will to choose. But what is the point of free will when there is no alternative? In the end our lives are desperately unfulfilled because of it."

"But wasn't it the same great possibility that drove these artists to create these beautiful paintings?"

"No, I think they were trying to retreat or escape from the relentless assault of chaos." Her palm started rubbing on the fabric of her jeans. "Fate is a bully. It feeds on the fear of what might be. It is always in our blood and psyche, waiting, preparing and perpetually fulfilling its own meaningless obsession."

She paused, her hand stopped moving. Then she smiled at Jacob. "And that's why I like this painting. Because fate has been sealed inside the frame forever. The future is locked up and safe; dried out and stretched across the canvas. I find it comforting to know that there is at least one thing in life I can cling to as a complete certainty, a moment perfectly frozen and impervious to the abusive nature of fate."

She wiped the tip of her nose with her finger. Jacob reached into his pocket and produced a packet of handkerchiefs.

"Thanks." She blew hard and the sound reverberated around the room. She offered it back to him.

"Keep them."

"Sorry I went on. Once I start I find it difficult to stop."

"I noticed."

She giggled and blew her nose again. "I suppose I've got a bit of a thing about fate."

"I could have told you that." They smiled and their eyes met for the first time. There was something very sad and deeply troubled about her. He wanted to wrap his arms around her shoulders and make her feel better about herself and the world.

"Would you like to go for a drink?" The words spluttered out of his mouth and were airborne before he could stop them.

She hesitated for a moment. "OK, I'm Jude, by the way."

"Hi Jude, I'm Jacob. Good to meet you." They shook hands awkwardly and stood up to go.

***

The pub was half empty. There were a few regulars propped up at the bar and a couple in a far corner were engaged in an animated argument. Jacob suggested they sit in a booth well away from the noise. It was a warm softly-lit retreat from the seediness of the main bar. A stained glass window filtered and transformed the grey light from outside into a delicate lilac glow. They both felt immediately at ease with each other.

"What would you like?" Jacob reached for his wallet.

"No, let me. You had to sit through my rant. It's the least I can do."

"I'll have a double whisky then. I'll get the next one."

"Next one?" She smirked and went up to the bar.

When she returned, she sat close to him and he felt the warmth of her leg against his. He glanced down at her bag and tried again to read the inscription on the triangular-shaped badge attached to the front pocket, but it appeared to be in another language that Jacob didn't recognise.

"What does this say?" He touched its smooth surface with his finger.

"Oh, that's my lucky charm."

"What does it mean?"

"If I told you that it wouldn't be lucky any more." She

sipped her drink and Jacob attempted some more small talk.

"So, are you a student, or an artist?"

"Jacob, why do you do it?" she cut in.

"What?"

"Why do you work so hard at trying to understand your painting?"

"Well," he hesitated, sifting through words and phrases that wouldn't alarm her or make her think he was a basket case.

"Go on. I told you why I do it. Now it's your turn to embarrass yourself." She dug her elbow into his ribs.

"I suppose it's about mystery really, the value of it and the secrets and symbolism that you can find, not only inside the canvas but all around us, in the world we inhabit every day. I think mystery is something we've lost touch with. We live in very concrete times, and I suppose it's been relegated or rejected as something superfluous to our materialistic needs." He shook his head. "Sorry, that sounds a bit pretentious. What I mean is, we might believe that we have no need for mystery, we might even think that we have abandoned it for something better, more modern and rational, but it's still there at the centre. It informs and influences our thoughts, our culture, our essence. We are saturated in it, yet we don't even know it." He gulped a mouthful of whisky and continued. "I study the painting because I want to show that mystery does still exist. It continues to have a place, and play a vital part in our world. If I can unlock the enigma and highlight the force of its impact on everyone who studies it – even those who might just glance at it on their way to your Rubens opposite – then it could open doors to all sorts of other possibilities and other ways of being."

"What do you mean?" she asked.

"I'm attempting to establish a mathematical and geometrical relationship between line, light, colour, position and perspective. I've been developing a series of—" He stopped. He had never actually vocalised the exact purpose of his research and he began to feel vulnerable.

81

"Go on. It's all right." She nudged his elbow and smiled.

"Well, I was part of a research team, working on a project to improve earthquake prediction rates."

"At the University?"

"Sorry, yes, I thought I'd mentioned it. I'm a lecturer in Earth Science, or maybe I should say, that's what I used to be."

"Have you left, then?"

"It's a long story. Anyway, it is a notoriously complex phenomenon to measure and calibrate so we were having on-going problems making any kind of headway." He stopped and searched his pockets "Do you mind if I smoke?" he asked.

"No. Go ahead."

He offered her one but she declined. He lit up, took another sip of whisky and continued. "As I said, we'd been working on the project for a number of months and I was becoming increasingly frustrated, bored even by the lack of progress. So, I began dropping into the museum on my way to work for a coffee and a look around, delaying the inevitable failures and disappointments that awaited me each day at the office."

"I can identify with that," she said.

"But my visits grew more frequent, as I became more and more intrigued by this particular painting."

"What was it that attracted you?"

"At first, I suppose it was the glass goblet; the idea of an object or an event on the brink, and the symbolism of an uncertain future. For me, these were concepts very similar to my research in seismology."

"So what happened then?"

"I began to see that the painting was more than simply a beautifully crafted image. That there were a whole range of hidden and complex patterns and structures present within the composition. So I started to try and unpick the work, applying similar mathematical models that we had been trialling on the research programme."

"How did you do that?"

"Well, basically through systematic analysis of the entire composition. Over the last few weeks, I have been observing, measuring and accumulating data, and slowly developing a series of equations, formulae if you like, that I hope will eventually reveal and unmask the mysteries, and the allegorical representations and riddles buried in the portrait."

He half-looked at her, afraid that he'd said too much. She ran her finger round the rim of her glass. The booth swelled and the silence pushed between them, until finally she spoke.

"And you think that you can use this formula to deconstruct and explain things out here, the movements in the Earth?" she asked.

Jacob nodded. "That's the plan."

"But didn't Fibonacci do that? Doesn't his theory try to show that the world is created by a single formula?"

Jacob sat back, surprised. "How do you know about him?"

"Fate, remember?"

"But Fibonacci was wrong," he went on, "because there's more than one formula, and the rules keep changing, or at least, evolving."

"I don't understand."

"You see, you long for stillness, but for me the painting is not still, it's just like the Earth, it's in a perpetual state of movement, and this makes it challenging to pin down. It's like discovering pieces of a jigsaw puzzle, but the puzzle is made of some kind of fluid. You fit one clue into the other and slowly the picture, the story, starts to form and take shape. But then the current changes and forces the whole riddle inside out. It swells and recedes, and yields to the weight of expectation and the levels of attention it receives."

She sipped her drink and said nothing.

"So here we are," he said, "you longing for stillness and me looking for movement. A right pair, eh? What do you think?" He scratched his forehead and waited for her response but she remained silent.

She put the glass down gently on the table.

"But, you've overlooked one other possibility," she said, finally. "What if there is only mystery?" The whisky started swimming around in Jacob's head. He remembered his wife's fury the night before. He tried to remove her image from his mind, but her words resonated inside his skull, her mouth widening to articulate a high-pitched scream, the flames leaping up her dressing gown and engulfing her body, her face and her hair. He gripped the side of the chair in an attempt to relocate himself in the bar.

"Are you OK?" She touched his hand and he nodded.

"It's nothing, a bit of a whisky rush. I'm fine, please. You were saying?"

"But it's still just a freeze frame of a moment, an artificial two-dimensional constructed image. Can I be honest with you?"

"Of course, go ahead."

"Forgive my metaphor but don't you think you're falling through the cracks in your own rationale?"

"In what way?"

"Suppose fate has pushed you into a hole and you just can't see it."

Jacob shook his head and searched for an answer but the alcohol crowded out the words. She raised the palm of her hand.

"It's like this, Jacob. We have one moment. Right here, right now." She clicked her fingers close to his face. He pulled his head back to avoid contact with her knuckles. "And this moment may be more complicated, more devastating, elusive or sublime than a whole lifetime of living, or the dried up static combinations of colour on paper that you so admire. That's the grotesque beauty of fate. In life every millisecond is fraught with possibility. It's only fate that holds the key to certainty. In your painting, just like mine, all possibility has been removed and only certainty remains. But you want to take that away. If you are telling me that nothing is certain, including the static peace that I find in my painting, then I have nothing to hold on to."

84

"Sorry."

"And what happens when your measurements are taken, your formula is established and you find all the pieces of your forever-flowing puzzle? What then, Jacob? Do you control fate? Does it go away? Does it stop interfering? Is that how you see it?"

"Well, there is that chance. If I can prove that uncertainty is measurable then I suppose fate is rendered obsolete." He was beginning to feel nauseous.

"You're living inside a tight little lie. You're fooling yourself if you think you can win. You'll never win. You are up against something too powerful and too cunning. Reason and rationality, enlightenment, all of those great movements, great ideas put forward by brilliant minds. They all tried to resist, deny or destroy fate, to argue their way out of the dark corners they had created for themselves. But they all failed. What makes you think you can succeed?"

"I just know that somehow uncertainty can be measured and understood. Surely that would provide at least a sense of order and safety. Just think of the suffering that could be avoided if we could predict when and where an earthquake was about to strike. Wouldn't this act as a counter to your theory of chaos?"

"So your research is driven by altruism?"

He put his hand on the sleeve of her jacket. "Hey, let's not argue about it. Why don't we have another drink?"

"I've got to go," she said, standing up.

"What?"

"I've got to be somewhere."

"Don't you want another?" He held up his glass.

"Sorry."

"I haven't upset you, have I?"

"No, it's just I have to be somewhere else."

"What, right now?"

"Yes."

"Can I see you again? I mean, will I see you in the gallery?"

He stared at the door as it rattled back and forth in its frame, hoping for it to swing open again, but after a few moments it settled on its hinges and stopped moving. She had gone. He drained his glass and contemplated another. His body filled with the desire to obliterate itself, to shatter and fragment into a thousand pieces. But he resisted, put on his coat and went to the toilet. He stopped at the sink and examined his face in the mirror.

After a moment or two, the features started to fold in on themselves, his nose retreating into the swelling mass of his cheeks. The skin around his eyes puckered and swelled and his forehead sagged down over the eyes towards the tip of his nose. It was as though he was melting or mutating into some other person. A rush of bile flooded his throat and mouth. He gagged and spat a long string of clear fluid into the sink. Rinsing his hands under the cold tap, he glanced back at his reflection. His contorted features seemed to judder and spring back into shape.

Perhaps Ella's mother was right and some disease was eating away at him; the numbers, the painting, all of it some elaborately cloaked symptom of impending madness. He was on the brink of losing his job and worse still, he had abandoned his grieving, depressed wife when she needed him most. He pulled at the loose lid beneath his left eye. The exposed flesh was pale and yellow. What kind of monster was he turning into?

He hurriedly grabbed his things and left the bar, heading for home.

'g'

He was about to put the Yale in the lock, but the door was already open. He pushed it with his fist and it thumped against the inside wall.

"Ella?"

He inched down the hallway anticipating an intruder. When he reached the lounge, he flicked on the light. The room was empty. He grabbed the poker from the fireplace and searched the rest of the flat. There was no-one there. He tried to focus his thoughts. She'd probably popped out for a second. Maybe she was next door with Rhona. That would explain why she hadn't left a note. But then threads of doubt started to flutter in his head. What if she'd gone, really gone? What if he had misjudged her discontent, underestimated the depth of her sadness?

He went into the bedroom and opened the wardrobe. All her clothes were still there, her skirts, dresses and trousers racked up on the railing, and the drawers crammed full of her things. The bed was made. The eiderdown hugged the mattress to form a perfect, creaseless shape. In the bathroom her toiletries and make up sat in neat little rows on the shelf. Her toothbrush lay next to his on the sink. Her shoes were in the hallway, her coat was on the hook, the umbrella folded in the stand. He counted the suitcases in the cupboard and checked the bookcase and CD tower. Everything was in its place, except her. He returned to the lounge and steadied himself against the fireplace. The panic refused to subside. She would never leave the door wide open, not for a second. And she would always leave a note, to let him know where she was. Something was wrong. He wiped the sweat from his brow. He would wait five minutes and if she didn't appear he would try upstairs. He stabbed at the ashes in the fire with the poker. The charcoal disintegrated and the powder fell onto the hearth. Some fragments of the gown still remained, scattered on the tiles around the fireplace. He knelt down and with the back of his hand, pushed them under the grate. Something sharp snagged on his skin. He lifted up a piece of charred cotton, and underneath was a small metal object. The fire had blackened its surface. He picked it out of the debris and placed it in the palm of his hand. He wet his thumb and rubbed off some of the smoke stains and soot.

It was a knife, about four inches long, made of silver or pewter with a pearl embossed handle. He had never seen it before. It must have been in the pocket of her gown. He searched the rest of the remains, but there was nothing else. He held the knife under a table lamp. There appeared to be some markings on the reverse side of the blade, but they were too small to make out.

He went to the kitchen and rinsed it under the tap. The water washed away the remaining dirt and the metal glistened like new. It was quite beautiful. He noticed that the tip of the blade was slightly curved with a rounded point. He stretched his legs and his heel slid on something soft. He leaned over and peered under the table. There was a puddle of dark crimson liquid around his left foot. Shocked, he pulled his leg back and some of it clung in strands to the sole of his shoe. He jumped up and pushed the table away. It was around six inches in diameter, a thick wet circular glob of red fluid. He knelt down and touched it. It was warm. In panic, he dropped the knife and ran out onto the landing. He leaned over the banister and shouted out his wife's name, over and over, his voice reverberating around the stairwell. He ran back into the flat. The circle of red fluid was still there, but now, the handle of the knife, half-submerged, was protruding from its centre. He picked up the phone to call her work, her friends or her mother, anyone. He put it down. He picked it up again and put it down.

Rushing back out into the close, he ran down the stairs onto the next landing. He imagined her coming back. Cursing and swearing,

"Why do you never have anything fucking useful in that so-called first aid fucking kit of yours," she would say and he would help her to the sink to clean the wound and rub at the blood until it stopped. And she would smile and embrace him gratefully. But the landing was still empty.

Frantic now, he ran back upstairs, past their flat and banged on the neighbour's door. No reply. He thumped it again. Andy answered.

"Hello, Jacob."

"Have you seen Ella? Is she here?"

"No, she's not. Are you OK? You don't look too good."

"It's just that I got back and the door was wide open. I thought maybe she'd come up here for something or that she was out somewhere with Rhona."

"I don't think she's with Rhona. She's on a late tonight at the office. I suppose they could have arranged to meet afterwards, but she didn't say anything to me."

Jacob flinched and rubbed his cheek with his knuckles.

"Jacob, don't worry," Andy continued, "she's probably just getting a paper or some milk. She'll have forgotten to pull the door. Come in for a minute and wait for her."

"There's something else." Jacob hesitated. "I think there might be some blood."

"Look, let me get my keys. I'll come down with you, OK?"

Andy stopped at Jacob's door and inspected the lock and the frame.

"So it was open like this?"

Jacob nodded and they went inside. He took him into the kitchen and Andy stopped in the doorway.

"Jesus, Jacob." He squatted down to look at it. The knife had completely disappeared into the mass of liquid.

"Is it blood?" Jacob asked.

"I don't know."

"Oh Christ, what's happened? Where is she? We had a row last night. A stupid argument, you know? But we sorted it out, all her stuff is still here. She's not gone. She wouldn't go without her stuff. Do you think we should call the police?"

"Let's wait a few minutes or so and then if she doesn't show up—"

"Fucking hell, you said she was with Rhona."

"I said she might be with her but I don't know. I tell you what, let's go back to my flat and I'll try Rhona on the mobile. We could ring round a few of your friends and see if they know nothing then—"

"It's just that she's still very upset about her dad," Jacob interrupted. "I'm worried that she might do something stupid, you know?"

"Come on. I'll get you a drink and we'll sort this out," Andy said.

"No. I have to stay. She might come back or phone."

"Come on, Jacob, just five minutes." He took him by the arm and led him upstairs.

***

Rhona arrived soon after Andy had poured Jacob a large whisky. Jacob approached her as she came through the door.

"Where's Ella?" He looked over her shoulder. "You two were together, weren't you?"

Andy came out of the kitchen. "Calm down, Jacob," he said, putting his hand on his shoulder. But Jacob shifted out of his way.

"What's wrong?" Rhona dropped her bag onto the floor and looked over anxiously at her husband.

"Where's Ella?" Jacob repeated.

"I don't know. I've been working late. I've got so much on at the moment. The Inland Revenue are all over us."

Andy shook his head and she shut up. "Something might have happened to Ella," he said.

"What? How do you mean, 'happened'?"

"Jacob's door was open when he got home and there's," he paused, "well, it's a bit odd. We thought she was with you."

"No, I haven't seen Ella since last Saturday, you know, when we went out to the – the what do you call it, and had lunch."

"But you were out together a couple of nights ago!" Jacob broke in. "She left me a note saying that she was with you. She got back late."

"No, Jacob. Tuesday night, Andy and I went to the pictures, didn't we Andy?"

Jacob downed the whisky. "I don't understand. She left me a note. It said, "Out with Rhona". Why would she lie? She never lies. I don't get it. Why would she write that?"

"Is there anywhere else she could be? What about at her mother's? You said you had a row. Would she go there?" Andy asked.

"No, I told you we made up. Her stuff, her clothes, her books, even her fucking toothbrush – it's all there!"

"You had a row?" Rhona asked.

"So you two don't fucking row, then? Mr and Mrs fucking perfect, is that it?"

Rhona let a moment or two pass and then put her hand on his arm and spoke softly, "Why don't we ring a few people, just to check, OK?"

But Jacob didn't respond. He was staring out the window, across the broken lines of chimney pots that stretched beyond the tenements, and out into the fading murky blur of the early evening sky.

**

C.I.D. arrived about forty minutes after Andy called.

"Chief Inspector Tagert, Strathclyde Police," the detective said, holding up his badge. Andy bit into his lip and looked at his ID. "I know, I know. It's very amusing, but that's Tagert with one 'g' and an 'e'. It's French, apparently." He spoke with a Southside twang that sounded a little forced. He was unfeasibly thin, the skin around his face pulled tight around pronounced cheekbones. He was wearing a slightly oversized suit and the end of his tie was sticking out through his buttoned up jacket. Andy ushered him into the living room.

"Jacob, this is Chief Inspector – er – Tagert." Rhona turned, half-expecting the full complement of a Scottish television film crew. The inspector approached Jacob.

"How do you do? It's Tagert, with one g and an e, by the way."

He held out his hand but Jacob didn't move. He fumbled in his pocket for a notepad.

"So – Jacob, isn't it? And your surname?"

Jacob didn't respond. The inspector coughed and tapped the pad with his pencil. "Jacob, your family name?"

"Boyce," Jacob said, finally turning round.

"Are you Welsh, Mr Boyce?"

Jacob shook his head.

"So, anyway, at what time did you arrive tonight? When did you make the grizzly discovery?" Jacob looked up. Tagert was smiling. "Only joking, nine times out of ten this is a waste of bloody time. Have you and your wife had a bit of a domestic?"

Jacob fixed his gaze on the inspector's protruding tie.

"Jesus! My wife is always on at me about being smart, creating a good impression. Power dressing she calls it. She watches a couple of episodes of NYPD Blue and that's it I have to dress like Sipowitz or what do you call him, you know, the Puerto Rican?" He looked at Rhona for help. "Anyway, I never seem to live up to her estimations. I'm always the embarrassing scruffy bastard, pardon my French." He tucked his tie into his suit and continued. "So you got home, at what time exactly?"

After a moment's silence, Andy replied, "Just after nine, wasn't it, Jacob?"

"Just… after… nine." He wrote the information in his pad. "And the door was open, is that correct?"

"Yes, slightly ajar." Andy said. "No sign of forced entry."

"No… sign… of…" He looked up from his pad. "Well, let us be the judge of that. And then what did you do, Mr Boyce?"

"He went in," Andy replied again.

"Yes, and after?"

"He— What did you do Jacob?"

"I looked for my wife."

Tagert stepped back, feigning surprise at Jacob's sudden cooperation.

"Good plan. Glad to have you back with us. And your wife is Elizabeth, is that correct?"

"Ella."

"As in Fitzgerald? What a voice." He tapped his pad lightly with the pencil. After a few moments of silent contemplation, he continued, "Could you show me what you did exactly? Could we go down there now?"

Jacob hesitated.

"Don't worry, you'll be OK," Tagert said and gestured towards the hallway. As he did so, he noticed a trail of brown marks leading from the living room door across the cream carpet to the where he stood.

"Oh Jesus." The inspector lifted his left foot and pulled at his shoe to inspect the sole. "I am so sorry. I seem to have trodden in something." He removed his loafer and sniffed the bottom. "Yes, it's me, I'm the guilty one." He shook his head. "I don't know, it's like wading through a bloody quagmire of animal waste out there. The world is full of defecating pets and irresponsible dog owners. If I had a gun, I'd shoot every last one of them."

He hobbled to the door and apologised again to Rhona.

Jacob stepped round the stains and took him to his flat. The detective whistled down the stairwell and two uniformed policemen came up. As he examined the doorframe and the lock, he scribbled another note in his pad. Jacob continued down the hall. The detective limped as he walked, his soiled shoe upturned in his left hand.

"So where did you go first?"

"I went into the lounge."

"Show me what you did."

"Well, I came in here, picked up the poker and then searched the flat for Ella."

The detective limped over to the fireplace and examined the stand.

"Why did you do that, Jacob?"

"I thought there might be a burglar or an intruder of some kind."

"I see, and you thought you'd sort him out with this." He picked up the poker and swiped it through the air and as he did so, he lost his balance slightly.

"Very dangerous game, that. These guys are professionals, you know. You might fancy yourself as a bit of a Charles Bronson, but a hardened criminal would have you flat on your back on life support in the Royal Infirmary before you could even sneeze at him. What's all this?" He stabbed at some of the burnt fabric.

"Oh, I couldn't find any paper to light the fire with so I used an old tea towel." Jacob decided to keep things as simple as possible.

"So you picked up the poker and searched the flat?"

"That's correct, yes."

"And where did you go next?"

"The bedroom."

The inspector put the poker back on the stand but it missed the hook and clattered onto the tiles. They carried on through to the bedroom.

"And what did you do in here?"

"I checked the room and I looked in the…"

"In the?" The inspector looked up from his notepad.

"The wardrobes – to check that our stuff was still here."

"Perhaps you mean Ella's stuff."

"No, well, yes."

"So you did have a barney?"

"No," Jacob retorted. "It's just that she's been a little depressed recently following the death of her father and I've been so busy with my work, I suggested she go to her mother's for a couple of days."

Oh, her mother's," the inspector said, sarcastically. " So you thought the best thing to do, to make up and placate her, to support your grieving, neglected wife was to send her to her mother's? That makes perfect sense. Very new man."

Jacob shrugged.

"And what is your line of work?"

"I'm an Earth scientist. I work at the University."

"An Earth scientist," the inspector said. "What is that exactly?"

"It's a scientist who studies things relating to the Earth."

The detective frowned.

"Look," Jacob said, approaching the detective. "She hasn't left me. She would never leave me." Jacob tried to control the tone of his voice.

"So, there was no barney then?"

"No."

"No row?"

"No."

"No tiff or minor disagreement?"

"No, nothing!"

"You seem a little agitated, Jacob. Are you easily roused?"

"No! Look, I've been working hard. My job is stressful. And stress, well, you know, it can make you say things."

"And do things?"

"No, say things, stupid things to each other. But we didn't

95

have a row, a discussion maybe, and then an agreement."

"OK, so you had an 'agreement', and it was so constructive and positive, the first thing you do when you get home is come in here to check that your wife's clothes are still in the wardrobe."

"That's the way it was. I'm not a psychologist."

"Apparently not. So you opened the wardrobes and they were?"

"Full," Jacob said, opening the doors to show him.

"And the drawers?" Jacob nodded but the inspector was over by the bed. "And have you tried her mother's, have you contacted her?"

"Well, I think Rhona phoned, and no, she's not there."

"This is a very nice quilt. Is it handmade?"

"What?"

"Somebody likes to sew. Look at all that cross stitching."

"Yes, it was a wedding present from Ella's mother."

"Ah, the mother again. You'd have to like it, wouldn't you? The detail and the patience you'd need. I'd be off my head with it in no time." He stroked the surface, "It's a thing of beauty. And it fits the bed very well. Very... snug and tight. There's something quite reassuring about an old fashioned eiderdown, don't you think? I can't stand these Swedish contraptions, what do you call them?"

"Duvets." Jacob rubbed his eyes.

"Yes," he clicked his fingers. "Duvets. Must have been a sadistic bastard or a trained contortionist who came up with that idea. They're full of brilliant ideas, the Swedes, aren't they? Abba, Volvo, Ikea, free love. But they definitely lost the plot with continental quilts." He sat down on the bed and gently bounced up and down. "Comfortable too, this is a nice bed."

There was a knock at the door and one of the uniformed policemen came in.

"Excuse me, sir, there's been a call from the station. You're wife wants you to give her a ring, something about the plumber.

96

He needs a bigger tool and won't be able to fix her block until Tuesday?"

"Fine, fine." The detective got up and handed him his shoe. "Do something with that, will you?" The policeman grimaced. "That'll be all, officer. So where did you go next? Can you show me?"

"I went into the study to check the answer phone."

"Show me, please." As they left the room, the inspector stopped for a final look at the quilt.

"This way," Jacob repeated. In the study, Jacob directed him to the phone but he stopped at the large poster on the wall directly in front of the desk. He glanced round the room and noticed another four or five versions of various sizes and details with post-its and scribbled calculations all over them.

"My, oh my, what have we here? You do work hard, don't you? What is this?"

"It's a painting."

"This is fascinating. Is it, let me guess, Italian?"

"Spanish."

"Spanish!" He clicked his fingers again. "Yes, now I see. I used to be a bit of an art connoisseur. I subscribed to that magazine, Great Artists and Their Work – you know the one they advertise during the break in Take the High Road. I don't watch it by the way, it's the wife's favourite. She's obsessed with it. Anyway, I built up quite a collection. They liked their paintings big, didn't they, the Spanish?"

"I suppose."

"But what are you doing with it? And what in God's name are all these notes and these numbers everywhere?"

"It's part of my research for the University."

"Really? I thought you said you were an Earth scientist. I didn't know you lot were interested in Spanish art."

"Well, I'm exploring links between the arts and science. It's part of my research," Jacob repeated nervously.

"How interesting." He went over to Jacob's desk. "Jesus, you do love this picture, don't you?" He picked up a pile of postcards. "And in here, too?" He pulled the drawer open and a bundle of postcards tumbled onto the carpet.

"Please don't touch those," Jacob said, bending down to pick them up.

"If you don't mind me saying, Jacob, it looks a bit, how can I put it, and I don't mean to offend, but isn't it just a tad, ever so slightly obsessive? You've not gone a bit nutty have you, a bit Russell Crowe?"

Jacob gathered up the stray cards and replaced them in the drawer. "Don't you think we should go to the kitchen?" he said, gesturing to the inspector.

"Let's do that." The detective smiled. "Lead the way."

When they reached the doorway, Jacob started to shake and he felt his legs begin to buckle under him.

The inspector caught his arm. "Calm, Mr Boyce," he said.

"It's over there, by the table?" Jacob leaned against the door. The inspector approached the puddle and knelt down. He put his face close to the surface of the floor and sniffed. From his coat pocket he produced a small plastic spatula and prodded the substance once, then again. Jacob turned away.

"Mr Boyce, can you come over here?"

"No, I don't think I can."

"It's all right, you'll be fine." He smiled. "Come on."

Jacob edged towards him.

"Come on, it's OK." He held up the spatula. Jacob recoiled.

"You see that?" the inspector asked.

Jacob opened his eyes and squinted at the end.

"That's right. There's nothing there. Do you know why?"

"No, I—"

"This – how did your friend report it, what were his exact words? – Ah yes, this pool of blood that you found. Well surprise, surprise, it's not blood."

"What?"

"See for yourself." He pulled him down next to it. "It's wax.

98

"Solidified candle wax." He tapped it with his knuckle. "You see, hard as a rock. Touch it."

"I can't."

"Touch it, please." The inspector grabbed his hand and forced it down onto the surface. He stood up. "You seem to have been wasting our time, Mr Boyce."

"No. It was warm and wet."

"It's a criminal offence you know, wasting police resources. We are busy people. My wife doesn't seem to think so, but believe you me, we are run off our feet." He looked down at his sock.

"But what about the door?"

"There's no crime in leaving a door open. A bit foolhardy maybe in this part of the city but nothing's been stolen or damaged and like you said, no sign of forced entry. No, Mr Boyce, I think you are playing silly buggers with us. You had a barney, your wife thinks you've gone doolally, and quite frankly, so do I, and she's run off and you can't face up to it. She's not dead. She's not been kidnapped. She's not lying in a pool of… molten wax somewhere. She's grieving for her dad and you haven't given her your support. So she's pissed off and left you to it, and quite frankly, I don't blame her. You might patch it up, you might not, but it is not our business. It's not our problem, it's yours." He straightened the buttons on his suit and reinserted his itinerant tie. "If your wife doesn't show up in the next three or four days, give us a call and we can start again. Here's my card. Hopefully, we won't meet again." He hobbled out of the kitchen and Jacob followed him to the door. "You know," the inspector paused to formulate his thoughts, "women need love, Mr Boyce." He gestured to the two uniforms and as they disappeared down the stairs, their laughter resounded in the stairwell.

Jacob closed the door and pressed his head into the wood. His thumb touched the smooth layer of hardened wax on the tip of his forefinger. He looked down at his shoe. It too was covered in a firm crimson residue. His skull felt as though it was about to crack open and he closed his eyes to try and stop the hall from spinning. The clock chimed loudly and he fell back onto the wall opposite. He counted nine strikes and then the mechanism seemed to freeze, the pendulum remaining suspended at a thirty degree angle inside the casement. He staggered into the living room, slumped down in a chair and waited for the sensation of drowning to subside.

***

There was a loud knock at the door and Jacob heaved his weary limbs out of his chair to answer it.

"Rhona, what's the matter?" She clearly had been crying.

"Can I come in for a moment?"

"Of course," he said and she pushed past him.

"Andy said I shouldn't bother you with this."

"What?"

"I don't know if it's important." He followed her into the living room and invited her to sit in his chair. "You know that I said I hadn't seen Ella since last Saturday."

"Yes?"

"Well, that's not entirely true. I saw her yesterday."

"When?" He sat down on the sofa opposite.

"We didn't meet or go out or anything, I mean I didn't speak to her. I just saw her."

"Where?"

"In the close, outside your flat."

"Yesterday?"

"Yes."

"What time?

She paused for a moment.

"Rhona!" Jacob said, feeling both relieved and agitated at the same time.

"She was on the landing outside your flat." She repeated. "I'd

100

forgotten some papers and had popped back for them. I heard a noise in the close and had a peek through the spy hole."

"Jesus! Why didn't you say anything to me, or to the police."

"I didn't want to embarrass you."

"What do you mean, embarrass me?"

"She was with someone."

"Who?"

"A man."

"What man?"

"I promised her," she said, shaking her head.

"Come on, Rhona, the cat's out the bag. What man?"

"When we met on the Saturday, she told me about this guy she'd met."

"Fucking hell, was she seeing someone, I mean, an affair?"

"I don't know. She didn't get into it too far. She just said that she'd met this really interesting man."

"I can't believe it," he said. "When did this all start?"

"A few weeks ago, I think."

"Weeks? Fuck me."

"Then yesterday, I saw her with a man in the hallway outside your door, and then they went in together."

"He was in here, with her?"

"I think so."

"Oh, Mother of God," he said, dropping his head into his hands. "Did she tell you anything about him, where they'd met? What the fuck she was doing with him?"

"She didn't say much."

"Don't lie to me," he snapped.

"Honestly, Jacob. I'd tell you if I knew anything. The only thing she said was that he was interesting."

"What did he look like?" Jacob said, struggling to control his growing sense of rage.

"I couldn't really see him very well, you know, through the spy hole. To be honest, I was feeling a bit intrusive so I only watched them for a second or two. He was standing behind her,

101

kind of leaning on her slightly. He was tall with long dark hair and dressed from head to toe in black. I could only see a little bit of his face but he looked the Mediterranean type, you know strong features." She paused again and looked over at Jacob. "The thing is…"

"What?"

"Just before they went in, he put his hands on her shoulders and kissed her. I'm sorry, Jacob." She bit into her lower lip.

Jacob got up and went over to the door.

"Should we call the police again?" she said.

"Thanks Rhona, I really appreciate you telling me. It must've been hard for you, betraying your friend like that?"

"Jacob," she said, approaching him.

"I'd like you to leave now."

"Are you OK?"

"Please, Rhona. I have to think this through."

"Are you going to call Tagert?"

"Please," he repeated, gesturing towards the front door.

"Just knock if you need anything, OK? You can talk to either of us any time. I'm so sorry." She reached out to hug him but he pulled away and shut the door on her.

The Law of Sines

He picked up the phone and called Ella's mother. But after a couple of rings he hung up. He hadn't spoken to her for months and he momentarily lost his nerve. He rang again and after a dozen or so rings, she finally answered.

"Sylvia, it's Jacob," he said tentatively.

She didn't respond.

"Is Ella there?"

"No," she replied, finally.

"Please, Sylvia, if she is there with you, could you please put her on. I'm worrying about her."

"Jacob, she's not here. I'm sorry but I'm in the middle of something so I'm going to have to hang up."

"I just need to know that she's safe. When I came home the door was wide open. She doesn't have to talk to me if she doesn't want to. I just want to know."

The line went dead and Jacob re-dialled. It rang and rang until Jacob gave up. He ran back through to the bedroom and searched her things again. At the rear of the walk-in wardrobe, he rifled through the pockets of her coats and jackets but they were all empty. On a shelf above the rail he searched piles of books and shoeboxes full of trinkets, and as he pulled at them, a box of photographs toppled over and the contents emptied out onto the floor. At the back of the shelf, he found the photo album she'd been working on. Flicking through the half-finished collages of scenes and faces, a scrap of paper fell out into the mess at his feet. It looked like the stub of a receipt for a flight booking.

Sept 23 - BA 2032 Dep: 09.23, Arr: 13:02

"Of course!" He ran back into the kitchen and as he ransacked the contents of a drawer, the cat jumped in through the window and onto the worktop. It brushed up against his shoulder and face.

"Not now!" Pushing the cat out of the way, he yanked the drawer out of the unit and emptied its contents onto the floor. Amongst the pile of kitchen clutter, he spotted the distinctive pale blue cover of Ella's old address book. He ran his finger down the a-z on the side and at the bottom of the relevant page he located the contact details for Ella's mother's holiday home in Spain. If Ella had left this morning, she would be there by now. He picked up the phone and began to dial but his hands were shaking so much his fingers kept missing the buttons. At last, the line clicked and whirred as the signal bounced off satellites and shot through cables, searching for its long distance recipient. It started to ring and within a few seconds someone answered.

"Ella!" Jacob said.

There was no response.

"Ella, it's me!" Jacob repeated. He pressed the receiver into his ear. Through the hiss and static he thought he could hear the sound of someone breathing.

"Please, Ella. I know it's you, speak to me. He put a finger in his other ear and pushed the receiver tight against his head. The breathing was soft, slow and rhythmical.

"Just say something. Let me know that you are all right. I'm worrying about you."

Again there was no response.

"Christ sake. I've had the police out. Come on, Ella. Is it so bad that you can't even say you're OK?" He pushed the earpiece further into the side of his head and put a finger in his other ear to try and isolate the sound.

"Listen, I know what's been going on and it doesn't matter. I'm not angry with you. It's my fault, I understand that now. Just come home and we can sort it out. I love you." The breathing stopped for a moment, and when it resumed, each inhalation was punctuated by a faint wheeze followed by a small resonant click in the throat. He forced the words out.

"Jude?"

But the line was already dead.

One Six Seven

In the first hours of daylight, he checked the quadrangle and the café and then searched the aisles and study desks in the library, but she wasn't there. In the museum, he took the stairs two at a time and scoured the Baroque room but she wasn't there either. He needed to know that he'd got it wrong, that Jude was not implicated or involved in his wife's disappearance, that she would walk in and sit in her place and that all of this madness would stop. He paced up to the end of the gallery, avoiding eye contact with the painting, trying to control his breathing. He visualised small electrical impulses shooting down his spinal cord, into his legs and ankles, the fibrous tissues expanding and contracting, the muscles pulling the bones forward. When his right foot touched the rear wall, he turned left and followed the skirting board to the next corner. When he reached the entrance again, he crossed the gallery diagonally until he came to the furthest exit. Then he retraced his steps back to the centre of the room. The sun shone through the skylight window and a single beam of light struck the marble tiles directly in front of his shoe. He edged slowly forward and craned his neck upwards to catch the ray as it fell. With eyes closed he held the position and waited, the light penetrating the thin membrane of his eyelids, the skin on his face beginning to warm and relax. He longed for stillness, for all movement and the accumulation of mystery to cease. He held his breath and counted.

One – two – three. The air in the chest cavity seeps further into the branches and tributaries of the lungs. Four – five – six.

Chemicals attack the oxygen molecules and convert them to carbon dioxide. One minute. The pulse thumps behind the cranial wall and pushes against eardrums and eye sockets. One twenty-six. The lungs ignite, searing pain spreading from the ribcage, up through the windpipe and down to the pit of the stomach. One forty-eight. The mind is overwhelmed by the instinctive will of the body to survive.

At one forty-two, he exhaled. He staggered forward out of the light and breathed in, his body straightening and stretching to allow the air to penetrate the oxygen-starved core of his lungs. Out and in again. His heart rate began to slow and the flush of blood drained from his cheeks. He thought he was going to topple over. He staggered to the bench and slumped down. He placed his hands on his knees, upturned as she had done. His pulse throbbed and the forefinger in his right hand twitched erratically. He concentrated on its movement. It slowed and then stopped. He clenched his fist and spread the fingers out, stretching the tendons as far as they would go. He relaxed his hand again; the spasm had gone.

He glanced back at the entrance. He needed her to be there right now, framed in the doorway, standing over him, in his way, blocking the painting, pressing her hips close to his face. He needed the smell of her wet clothes in his nostrils and the movement of her finger as it rested on her knee. But still she wasn't there.

Finally, he lifted his head and looked up at the painting. Its familiarity provided a moment's reassurance, but something wasn't right. He shifted along the bench. The glare from the halogen spotlights bounced off the surface. He moved back. His eyes followed a line from the girl's left shoulder, down her dress to her ankle. Her left foot turned out, one shoelace touching the floor, the other, obscured by the outside of her foot. There was something different about the reflection of the courtier, to the left of her leg. He was on one knee with his head bowed and his left hand resting on the scabbard of his sword. His right arm

107

was outstretched with a jewel-encrusted crucifix dangling from a thick golden chain.

There seemed to be more of the cross visible in the reflection and one of the rubies appeared to gleam with a greater intensity. He stood up and changed the viewing angle. He leaned in closer and then stepped back again, but it made no difference. The girl had moved; a partial, almost intangible shift to the left that altered both her posture and the juxtaposition of light and colour in the area surrounding her. He searched his pockets for his notepad to check previous entries but he'd left it on his desk at home. He tried to remember.

"Relative 2.4 (foot – lower frame) x 6.2 (foot to doorframe) x – to the right... Fuck!" His voice reverberated around the gallery. An attendant by the emergency exit was staring at him. He approached and Jacob shook his head.

"Sorry, I'm just a little agitated. I won't… eh, it won't happen again."

The attendant nodded.

"Does this look different to you," Jacob said, before the attendant could leave.

"Sorry?"

"Here, the foot." He tapped the canvas.

"Please, sir, don't touch the paintings." The attendant looked around the gallery.

"Does it look different to you?"

"How do you mean?"

"Different, you know, altered, changed?"

"Well, it hasn't been moved if that's what you mean?"

"No, I mean the foot, has *it* moved?"

The attendant laughed.

"I don't think it can move, sir, not really. Maybe it's the light. It's very bright outside today. It could be affecting your eyes."

"But the angle, is it pointing further to the right?"

"Maybe you should go for a cup of tea and come back to it. You'll probably find that it's just a trick of the light." The attendant looked nervously at the entrance again.

"I don't want a cup of tea."

The attendant shrugged his shoulders and returned to his seat by the entrance. Jacob looked back at the painting.

"Relative 2.4 (foot – lower frame) x 6.2 (foot to doorframe) x 3.35 (foot to right fingertip)." He repeated under his breath again. "Left foot alignment 1.5 degree from vertical elevation."

The angle had changed by at least two degrees. He went over and examined the lace on the girl's left shoe. The end was now visible on top of the buckle. He stepped back slightly and took in the whole of the girl's frame. She was leaning at an awkward angle against the mirror. He looked down at the glass on the table. A section of its base was now slightly elevated above the surface and appeared to be closer to the tipping point and the brink of toppling over. He followed the line down her dress to the left foot and sandal. The pointed end of the lace was now directing the eye to the dead pheasant that lay in the foreground. He continued from the tip down towards the bird. It passed through the tail, entering its body by the ribcage and the lace was pointing directly at the malformed V on the outstretched wing. The movement of the foot had somehow altered the alignment of the bird. It was as though the room had swivelled to the left slightly, changing angles and revealing more of the letters superimposed on the dead carcass. He looked round the gallery and spotted an elderly woman standing by a small Vermeer at the back of the room. He ran over to her.

"Have you got a mirror?"

The woman stepped back. "Sorry?"

"A compact, you know, for make-up?"

She looked him up and down for a second and started to reply. "I'm afraid—"

"Please, I didn't mean to startle you. I just need it for a second. It's important. I promise I'll return it." She examined his expression again, smiled nervously and opened her bag. He returned to the painting and placed the mirror close to the surface at an angle that would capture the reflection of the two letters. His hand shook as he tried to find the correct position and the scene flickered in and out of the tiny frame. Finally, the letters appeared. He held his breath. The incomplete and malformed D and V were now inverted and transformed into 'P' and 'M'. Jacob snapped the compact shut and slumped down on the bench. The elderly woman cautiously approached him. Her movements were measured and precise. Each carefully placed step was preceded by a slight twist of the hip that turned her left foot outwards as it made contact with the floor. She stopped three feet from him.

"Did you find what you were looking for?"

"Yes." He handed her the compact and she dropped it into her handbag.

"I hope you don't think it too presumptuous of me to ask," she continued, "but what was it exactly that you were looking for?"

He studied her expression for a second and then replied, "The truth."

She shifted her weight onto her right leg and, as she turned to leave, muttered something under her breath.

"What was that?"

"God bless you, son."

The Chaliced Hand

Back at the flat, he put the notebook down on his desk and flicked through the pages until he found the entry.

"Relative 2.4 (foot – lower frame) x 6.2 (foot to doorframe) x 3.35 (foot to right fingertip)."

He checked and re-checked numbers and calculations and scanned the scribbled formulae on the posters behind his desk and around the walls of his study. There was no doubt, no possibility that he had been mistaken, no trick of light or hallucination. The painting had moved. There had been an inexplicable yet significant shift to the left.

He sat down and searched a drawer for cigarettes but he couldn't find any. His office phone started ringing but it wasn't on his desk. The sound was coming from somewhere on the floor. He scrambled and kicked at the mess of papers and debris until he found the cable, and following the line across the room, he finally located the handset buried under a pile of notes. As he reached for it, the ringer stopped.

"Jesus Christ!" he hollered into the empty room.

The light on the front was flashing two messages. He pressed the recall button. The first was recorded yesterday at 3.29 pm. The machine whistled and the message began;

"Jacob, David Colby. I was hoping that you would come to see me today. I regret that due to your lack of willingness to deal with the issue of your work commitments, you leave us with no other option but to begin disciplinary proceedings."

From the tone of Colby's voice, it was clear that he was rather emotional. The message continued,

"Once again, I urge you to call me as soon as you possibly can or arrange an appointment with Mrs Skinner so that we can attempt to resolve this rather unfortunate matter."

There was a pause in the recording and then he concluded,

"I'm sorry. Bye."

Jacob pressed the delete button. The mechanism clicked forward to the second message, left the previous evening at 9.23. He must have missed it while he was next door with the detective. The speaker unit hissed and cackled for a few seconds and then a voice broke through the static.

"Jacob, it's Jude."

Jacob grabbed the phone and turned up the volume. The room filled with the roar of white noise.

"You need to find the letter opener. You need to find it and bring it to me."

The line sizzled and screamed again and Jacob leaned in closer to the speaker.

"Ella," Jude continued, but a sudden screech of feedback cut off the rest of the message.

In panic, Jacob picked up the phone and shook it violently, pulling the mains plug out of the back.

"Fuck!" he screamed and rammed the end of the lead back into the phone, but the loss of power had automatically erased all the recordings. He threw the phone across the room and it smacked against the rear wall.

In the kitchen, he searched the drawers for a suitable tool, and with a skewer he knelt down and stabbed at the surface of the hardened wax on the floor until it began to crack and break up around the edges. Fragments shot into the air and across the room. He gouged out piece after piece until only the thickest part remained. He jabbed into the centre and it split apart, but there was nothing there. The letter opener had vanished. He stood up and scanned the rest of the kitchen, the work surfaces, the sink and the table, but there was no sign of it. His chest tightened again and his eyes began to rotate inside their sockets. He felt his knees buckle under him and he grabbed for the table but it seemed to slide away from his hand. Falling sideways, he hit the floor hard, his head clipping the edge of the skirting board. In an instant, he was unconscious.

***

Luminous electrostatic filaments shot from one side of the gallery to the other, from the ceiling to the floor, from the window frames and skylights to the door. Tangible interdependent paths weaved between the painting, the girl, the book and the knife. Objects, flesh, thoughts and occurrences criss-crossed, and entwined. The room filled with a dense web of bright light.

Ella's face appeared. Her features distorted, her cheeks streaked with mascara and tears. She was trying to say something, her mouth contorted to form a word but the lips wouldn't part. He attempted to turn onto his side but he couldn't move. She pressed down on his eyeballs, forcing them back into their sockets. She was moaning, a low-pitched repetitive drone that grew louder and louder as she pushed her face into his.

He stopped breathing. There was something lodged in the

113

back of his throat. He tried to cough it up but his windpipe was completely blocked. He grasped at her face but his hands disappeared and melted into the soft warm tissue of her cheeks.

His lungs were on fire. He woke up and hauled his lifeless limbs from the floor and staggered out of the kitchen into the bathroom. He tugged at the light cord and the fluorescent tube spluttered off and on. Reaching for the sink, he turned on the cold tap and threw water at his mouth, swallowing whatever he could. The lump began to dislodge. His ribcage jolted and a small amount of air wheezed through the obstruction. He managed to get some more water down and this seemed to open the airway. His throat started to spasm and he retched into the sink. The intensity of the convulsions forced bile and vomit through his nose until, at last, the coughing eased and then stopped. He slumped over the sink and, wiping the tears from his face, he searched the bowl to find what had made him choke. Half way down the plughole a single black hair protruded from the metal grill. He pulled at it and a thick matted lump slowly emerged from the drain. The end squeezed through and popped out. He held it aloft and it swung on his finger like a pendulum. The hair was connected to something solid underneath. He held it higher and cocked his head to see. It was fleshy and pale yellow in colour, like over-cooked chicken. He dropped it in the sink and his stomach heaved. It was a neatly sliced triangle of skin.

In the cold grey emptiness of the living room, he dropped down into a chair and waited for the nausea to recede. "What's happening to me?" he muttered, staring at the blackened remains of the dressing gown in the fire grate. The door creaked and he turned.

"Ella?"

But it was the cat wriggling through the narrow gap. It jumped up on his knee and he stroked the softness around its neck and under its chin.

"Where is she?" he said, gently pulling the cat's tail. The cat purred and after a few more turns on his lap jumped down onto the floor and sat on the hearth by his feet. For the first time, he began to cry and the emotional release seemed to ease the fear and anger gripping his chest. Soon he was sobbing uncontrollably as the events of the last few weeks and months poured from him. He let all of it out, wailing freely like an infant or an injured animal waiting to die. Finally, when his body stopped shaking, he placed his hand on top of his leg, stretched out his fingers and followed the lines of tendons as they spread from the wrist to the first knuckle of each digit. He located the small crimson puncture mark where the letter opener had pierced the skin, a neat triangular incision in the centre of his hand. He pressed it with his thumb. The scar blushed and stood out against the pale yellow of the surrounding flesh. He closed his eyes and tried to visualise his wife's face, but his mind would not permit it. Instead, his thoughts fixated on the sound of Jude's voice rasping through the howl of feedback on the answer phone; her words reverberating inside his eardrums and pounding on the walls of his skull, tumbling over and over, repeating the same, unremitting mantra.

"Find it. Find it. Find it."

A hand grips the edge of the door, small bony fingers with knuckles white against pale yellow skin. The flames illuminate portions of the face and features begin to emerge from the darkness: Large intense eyes and piercing black pupils, the contorted line of the nose, the pale shape of a cheek, and the mouth with full pronounced lips upturned at the corners, smiling or grimacing. The girl twists, a sharp sensation of heat in her right side. She inhales. Her finger pushes against the goblet as she tries to control the pain. At first the rim resists but then slowly begins to move. She tries to pull it back, to force realignment, but the goblet refuses to return. Minute changes in colour, tone and light flutter across the surface. The wooden frame groans as nails and joints are stretched and tested to the limits of tolerance. In panic, she forces her head to turn to plead with it to cease, but her mouth will not open. The tendons and sinews in her jaw remain locked and frozen. The goblet hangs on the verge, between the ceiling and the floor, poised and prepared for the inevitability of the fall.

Part II

La Reina de Los Gatos

The side of his head rattled against the window of the carriage, and he fell forward onto the seat in front. Wiping a thin sliver of drool from his chin, he reluctantly opened his eyes and stretched his aching neck muscles. He had been asleep for almost the entire length of the journey and his brain was refusing to re-emerge from the befuddled fog of unconsciousness. He stood up just as the train shuntered to an abrupt stop and he tumbled back down into his seat. Peering through the window, he tried to decipher the name of the station on a sign at the rear of the platform, but his view was obscured by layers of dust and grime covering the outside of the glass. He stood up again and spotted a solitary figure at the other end of the carriage.

"¿Dónde estamos?" he called over to the man, who appeared to be asleep.

"Señor. ¿Cuál es esta estación?" he repeated.

Finally, the man looked up for a moment and shrugged his shoulders. Then, glancing out the window, he finally shouted back, "Los Gatos."

"Shit, my stop."

He quickly bundled up his belongings and stumbled along the aisle, through the door and out onto the platform. The heat of the late afternoon sun almost knocked him over and, dropping his bags to the ground, he held up both his hands to shield his eyes from the intensity of the light. Slowly the world around him began to materialise out of the glare. He squinted along the platform but he appeared to be the only alighted passenger. The train lurched forward and he stepped back as it rumbled reluctantly out of the station and melted into the shimmering blur of the horizon line. The station was now completely deserted except for a solitary cat stretched out on a bench by the small station building. It lifted its head briefly to scrutinise the new arrival but then returned to its nap. He picked up his coat and bag and made for the exit through the station building.

Inside, the air was considerably cooler. He paused for a moment to regain his composure. The walls were covered in heavily stained mahogany panelling and a large and rather incongruous ticket booth stretched the length of the room. Art Nouveau swirls and loops were carved along the outside of its frame, and above the counter, intense sunlight streamed through a tiny ticket booth window. He approached the hatch and peered into the office on the other side, but like the rest of the station, it too, was deserted. Behind him on the rear wall, the clacking movement of an ancient station clock resounded loudly around the room. He turned to look. The yellowing surface of its face was cracked and worn with heat and age. It was three minutes to six. His tongue rasped against his windpipe and, drawing the back of his hand over parched lips, he searched his bag for his bottle of water. He gulped at the remainder of the tepid liquid, swilling the last mouthful around his mouth before swallowing. Glancing round the room again, he quickly removed his sweat-sodden shirt and replaced it with a clean t-shirt. The dry cotton on his skin felt cool and soothing. He stretched and sighed, allowing his body a little more time to recover from the journey. Suddenly the clock began to chime; six loud and discordant notes that announced the arrival of the hour. Gathering up his belongings again, he hurriedly left the station.

About half way up a steep incline he stopped to catch his breath. It had been over three years since his last visit to La

Reina de Los Gatos, but it appeared to be more or less as he remembered it, a reassuringly preserved backwater that had managed to escape the ravages of tourist developments which blighted the towns and new developments along the nearby coastline.

As he pressed on towards the village centre, the rows of whitewashed houses on either side of the road seemed to lean in towards him, their stark smooth surfaces intensifying the glare of the sun. Eventually, he reached the small, deserted main square festooned in what looked like the remnants of a fiesta or some kind of wild exuberant party. Colourful bunting stretched from lamp posts and balconies around the perimeter, criss-crossing to a central axis point on top of a somewhat disused and dilapidated fountain in the centre of the plaza. A small stage had been erected under a giant rubber tree and enormous PA speakers were stacked up on either side of the platform. Around Jacob's feet there were tangles of multi-coloured streamers, confetti and spent firecracker carcasses. More decorations dangled drunkenly from the branches of tall potted olive trees and balustrades. On the other side of the square there was a temporary bar with rows of tables and high backed chairs stacked up precariously by its side, while others lay upside down and abandoned or congregated together in small intimate circles. Half empty glasses, discarded beer bottles and overflowing ashtrays were everywhere; on the table tops, around the bar area and even resting on the walls of the fountain. And on the far side, a large banner hung loosely across the front of the Ayuntamiento building. The inscription, in bold crimson lettering declared,

¡NUNCA MAS!

He carried on through the square and took a narrow side street adjacent to the cultural centre, and then down a steep hill that led to the house of Señora Vigo.

123

The señora had looked after Sylvia's property for over thirty years. Between family visits, the Professor's sabbaticals and holidays, she would air the rooms each week, give the place a once over with a mop and duster and sort out any maintenance or minor repairs that were required. Over the decades, Sylvia and Señora Vigo had become close friends and the señora had long since refused any payment for her time and efforts. In many ways, she considered Sylvia and her family as part of her own, and the feeling was reciprocated.

He approached the town house and thumped the big brass knocker against the weather worn front door. There was no reply. He tried again, this time a little harder but still with no response. Stepping back onto the road, he cleared his throat and shouted up to the balcony on the first floor.

"Señora Vigo." His voice bounced off the walls on the other side and then escaped out into the fields beyond the village. He tried again.

"¿Señora Vigo, está en casa?"

A dog started barking on the other side of the door. He waited a couple of minutes more, searched his bag for a pen and, rubbing his brow to try and re-animate his dormant Spanish, he scribbled a note on the back of his used boarding pass.

Señora Vigo. Acabo de llegar del Reino Unido. Estoy buscando a Ella. Voy a estar en la casa. Por favor, venga lo más pronto posible. Jacob

He folded the card in two and pushed it halfway into a small letterbox attached to the wall. He carried on further down the hill until he finally reached Sylvia's place, a large townhouse at the very edge of the village. He peered through a ground floor window but the shutters on the inside were closed. He was about to knock the door but changed his mind and instead went round the side of the house and down a long flight of steps to the rear. He tried the gate but it was locked. Kneeling down by the garden wall, he pulled at a couple of bricks until he located one that was loose. Carefully prising the brick out of its socket, he reached into the hole and retrieved a set of keys. The security grill across the back door was heavily rusted and it took all of his strength to shift it. As he yanked and tugged at the handle, it squealed and screeched in protest, until it finally swung open. He unlocked the door and stepped cautiously into the darkened space beyond.

"Ella?" he said, almost whispering.

Moving further into the blackness, he tripped over something at his feet and fumbled along the near wall for a light switch.

"Ella?" he repeated, stumbling over another object.

At last he found the switch and the fluorescent strip stuttered on. The room was crammed full of overfull boxes, piles of folded clothes and tangled heaps of recliners, deck-chairs and other garden paraphernalia. At the back of the room, there were two sinks and a washing machine, pulled out from the wall, its innards dangling out the back.

He glanced down at his feet. He had tripped over a box of shoes and various pairs lay scattered around him. He picked his way through the debris to the internal door that led up to the main part of the house. He slid a couple of boxes out of the way and, inching the door open, squeezed through the gap into the hallway. Again, it was pitch black and he cautiously negotiated the narrow stairway up to the ground floor. When he reached the top, he called her name again but with no response. He pushed the door to his left and intense bright sunlight flooded onto the landing. Shielding his eyes, he stepped inside and closed the shutters until the light was bearable. The kitchen was immaculately tidy with everything clean and neatly in its place. He went over to the kettle and touched its metal side. It was cold. Crossing the hall again, he went into the master bedroom. The bed was made and the dressing table was bare. He ran his hand along the cool surface of the quilt and then opening the cupboard, rattled the row of empty coat hangers.

He continued on to the salon. The last of the evening sunshine was streaming through floor-length drapes that hung across elegant balcony doors, filling the room with a warm orange glow. A large ancient leather sofa occupied most of the floor space, and on either side of a stone fireplace, two large book cases were crammed full of hardback volumes of journals and academic text books. A mahogany cabinet was pushed against a side wall and there was a large oval dining table with chairs over by the balcony. As in the kitchen, the orderliness of the room was a little unsettling; precisely stacked magazines on the side table, a selection of fruits carefully arranged in the fruit bowl as though waiting for an artist to paint them, cushions on the sofa fluffed up in near perfect symmetrical alignment. He went over to the fireplace and, kneeling down, touched the top of the empty fire grate. It was cold, but underneath, he spotted the half-charred remains of a cigarette end. He reached under and picked it up between his nails to examine it. There was a tiny pink smear of lipstick just visible on the end of the filter. He flicked it back into the fireplace and glancing round the room again, spotted some documents on the dining table. But before he could investigate, he heard someone shouting in the street below. He stepped out onto the small terrace and into the full glare of the sun. Leaning over the railing, he peered down into the street, but there was no one there. He went back inside and immediately heard the woman calling out again. This time he could see her standing on the pavement, partially hidden by the protruding lip of the balcony. It was Señora Vigo. She waved up to him when he saw her.

"Hola Señora Vigo," he said, waving back. "Voy a bajar a abrir la puerta." When he opened the front door, she greeted him with a prolonged embrace accompanied by three or four kisses on both cheeks.

"Ha pasado tanto tiempo, señor," she said affectionately.

"Lo ha hecho. Te ves muy bien," Jacob said, feeling slightly unnerved by the intimacy of the señora's greeting.

"No no, this is not true. My hips are worse than before and now my doctor say I have – sciatica, crónica," she said, switching to near fluent English.

"Please, señora, could you speak in Spanish. I'm a little rusty and I need to practise," Jacob said.

"False modesty, Señor Boyce," she said, switching back to Castilian. She studied his face for a moment. "So how are you? You look tired."

"Your transportation system is not the best."

"Ah, you came on the funeral march." She rolled her eyes.

"Unfortunately, yes. The service seems to be getting worse."

"Our little train is in the twilight of its days, I fear. You have been away too long, señor." She slapped his arm gently with the back of her hand. "We all miss you in the village."

"I'm sorry. I've been very busy you know. Life gets in the way of the important things."

"True."

"So what's been going on in the square?" he asked. "All those," he paused for a moment searching for the correct vocabulary. "Forgive me," he said, shaking his head.

"You mean the serpentinas?"

"That's the word I was looking for, the banners, yes."

"Oh, some political nonsense," she said. "I don't understand any of it. To be honest, I think I'm getting too old to care."

"I was sorry to hear about your husband. He was a good man," he said, inviting her to sit down.

"I'm still angry with him for leaving without me," she said, "but we carry on and that's all we can do."

"That's what he would have wanted you to do."

"Oh, I'm not worrying about him," she said, biting on her lower lip as though to censor further comment. "Now, señor,, we were expecting you yesterday. Where were you?"

"Yesterday?"

127

"With Ella."

"She was here?" he said.

"Of course she was here."

"You've seen her then?"

"Well, yes, I mean no, not exactly. She called me the day before yesterday to say that she would be arriving that night. She asked if I could prepare the house."

"Didn't she call in to see you on the way down?"

"No, I think it was very late, perhaps her flight was delayed. I called round the next morning but when I knocked there was no response."

"I don't think any of her things are here."

"She was definitely here, or at least someone was because you know I can see your kitchen window from my bedroom and the light was on. Maybe she's gone back to Barcelona for something. I can't believe she would leave without calling in to see me before she goes."

"I'm sure you're right." Jacob said, attempting to reassure her. "Did she say why she was coming to Los Gatos?"

"No," she paused again, "only that I should prepare the house. Of course, I said I would be delighted and as always it would be wonderful to see her again. I never thought she would just go," adding, "Did she not tell you she was coming?"

"It's complicated." He rubbed his eyes wearily. "Is it all right if I stay here tonight?"

"You don't have to ask, señor. This is your family home."

"Thanks. I used the spare key in the garden. I hope you don't mind."

"You don't have a key?"

"I think Ella took it with her." He sat down on the sofa and leaned back.

"Señor, you are tired. Please let me make you something to eat. I have some bread here in my bag."

"No, I'm fine. I had something to eat in Barça."

"But that was hours ago."

"I'm fine, honestly."

"At least allow me to make you a coffee."

"That would be great. I'm not sure that there is any."

"I'll go and see."

When she left, he pushed himself deeper into the sofa and closing his eyes, his wife reappeared for a moment, smiling and holding out her arms towards him affectionately.

"Black, one sugar?"

Jacob looked up with a start. The señora was standing over him with a cup. "Sorry, I think I must have fallen asleep."

"Just ten minutes or so, you must be very tired. Black with one sugar. Is that correct?"

"You have a very good memory, señora," he said, taking the cup from her.

"Now, would you like some ham and eggs, English, I mean, Scottish style?" She smiled.

"No, the coffee is fine, honestly. I'll go to Las Olas later."

"If you are sure?"

"Positive," he said, sipping slowly on the hot liquid. "You've done enough for me. Anyway, I think I need to shower and change."

"Very well, señor, but please come and see me tomorrow morning. And if Ella returns, please bring her with you and I will make you both some breakfast."

"I will, I promise. Thank you."

"I'm so glad that you are both here. This can only be good." She smiled at him affectionately.

Jacob nodded and carrying her heavy bag of shopping, he followed her back down the narrow staircase, through the lobby and to the front door. She hugged him again and he handed her the bag.

"Do you want me to take that back to your house?"

"No, no," she said, shaking her hand. "Hasta mañana."

"Mañana," he repeated and she kissed him on the cheek again.

129

He watched her as she slowly made her way back up the hill. About half way, she stopped and turned. He waved to her, but instead of waving back, she pointed at something above and behind him. Turning round, he leaned out over the balcony to get a better view. An ominous black cloud had engulfed the line of hills that encircled the village. As it rolled in towards him, the air suddenly cooled, the sunlight faded and there was a distant rumble of thunder. Turning back, he waved to her again, but she had already gone.

Las Olas

The solitary village bar was often described by the locals as the heart and soul of La Reina de Los Gatos. Miguel Figueras had inherited the business from his father, ex-mayor and a respected elder in the village. Like his father, Miguel was a powerful and equally venerated figure who seemed to have his finger in most pies and puddings of village life. But tonight, the bar was quiet. The thunderstorm had probably dissuaded most from leaving the shelter and safety of their homes. As Jacob stumbled in through the door, the wind sent beer mats and paper table cloths flying across the room. He slammed the doors shut and removed his dripping wet coat. When Miguel saw him he smiled broadly and shouted over to him. "Hey escocés. ¿Dónde estabas, escondido?"

Jacob approached him and Miguel extended his arm over the bar.

"Good to see you, Miguel," he said as Miguel took his hand and shook it firmly.

"You brought your lousy Glasgow weather with you."

"Looks like it."

"That's the first rain we've had for eight months, so well done. Hang your coat on the stand and I'll get you a beer."

When Jacob returned, he picked up a napkin from the counter and wiped the moisture from his face. He glanced round the bar. Three old guys were sitting together in silence at a table in the far corner. While at the other end, a group of well-fed, red-faced builder types were engaged in a heated argument

131

about some quiz show that blared out from a small black and white TV high above the bar.

"So how are you, my friend?" Miguel said, handing him a beer in an ice-cold frosted glass. "You look fucked."

"Thanks," Jacob said, holding up the glass. "How's business?"

"Shit. It's always shit. No one wants to drink any more except those assholes," he said, pointing at the builders. One of them turned, smiled and then gestured obscenely at him.

"How's Rosa?" Jacob asked, gulping on his beer.

"The thorn in my rib? She's fine. And before you ask, she's off tonight so there's no food except olives and bread."

"You've given her a day off?" Jacob said, smiling. "You must be getting soft in your old age."

"She's gone to Barça with friends for a weekend of shopping and whatever shit women do when they get together. God preserve my credit card balance."

"That's a shame. I like Rosa. She's prettier than you."

Miguel shrugged his shoulders. "She's back tomorrow. Are you here for a few days?"

"I don't know yet," Jacob said, finishing his drink.

"Did you hear about Paco?" Miguel said, pouring Jacob a second beer.

"Which Paco is that?"

"Paco Ibañez, you know, he owns the garage out on the Fincas road."

Jacob nodded.

"He won the loteria, forty-eight million pesetas."

"Really? That's fantastic."

"No, it was a disaster. The day after he won, he dumped his wife and then torched the garage. The village was lit up like Las Fallas for about a week. Then the fucking asshole disappeared. Nobody knows where he went. And about two days after that his wife and kids vanished too, but the strange thing is, the cheque was never cashed."

Jacob shook his head and took another sip of beer.

"What was all that about, eh?" Miguel continued."Give me the fucking cheque, I'll show that asshole how to spend the money."

"Would you torch this place?" Jacob quipped.

"Yeah, with all these fuckers in it."

"Jacob glanced back at the builders. "Evening, Manolo," he said, spotting a familiar face.

Manolo turned and shrugging his shoulders, muttered something to him in Catalàn that he didn't understand.

"What did he say?" Jacob asked.

"Don't ask." Miguel grinned." So, food?"

"Yes, that would be good."

While Miguel went out the back to make up the order, Jacob sat down at a table by the wall and searched his pockets for his cigarettes. Puffing heavily on the end, he peered out the window to see if the rain had stopped yet. But if anything, conditions outside had worsened. As gale-force winds sent debris flying in every direction, marble-sized hailstones were now raining down on the square, smashing into puddles and car windscreens and rattling the roof of the bar like rapid machine gun fire. Every couple of seconds a series of lightning flashes illuminated the village, followed by a loud crack of thunder. Miguel returned with a plate of food and an ashtray.

"It's going mad out there," Jacob said.

"Ella will get soaked," Miguel replied. "Has she made it back yet?"

Jacob spat out an olive stone onto the plate. "You've seen her?"

"Of course." Miguel grimaced. "She was in last night."

"When?"

"Last night."

"Yes, but when?"

"It was late. Rosa had already closed the kitchen but as it was Ella, she made them something anyway. Is he one of her work colleagues?"

"Who?"

"The guy she was with."

Jacob stood up. "What guy?" he repeated.

"The Sevillaño."

Jacob's head began to spin and he grabbed the table to steady himself.

"Tranquilo, Jacob. What's the problem?"

"What—" Jacob began, but his voice faltered.

"Sit down, my friend, I'll get you a Soberano."

Jacob slumped back down in his seat and stretched his left hand out on the table. The small puncture mark was now barely visible on the surface of the skin. He rubbed the scar backwards and forwards until its shape and colour intensified. Miguel returned with a large glass of brandy.

"It was a real tragedy, you know, about her father," he said, handing him the glass. "How is she now?"

Jacob took a couple of sips and put the glass down on the table. "What's she doing here?" he said finally.

"You didn't know she was here?" Miguel said, sitting down next to him.

"She disappeared a couple of days ago."

"What do you mean, disappeared?"

"When I got back from work, she'd gone."

"And she didn't say anything, you know, ring you or leave a note or anything like that?"

"Nothing. The door of the flat was wide open. I thought something terrible—" He stopped and picked up the glass.

"And this guy, you didn't know about him?"

"No."

"Fuck," Miguel said, dropping his head.

"Fuck indeed."

"I thought she was acting a bit odd. Well, Rosa said to me afterwards that Ella wasn't herself. I said that she was probably still mourning her father, but, you know my wife," he said, shrugging his shoulders. "Nothing gets past her all-seeing eye.

She thought she was—"

Jacob looked up from his brandy. "What?"

"She said she thought she seemed afraid."

"Of what, the Sevillaño?"

Miguel thought for a moment and then answered, "Perhaps preoccupied is a better word."

"Were they arguing then?"

"No, but she seemed nervous, not the confident Ella we know."

"What was he like then, the Sevillaño?"

"What can I say, he was tall, long hair, a Sevillaño, you know, a quiet guy, maybe a bit older than you. When she introduced him, she didn't say his name, just that he was a work colleague."

"So did she say why she was here?"

"She said she had some work to do in Barça, some corporate case or other."

"How were they with each other? I mean, were they affectionate or physical or—"

"Jacob, my friend," Miguel interrupted, "don't bother with this. I'm sure it's someone connected with her work. She's probably forgotten to tell you about it. Rosa made them a meal, they had a couple of drinks and they left."

"Did she say anything about me?"

"I asked her if you were coming out and she said, maybe."

"So they stayed at the house?"

"Where else would they stay? She doesn't have a car and the last train out of the village is 8.00."

Jacob downed his brandy and, standing up again, searched his pockets for some money.

"What are you doing?" Miguel asked.

"Thank you very much," he said, putting a couple of notes and a handful of coins down on the table.

"Jacob, you can't go. The weather is terrible out there. Stay and have another drink."

But Jacob didn't respond. Instead, he retrieved his sodden coat from the stand, pushed his arms through the crumpled sleeves and turned up the collar.

"Jacob, come on," Miguel repeated.

Jacob pulled at the door but it refused to budge. He tried again and this time, it flew open and the wind howled in. He stumbled out into the street, and pushed headlong into the tempest that had now completely engulfed the village. As he waded ankle-deep across the flooded square, his mind raced and raged against the elements and what Ella had done to him. He felt like a fool. She had been seeing this man for weeks, right under his nose, in his own bed and he hadn't even noticed.

And what of Jude, the painting and its movement, how did they figure in all of this? The questions tumbled over and over in his mind as he ploughed on through the wind and hail.

Approaching the house, he could see a faint light flickering on and off in one of the first floor windows. A fork of lightning suddenly skittered across the sky, and the burst of white light penetrated the darkness, momentarily illuminating the side of the building. He thought he saw a figure moving around inside. He ran down the hill to the front door and thumped it wildly with his fist.

"Ella!" he hollered, but his voice was drowned out by a prolonged roar of thunder. He pounded the door again and then ran round the side of the house, down the steps and in through the side gate. He fumbled with the keys and dropped them into the darkness at his feet. Down on his knees, he frantically scoured the sodden ground around the doorway, swiping his hands back and forth until he finally located them. With another flash of lightning, he unlocked the door and pushed it open.

Inside, he forced the door against the wind until it shut with a loud clatter. The noise and chaos of the night suddenly ceased and the storeroom fell almost completely silent. He turned on the light and pushed through the piles of boxes to the door up to the main house. Running up the stairs, he called out to her again. On the first floor, the living room door was shut. He tried the handle, but it wouldn't turn.

"Ella, let me in!" he screamed, hammering at it with clenched hand. Stepping back, he turned sideways and rammed the door with his shoulder. The frame creaked and cracked but still it wouldn't budge. In the kitchen, he searched a drawer for something sharp to force the lock and grabbing the sharpest knife he could find, he returned and thrust the end of the blade into the lock. He levered it up and down, pushing the knife further in towards the mechanism. But when the tip reached the hard metal bolt it refused to go any further.

"Fuck!" Jacob cried. "Open the door,, please."

The knife handle suddenly snapped and Jacob fell forward onto the door. And as the weight of his body pressed against the frame, the hinges creaked, the lock clicked and the door swung open.

He stumbled into the pitch-black room and, reaching for the light switch, he flicked at it but the power refused to come on. The storm must have tripped the electricity. The room was filled with a sweet pungent aroma of jasmine. Jacob recognised it immediately. It was Ella's favourite perfume.

"Ella!" he called to her again but there was no response. Feeling his way around the sofa, he reached into the darkness, and as his hands searched for the end of the dining table, something soft brushed against the tip of his fingers.

"Is that you?" he said, straining his ears to hear, but there was only the sound of the hail outside rattling against the French windows. He let go of the sofa and moving further into the room, he swiped his arms from left to right. But as he inched forward, the back of his hand struck something hard, sending a sudden jolt of pain shooting up his arm and into his shoulder. He stopped and rubbed at his wrist until the pain receded. By now his eyes were beginning to get accustomed to the dark. He could just make out the shape of the table in front of him and as he reached for the back of the dining chair that he had just hit, the power came back on and the lights suddenly burst into life. The room was empty. Running back across the hallway, he checked the kitchen and then both bedrooms but there was no one there. He returned to the living room. Everything seemed to be exactly as he had left it an hour or so ago. He sat down at the table and ran his hand though his wet hair. As he struggled to pull his arms out of the sleeves of his coat, he noticed his briefcase, upturned on the sofa with its contents spilled out over a cushion and onto the floor. He jumped up and the chair toppled behind him with a clatter. Grabbing the bag, he searched inside for his notebook. But it was missing. In panic, he emptied the remainder of the contents out and scattered them with the back of his hand, but the book wasn't there. He thought for a moment and tried to remember if he had been reading it. Perhaps he had put it somewhere else. But the last time he looked at it was on the plane on the way over. Removing the cushions from the sofa, he thrust his arm down the back and then the sides of the frame, but apart from an empty cigarette box and a few pesetas, there was no sign of it. Grabbing the end, he yanked the sofa as far as it would go over to the other side of the room, and as he clambered over the back to inspect the vacated space, he spotted the book lying face down and open on the sideboard by the door.

As he picked it up, two or three pages fell out on to the floor. The book was damaged. Its cover looked as though it had been crushed or twisted in some way and a few threads of binding were sticking out the top of its cracked spine. Inside, more pages were loose, or held together in collective clumps by the remnants of the stitching and glue. Kneeling down, he carefully reinserted the itinerant pages and flicked forward through the notebook, checking each page carefully. But when he reached the last of the entries, the section containing his notes on the observed movement of the painting had been clumsily torn out, with only ragged fragments of paper clinging desperately to the binding. He searched around his feet and behind the sideboard but they had vanished. Running down the stairs, he unlocked the front door and threw it open.

Outside the storm had passed and the sky was clear. The stars and a three quarter moon glistened brightly as though nothing had happened. He stood in the middle of the street and shouted out her name over and over. Two dogs began barking in a house opposite and a few lights came on. He went round the side and checked the steps down to the backyard, and then back up the hill as far as Señora Vigo's. He thought about knocking on her door but all her lights were out. He searched doorways and nearby side streets but everywhere was completely deserted. Even Miguel had shut up shop and closed Las Olas for the night. Exhausted and broken, he went back down the hill to the house.

In the bedroom, he re-examined the notebook and the tattered remains of the missing entries. He closed his eyes and tried to visualise the numbers, calculations and formulae he had documented but nothing appeared except an image of rolling black clouds encircling the house. He carefully closed the notebook and placed it down on the bedside table. As he lay down on top of the duvet, an image of Ella appeared from within the cloud. Once again, she moved towards him, smiling and holding her arms out. He focused on her features, her pale skin and pronounced nose and full sensuous lips. But as she approached, her face began to melt into itself, her features mutating and then disappearing until there was nothing except her left eye peering out of the impenetrable blackness of the cloud. He opened his eyes and the vision evaporated. He leapt out of bed, threw back the duvet and ran his hand across the base sheet, looking for the evidence and the stains of her betrayal, but the bed linen was clean and freshly laundered. He sat down, held his hands up to his face and breathed slowly into his cupped palms until the rage and confusion receded. Pulling the duvet cover over him, he lay back down on the bed, curled up in a tight ball and waited for the first waves of sleep to roll over him.

***

He was surrounded by a thick impenetrable blackness. His body felt heavy and restrained by something he couldn't see. He was on his back, though perhaps his head was closer to the floor than his feet, as he could feel the blood pounding in his temples. He rolled his eyes back and forth to see if he could locate an object or a person, but there was nothing, only the impenetrable gloom of the imposing space. He was aware of a sound, faint and indistinct at first, but growing imperceptibly louder as the seconds and minutes passed. It was a low-pitched hum that seemed to emanate from somewhere behind his head. He closed his eyes for a moment and focused on it. It was a human voice, a slow repetitive chant broken only by short inhalations of air. He counted the length of the drone. Each one was exactly twenty-three seconds.

He felt the panic rise in his throat. He attempted to speak but his mouth wouldn't open. He forced his tongue through his lips and it pressed against a cold metal surface. There was some kind of obstruction, a mask strapped to his face. He arched his back, but the restraints cut into the skin around his ankles, thighs, wrists and shoulders. The drone had now been joined by two, possibly three other voices. They began to articulate a repeated phrase that Jacob didn't understand. The straps around his forehead tightened, forcing his head back onto the hard surface beneath him and eliminating the possibility of even the slightest movement.

Suddenly there was a burning sensation in the top left of his skull. A hard, sharp object was being inserted under his scalp. As it penetrated the thin layer of flesh, it tapped and scraped against the cranial wall. The pain was unbearable. He bit down on his tongue as shards of white hot searing pain exploded

140

behind his eyes and shot down the length of his body, causing muscle and sinew to spasm and jerk against the restraints. But just when he thought he was about to black out, the humming stopped and the pain subsided. The hand lifted from his forehead and fingertips lightly brushed against his left cheek and lips. Someone was breathing close to his left ear. It was warm and slightly moist, and its gentle sensual rhythm seemed to instantly remove all sensation of fear or anxiety. It paused, and a moment later, whispered,

"Thank you."

His head was pounding. He sat up in bed and rubbed his temples to try and relieve the pressure. The morning sun was peeking through one of the half-closed shutters, filling the room with ribbons of light that illuminated dust particles as they danced and swirled around in the air. He stood up, but the hammering in his head intensified, and he staggered over to the window to push the shutters closed. At some point in the night, he'd managed to get out of his wet clothes and they lay in a heap at the end of the bed. The room was cold and he grabbed the duvet, wrapping it around his nakedness, and shuffled out the door. In the kitchen, he made himself a strong black coffee and slumped down at the table, the duvet cover bundling up around his head. After a few sips, his thought processes started to function again and the previous night's events began to play out in his mind like a relentless feedback loop. Reaching for the ashtray, he lit a cigarette and blew smoke high into the air. The combined caffeine and nicotine hit cleared his headache almost immediately. He took another long drag and glanced out of the window. The morning sky was blue and cloud free, and the back courtyards and gardens appeared to be completely dry. It was as though the storm had never happened. Finishing his coffee, he went back to the bedroom to get ready.

After a long shower, he returned to the living room with the notebook and examined it again. In the sober reality of the morning there was no doubt, no possibility that in his tired and drunken stupor he'd got it wrong. Someone, possibly Ella, had attempted and partially succeeded in destroying his work. Lighting another cigarette, he sat down at the table and felt the anger and bile return again. He slammed his fist down on the table top, his knuckle catching the edge. He howled in pain and his cigarette fell from his lips into his lap. He flicked at it frantically, sending a shower of sparks up into the air and the cigarette onto the floor. As he bent down to retrieve the half-extinguished remains, his finger brushed against something solid, protruding from the surface of the floor. He got down on his hands and knees to take a closer look. It was a small lump of something warm and hard. He pushed his finger into it and a section broke off. Clambering back to his feet, he examined the shard in the light of the French window. It was a small chunk of hardened wax, deep crimson in colour, with a portion charred black by smoke. He dropped it down onto the dining table, grabbed his bag and house keys and hurriedly left for the señora's house.

He rattled the large brass knocker on her door repeatedly until she finally came.

"Señor Boyce?" she said, looking a little flustered. "Is there a problem?"

"Can I come in?"

She ushered him in and he followed her into the living room which opened out into a beautiful sun drenched courtyard, overflowing with exotic plants and flowers.

"Come and sit outside," she said, and they continued to the patio area laid out with a couple of large wicker chairs and coffee table. She invited him to sit down and he slumped into one of the chairs.

"I'll bring you a glass of water. Wait a moment."

He leaned back and closed his eyes for a second.

"Señor Boyce," she said, leaning over him with the glass.

"Sorry," he said, taking the glass from her.

She sat down next to him. "What's happened?" she asked.

"Did you come to the house last night?"

"Of course, I met you there."

"No, I mean later, about 12.30?"

"What?" the senora said, confused. "I was in bed trying to sleep through the storm. It was awful. I was afraid that my roof was going to blow off. Is the house OK?"

"Are you sure you didn't forget something, or needed to drop something off," he said, ignoring her question.

"Señor, with weather like that it is always best to stay indoors. You weren't flooded out were you, in the basement?"

Jacob shook his head.

"Where's Ella? Did she come back last night?" she continued.

"No, but someone was in the house."

"Who?"

"I don't know. That's why I'm asking you. I saw a light on when I was on my way back from Las Olas. But when I got inside, the house was empty."

"Are you sure? It might have been the lightning. I mean, if Ella wasn't there then who—"

"The contents of my briefcase were all over the floor," he interrupted.

"Oh my God, you mean an intruder? Was anything taken?"

"No, just some of my work notes were—" he stopped. Señora Vigo had picked up the phone and was about to dial. "What are you doing?"

"I'm calling the police."

"No, don't do that."

"But a thief has been in the house. They could have taken anything. I mean, did they break in?"

"No, all the doors were locked."

"And you didn't see anyone when you went in?"

"The electricity had tripped the lights so it was pitch black, and when it came back on the house was empty."

She started to dial.

"Please, señora. I don't want to involve the Police in all of this."

"But, Jacob, if the thief has keys, he might return."

"It's just…" He paused. "I think it might have been Ella."

"What? But you said—?"

"Her perfume, I could smell it when I went in. The whole house was reeking of it."

"But why would she do such a thing?"

Jacob looked at the señora for a moment before answering.

"We've not been getting on," he said finally, sitting back down. "I haven't been the best of husband's recently."

"Oh, come on now," she said, sitting down next to him. "You've both been through a great deal. A death in the family, one so tragic can cause so much pain and some conflicts between you is unfortunately inevitable, but Ella is your wife. Why would she break in and steal from you, and then leave without…"

"I don't get it. Why here?" he mumbled, almost to himself.

"Did you hear what I said, Jacob?" She reached for his arm. "Maybe she needed to get away for a while."

"Get away from me, you mean?"

"She just might need the space to come to terms with her loss."

He shook his head in dismay.

"Listen, señor. Have you had any breakfast? I will make you some eggs, OK?"

"There was a man here with her," he said suddenly.

She looked up surprised, and her cheeks began to flush. "Did Miguel say something to you?"

"So you knew?"

"Sorry."

"Why didn't you tell me?"

"I thought he must be a friend of yours."

144

"They were in the bar together the other night, Ella and her mysterious Sevillaño colleague," he said, sarcastically.

"So you don't know him?"

Jacob didn't respond.

"Let me make you some eggs. Then we can think what to do. If you like, I can go and talk to Miguel again. He might tell me more."

Jacob nodded and the señora disappeared back into the house. From his bag, he removed the note he'd found at the flat with flight times scribbled across its centre. He was beginning to fear that it looked like some kind of premeditated plan Ella had been devising for some time. But it was unclear why she would come here, to her mother and father's holiday home ,with this man. He stretched the note between his hands and it began to tear down the middle. Resisting the temptation to rip it into tiny pieces, he folded it in two and put it back in his bag.

A short time later, the señora returned with a large plate of scrambled eggs and another coffee.

"Please eat," she said, setting it down on the coffee table in front of him. As she watched him eat, she began to click her nails together nervously. Jacob paused and put his fork down.

"Is something the matter, señora?"

"Ella was here a few weeks ago."

"What?"

"Normally Ella or her mother would telephone to let me know they were planning a visit but she just turned up without warning."

"When was this?"

"It was about three weeks, I think. Yes, September 1st."

"Are you sure?"

"Yes, because the train company was on strike and she complained about the extortionate cost of the taxi from the airport."

"But she was at a conference in Manchester at the beginning of the month," Jacob said after a moment's thought.

"I'm afraid she was here, señor."

"Did she stay at the house?"

"Yes, for two days and then she went back to Barcelona."

"What for?"

The señora stared at him for a few moments.

"What for?" Jacob repeated.

"To make arrangements."

"For what?"

She sat down next to him. "To live there," she said, finally.

Jacob dropped his fork and it clattered across the stone floor.

"What?"

"Let me get you a clean one."

"Fuck the eggs. What do you mean, live there?"

"Señor, please calm down."

"Why didn't you tell me this before?"

"I feel it is not my business."

"But I'm desperate, señora. You have to help me. What did she tell you?"

The señora reached under the coffee table for the fork.

"Leave it!" he barked at her.

She held her hand up to her eyes and Jacob leaned over and touched her wrist.

"Sorry. I am a little agitated. I didn't mean to upset you," he said.

"When my husband died," she began, trying to take control of her emotions, "I found out that he had been having an affair."

Jacob withdrew his hand and sat back in his chair.

"Some old letters in with his belongings, in amongst the stuff that dead people leave behind." She wiped her face and sat up straight.

"Who was it, do you know?"

"Oh, a woman from the city that he'd meet on his business trips. But, you know, the thing that got to me?' It wasn't that I never knew or even suspected, or that it had been going on for years. It was that she used his middle name, Francisco. Why did she call him that? No one called him Francisco. It was as though there was a whole part of his life that went on elsewhere and it had completely eluded me."

"I'm sorry."

"So then when Ella told me about her plans, I was very upset and I didn't know if telling you was the right thing to do. Knowledge can be a terrible thing."

"Did she say why?"

"She said that she needed to get out and that her life in Scotland was impossible."

"Impossible!" Jacob shrugged. "So this man, was he going to make it all possible again?"

"I don't know, she didn't say anything about him to me. The first I heard about it all was from Jorge, the butcher, who had seen them together in the bar the other night."

"And she said nothing else, about where she was in Barça or…"

"She asked me about a hotel. I can't remember the name."

"Please try and think, señora," he said, impatiently.

"La Fovea, a strange name." She paused again. "I think that was what it was called. Wait a moment." She went over to the side table and opening a drawer, removed a páginas amarillas.

"Let me see if I can find it in here." She opened the book and after a few moments of flicking back and forth, her finger stopped about halfway down a page.

"There it is, Hotel Fovea, two stars. It's in Barrio Gótico. I thought it might be a little run down so I suggested one or two of my own trusted places but she was insistent. Do you want the number?"

"Could you write it down with the address as well?"

"Please remember, señor, this may lead you nowhere." She folded the note and handed it to him, "I don't know where she stayed in the end and she never told me."

Jacob shrugged.

"She did say one thing though before she left," she added.

"What?"

"That she was afraid."

"Of what?"

"What you might do?"

"To her?"

"No, to yourself." She stopped and looked up at him. "Are you unwell, Jacob?"

"No more or no less than her," he said. "I think our marriage has been sick for quite some time."

"I mean, in your mind."

"Right now I feel numb," Jacob said, standing up. "I think I need to go back to the house and work out what to do next."

"I don't want to leave you alone," she said, reaching for his arm again.

"I'm not going to do anything stupid, if that's what you think." He moved away from her.

"Let me make you some more coffee and we can talk some more."

"No, señora, I'm all done," he said, picking up his bag.

The señora followed him to the door and, showing him out, she gave him another hug. "Let me know what you are going to do, OK?"

"Thank you," he said, and he set off back down the hill to the house.

When he had finished packing up his small travel bag, he sat down at the dining table and smoked the last cigarette in the pack. Leaning over, he spread out the neat pile of papers and scanned the various tourist brochures, leaflets and restaurant menus that Sylvia had collected over the years. About half way down, he picked out a brochure for a gallery in Barça. The cover detail was of a vaguely familiar Baroque painting. He studied the image for a moment and then pushed the brochure back into the mess of leaflets on the table. Drawing on the last of his cigarette, he flicked the glowing end into the fireplace and it bounced off the grate onto the hearth. He got up and pressed down on the fading ember with the toe of his boot, grinding it slowly back and forth into the marble until the filter was all but obliterated. He kicked the fragments under the grate and went to look for the house keys.

When he reached the señora's house, he dropped a note in her post box;

Dear Señora Vigo,

Thank you for your hospitality and kind words. I have gone to Barcelona to try and tidy up this mess. The house is locked and I have returned the spare keys. I have left the bed linen in the laundry basket.

Please don't worry about me. The truth will prevail.

Gratefully yours,
Jacob

Carrying on up the hill, he could hear the whistle of the train approaching the station, and he quickened his pace.

Café Madrileño

"Habitación ciento trenta y nueve."

"Are you sure?" Jacob said, staring at the hotel receptionist.

"Mira." The receptionist turned the guest book around so that Jacob could read it. "Tres noches, Septiembre tres a seis, Señora Ella Boyce, habitación ciento trenta y nueve."

Jacob studied the entry. It was definitely her signature. He ran his finger across her name.

"A single room, you say?" Jacob said.

"Single room con baño."

"And she checked in alone?"

"Si." The receptionist was growing increasingly impatient with Jacob's relentless questioning.

"I'd like to book this room please," Jacob said, removing his wallet from his coat pocket.

"Un momento." The receptionist leaned over and checked the latest bookings in his ledger. "OK, the room is free. How many nights?"

"Just the one for now."

"Una noche con desayuno," the receptionist said, handing him his key.

Jacob slid his bag over to the lift and pressed the button.

"No funciona," the receptionist said without looking up from the sports pages of his paper. "Not working. Escala – after the door."

When he reached the second floor, Jacob took off his coat and wiped the moisture from under his chin. He followed the numbers along a gloomy corridor until he reached his room. Inside, it was claustrophobically small and the hot, stale air reeked of bad plumbing and sweat. He dropped his coat on the bed and opened the window. The sounds of the city wafted in and swirled round the room; car horns, screams, and whistles, punctuated by the persistent thump, thud and hammer of urban regeneration. He lay down next to his bag and dropped his head into his hands. In a corner of his brain, he had half hoped to find Ella here waiting for him, her voice greeting him as he opened the door, but instead the emptiness of the space reaffirmed his ever-increasing sense of confusion and loss.

He got up and scoured the room for any sign or fragment of her life that she might have left behind. But aside from a tatty Gideon's Bible and a pile of dated tourist paraphernalia tucked away in the bedside drawer, the room was austere and bare. In the bathroom, he ran the tap until the water was cool enough to drink, and leaning over the sink he gulped greedily at the liquid as it gurgled out of the spout. He looked up and studied his features in the mirror. The shadows and cracks around his eyes had deepened and intensified, and a cold sore was beginning to form on his lower lip, the cluster of pale pink blisters glistened through a matt of thickening stubble. He looked at his watch: ten to five. He quickly removed all of his clothes, turned on the shower and stepped under a pitifully weak spray of tepid water.

When he had washed, shaved and changed into clean clothes, he returned to the bedroom and emptied the contents of his briefcase onto the bed. Gathering up the collection of objects, he laid them out methodically on top of the bedspread, his notebook in the centre, a photograph of Ella directly above and a selection of postcard images of his painting placed in a circle around the perimeter. He carefully unfolded various fragments of paper that he had accumulated over the months, tiny scraps covered in scribbles and observations, some perhaps still to be catalogued in his notebook. He placed each one between the postcards, eventually forming what resembled the pattern of a flawed snowflake. When he couldn't find anything else in his bag, he opened the notebook and turned to the torn pages of the missing part. He stared at the ragged corners for a couple of minutes, trying to activate his brain and remember his calculations of the observed movements within the painting. He scrutinised the scribbled notes for clues but they all pre-dated his final entries. Flicking back a couple of pages, he re-read his notes on the Professor. At the bottom of the page, he'd written out the equation $V=mP^3$ in bold red lettering. As he stared at the formula, he attempted to visualise the logical pathways he had travelled along, and the data he had calibrated. But every direction he tried was blocked by an impenetrable, unyielding blackness.

He closed the notebook with a loud thump and reached for a fresh pack of cigarettes, hastily purchased from the machine in the hotel foyer. Unable to find his lighter, he rummaged around in the bedside drawer and found a book of matches under the bible. He removed both and quickly lit the end, puffing repeatedly until the nicotine craving began to recede. Picking up the bible, he casually flicked through until he came to a leaflet that had been tucked between two pages. It was a flyer promoting one of the many Art Galleries in Barça, Galería Regional de Català. The image on the front depicted an aristocrat on horseback with hunting dogs by his side. But in a large tree next to him, there was a boy hanging from a branch by his neck. A rather unsettling image to put on the front of a promotional leaflet, Jacob thought. He glanced at the name of the gallery again and, searching his pockets for the paperback he'd purchased a few days ago, turned to page 239 and found the citation:

In *"La Mano Chastite"*, *(Manuel Piñero (1637), Galería Regional de Català, Barcelona), an infidelity is symbolised by the inclusion of the blood stained letter opener.*

He flicked the leaflet over and on the back there was a few lines of promotional blurb in Catalán. Jacob attempted a translation but could only decipher parts of it.

... a unique and highly unusual collection... important and influential works from obscure and lost artists from the 16th – 20th Century...

Beneath the blurb, a few of the represented artists were listed along with the contact details for the gallery. The address had been heavily circled in bold red pen and, along the bottom margin, a few handwritten words had been scribbled out. Jacob peered at the scrawl but couldn't make out any of the letters. He turned the leaflet over again and examined the imprint from the other side. Holding it up to the window, he could just make out the inverted impression of the original letters. There appeared to be two words pressing through the thin card. He searched his briefcase for a pencil and lightly rubbed the nib across the letters until their darker shapes stood out against the grey background; an inverted D N A and H, followed by D E S A H and C. The other letters were too indistinct to decipher. He put down the leaflet and, opening his notebook, copied down the inverted letters. Within a moment he realised that the near-obliterated characters were forming the phrase, CHALICED HAND. Grabbing his keys, he quickly returned to the reception.

***

There was now a young woman behind the desk who appeared to be equally disinterested in him.

"Excuse me," Jacob said impatiently, "do you have a street plan?"

The girl finally looked up.

"Tourist Information," she said, gesturing towards the hotel entrance.

"And where might I find that?" he asked, responding to her sullenness.

She sighed and went into the small office behind and returned with an A3 map of the city.

"We are here," she marked the hotel with a large cross, "and tourist information is here."

"Can I have this?" he asked.

She thought for a moment, shrugged and then handed it to him.

"Thank you," he said, sarcastically.

"And the Galería de Català?" But this was a question too far. She shook her head, closed her gossip magazine and retreated to the office, slamming the door behind her.

On the back of the plan was a list of sightseeing attractions. He scrolled down the column until he found the gallery and its co-ordinates on the map. He followed the network of streets from his hotel in the Barrio Gótico, along the central spine of Las Ramblas and then up into Eixample. Finally his finger stopped on a cul de sac about two km from the hotel. He folded the map until he could fit it into his pocket and left the hotel.

Out on the street, the early evening air was humid and oppressive. He negotiated the labyrinth of alleyways and decaying gothic buildings until he reached the main part of the barrio. He cut across Plaza del Pi which was just starting to come to life again after the siesta. Waiters were busily preparing tables for customers while stall holders, buskers and street peddlers were setting up for the evening trade.

When he reached Las Ramblas, his shirt was already drenched in sweat. The main thoroughfare was packed with tourists and locals returning to offices after their prolonged lunch break. He fought his way through a large group of overweight elderly Americans, who were all bedecked in identical blue nylon sports jackets with *Philadelphia Old Timers On Tour* emblazoned across the back. They had gathered around a particularly loud tuba playing busker who was wearing an ill-fitting clown's outfit. Most of his make-up had been washed away by a torrent of sweat pouring down his face, and as he blew on the horn, his cheeks inflated to an unnatural size. After a moment of cacophonous noise, a large bubble appeared from the end of the instrument, floating gently out through the crowds and up into the cloudless evening sky. A child standing nearby began to wail hysterically and she buried her face in her mother's skirt. The mother picked her up and quickly moved away.

Jacob continued through a relentless sea of people who all seemed to be pushing in the opposite direction, until finally he reached Plaza Catalunya. As he stopped to get his bearings, a man approached him from behind.

"You have money?"

"What?" Jacob said, turning round. A down and out was standing close to him, with his arm extended. The stench was overpowering and Jacob instinctively stepped back from him.

"You have money?" the man repeated in English. He was wearing a couple of filthy plastic bags on his feet that were tied round the ankles by a pale string-like substance that looked like long strips of skin or internal tissue. His hair was long and matted with black oily clumps dangling over his face, obscuring most of his features.

"Dinero," the man growled.

"No," Jacob retorted and stepped further away from him, partly to escape the sensorial assault. The man followed.

"Borracho, dinero?" he said again, holding out both hands now.

"No." Jacob increased his pace.

The man persisted and grabbed Jacob by the arm. Jacob pulled away with some force and as the man staggered backwards, his long hair fell from his face for a moment, revealing an empty eye socket that resembled a large bullet hole in his forehead.

"I have no money, now fuck off!" Jacob shouted, staring

morbidly into the dark void of the empty cavity.

"Aquí," the man roared, pointing at the ground.

Jacob ignored him and carried on.

"¡Aquí! Terra firma, mira."

When Jacob looked back again, the tramp was stamping on the ground with his left foot.

"¡Aquí, aquí!"

Jacob finally spotted a break in the traffic and ran to the other side of the square. When he reached the safety of the pavement opposite, he turned again to check that he hadn't been followed. The man had gone but there seemed to be a space in the crowd where he had been standing.

"Fucking lunatic," Jacob muttered and continued on into Eixample.

Passing through a wide tree-lined avenue, he came to an intersection. He looked across the wide expanse of road and the various junctions and routes available but soon realised he was lost. He removed his map but was wary about opening it out for fear of attracting the unwanted attentions of pick pockets or more insane vagrants. He turned it over and back again but he couldn't find the junction he needed. He was tired and uncomfortable and the bitter taste of the traffic was clinging to the back of his throat, making it painful to swallow. On the opposite side of the avenue he spotted a cafeteria sign, tucked away at the end of a narrow side street. He picked up his bag and waited for a break in the flow of cars.

Jacob stepped into the bar and immediately wished he hadn't. The room was gloomy and reeked of a sickly sweet stench of rotting flesh, not dissimilar to the repugnant aroma emanating from the tramp. His nose led him to a collection of ham joints hanging on the wall behind the bar. They were skewered on hooks in a long row above bottles of spirits and liqueurs. Each dismembered thigh was covered in a yellowish blue mould with blackened trotters sticking out the top. The nails were curled and tied together with rotting string, and thick congealed globules of fat oozed out of protruding arteries and dripped onto the bottles and surfaces below. They were everywhere, little mounds of hardened lard splattered on shelves and on top of the till. He was about to turn and leave but the lure of a cold beer and a rest convinced his body to reluctantly remain. He scanned the rest of the bar. The walls were plastered in shiny, fading posters of ancient bullfighting events and football teams. In the corner, a TV blasted out an afternoon game show, a Real Madrid scarf was draped over the screen with a small plastic replica trophy balanced on the top. The bar was half empty, for any number of reasons, Jacob supposed. A couple of seasoned drinkers had spread themselves out at the counter. They were engaged in an animated conversation in Catalàn. A thin, pale-looking man sat in the furthest corner reading a local paper. Every few seconds he took a sip from a large brandy glass and puffed heavily on a fat cigar. Jacob pulled up a stool. He turned to the barflies.

"Perdon, ¿Usted sabe dónde está el barman?"

They broke off their argument for a second, scrutinized him, and then resumed their conflict. He called out, hoping that the barman would appear from the toilet or from a back room, still nothing. He tapped the counter with a beer mat and was about give up and leave, when the man in the corner folded his paper, put his cigar out in an ashtray and went round the other side of the counter.

"¿Dígame?"

"Cerveza, por favor," Jacob said at last.

"¿Caña?"

"Si."

The barman slowly poured a beer from a large silver pump. As it spilled over the top, he ran a small knife across the rim of the glass, flicking the froth to one side. When it was finally ready, he placed it down on the counter. Jacob seized the glass and guzzled impatiently on the ice-cold liquid, choking slightly in his haste.

"¿Otra?"

"Si."

About half way through the second he began to feel a little better, and he picked at the pistachios the barman had put down in front of him. He split one and was about to pop the contents into his mouth when he spotted a dribble of fat trickling down a bottle of Jack Daniels just behind the barman's greasy head of hair. He dropped it on the floor and took another sip of beer.

"¿Sabe cómo llegar a la Galería Regional de Català?"

The barman shrugged and wiped the counter with a filthy tea towel.

"No sé."

Jacob turned and asked the two combatants at the other end of the counter. One grimaced and the other pointed to the door, perhaps suggesting that Jacob should use it. He unfolded his map and laid it out on the bar.

"¿Galería de Català?" he repeated.

The barman picked up the map and turned it this way and that, then put it back down again. "No sé ," he repeated.

Jacob raised his glass. "Salud - no pasa nada." He downed the remains and tapped the rim. "Una mas."

About five minutes later, a man entered the bar and went over to the cigarette dispenser. As Jacob turned to look, he wobbled unsteadily on his stool. The beer was beginning to take effect. The man dropped three or four coins in the machine and a packet clacked out the bottom. He repeated the procedure again, and then again, until he had collected three. He approached the counter and stood next to Jacob. He pulled at the cellophane wrapping, removed the silver foil and tapped the end of the cigarette on the back of his hand. He spotted Jacob looking at him and held up the pack.

"No, gracias."

The man lit his cigarette, inhaled and blew the smoke high into the air. "¿De dónde eres? De Inglaterra?"

"Yes, well, no. Escocia. Soy escoces nuevo."

The man attempted some English. "Ah Scotland, what beautiful, very nice personas."

"Uno o dos de ellos son." Jacob nodded.

The man pulled himself up onto a stool, manoeuvring his buttocks until he was comfortable. Jacob swivelled round to look at him. He was seriously overweight, his large frame bulged against the fabric of his suit and his gut, which had partially escaped from his shirt, engulfed the top of his belt. His eyes were bloodshot and watery, and the lids looked painfully swollen, as though they had been cooked.

"I go there with my mujer… to Edimburgo y Foat Wilyam, before the año."

"Ah." Jacob sipped his beer. He didn't want to get into it.

"Are you doing holiday here en Barça?"

"No, estoy en el negocio."

"Business? What business is it of you?" The man persisted in English.

"I'm an Art Historian," Jacob said, avoiding the truth.

"¿Cómo?"

"Un profesor de Historia del Art."

"Ah, I am interesting."

Jacob pointed at the unfolded map on the bar. "Perhaps you can help me? I'm trying to get to the Galería Regional de Català. Do you know where it is or maybe which bus I could catch?"

"To cash?"

"To take, what number do I take?"

"Galería de Català, you say – ah I know this Gallery. Mira. It is – I'm sorry. My English is very difficult."

"It's very good," Jacob lied. "Pero yo hablo español así que no es un problema para mi entender."

"I want to practise because I study until many years, for School, to University, but is very – how do you say – duro?"

"Hard?"

"Yes, I am very hard."

Jacob stifled a grin.

"And I have…" He shook his head. "¿Cómo se dice, like a donkey?"

"Big ears? Hung?"

"Lazy!" He held up his hand, and paused, his brain formulating another tortuous translation. "I have is fucking lazy."

Jacob laughed. "My Spanish is OK, honestly, so I don't mind, if you'd prefer."

"Vale, when I speak English, I have five years." He switched to Castillian. "The gallery is part-financed by CAC."

"CAC?"

"You don't know CAC? Caja de Ahorros De Català? CAC is one of the largest banks in Catalunya. I work for CAC, so I am familiar with this gallery. The bank purchases works and funds some exhibitions there." In Spanish, the man's accent was soft and refined.

"So is that what you do?"

"No, I wish I did. Unfortunately, I am in charge of freight. Essentially, I am Head of Transportation and consignment allocation. That's my official title. I prefer 'fucking lazy', but I like to keep up to date as much as I can with CAC's cultural programme."

"What's that?"

He took another long drag on his cigarette. "Well, the bank sponsors and promotes activities in Barcelona and around Catalunya – museums, galleries, films, theatre, music, artists, installations, and so the list goes on. They like to invest a lot of money in the preservation of traditional Catalunyan culture."

"Why? What's in it for CAC?" Jacob said, warming to the conversation.

"Ah, I see you really are Scottish. I suppose the bank would say they want to be seen as a philanthropic organisation. But if you are a cynic like me, then they are in the business of selling an elaborate white lie. Their support of the arts perpetuates a myth, a sophisticated illusion that CAC is cool, a supporter of Catalunya, a purveyor of high cultural refinement. And so the more they sponsor, the more their customer base expands as the people of Catalunya buy into the logo and the myth. And when the hazy heady mist of altruism clears and the customer finds himself mortgaged up to his eyeballs, and his credit card debts spiralling out of control, at least he can say, I may be homeless and hungry but I supported the Arts. You think I am a little bitter, no?"

"Not at all, you sound more like an anti-capitalist."

"Aha, you have found me out. I'm afraid it's true, the one and only anti-capitalist banker, a Marxist hypocrite caught in the jaws of a ravenous and rampaging bourgeoisie, public enemy number one!" He leaned over and whispered, "Is it that obvious?"

Jacob laughed and extended his hand. "How do you do? I am Jacob."

"Oh, very English, or should I say, British. How do you do? My name is José, José T. Miro." They shook hands and nodded in unison.

"So what about the Galleria Regional de Català?" Jacob asked.

"Yes, this is a very special place for CAC because it was one of the first galleries in the city to benefit from the bank's support. The relationship goes back a long way, well, to 1987 when CAC had to write off some tax and so they thought that the galleria would be the best place to launder the money."

Jacob smiled.

"Forgive me, there I go again. I shouldn't say such terrible things about my place of work." He sipped his beer. "I can tell you exactly how to get there," he said, turning the map around. "We are here." As he pointed, a column of ash fell from the tip of his cigarette, covering the south side of the city centre. "And you need to walk a little further, up to here, take the number 19 and you are within two blocks of the Gallery. Then it's a short and pleasant walk through Eixample and you're there, or here." He tapped the plan and pulled a pen out of his suit to mark the route.

"What about the bus stop?" Jacob asked.

José leaned over the bar and called to the barman who was wrestling with one of the beer pumps at the far end of the counter. The barman looked up and replied in garbled Catalàn that Jacob couldn't understand.

"A couple of blocks away, I will show you when you leave."

"Thank you very much. Let me buy you another beer." Jacob touched the rim of his glass with his forefinger.

"I shouldn't really." José winced. "I'm supposed to be in a meeting but, hey, I'm the boss so I can be late. I'll reprimand myself later. Same again, thanks."

The barman poured another couple of beers and José continued. "I am a great art lover you know. Well, I am now, after my eye operation. Perhaps you noticed that my eyes are a little red. I've just had treatment to correct the focal length of my lenses."

"Both eyes?"

"Yes. My God, it was painful. It took six visits, each one more agonising than the last. But it was worth it. Now I have twenty-twenty vision. Or I will have in a couple of months when the swelling goes down and the retinas recover. So art for me is like a whole new experience. I can see colour, lines and detail like I never could before. Of course I always loved painting and sculpture but now I don't have to half-imagine their beauty, I can see it all as clear as day and it really is a magnificent thing. It is so incredible."

"But didn't you wear glasses or contacts."

"Yes, but I have a degenerative problem with my retinas, so glasses and contacts were never quite right. I looked like, what's the name of that cartoon guy, the old man?"

"Mr Magoo?"

"Señor Magoo, that was me six months ago. The laser surgery has hopefully removed the problem and my eyes will remain stable. So, Señor Jacob, today you have met the right person. I am like a child in a sweet shop. I can't get enough of my new eyes. I can see the world as it really is. What is it you are looking for in the Gallery?"

"Well, it's a painting by a lesser-known Baroque artist called Manuel Piñero." Jacob fumbled in his briefcase and removed the book he'd purchased in Glasgow. He turned to page 239 and handed it to him. "Here is a description of the work. The painting is called The Chaliced Hand. Do you know it?"

As José read, he rubbed his left eye gently. He looked up. "I'm not sure." He puffed on his cigarette and blew out another long stream of smoke. "No, sorry, it's gone. That's what you get when you work in a bank, fucking dementia! I can't say I'm familiar with him or this painting. What did you say it was called?"

"The Chaliced Hand."

José shrugged his shoulders.

"Don't worry. He's a little obscure."

José flipped the book over and looked at the cover.

"This is pretty old. Did you buy it in Scotland?"

"Yes, I got it in a second hand bookshop. The book-keeper said the author was once an authority on Spanish Baroque Art." José shrugged and flicked through the chapters. "You've been working hard, haven't you?"

"Oh, those are not my notes."

"This entry here looks like Catalàn. "A la vida – busquem l'alegria de la – verita," he said, trying to decipher the hand writing. He closed the book and put it down on top of the map. "There are a few Baroque artists in the gallery. Let me think, we have one tiny Velázquez and something that could be an El Greco. The rest were plundered by Franco and his cohorts and shipped back to Madrid. Of course, if you are looking for

Baroque art, then you really have to go to the Prado museum in Madrid. But you have already visited, no?"

"No."

"What? An art historian who has never visited El Prado?" He lit another cigarette with the end of his last. "If you are going to find your Señor Piñero, then El Prado is the place to do it. But this specific painting you are looking for is maybe in the Galería Regional de Català, I don't know." He shifted his weight onto his left buttock. "So what is your fascination with this character Piñero?"

Jacob thought for a moment. "I'm trying to establish a link between him and an anonymous painting in Glasgow."

"And you think he may have painted it?"

"It's possible. The museum has it down as a Velázquez but I'm not convinced."

"Ah, they would say that, wouldn't they? A nice little crowd puller. So you have come to Barça to find the evidence and the truth."

"I hope so."

"Well, this is the best city in the world to find truth. Great artists and writers have been doing it for centuries."

"You seem very passionate about Barcelona."

"You think so?"

"So why do you drink in a bar called El Madrileño?"

"A-ha, you have found me out again." He waved his finger at him. "I will be honest with you, I am a Madrileño. I was born in Madrid, but when I was seven, my father moved us to Barcelona. I suppose I am like a spy. I have perfected the accent, I speak fluent Catalunyan. I even sing its praises to passing Scotsmen. But deep down I am a Madrileño and I can't escape my past, you know?"

"I don't think any of us can. But listen, you aren't much of a spy if you come in here every day."

"Ah yes, but it's like a double bluff. My friends think I am like a double agent, checking up on the enemy."

164

"So your friends don't know you are from Madrid?"

"No, I could never tell them. It would break their hearts. They are all so proud of their culture, their language, food, beer, and their fucking football team."

"But isn't that a little sad, to live a lie like that, deny your roots?"

José paused and then started to snigger. He slapped Jacob on the shoulder.

"Do you really think I could hide my identity like that in Barcelona! Catalunyans can smell a Madrileño coming from a thousand kilometres away. Surely it is the same in your country with the English. Madrid is in my blood and there is no way I could conceal it, not from them."

Jacob shook his head and drained his glass.

"Another?" José smiled mischievously.

"Well, I shouldn't really."

"No," he clicked his fingers, "I tell you what, let's have a real drink." He gestured to the barman. "Two Glenmorangie, is that how you pronounce it?"

"Yes, you've obviously practised, but I think I've had enough."

"Oh come on, it's not every day I meet a Scotsman, and you don't want to offend me, do you?" He smiled.

The barman flicked off a blob of semi-dissolved tendon stuck to the side of the bottle. He poured two enormous measures. Jacob attempted to stop him but José brushed his hand aside.

"Cheers."

"Salud."

Jacob winced as the liquid scorched his throat. José took two or three large mouthfuls and let out a loud sigh.

"I love Scotland," he said in English and took another couple of mouthfuls. Wiping his mouth, he returned to Castilian.

"So where are you staying?"

"The Hotel La Fovea. Do you know it?"

"It's in the Barrio Gótico, no? Is it OK?"

"Shit hole."

"Isn't that the hotel with the eye in the basement?"

"What?" Jacob said.

"I'm sure it is," he replied. "A few years ago, when they were renovating the building, they unearthed some kind of eye-shaped well in the cellars. It dates back to the Moors or even earlier. It's quite famous because it's so unique. I can't believe they haven't told you about it." He let out a loud chortle. "Hey, now there's a coincidence. I've got my eyes back and you've got one big one buried in your hotel basement. Check it out before you go back to… is it bony Scotland?"

"Bony it is."

"To bony Scotland," he said, raising his glass. "I wish you the best of luck, señor. I'm sure your trip will be fruitful."

"Thank you," Jacob said, downing the remainder of his drink in one.

"So now unfortunately, I must return to the workhouse," José said, slamming his empty glass down on the counter. "I will show you the way to the bus stop now."

José slipped off his stool and flicked at the ash on his jacket. "I have to chair a meeting on cost-cutting strategies for the internal post. I'll be thinking of you wandering around our beautiful gallery." He gestured to the barman and handed him some notes.

Jacob tried to intervene. "Please José, you have been so helpful. Let me pay."

"Are you crazy? I am a banker. When is the last time you got something for nothing out of one of those fuckers."

Jacob smiled and pushed his wallet back into his trouser pocket.

***

Out on the street, the late afternoon light was still intense. Jacob reached for his shades but in his haste dropped them on

166

the pavement. José bent down and picked them up.

"You see that? Six months ago, I'd have been fumbling around on the ground for hours."

Jacob felt a sudden loss of composure. He couldn't remember how many he'd had but his body swayed from one side of the pavement to the other.

"I think you might need a coffee, señor," José said, grabbing his arm.

"It's drinking in the afternoon, my body can't take it."

"You won't last long in Barça then. Afternoon drinking is our religion."

They staggered along for a few blocks until they reached the bus stop.

"This is the one, remember, number 19 to Calle Pachego, then a short walk to the gallery, OK?" He held out his hand and Jacob took his arm as they shook.

"Thank you again, José."

"De nada. Hasta luego." He walked up to the end of the street, waved for the last time and disappeared. Jacob slumped down on the bench and waited for his bus to come.

Semáforos

His head was full of thick yellow smog. A toxic cloud swirled around inside his skull and pressed against his eyelids as the confusion of incoherent thoughts rattled between delirium and the hard discomfort of reality. A sudden sharp pain in his side forced him back to complete consciousness. He opened his eyes. An arm was moving backwards and forwards, thrusting something into his ribs. With each jab, the wrist twisted and recoiled. The pain intensified and he shifted sideways to escape the assault, but the arm followed and the torture continued. His eyes began to adjust to the light. He could make out a face. There was a man standing over him. The smog began to recede and he heard a voice.

"Despierte, borracho. Wake up!"

He couldn't feel the lower part of his body. He turned his neck to look for his legs. They appeared to be folded under him.

"Despierte. ¡Vamos, Borracho! Es el final de la línea. Usted tiene que irse - last stop."

Jacob attempted to reply but instead let out a loud belch that only seemed to exacerbate an overwhelming desire to vomit. He could feel something pinning him down to the hard metal surface of an unfamiliar floor. He reached into the dark void where his feet should be. A cold metal rod was pushing down against his ankles. He widened his focus. His legs appeared to be squeezed under the frame of a seat. The man started pulling him out. His feet appeared, but he had no shoes on.

"¿Dónde estan mis zapatos?"

"No sais, borracho ingles." He hauled Jacob out into the aisle and sat him up. Jacob looked down at his socks. One had turned round on itself and the other was dangling from his big toe.

"¿Dónde estan mis zapatos?¿Dónde estoy?"

"En la parada final. Debe bajar del autobús ahora. You must leave."

"¿Un autobús?" He racked his brains in the hope of skewering out a recognisable memory. Then he remembered. "¿Number 19 - Diecinueve?"

He looked down the aisle, and back up at the man. He was dressed in a blue uniform and in one hand he was holding a small, pantomime-like broomstick and in the other a large overfull bin bag. "¿Dónde estoy?"

"Al final de la linea señor. Usted tiene que bajar del autobús. Tengo que limpiar y se va. You must go."

"But where am I?" Jacob repeated in frustration.

"Barri Sant Joan. Por favor, vamos, get up – go."

Jacob tried to stand up, but his legs were still numb. "Un momento, señor."

"No, ahora. ¡Vamos!"

Jacob rubbed his thighs and calves to stimulate the circulation. The blood began to return. He got up on one knee and then, using the seat arms on either side, pulled himself up. He swayed from one side to the other, and the man caught hold of his arm.

"I think I'm still a little pissed. I'll just look for my shoes and my bag and then I'll be out of your way." He found his bag, and his jacket but his shoes had vanished.

"Señor. Por favor, rápido."

"Look, I need my fucking shoes. I can't get back to the hotel without them. Muy importante."

"No sé, señor! I am going to close the bus now."

"Fucking hell." Jacob's head pounded and he could feel bile rise in his gullet. He picked up his things and hobbled to the

169

door. Outside, it was dark and the temperature had dropped significantly.

"¿Que hora es?"

"Una menos diez." He'd been out for five hours.

"Are you sure it's ten to one?"

"Si. I finish at 12.30 so you are making me very late."

"Vale, vale."

The cleaner opened the door and Jacob stepped out into the street.

"How do I get back to the city centre?"

"Autobús a la noche. There should be one in about half an hour or so."

Jacob turned round. The bus stop and the nearby walls were covered in graffiti. The glass window on the shelter was missing and the plastic timetable had been melted off the pole. The buildings across the street looked derelict, with boarded up shop fronts and vandalised doorways. He tapped the door of the bus, but the cleaner was at the back, sweeping up where Jacob had been lying. He limped to the corner and looked up the next street. But he couldn't see beyond the third or fourth doorway. He returned to the safety of the bus. The doors hissed open and the cleaner dropped the refuse sack onto the pavement.

"Half an hour, you'll be ok," he said, switching off the lights and shutting the doors. He picked up the bag of rubbish, gestured at Jacob and disappeared into the night.

Jacob looked down at his shoeless feet. His stomach heaved and he retched onto the pavement. When the nausea had subsided, he put on his jacket, picked up his bag and started to walk. After a few minutes, he came to a large avenida. It was deserted. He walked on. His socks kept slipping off so he removed them and continued in his bare feet. Up ahead he could see a brightly lit set of road signs. An arrow indicated that the city centre was next left so he crossed the road and staggered on, hoping that he would come across a taxi rank or a bar. The soles of his feet slapped and scraped against the concrete. He stopped, sat down on a doorstep and massaged the muscles and tendons until they had recovered, and then continued.

About fifty yards ahead of him, a figure appeared on the other side of the street. It seemed to materialise out of the gloom of an unlit building, move towards the edge of the pavement and stop. Jacob raised his arm and was about to call out but hesitated. Instead he ignored the pain in his feet and quickened the pace. As he approached, he could now see that it was a young woman, but most of her features remained obscured by the inadequate street lighting. She seemed to be teetering on the edge of the kerb, just managing to maintain her balance. At first, Jacob presumed that she was drunk, but after a few moments realised that this was a controlled, deliberate manoeuvre. He called to her, but she didn't respond and continued to arch forward into the space and light of the open street and then back into the shadows. Each movement outward revealed a little more of her face. He could just make out her pale complexion and pronounced cheek bones. And her hair was either cropped short or tied back tight against her skull. He was now within ten metres of her. He called again,

"¿Perdón señorita, puede decirme donde estoy?"

She stopped rocking for a second and turned towards him. As she did so, a voice whispered behind him.

"Aquí."

Jacob swung round but there was no one there. He started towards her again but as he placed his left foot on the pavement, the voice returned, this time close enough that the breath of the words vibrated the hairs around his ear.

"Aquí."

He dropped his bag and the contents spilled out onto the pavement. As he knelt down to retrieve them, the girl smiled. It was Jude. He jumped up and called after her. But she turned away and in one eloquent movement, twisted her body sideways and dropped off the kerb onto the road. In that instant, a bus careered past. Its airbrakes screeched, tyres squealed and it shuddered to a halt. It let out a long sigh and the wheels seemed to sink down below the surface of the road. Jacob ran to the front and searched under the chassis. She wasn't there. He ran around to the other side and frantically scanned beneath and behind each wheel. Still nothing. He knelt down and examined the bumper, muttering her name over and over. The driver sounded the horn and Jacob fell back onto the road. He got up and went to the open door.

"Señor, you have just hit someone. Didn't you see her fall in front of the bus?"

The driver smiled and gestured to him to get on.

"Señor, you need to come down and help me look for her." He stepped up inside and looked down the length of the vehicle. "Consiga un cellular, necesitamos pedir una ambulancia. Can someone call for an ambulance? ¡Ambulancia!" The three or four passengers on board looked bemused and remained motionless. "For Christ sake, there's a girl under one of the wheels! Didn't you see her?"

The driver continued to grin and then started speaking in a language or dialect he didn't recognise.

"Please, señor, speak Spanish. I can't understand." Jacob pleaded with him. "Why are you smiling? Don't you understand how serious this is? You might have just killed somebody."

The driver shook his head and continued to mumble an incoherent babble.

Jacob spat back at him. "Fucking hell, call an ambulance!" The driver let out a sustained laugh and hit the steering wheel with the palm of his hand. Jacob jumped back down onto the road and pointed under the bus.

"There's a girl seriously injured or worse under the wheels of your bus. Please, you have to come and look!"

"Chill, man, tranquilo. What girl? Is it your girl? Did you push her?" He smirked.

"Don't be fucking stupid. Please."

"OK. I'll do this just for you because you make me laugh.

But I can tell you right now I didn't see anyone." He climbed out of his cab and as he descended the stairs, one of the passengers shouted to him. "Chill guys, it'll only take a moment." He followed Jacob to the front of the bus, Jacob pointed to the kerb.

"She was standing over there on the edge of the kerb and she fell right in front of you. She just let herself go. I can't believe you didn't see her."

"I'm telling you, there was no one there, but let us have a look. The driver squatted down on one knee and peered under the bus.

"Oh my God!"

"What?"

The driver stretched his arm under the chassis. Then his head and shoulders disappeared.

"Can you see her? Is she dead?" Jacob got down next to him but as he tried to look, the driver remerged from under the bus and sat up. Jacob scanned his face for any kind of answer. But the driver didn't respond immediately. Instead, he held out his hand.

"Fortuna. El Gordo!"

"For Christ sake."

"Chill, man. Don't you know it is good luck to find a full packet of cigarillos? Here, have a smoke. It'll calm you down. He pulled one from the slightly squashed pack and offered it to Jacob. "Sorry it's a bit – flat, like your chica under the left rear wheel." He laughed. "I tell you what, you keep them as a souvenir of our encounter with the invisible girl." He stuffed the pack into Jacob's jacket pocket and stood up.

"But, she has to be there. I saw her fall."

"Sorry to disappoint you. Now, shall we get you back to the centre of civilization before you lose it completely? You look like you could do with a lie down for a day or two. Where are your shoes?"

Jacob shook his head.

"See what I mean? Bare feet, alcohol and dead girls. Time to call it a night, don't you think?"

"I don't understand. It was Jude."

"Oh, so you know this dead girl? Did she steal your shoes?" He smiled.

"But why did you stop so suddenly?"

"Semáforos." The driver pointed the set of lights up ahead. "Come on. Let's go."

Jacob followed the driver up the stairs and sat adjacent to him in the first row. The doors slammed shut and the bus accelerated down the avenida. Jacob leaned back into his seat and tried to control his breathing and slow his heart rate, and immediately started to slip into the first stages of sleep, but within a few seconds he was wrenched back by a sudden explosion of noise. At first, he thought there might be a mechanical problem with the bus but then, after a few painful moments, realised that it was some form of demented music. It was so loud, the intensity of the bass notes started to vibrate his internal organs. The driver pounded the steering wheel and wailed along to the discordant clash of instruments and percussion. He shouted at Jacob over the din.

"Fuck me. This is supreme!" He swivelled round in his seat. "Do you dig?"

"Sorry? Mind the road!"

The bus swerved from one side to the other as the driver rocked and bounced insanely in his seat following some secret time signature that Jacob couldn't locate. Jacob began to feel sick again. He attempted to speak but his voice disappeared into the cacophony.

"Do you think you could turn it down a little?"

"Huh?"

"The music!"

The driver reached under the dashboard and the sound level dropped slightly. He pointed at Jacob.

"Rydych chi Cymru, nad ydych?"

174

"What?" Jacob said, straining to understand him.

"Oh, so where are you from then?" The driver asked, looking a little puzzled.

"Scotland."

"I knew it, a Celt. At least I was part right. That explains everything." The music hit a crescendo of aural insanity and the driver turned up the volume again.

"Fuck, this is so fucked!" He put his foot down and the bus accelerated forward with such force that Jacob smacked the back of his head on the head rest behind. Jacob looked back at the other passengers who seemed completely ambivalent to the sensorial assault being inflicted on them. He grabbed the sides of his seat to avoid falling into the aisle.

"This is the night bus to the city centre, isn't it?"

"You are a lucky man. Another ten minutes in this neighbourhood and you'd have been dog food. So really, tell me, what happened to your shoes?"

"I don't know. I lost them."

"You Celts, you like to drink, no?"

Jacob fumbled for some change.

"Forget it man. I don't take money from Celts."

"What?"

"No, no, sit down. Enjoy the ride back to civilization."

"Thanks."

"Do you like Free Jazz?"

"What?"

"This, do you like it?"

"I don't know."

"The Shape of Jazz to Come. Ornette Coleman, my favourite."

"Is this it?"

"This is Mr Albert Ayler." The driver reached down and pulled the handbrake. The bus careered to the left and Jacob's lost his balance completely and tumbled down into the aisle. The bus spun round in a near 180 degree turn and the rear end slammed into a bin by the side of the road. The driver switched off the music. "¿Todos bien? Everyone OK?"

The other passengers nodded and shrugged their shoulders, and Jacob picked himself off the floor.

"This fucking music is so fucking bad." The driver continued, "I get locked in and carried away sometimes. It makes me do fucked up things. But what a fucking ride. Eh? Wasn't that a miraculous turn? Extreme, supreme!"

He re-started the engine, slammed the bus into gear and rolled the bus backwards and forwards until the rear bumper disengaged from the bin. He turned the music back on.

"So what part of Scotland are you from?"

"From Scotland, yes."

"WHAT PART?"

"Glasgow!"

"Edimburgo?"

"NO, GLASGOW!" Jacob could feel his tonsils rasping against his windpipe.

"Ah, fucking hot."

"What?"

"Edimburgo Jazz is excellent. We played at the festival last year."

"I.M. F.R.O.M. G.L.A.S.G.O.W."

The driver pummelled the dashboard with his fists and yelped in unison with the screech of a trumpet. As the bus reached the outskirts of the city centre, Jacob began to recognise a few familiar landmarks. He closed his eyes, anticipating a warm bath and bed. The screech of brakes accompanied the last bar of a number. The bus and the music stopped, but the roar, clacks and whistles continued in Jacob's ears. A young couple got off and the journey, along with the next deranged track, recommenced. When they reached the Plaza Catalunya, the bus swung round and stopped outside El Corte Inglés.

"End of the road." The driver opened the doors and the remaining passengers descended and wandered off into the night. Jacob stood up to go. "Hey man, are you gonna say goodbye?"

"Sorry, I've had a bad day and I could really do with lying down."

"Nobody has a bad day in Barcelona. Every day is bad, you know what I mean?"

Jacob had no idea what he meant. "Thank you for the free ride," he said, wearily.

"Hey – free ride, free jazz – I can use that. So did you like it?"

"What?"

"The jazz! Shit, you really are wasted, aren't you?"

"It was – interesting."

"Yea yea, that's what they all say at first. But I tell you after two or three listens, you'll be hooked. You won't want to listen to anything else."

Jacob shook his head. "No really, I thought it was very unusual, maybe a little loud."

"Too loud?" He held up his arms. "Woah, Free Jazz can never be too loud. So what was that shit about the girl under my wheels?"

"I don't know. She was there and then she wasn't. Too much booze, I suppose."

"I think you just need to sleep it off. Your girl will turn up in the morning, I'm sure. So what brings you to Barcelona and how did you end up in Saint Joan?"

"I'm here to see a painting. I was drinking in a bar with this guy and the next I woke up on the floor of a bus without my shoes."

"Well, it could have been worse. At least it was only your shoes you lost and not your feet. A painting, you say?"

"Yes. I was trying to get to the Galería Regional de Català when I ran into a Spanish measure of Malt Whisky."

"Ah, the Scottish Cure, eh? So you're trying to find this painting and then what?"

"I don't know. I'm hoping to find answers to a few things."

"Aren't we all? So you've come to Barcelona to see a fucking painting? Are you loco? Get a life, man. I mean, Barça is the happening capital of the world and you want to go and sit in some shit-turd tedious gallery?" He pointed at Jacob's bare feet. "You see, that's what you get for being a boring bastard in Barcelona. If you carry on like that, she'll be after your soul."

"Maybe you're right." Jacob sighed.

"Of course I'm fucking right." He put on his jacket and stepped out of the cab into the aisle. "So you liked it, yes?" he asked, approaching Jacob who had slumped back in his seat.

"What?"

"Not again, the fucking music."

"I'm pretty hungover though so it may be clouding my judgement."

"That's the best way to listen to it." He knelt down next to him, reached into his jacket and produced a small triangular card. In the centre of the ticket was a scanned print of a Jackson Pollock painting. Below was written,

Bombissimo
Café Wha?
21 Setiembre 2.00am

"What's this?" Jacob asked.

"It's my band. We're playing tomorrow night." He handed it to Jacob.

"What do you play?"

"Take a wild guess, memory man."

"No, I mean what instrument do you play?"

"Trombone mainly, but also a little trumpet, some percussion and – eh – broken glass." He smiled.

"What?"

"You'll see. You must come. You have no choice."

"Vale," Jacob lied.

"My name is Alvaro." He held out his hand.

"Jacob. Pleased to meet you." They shook hands. The driver's grip was tight and reassuring.

"What was that you said to me when I got on? Was it Catalàn?"

"Shit, no. It was Welsh."

"Welsh?"

"Yea, it must be your Tom Jones nose. That's why I stopped the bus. If I'd known you were Scots I would have run you over."

Jacob smiled. "So, you speak Welsh?"

"You heard me, didn't you?"

"It's just a little unusual, you know?"

"Why?"

"Well, for a Spaniard to speak... I mean... you're not Welsh, are you?"

"Do I look Welsh?"

"I don't know, maybe."

"For fuck's sake, of course I'm not. I lived there for four years. I studied music at Bangor University."

"You went to Bangor University?"

"University of North Wales, why not? They had a course I wanted to do so that's where I ended up. It's a great place, so long as you're not English or from Cardiff."

"So how did you end up a bus driver?"

"I haven't 'ended up' anything. You should never think like that," he said, helping Jacob to his feet.

"Well. Thanks for the ticket. I'll try and make it." Jacob said shaking his hand again.

"Don't try. You have no choice, remember? Anyway, you owe me some money." He winked.

They stepped out onto the road and the driver pointed at him.

"I mean it, come. Puede ser que incluso encontremos sus zapatos."

179

"What?"

But the driver had shut the door. The music recommenced, the gears crunched and the bus drove off into the night. Jacob picked up his bag and as he made his way across the square, he realised what the driver had said to him. 'Puede ser que incluso encontremos sus zapatos.' We might even return your shoes.

He smiled and limped slowly back to his hotel.

El Siglo de Oro

The Galería Regional de Català was at the end of a long tree-lined cul de sac. It looked as though it had once been a private home, but the large bright yellow and pink CAC banner dangling from the second floor balcony clearly marked it out as a corporate acquisition. Inside, the air was cool. The intense heat and light from outside seemed to have been diffused and filtered through the thick stonework and elaborate stained glass windows. It took a few moments for his eyes to adjust to the sudden atmospheric alteration, and he rubbed at them frantically until his temporary blindness dissipated.

"Buenas tardes, señor." An elderly woman emerged from the gloom directly in front of him. She was sitting at a small reception desk.

"Lo siento señora," he said, clearing his throat. "No podía ver nada por un momento. ¿Cuánto?"

"Es gratis." She handed him a plan of the gallery.

"I'm looking for a painting."

"You've come to the right place," she said, with accurately delivered English intonation.

"It is La Mano Chalise by an artist called Manuel Piñero," Jacob continued.

"Is he modern?" she asked, looking increasingly perplexed.

"Baroque. It could be called something else."

"I'm not sure. We have a few Baroque paintings on the second floor; perhaps you could have a look up there?" She stood up and leaned over her desk. Jacob stepped back in order

181

to avoid bumping into her. "Go up the spiral staircase and the baroque room is number XII. It is marked above the—" She paused for a moment, distracted suddenly by his hastily purchased polka-dotted espadrilles that adored his feet.

"—above the door," she said, trying to conceal a smile. He folded the plan and pushed it into his pocket.

The staircase was a large metal construction that spiralled up to a stained glass dome at the top of the building. The iron work was so intricate and ornate, it was difficult to determine where the art nouveau swirls and loops ended and the bannister began. When he got to the top, he paused to catch his breath. The corridor extended to his left and connected to two large rooms, one bright and the other dark. He checked the Roman numerals above the doors and entered the first. The gallery was filled with natural light which cascaded down from a large oval skylight that spanned the entire ceiling. The room had been recently refurbished and sections of the walls had been knocked out and replaced with large tinted windows. As he entered, he noticed a small Velázquez painting at the far end of the room. Despite its diminutive size, the intensity and richness of its colours dominated the space around it.

He turned away and looked to his left. On the side wall, there were a number of works hung symmetrically together as though part of a larger theme, all displaying scenes of domesticity and family life. He glanced over his shoulder at the opposite wall. In the near corner next to the entrance a single colour caught his eye. In the centre of an isolated painting, he recognised a deep crimson sheen.

He approached it slowly, his eyes remaining focused on the intensity of the pigment. He positioned himself within two feet of the work and slowly allowed his focal field to widen and take in the whole of the canvas. A single figure, a young girl, was standing by a fire in a panelled room. Jacob exhaled and leaned in towards the work. It was her, the same girl occupying the same space in the same room. She was leaning on the fireplace,

182

holding a piece of paper up to her face as though taking in the scent of something sweet. She was smiling, almost caressing or kissing its surface. Her left foot was extended outwards to indicate joy. Her right hand was resting on a large wooden mantelpiece. But there was something different. The girl's features appeared altered in some way. Her nose was larger or more elongated and the gentle laughter lines around her eyes were deeper or more pronounced. She was older, perhaps by five or six years. Jacob stood back again to take in its entirety. She was wearing an unfamiliar tunic. It gripped her tight around the chest and waist. It was dark blue, almost black in colour with a deep crimson crucifix embroidered on the front. The cross stood out against the dark fabric behind and appeared to hover or float above the surface of the painting. Jacob studied it for a moment and then realised that its shape was identical to the crucifix dangling from the courtesan's open fist in The Loss of Innocence. Her right hand was resting on the mantelpiece and to the left of her slightly extended little finger was a small metal object.

Jacob moved closer again, his face almost touching the canvas. Now he could see a long thin blade glistening in the light of the fire and just visible, protruding from within the girl's palm, was the corner of a cream coloured handle. It was the letter opener.

A sudden sharp pain made him jerk backwards. It was as though an unidentified object had penetrated his left eye. The sensation of intense heat shot from the outside edge of his eye socket to the back of his skull. He instinctively raised his hand to protect his face and slumped to his knees in an attempt to escape the invisible assault.

"¿Esta bien?" The attendant was standing in the doorway, looking a little flustered. He turned but he couldn't open his eyes.

"You were shouting," she continued. "As courtesy to other visitors, could you please refrain?"

"Sorry," he said, struggling to his feet. He stepped towards her but she retreated back into the corridor.

"Por favor, señor."

"Lo siento – bad headache. You know, MI-GR-AINE," he said, finally managing to force his eyelids apart. "I was just looking at this painting and I got it right in my eye. Something went right in."

"I'm sorry, sir, but you shouldn't be in there. The room is closed."

"What?"

"Por reformas."

"But what about the paintings?" Jacob interrupted.

"They are on temporary loan to El Prado while we carry out the work."

"No, I mean the ones that are left." He turned and squinted back into the room. The floor was covered in paint splattered tarpaulin and the walls had spirals of electrical cables hanging out of hacked out holes.

"But there was a canvas here, of a girl in a blue tunic." He ran his hand up and down the wall.

"Is anything the matter, sir?"

"What have you done with it?"

"Sir?"

"The Piñero, it was there!" He slapped the surface with his hand.

"Calm down, sir. No, sir, I told you that XII, the baroque room, was closed. All the paintings are on temporary loan to El Prado."

"Look, you said Manuel Piñero was in XII, upstairs, here on the second floor."

"Sir, the paintings are not here. Look, I'll show you. Please come with me."

"But I was just looking at it," Jacob protested.

"Come please."

He followed her downstairs and she returned to her desk.

"I checked our records and I think the painting you are looking for has been sent to El Prado in Madrid. It is part of the exhibition Baroka Obskura which runs until the end of October. Unfortunately, it will not return here until December. I think there may be a study of the painting in one of our catalogues. I should have one, let me have a look." She opened a drawer and removed a pile of papers and postcards. She spread them out across the width of the desk and picked through one or two. "This one, mira." She placed a small booklet on top of the pile and began skimming through it. As he stared at the repetitive movement of her index finger flicking at the pages, he momentarily lost his balance and teetered forward into the desk. It rattled on its legs and the woman looked up in alarm.

"Are you all right, señor?"

"Sorry," Jacob mumbled, steadying himself on the desk.

"Please sit for a moment." She got up and gestured towards her chair.

"No, I'm fine. Please, keep looking."

"Are you sure, you don't look very well."

"I'm all right."

She continued to search the catalogue until finally her finger stopped.

"Yes, I was right. I knew it was here somewhere. I think the name is slightly different but I'm sure it must be the same painting, La Mano Chastite. By M. Piñero." She rotated the book so he could view the image. "One of the themes is the use and importance of hands in allegorical painting. I'm sorry it is only a small section of the work."

The detail was slightly blurred but showed a female hand clutching a small object. Jacob leaned in closer, but the image became too distorted to clearly identify what it was. He read the inscription beneath.

En el momento de violencia, el abridor de cartas se transforma en el mensajero del amor, el emblema fálico del placer sexual y el deseo erótico de un instrumento de dolor, de la venganza y de la muerte.

In the moment of violence, the letter opener is transformed from the messenger of love, the phallic emblem of sexual pleasure and erotic desire, to an instrument of pain and death.

"¿Cuánto es?"

"¿Cómo?"

"¿El Programa, cuantas?

"Es libre."

Jacob fumbled in his pocket for his wallet.

"No, señor. It is free," the assistant repeated.

He opened it up and thrust it towards her. "Do you recognise this woman?" he asked, pointing at a small photo of Ella tucked behind the plastic window.

The attendant glanced up at him anxiously, and then back at the picture. "Señor, many people visit the gallery," she said. "May I?" She took the wallet from him and studied Ella's features.

"She is my wife. She's missing. I think she came here, maybe even a couple of days ago?"

The attendant shook her head. "I'm sorry, señor. I don't know her. I work part-time so I may not have been on duty."

"Please. Are you sure?"

She looked down at the photo again, but then handed it back to him. "Sorry."

Jacob snatched the catalogue from the desk, and as he left the gallery, the attendant shouted after him, "I hope you find her."

***

On his way back to the hotel, he stopped at the tourist office

186

on the Plaza Catalunya and picked up a timetable for trains to Madrid. In his room, he checked evening departures but he'd missed the last train out of Sants station. He would have to catch one first thing in the morning. He began packing his bags but was interrupted by a knock at the door. It was the girl from the reception. She looked a little flustered and out of breath from climbing the stairs.

"Someone left a message for you this afternoon," she said between gasps, and she handed him an envelope. "My father told me to bring it up." As he ran his thumb through the seal, the girl continued to stare at him. He stopped.

"Thank you," he said abruptly and shut the door on her.

He opened it and found a sheet of folded paper with a card tucked inside. Along the top of the page was a bold yellow logo with the letters C.A.C. printed in the centre of the margin. It was from José. He read through the note, struggling to decipher his illegible handwriting.

A Talk tonight in La Case de La Cultural
History of Spanish Art
Could be useful
Free ticket enclosed
MOST IMPORTANT: Free beer!
See you in the bar at 7.00

And at the bottom he had signed it, The Madrileño Marxist. Jacob turned the ticket over and examined the front. The talk was entitled, 'How the Spanish invented Modern Art' and the speaker was a Professor Bárbola. Beneath, there was an image of Velázquez's Las Meninas juxtaposed with Picasso's version. Searching his pockets for his street plan, he unfolded it and laid it down on the bed. La Casa de la Cultura was located on the other side of Las Ramblas, only a stone's throw from the hotel. He put the note and card down on the bedside cabinet, closed the shutters and sank down onto the bed, the weight of his weary limbs pressing him deep into the folds of the duvet cover. He closed his eyes and was unconscious in a matter of seconds.

***

Ella appeared. She seemed to be trying to say something. Her mouth opened and closed, but she made no sound. Her arm extended and she pointed to her right. He opened his eyes and looked over at the door. There was a small notice pinned to the top right hand corner. He got out of bed to examine it more closely.

EN CASO DE INCENDIDO
Mantenga la calma. No corra.
No utilice los ascensores
Siga la ruta de salida de emergencia
Si su ropa se prendeen fuego, tirarse al suelo
Rodar para apagar las llamas

Stay calm. Do not run.
Do not use the elevators
Follow the emergency exit route
If your clothes catch fire, lie on the floor
and roll to smother the flames.

He turned the notice over and on the back there was a hand written word scrawled across the card. It read,

Aquí

There was something else. The door was warm. He pressed his palm flat against the wood and the heat raced from his wrist and up his arm like an electric shock. He stepped back. A tiny thread of smoke appeared through the keyhole and curled up towards the ceiling. He grabbed the handle but it too was unbearably hot. He pulled the cuff of his shirt down to protect his hand and snatched at the knob until the lock turned and the door swung open. The corridor was empty with no sign of fire or smoke. He stepped out and examined the other side of the door. There was nothing, no blistered paint, scorch marks or smoke stains. He walked to the end of the corridor and peered down the stair well. It was deserted. Returning to his room, he locked the door, closed the wooden shutters and climbed back into bed. Sleep returned like a swift hammer blow to the head.

***

He woke with a start and fumbling for the light switch, he squinted at his watch. It was 7.23pm. He'd been asleep for over three hours. He sat up and lit a cigarette. The headache that had been bothering him all day had gone, but the room was hot and his shirt was clinging to his back. He got out of bed and opened the shutters. It seemed that despite his absence from the waking world, Barcelona had carried on without him, and the familiar sounds and smells raced back in to the room. He leaned out the window and took in some of the warm dusty air. The evening sunset had turned the city skyline into a sepia soaked postcard. On the street below, a couple were locked in a passionate embrace. Jacob watched them for a moment as they kissed and the man slipped his hand under the waist band of his lover's skirt. She twisted slightly and raised her ankle to accommodate his wandering hand. Then, leaning further over her, he spun her round and his body seemed to completely consume her as she disappeared behind him. Then they broke off in fits of laughter and disappeared into a building opposite. Jacob flicked the end of his cigarette over the railing and went back inside.

El Engaño

The young doorman was visibly unimpressed with Jacob's excuse.

"Ninguna invitación, ninguna entrada."

"I tell you," Jacob explained, "Señor Miro sent me a ticket but I've left it in my room. Could you check, please?"

He looked at Jacob and sighed. "Un momento. ¿Cual es su nombre?"

"Voy-ees, Jacob Boy ees." Jacob said, hissing through his teeth.

The doorman went into the lobby and picked up a phone on the reception desk. Moments later, he returned looking a little flustered.

"Me siento terrible apesadumbrado, esta manera, por favor. Señor Miro says he will meet you in the bar."

Jacob followed him into a vast but rather austere entrance hall. For a centre of cultural excellence it seemed somewhat disappointing.

"This way, sir."

They continued through into a second chamber and the doorman stopped by the elevator. "Level seven, señor, and I apologise again." He touched the rim of his cap with his forefinger and returned to the reception area. Jacob pressed the call button and waited for the lift to come. As the door opened, a very small, dishevelled-looking man looked up at him and instantaneously dropped the papers he was holding onto the elevator floor. Jacob entered and helped him to gather them

190

together.

"Gracias, soy tan torpe."

As Jacob continued, he was suddenly aware that the man had stopped and was staring up at him. Jacob turned to him again.

"Extraño," the man said, shaking his head.

"Sorry?" Jacob replied,

"¿Ya nos conocemos? Have we met before?"

Jacob handed the man the remainder of the fallen pages, his tiny swollen hands struggling to grip the large bundle of papers.

"No, I don't think so," Jacob replied.

"Your face is very familiar." He scratched his head and almost dropped his papers again. "There I go again."

Jacob hadn't noticed but the lift had descended to the basement level. It stopped on -3. The doors opened and the man started to leave. He stopped for a second and studied Jacob again. The door began to close on him and he just managed to squeeze himself and all of his paraphernalia through before it trapped him completely. The lift jolted and continued its journey up to the seventh floor.

José was standing by the bar with three immaculately dressed men in dark suits. When he spotted Jacob come in, he bellowed over to him.

"You made it! Come and have a drink," his voice booming across the room. The bar was packed with similarly well-groomed bankers and business types, but amongst them were a few slightly less sartorially elegant people Jacob assumed to be academics and artists. The air reeked of a pungent and slightly nauseating cocktail of expensive aftershaves and perfumes combined with tobacco smoke and sweat. Jacob picked his way through the throng.

"My friend." José extended his hand. "God, you look terrible. What have you been doing?"

"Working. Good to see you too, José."

"Oh yes, we all have to work in Barça, don't we?" He smiled. "Let me get you a drink, beer?"

191

"Thanks."

He clicked his fingers and a barman stopped serving another customer to attend to José's order. In that moment Jacob realised, that José was perhaps a more important employee than he had been led to believe. "Glad you could make it," he said, handing him his drink."

"How did it go yesterday, at the gallery?"

"The painting I was looking for is on temporary loan for an exhibition in El Prado. I'm leaving for Madrid in the morning."

"So this is your last night in Barça?"

Jacob nodded.

"Well, we'd better make the most of it for you, my friend. Salut," he said, raising his glass. After a couple of large mouthfuls of beer, he toasted again. "And good luck with your research." He turned to a group of men standing behind him. "Jacob, please let me introduce you to some sad and, in English, bored or is it boring?"

"Both."

José laughed. "Yes very fucking boring managers from my office."

Jacob winced.

"It's OK, don't panic they can't understand English. This is Señor Giordano, Señor Calderón and Señor Velasco," he said, switching back to Spanish. "They work with me in freight."

Jacob shook their hands.

"Jacob is one of my spies here in Barça. He is going to find all your flaws and your weaknesses so that we Madrileños can take over your city once more."

The men laughed nervously.

"Oh come on guys we are not at work now, relax for Christ sake." He slapped one of his stooges on the back. Jacob looked José up and down. He was wearing a Bermuda shirt and shorts; his gut was sticking out from under the bottom of the shirt, the pale hairy flesh stood out against the bright red and purple flowers festooned across the fabric. The fly of his shorts was slightly undone and a corner of his underwear was peeking out of the opening. He was puffing heavily on his cigarette and every few seconds blew smoke in their faces. One of them coughed.

"Smoke?" He held out the pack. Señor Giordano hesitated, then took one. The second refused. "What? You haven't quit again, have you?"

His colleague nodded.

"When?"

"Three months ago."

"Mierda. Por todos los santos. I didn't take you for a quitter. Oh, hold on, yes I did, ha! How about you, Jacob?"

Jacob picked one out of the pack and accepted a light, drawing the smoke deep into his lungs.

"You see, gentlemen, now that's how to smoke a cigarette," José said, grimacing at his colleagues. "So anyway, Jacob, any luck at the gallery yesterday?"

But before Jacob could answer, José interrupted, "Fuck me, where is your badge?"

"What badge?" Jacob asked.

"Your badge!" He pointed at his three subordinates. They were all wearing small triangular enamel lapel badges with the words, ¡NUNCA MAS! across the centre.

"And look."

Everyone in the bar, including the staff, were wearing identical red and black insignias, and the same message was also displayed on a large banner above the entrance and another draped over the row of spirits at the back of the bar.

"I'm sorry, José. I've no idea. What is 'NUNCA MAS'?"

José let out a loud chortle. "My God, Jacob, it's worse than I thought. Where have you been?"

"I saw the same insignia a few days ago in Los Gatos. Have I missed something?"

"Now let me think for a minute. Jesus Jacob, only the fucking war."

"What war?"

José looked at the three managers and they smiled at him. "You are joking, aren't you?"

"Like I say, I've been kind of busy with things. I've not really had a chance to look at the news."

"I think you need a badge before you are taken out the back and shot." He reached into his shirt pocket.

"Here, have mine."

"But then you won't be wearing one."

José laughed again. "I couldn't give a fuck about the war. I'm neither for nor against it. It's a war. There have always been wars and there always will be wars. What's the fucking point of being for or against it?"

Señor Giordano shuffled nervously on his heels.

"Oh don't worry, Luca, this won't affect your promotion chances. It's my job you're after and it's my job you'll get." He gestured to Jacob. "Come here a moment." He took him to one side. "The thing is, my Scottish friend, if you don't wear one, then people ask questions, arguments start, fists fly, weapons are drawn and I wouldn't wish that on anyone, so please, wear the fucking badge and do yourself a favour."

"But what about you?" Jacob repeated.

He leaned in closer to Jacob's face. "Don't be fooled by my ridiculous clothes and my cynical attitude. I'm still a powerful guy round here. People fear me." He turned to the managers. "Boo! You see how they jump. So I can get away with it. But you, you're a guest here, a stranger. As soon as some of the idiots in here get within sniffing distance of that empty space on your lapel where your badge should be, you are fucked. You'll spend the entire evening and probably most of the next day locked in a loop with arseholes, corporate responsibility goons and opportunistic do-gooders."

"But I don't think I can wear a badge to support something when I don't know what it is."

"Now there's an intelligent statement, very noble. But this is

194

an anti-war sponsored evening and if you want to, shall we say, blend in, I suggest you wear the badge and avoid the grief."

"So CAC is sponsoring an anti-war event?"

"Oh yes, the great altruistic force of cultural and moral good is right behind the protest. As an institution we can't afford not to be. The whole fucking country is up in arms against the war, particularly up here in the north where the conflict is viewed as another move by Madrid to impose its will on the down-trodden separatists. Oh, and we do have a number of major assets and investments in the war zone, so the sooner it stops the better. The badge, yes?" Jacob shrugged his shoulders. "Good man." José stuck the pin through the lapel of Jacob's jacket and clipped it into the lock. He turned and twisted it until it was straight. "There you go, that should ward off any unwanted insects this evening."

"But what if anyone asks me about the war?"

"Just shout, '¡NUNCA MAS!'and they'll leave you alone. The thing is, they haven't really got a clue either. They're just toeing the company line." A loud bell sounded behind the bar. "Come with me, Jacob, the lecture is about to start. Let's see if we can get rid of the three stooges."

Jacob followed José through the throng of people to a small door at the side. José fumbled in his shorts for a second and removed a set of keys. He tried a few until he found the right one. He leaned in towards Jacob and whispered, "This is the VIP entrance." He opened the door and invited Jacob to go first. Jacob went in and José closed the door behind them.

Inside, the darkness was total. Jacob held his hand up to his face but couldn't see it.

"Now, where is the fucking light?" José was somewhere in front of him. Jacob held out his arms and shuffled towards him.

"Where are you?" Jacob said, reaching further into the blackness. A line of stark white strip lights flickered on, illuminating a long narrow corridor. José was about half way down.

"Come on." He gestured to Jacob to follow.

At the end of the corridor, José unlocked a second door. But before he opened it, he turned back to Jacob.

"I want to show you something."

On the other side, there was a gloomy stairwell that reeked of wet rot and damp. They descended to the bottom and into an enclosed windowless space with no sign of a door. José spotted the look on Jacob's face and reassured him. "Don't worry, my friend, all will be revealed." He searched his pockets again and removed what appeared to be a credit card. "This is a little tricky, please wait a moment." He slotted the card into a near-invisible slit in the wall and after a series of clicks and rattles, a hidden door swung open. "Please, can you help me push this? It can be a little stiff. Ha! That's what I often say to my wife." Jacob placed his hands on the door. The surface was warm and slightly damp. He pushed hard but the door refused to move.

"Come on, Jacob, put your back into it." José wheezed. They tried again and after further resistance, the door finally creaked, groaned and then swung open freely. José reached into the darkness and located the light. Inside, there was a large store room full of crates and boxes stacked up to the ceiling. After José had got his breath back, he turned to Jacob. "You see these. What do you think they are?" José asked.

"I don't know. Is it some of your freight – illicit whisky supplies?"

"They are all paintings, owned or acquired by CAC, wrapped up and ready to be shipped out."

"Are they selling them?"

"We've got everything in here," José continued, "from Goya to Matisse and Picasso. Only one thing wrong though."

"What's that?"

"They are all fucking forgeries."

"What?"

"Fakes."

"I don't understand."

"Remember, I told you about Franco and his thieving sticky fingers? During the war, Franco's best friend, Herr Führer, how shall I say, 'asked' him, as a favour, to relieve as many works of art as possible from those English loving partisans in the north. So Franco and his politically aligned comrades plundered thousands of great works from the region."

Jacob looked down at José's left foot that was tapping out an erratic rhythm as he ranted at him.

"But then, after the war," José carried on, "when we were all friends again, some people in Barça asked politely for their paintings to be returned. Now, if you had suddenly acquired priceless but plundered masterpieces and it looked like your country was about to lose the war, what would you do?"

"Sell them?"

"Spoken like a true Scotsman. Of course you would, so many of Barça's great works were sold on the black market to unscrupulous investors and wealthy gangland bosses. But to avoid another world war, the powers that be at the time instructed master forgers to come up with some pretty convincing fakes to keep the peace and maintain entente cordial within Europe. Of course, they were all involved, ex-Nazis, Allies, Brits, Yanks. The rewards were just too tempting to turn down."

"But how do you know all this?"

"Jacob, I've worked for CAC for over thirty years. I know a lot of things about a lot of things, and I know how to ship all manner of items all around the world without a sniff of suspicion."

"But why are you telling me this?"

"You're interested in art, aren't you? And you are looking for the truth, the integrity of the artists work and all of that?"

"Yes."

"Well, all this stuff in here CAC paid an absolute fortune for. They had to inflate their interest rates and rip off customers to cover the purchase and insurance costs. But they fucked up.

197

They bought hundreds of them and I mean hundreds of these counterfeit duds that were produced at the end of the war. And now they can't exhibit them in case someone spots their stupidity, and they can't admit to owning them because they are illegal and the scandal would probably bring down the bank."

"But what about the exhibited paintings, are they all genuine?"

"CAC has refused to allow anyone near them. They have their 'experts' who have written reports and produced validated documentation of authenticity that has been accepted by insurance companies and art historians as the real thing. I suppose the fascists ensured that forgers were the best they could find. And strangely, no one has questioned the integrity of any of the works on show, until now."

"But what about x-ray and carbon dating, surely that would reveal the truth?"

"As I said, state sponsored forgery and authentication is almost impossible to overturn. People just believe what they are told and leave it at that."

"But aren't you taking a risk showing me all of this, telling me. I could go to the papers."

"Jacob, you're not the kind of person who goes to the papers. And anyway, who is going to believe a mad Scottish alcoholic like you?" He leaned in towards him. "Listen, when you get to Madrid, there's a guy there you should talk to. He's one of the last of the original forgers. His name is Almir, but he's known as The Moroccan. He can tell you how it really is in the art world. He's been quietly 'advising', the bank for years on their unreliable acquisitions, he may even have painted a few of these."

Jacob went over to one of the crates by the side wall. Inside, there were half a dozen tightly wrapped and heavily taped frames squeezed together. Each of them was labelled and dated; this collection appeared to be full of Picassos dating from 1952 to1954.

"People say," José continued, "that in his time, Almir could paint any period and any artist, and his forgeries were so good they could fool even the most experienced art dealers and historians."

"Where can I find him in Madrid?" Jacob said.

"He's retired now, but he still runs a little shop near El Prado, selling legal fakes to the tourists. I think it's called," he stopped, "it'll come to me in a moment. He's a little shy of strangers."

"I'm not surprised, considering his colourful occupation." Jacob said.

"But if you tell him José sent you, I'm sure he'd be able to help you with your research. He's a smart guy." He gestured towards the door. "Come on, let's get out of here, the lecture's about to start."

Jacob's head was reeling from the revelation. He steadied himself on the stairs as José took Jacob deeper into the heart of the building, until finally they reached another door.

"Now, are you ready for this?" José smiled and pushed the door. It swung open to reveal the back of the auditorium. "I think the Partisans used these corridors as escape routes during the civil war. After a rousing political speech condemning the regime, the speaker would clear off down one of the exits and out into the night. Apparently there are nine or ten in the building but I've only found three so far. But hey, the more escapes we have in life the better. I'm thinking of having a few installed in my home, and a couple in the Café Madrileño would be handy."

They went down to the front of the lecture theatre and sat in the third row. José squeezed his buttocks into the seat and, turning to Jacob, said, "La Decoradora."

"What?"

"That's the name of Almir's shop. I knew it would come to me." He leaned back in his chair and the bolts creaked in their sockets. "I tell you," he continued, "you are very fortunate tonight, my friend, because Señor Bárbola is a leading expert in Spanish allegorical art. He is well-known throughout the art world for his very interesting and some might say controversial ideas. If there is anything you need to know about your artist, what's his name again?"

"Piñero."

"Then he's the guy to talk to, and I am the guy who can introduce you." He nudged Jacob with his elbow. "Anyway, I think we are about to start."

A woman approached the stage. She nervously introduced the speaker, but no one appeared. She apologised and accidentally hit the microphone with her hand, sending feedback screaming across the auditorium. Eventually, the speaker entered the stage from the opposite side. It was the same man Jacob had met in the lift. He stumbled over a cable as he took to the podium. Sifting through his papers, as though trying to locate a missing page, he shuffled up to the mic but his tiny frame disappeared behind the wooden lectern. The woman returned and laughing nervously, she grappled with the stand and the equipment and lowered it to an appropriate height. When she was done, she invited the speaker to start again.

Taking the mic from its stand, he thrust his left arm into the air and shouted into the mouthpiece, "NUNCA MAS!" His voice rattled the PA speakers, sending more shrieks of feedback through the system. The audience erupted in cheers, and hoops of approval, and stamped their feet in unison. José looked over at Jacob and rubbed his forefinger and thumb together.

When the noise had died down, he began his talk. His voice was quiet, helium-pitched and rather monotonous, and after ten minutes or so Jacob began to lose concentration. He looked round the hall. Most of the audience seemed half asleep or bored, some fidgeted in their seats while others struggled to stay awake. Jacob began to think that José may have over-hyped the event and the importance of the speaker's reputation.

But as he scanned the audience, on the far side he noticed a young woman frantically scribbling in a notepad. He couldn't see her face clearly as she was propping up her head with her elbow. But her right hand was working furiously to note down everything the speaker said. The movement seemed to have a rhythm of its own, like a typewriter or printer collating words. It flicked back and forth across the pad and when she reached the bottom of the pad, she quickly turned over onto a fresh page. As she did so, she dropped her left hand from her face and Jacob glimpsed her features. She was thin and pale with skin drawn tight across pronounced cheek bones. He recognised her immediately. It was Jude. But as he jumped up to call to her, the audience erupted again chanting, "¡NUNCA MAS. NUNCA MAS, NUNCA MAS!" The speaker had reached the end of his talk. The crowd applauded, cat whistled and cheered. He thanked them again, hesitated a moment, as though he was about to say something else, but then left the stage.

Jacob glanced down at José who was still in his seat.

"I would have given him a standing ovation, but I'm stuck."

"I'm sorry, José, but there's someone here I know. I need to try and find her before she leaves."

"Her?"

"It's a woman I met back in Glasgow."

"You don't need to explain to me, Jacob. You go and exercise your libido and I'll go and exercise my liver. I'll meet you back in the bar, but first, help me up."

Jacob pushed his way through the crowd. He could see her just ahead of him. He called again but she pressed on through the wall of bodies heading for the bar. When he got to the front of the queue, she had disappeared. He scanned over the tops of heads but he'd lost her.

"Jacob, over here!" José was at the other end of the counter waving at him. Jacob looked around the bar again but the number of people packed into the room made it almost impossible to distinguish where one person ended and another began. He gave up and pushed his way along the bar until he

201

reached José. He already had a beer and a whisky lined up for him.

"How did you get here so quickly?"

"Escape routes, remember? Any luck with your exercise?"

"No, I couldn't find her."

"Oh well, never mind. I've got a special treat for you."

"What?"

"I've arranged a meeting with our Professor Bárbola."

"Oh, I don't know, José."

"What's the matter?"

"The lecture was kind of…"

"What?"

"Well, it was interesting, but I just don't know if it'll be of any use to me."

"You are a liar. You weren't listening to him, were you?"

"I was."

"You were too busy with that girl. I can't believe you missed it. Didn't you hear all the booing?"

"What booing?"

"You randy old dog."

"OK, I found it boring. I switched off and got distracted. What happened?"

"It was all going well until he started talking about his latest theory."

"Oh, yes."

"You don't know, do you?"

"No idea, enlighten me." Jacob sipped his beer.

"He claims to have uncovered categorical evidence that Las Meninas, one of our nation's most revered and celebrated paintings, was not actually painted by our revered and most celebrated artist."

"What?"

"That's right. So I have your full attention now, do I?"

"Tell me."

"According to our diminutive friend on the podium, Las

202

Meninas was only partially painted, how did he put it, finished by Velázquez, but it was conceived by his student and protégé."

"Who?"

"Your mysterious amigo, Señor Manuel Piñero."

Jacob studied José's expression in disbelief.

"It's the truth. That's what he said. So shall I not bother introducing you?"

"No, please. I think maybe I should talk to him."

"Ah, so now you wake up? Ha! But first, a drink. Here, it's a Macallan. You like?"

Jacob downed the glass in one and chased it with a couple of gulps of beer.

After another round of drinks, the Professor finally arrived, clutching a large glass of red wine and looking a little more relaxed than he did before. Despite his size, he seemed to command the space around him and the drinkers at the bar moved politely out of his way to let him through. José introduced him to Jacob and they shook hands.

"We meet again," the Professor said.

José raised his glass. "Let's drink to a marvellous talk. Well done, Professor, you really shook them out of their collective comas tonight." He glanced at Jacob and winked.

"That wasn't really my intention."

"Oh yes, infamy and notoriety can do wonders for the bank account."

The Professor sipped his wine.

"You're not wearing a badge, Professor," Jacob said, looking at his jacket.

"No, my wife won't let me. She thinks it's too superficial."

"Quite right too," said José between puffs of his cigarette.

"But I do believe the war is unjust and unfair on the dignified people of—" he stopped.

"Aha, another one." José spluttered out a mouthful of beer, and it dribbled down his shirt onto the floor.

Jacob pressed on with a question.

203

"It was a very interesting talk, Professor Bárbola. Could you tell me a little more about your theory?"

"What is your interest exactly?" the Professor asked.

"Well, I've been studying the work of Manuel Piñero for some time. I believe that one of his paintings is hanging in the city art gallery in Glasgow, in Scotland."

"What's it called?"

"The Loss of Innocence."

"Now that's an interesting painting."

"You know it?"

"Of course. Do you think it's a forgery?"

"No, but there are doubts about its creator. Most critics have it down as a lesser known Velázquez, but I think, well, I believe it's by Piñero."

"And you are right to think this. In my view, this painting is an original work, conceived and created from beginning to completion by Señor Piñero."

"You know, Professor, you are the first person I have talked to who agrees with me."

"Well, not many people agree with me either. So we can be outcasts on our own island together. Salut." He held up his glass and Jacob sipped his beer.

The Professor continued. "Piñero is a very strange and mysterious character. It may take you some time to unravel the intrigue that surrounded his life. Did you know for instance that he was gay?"

"What?"

"There is a plausible theory that he and Velázquez were secret lovers."

José spluttered into his beer. "So now you see, Jacob, why the Spanish people have taken our beloved Professor to the bosom of their tradition-loving, Catholic guilt-laden, conservative hearts."

"Did you know that he was interested in the occult?" the Professor continued.

"I had read that."

"And that he had to flee Madrid because he was linked to a series of high profile murders in and around the city; ritualistic killings, torture, all sorts of gruesome things."

"Was he involved?"

"We don't know. He vanished for a while, so I suppose it's only fair to ask, why would an innocent man go on the run? But there is some contrary evidence that he was set up."

"By whom?"

"His ex-lover of course."

"Why would he do that?"

"The age old reason, and in many ways rather vulgar, blackmail. Piñero was driven by a desire to ruin Velázquez's flourishing reputation and he would have done anything to bring him down. So blackmail was a vulgar, yet simple solution. He threatened to reveal to the world and Velázquez's family the truth about their less than professional relationship."

"But why? What happened between them?"

"It's simple. He was jealous. As Velázquez's fame spread across Europe, Piñero's talents were being increasingly overlooked and ignored by the powerful and the good. He was disappearing into the shadow cast by his teacher's forever expanding empire of light and influence. And, of course, Velázquez was extremely arrogant, so he probably tormented Piñero and rubbed his nose in the dirt. Letters show that he was extremely critical of all his students. But it was Piñero who often bore the brunt of the severest of his attacks. Nothing could ever match or surpass the genius of Velázquez or the incalculability of his ego."

As the Professor talked, Jacob was aware that a circle of people had closed in around them, and they were hanging on his words.

"Piñero faced a relentless bombardment of critical and personal abuse." The Professor stared directly at Jacob. "His own original works were ridiculed and derided as hopelessly second

205

rate. And not only by Velázquez, but by the King, the aristocrats and courtiers, and those who commissioned paintings. You see, despite his genius, Velázquez's position at the top of the art establishment tree was highly vulnerable. Fashion is fickle, and he could have been toppled at any moment if the wind had changed along with the trends and ephemeral tastes of the court."

"I know the feeling," José interrupted.

The Professor took another sip of wine and continued. "So Velázquez may have looked upon Piñero as a potential rival for his extremely desirable crown. So it was not in his interest to let his protégé's talents shine too brightly. He would have exerted his formidable influence to ensure that Piñero never rose above the status of a chamber maid. So you can see why Piñero had every right to be angry. He vowed to avenge Velázquez's success and so became a master forger."

José winked at Jacob and gestured to the barman for another round of drinks.

"Why would he do that?" Jacob interrupted.

"Velázquez was a great teacher and had taught Piñero how to faithfully replicate his style and techniques, to help him speed up delivery of his commissions and so increase his wealth and social status. He had an extravagant lifestyle and a large demanding family so he needed a healthy income. He was also obsessed with position and power. Yet, despite being the country's most celebrated artist, he was still considered by many within noble circles as a servant." José handed the Professor another drink, and after a couple of sips, he turned back to Jacob and asked, "Shall I continue?"

"Please," Jacob said.

"So Velázquez used his money to aspire to noble status, and his art was his way into the club. It was the magic key that opened doors into the world of the court and inner chambers of the King. Piñero became his third hand, if you like. Velázquez would instruct him to complete paintings and touch up sections

206

of work that he had no time for or forgotten to finish. But what Velázquez didn't know was that once Piñero had mastered Velázquez's creative secrets, he had begun building up a supply of forgeries and replica works. Then, when the time was right, maybe once or twice a year, he would make up some tale about a sickly or dying family member in his hometown in Andalucia and that it was his duty to attend to them. Velázquez would reluctantly let him go. But instead of heading south he would travel north to France, Belgium or Holland, to sell his stash of fake but near flawless paintings."

"Classic supply and demand theory," José said.

The Professor continued. "When they fell out, he used these honed and perfected forgery skills to flood the market with counterfeit work and thus reduce the market value of the genuine paintings. But there was one other thing that Velázquez didn't know about Piñero."

"What was that?" Jacob asked.

"He had been secretly working on a painting he hoped would establish him as a major artist and help him achieve fame and fortune. This, I believe, is where Las Meninas comes in."

"You think Piñero painted it?" Jacob couldn't quite believe the premise.

"I believe he is the true author of the work."

José patted him on the shoulder. "Professor, you really know how to make a party swing."

"But why is it then considered Velázquez's masterpiece?" Jacob asked.

"Piñero was found out. Velázquez grew suspicious and had him followed, and when he discovered what he was doing, he was incandescent with rage. He felt betrayed and deceived. He denounced Piñero as a thief and a liar, and confiscated the painting. Piñero could do very little. He had no power. All he could do was plot revenge."

"So you think Velázquez finished it?"

"That is my theory."

"But where is the evidence?"

"You are familiar with Las Meninas, no?"

Jacob nodded.

"OK, who is the gentleman behind the two girls in the shadows, just to the left of the female dwarf?"

"There's been a lot of speculation," Jacob replied. "Isn't he supposed to be the King's bodyguard?"

"I see you have been doing your homework, Mr Boyce. Indeed, many have concluded that he must be the Royal Guardadamas. But no one really knows, do they?"

"No, I suppose not."

"This, I believe is in fact Velázquez."

"What?"

"The figure of Velázquez you see today, the artist standing proudly by his easel staring out at the world, posing for the viewer as though waiting to be photographed, I believe this was once Piñero. When Velázquez appropriated Las Meninas, he altered facial characteristics and added details. He effectively swapped places with his student. You see, one of the reasons why Velázquez was so angry with Piñero was because he had the audacity to place himself at the centre of the scene, while Velázquez is relegated to the rear. He was mocking his master. He was saying, you are only as important as the paint on the brush, and when your audience stop looking at you, they'll all be looking at someone else. The allegory is transformed. It's more radical, revolutionary even. It becomes a critique of celebrity and the perils of fame, a premonition of modernity or the post-modern condition. It could even be interpreted as a satirical swipe at the Royal Court of King Philip and, dare I say it, an attack on the state of Spain itself."

"But where is your proof?" Jacob shook his head.

"It's all in the perspective and the mathematical relationship between the figures of Piñero, Velázquez and, strangely, the dog in the foreground. Piñero had been working on a mathematical model to create a form of perspective that had never been seen before. And it wasn't until the invention of cinema that we would be able to replicate such complex trickery of light and line again. He had studied Da Vinci's use of the Fibonacci sequence to compose scenes, calculate perspective and play with the viewer's peripheral vision. Are you familiar with this sequence?"

"Oh, Christ!" José exclaimed. "Not another shitty airport novel. Spare us, please!" He lit another cigarette and brushed the ash from his shirt.

The Professor continued. "Good, then you'll understand the next part of my explanation. He had found, or stumbled on a mathematical formula, a code if you like, that blew apart Fibonacci and his predetermination theory. Velázquez, though a master of perspective still followed classical models, dividing up his paintings into quadrants, with separate yet inter-related focal points, which imitated the way the eyes process perspective. But Piñero was frustrated with the lack of truth in Velázquez's and other previous representation and interpretations of reality. He began to compile lists of measurements, relative distances between objects, relationships between space, light and structure, and using elaborate charts and models he came up with a series of equations that, when placed in a particular sequence and linked to pre-determined tones and hues generated what can only be described as a unique phenomenon, a number which expanded and contracted randomly above and below the figure of pi. He then began to work on Las Meninas, applying his formula to the canvas, positioning figures and objects in-situ as visual representations of the sequence and assigning appropriate pigments to exact locations within the composition. And, as a result, each element of the formula generated a form of visual magnetic energy, an ability to attract or repel neighbouring objects. It is this tension that creates the intensity of the visual experience. Our mind's eye somehow tunes into arbitrary shifts in line, light and colour, and it gives Las Meninas its unique sense of fluidity, and the mysterious

209

perception of movement."

"But that's just visual trickery, like the Mona Lisa smile," Jacob interrupted.

"No, it's more to do with the way the retina of the eye handles light, the relationship between peripheral, low frequency vision and how the fovea centralis."

"The what?" Jose interrupted.

"A tiny dimple in the centre of the retina that is the most responsive to changes in light."

"That means I've just had my dimple zapped," Jose said, rubbing his left eye.

The Professor continued. "So it's all about how the fovea interprets variations and subtle shifts in the refractive source. But in Las Meninas there something more complex going on than that."

"In what way?"

"We are talking about tangible movement within the structure of the composition."

"You mean the painting is moving?" Jacob interrupted.

"We don't consciously see it move, but tiny shifts occur due to tensions and stresses generated by the geometric relationships and interplay of shape, light, line and tone. Rather than multiple foci, the dog is the source, the starting point, or to be more precise the dog's front right paw."

"That's fucking ridiculous." José shook his head in disbelief. "You're trying to tell me that Las Meninas is moving?"

"Yes, miniscule, arbitrary shifts in the position of all brush strokes. They are almost immeasurable because they stretch and recede, within a microscopic timeframe, like tiny little earthquakes within a nanosecond of time."

"I'm sorry, Professor, you've lost me," José continued. "I can go with your marracon painter and forgery theory but moving paintings, come on. Your reputation is on the line here – again."

They laughed and finished their drinks. "I'll get another one. Vino tinto, Professor? And beer for my Scottish friend with a little whisky chaser perhaps?"

"No, please José. I need to stay sober tonight."

"That'll be a first." He disappeared into the crowd. Jacob picked up the conversation.

"I think I've seen it."

"What?"

"The movement."

"That's impossible. It is so small. It is something that is perceived rather than actually visualised. We don't really have the technology yet to measure such changes. It is like dark matter. In a rational, scientific sense, it doesn't exist."

"But I have seen it."

"Where?"

"The Loss of Innocence. It's moving, significantly."

"What do you mean?"

"I'm talking centimetres of movement in a few hours."

"I think you have misunderstood me, Señor Boyce, Piñero's code is all about the forces of nature and the ability to harness a tiny fraction of the kinetic energy required to produce physical movement from objects in stasis. The code would never induce such radical and extreme movements in a painting."

"It's moving and something is happening to the people who occupy the space around it."

José returned with the drinks. "Hey, what's with the faces?" he said, studying their expressions, "You haven't been arguing while I've been away, have you? Jacob, you look like you've been hit by a bus. What's up?"

The Professor sipped his wine and turned to Jacob. "A young woman came to my room tonight, just before my talk."

"What?" Jacob looked up from his drink.

"She was very distraught."

"Jude! I saw her in the auditorium."

"Ah, your imagined beauty is real after all, Jacob," José interrupted.

"So you admit that you know her?"

"Yes, as I say, I saw her in the auditorium. I don't know why she is here in Spain. I think she might be following me."

"She wanted to warn me."

"Warn you, about what?"

"About you, she said you had a dangerous mind."

"But I hardly know her. We met only once in Glasgow and we had a conversation about paintings. Why would she say that about me?"

"As I said, she came to warn me. She was extremely agitated, afraid even."

"I don't understand."

"Now, as you can imagine, Mr Boyce, I have many enemies and I wanted to find out what kind of enemy you were."

"I'm not your enemy, I don't even know you. I am trying to tell you that your theory is true."

"There are two types of assassinations, Mr Boyce, the critical and the physical. Which one do you subscribe to?" the Professor continued.

José stepped between them. "Come on, Professor. Jacob isn't an assassin. He can kill a whisky or two in quick time but he's no fucking hit man." He slapped Jacob on the back with such force, Jacob fell forward into the Professor's chest, knocking his wine glass to the floor. The contents sprayed over his suit and the glass shattered on the marble tiles, sending fragments in every direction across the bar room floor. The Professor panicked.

"Call security, José."

"I'm so sorry, Professor." Jacob wiped clumsily at the large crimson patch rapidly spreading across the Professor's jacket.

"Don't touch me. Call security, José."

José shook his head. "Sorry about this, Jacob."

"If you don't call them, then I will," the Professor threatened.

"Oh please, Professor, it was an accident," said José, who was now also attempting to clean the wine from the Professor's clothes.

"Security!" The Professor's high pitched shrill cut through the loud rumble of conversation and the people around him turned to see what had happened. Jacob, now gripped by a rush of disorientation and panic, pushed past José and fled the scene.

X

He ran out of the bar and forced his way through the crowd of drinkers gathered in the entrance hall. When he reached the doorway, he spun round and scanned the sea of faces in the room, but she wasn't there. He left the building and looked down the spiral staircase leading onto the street. He spotted a figure about a hundred yards away, a woman searching in her bag for something. It was her.

"Jude!" She looked up for a second, then disappeared down a side street. "No wait!" He took the stairs three at a time and sprinted to where she'd been standing. The street was deserted. On the right, there was a large five star hotel, with a doorman looking rather perplexed at Jacob's behaviour. Jacob approached him.

"Did you see a girl go past?"

"A girl, sir?"

"Yes. Thin, pale, hair tied back, kind of beautiful."

"There's someone over there," he said, pointing at the building opposite. Jude was standing in front of a doorway, on the edge of the kerb. She looked right at him and then turned and disappeared into the darkness behind her. Jacob ran across the Avenida narrowly missing a taxi. It sounded its horn and swerved to avoid him. When he reached the place she'd vanished. He paused and then stepped into the darkness.

He stumbled down a flight of stairs, almost losing his balance. At the bottom, there was a steel door. He tried the handle but it was locked. He searched around the space for any sign of her. But there was nothing. As his eyes began to adjust to poor light, he noticed that the surface of the door appeared to be shiny and wet, and there was a small dark-coloured cross painted neatly in its centre. He reached out and touched it lightly with his finger. It was warm. Placing the flat of his palm directly over the cross, he pressed down on the surface and his hand began to sink slowly into the steel. Soon, his arm had submerged up to his elbow and then his shoulder He could hear muffled sounds coming from the other side; someone breathing, the wheeze and click of mucus in the windpipe. But then something grabbed hold of his wrist and yanked at it violently. The side of his face smacked against the rippling membrane and as he was sucked under, a thick sour-tasting fluid surged into his nose and mouth, blocking his airways. He made one last futile attempt to resist but the force pulling him in was stronger. In an instant, the rest of his body disappeared into the interior of the door and he lost his grip on consciousness.

***

The muzzle tightened around his jaw and cut deep into his lower lip. The blood ran back into his mouth and slipped down his throat. The chanting continued but he could make out only one word within the complex sequence of vowels and consonants. A-Q-U-I. The pain in his head had stopped but he could still feel something moving around inside the top left corner of his skull. His eyes rolled back into their sockets and he sank deeper into the darkness of the space around him. Now he was ready to accept his fate and wait for the final moment to arrive, that critical point when nothing is truly revealed until it all comes finally to an end.

***

Jacob opened his eyes. It was pitch dark but ahead in the

near distance he could just make out a tiny pin prick of pale yellow light. The side of his face was half submerged in a puddle of cold foul-smelling liquid. Turning over, he slowly eased himself up. His left cheek began to sting and he was aware of a throbbing pain in his left foot.

Staggering to his feet, he fumbled for something to support the weight of his heavy limbs until his hand finally connected with a wall. And as he hobbled towards the light, the rectangular shape of a doorway emerged out of the hazy blur. He stumbled on and out into an alleyway illuminated by a nearby street lamp and slowly climbed the steps back up into the world. His face was burning now and as he rubbed at it, he felt a long narrow gash just under the cheek bone. Blood was pouring from the wound and splattering down his sodden shirt and onto the pavement. He must have hit his head on the ground as he fell through the door. He searched his sodden trouser pockets for a cigarette, but the saturated pack disintegrated in his hand. Wiping the blood from his face with the bottom of his shirt, he slowly re-traced his footsteps back to the cultural centre.

The building was in darkness and the doors were closed. He carried on to his hotel and slipped past the manager who was fiddling with the TV aerial in the back office. In his room, he went into the bathroom and examined his injury in the mirror. Although there was plenty of blood, the gash didn't look too serious, but then he noticed that a section of his hair was heavily matted with congealed blood. Probing the scalp with his fingers, he located a small slice in the skin about three inches above his left ear. Turning his head sideways, he parted the hair around the wound. It was a triangular shaped abrasion about half an inch in length, and as he stretched the broken skin, thick globs of blood oozed out and ran down over the back of his hand. With a damp towel, he gently dabbed at it until the bleeding slowed and then stopped. Finally, he got out of his wet clothes and climbed into the shower.

***

In the morning, he packed his belongings and went downstairs for a quick coffee before leaving. In the restaurant the manager's daughter stared at his injured face as she served him.

"Do you have a cigarette?" he asked.

She shrugged dismissively, but then a moment later, reached into the pocket of her skirt and produced a pack of Fortuna's. "What happened?" she asked, still staring at his battered face.

"Do you have a light?" He tapped the end of his cigarette on the table impatiently.

She searched her pockets again for her matches. "Were you mugged?" she persisted.

"Thank you," he said, taking the box from her. "I fell through a door."

"Don't you think you should have it checked out?"

"It looks worse than it is." He took a long drag on the end and blew the smoke high over her head.

"Do you want anything else, breakfast, I mean?" she said, pointing at a rather sad looking buffet of bread, orange juice and preservatives laid out at the back of the restaurant.

"More coffee, if you have some."

As she poured, he ventured another question. "Did you see my wife when she stayed here?"

"Your wife?"

"Wait, I have a photo." He searched his pockets for his wallet. "This is her. Ella Boyce. She was here a couple of weeks ago." The girl studied the image for a moment. "She was on her own, or with a Spanish man, a Sevillano."

She looked back at Jacob. "There was an English woman here, but I can't remember exactly when. You could check with my father in reception."

"I already have."

She glanced back at the photograph. "The girl who was here looked a bit like this, but she was younger, her hair," she paused to think, "it was straight and she dressed kind of scruffy, like a student?"

"Jude."

"I thought you said your wife was called Ella?"

"Was she thin and pale?" he continued.

"Yea, maybe. Is she your daughter or something?"

Jacob didn't respond.

"I do remember some guy came looking for her, though," she continued, "just after she'd checked out. He might have been from Seville. He was definitely not from Barça, but I'm not sure about his accent. He was a bit strange."

"What do you mean?"

"I don't know," she said, shrugging her shoulders. "You know how you get a feeling about some people. I didn't like the way he looked at me. I mean, why would a middle-aged guy like him be looking for a young English student on holiday? It all seemed a bit weird, you know?." She stopped. "Sorry, I didn't mean to—"

"It's OK, so why was he looking for her?"

"I can't remember, but he really wanted to see the well. Have you heard about our famous sacred well?"

Jacob nodded. "So did he?" he asked again.

"What?"

"Visit the well?"

"Oh, I don't know. As I said, I didn't want to get involved with the guy. My father dealt with him."

"So would he have let him in to see it?"

She scratched the back of her head nervously. "We normally only allow paying guests down there, so I wouldn't think so. But you would need to ask him."

"Can I have a look, before I check out?"

"Up to you; you'll have to speak to my father."

"Thanks again for—" he stopped. The manager was peering

round the kitchen door. "Anna, vamos!" he shouted to her and she followed him back into the kitchen.

***

When he'd finished packing, Jacob went back down to the reception to pay his bill. There was no one at the desk or in the office. He leaned over and, opening the guest book, checked Ella's details again. Although the signature looked authentic with her distinctive flamboyant movie star E encircling the rest of her name, looking at it again, he realised she'd used her maiden surname Brown, rather than Boyce. He had quickly checked the entries a couple of days previously, and one or two days after, but no other guests had checked in.

"What are you doing?" the manager said, approaching him from behind.

"I'd like to settle up please," Jacob said, closing the register quickly.

The manager frowned and returned to the other side of the desk. As he made up the bill, he glanced up repeatedly at Jacob's battered face.

"I fell through a door." Jacob smiled, removing a bundle of notes from his wallet. "Is it possible to see the well, before I leave?"

The manager sighed and shook his head. "The well is closed for refurbishment."

"Your daughter didn't mention that it was closed."

"It's not my daughter's business. It's closed, and anyway, I'm very busy. I couldn't take you down today even if it were open." He rustled some papers on his desk impatiently.

"So when did this refurbishment start?" Jacob said.

"It's been over three months. I'm waiting for my useless electrician to fit new lights."

"But what about that guy you allowed in to see it a few days ago?"

219

"What guy?"

"The man who came in off the street looking for one of your guests, the young English girl?"

"Sorry, I don't know what you are talking about."

"From Seville. Your daughter didn't like him."

"Oh him." The manager said finally. "That was a private arrangement."

"And how much does a 'private arrangement' cost?"

The manager looked at him for a moment, as though mentally calculating how much Jacob could afford. "2,000."

"What about 1,000?"

"OK."

"Let's go, then."

"Money first," the manager said.

After Jacob had handed over the last remaining notes from his wallet, the manager disappeared into the office and returned moments later clutching a key and a torch.

"This is strictly a private viewing, OK?" he said. "I don't want the ayuntamiento on my back."

"No problem."

"The key opens the door at the end of the corridor, and you'll need this when you get down there." He handed him the torch. "The lights in the main cellar are OK, but there's only one connected by the well. Be careful of the cables; none of them should be live but I wouldn't touch them if I were you."

"Thanks," Jacob said.

"You can leave your things here under the desk." The manager ushered him through the office and out into the corridor behind.

"It's at the end on the left," he said. "When you get down to the cellar, follow the arrows on the wall. The well is in the second chamber. Remember, it's dark down there, so try not to fall through the door." He sneered at Jacob and returned to his office. Jacob carried on down the corridor, and unlocked a small door under the stairs. He turned on the torch and stepped inside.

The steps were narrow and steep, and he could see why the Council had health and safety concerns. As he carefully negotiated his way down, the torchlight flashed and danced around his feet. At the bottom, he pushed open a second door and located the light switch. The cellar was smaller than he expected and reeked of rising damp and wood rot. In the far corner there were wine bottles racked up alongside a collection of casks and beer barrels. On the wall by the door he spotted an arrow pointing to the other side of the cellar. When he reached the back of the room, he opened an iron gate and, continuing into the second chamber, the smell of damp disappeared and the ambient temperature increased significantly. Within a few moments he was sweating copiously.

The second room was smaller than the previous and it was inadequately lit by a single light bulb that hung down from a low curved ceiling. Jacob had to step around the cable along with a few other wires that dangled dangerously close to his head from hacked out holes in the brickwork. Using the torch to guide him, he moved further into the gloom and approached a wooden barrier at the far end. Peering into the shadowy space on the other side, he still couldn't see the well. He scanned the area with the torch until the beam settled on a large dark patch on the floor just beyond of the barrier. Climbing over, he moved tentatively towards the unidentified shape that was slowly emerging out of the murky half light. Directly in front of him, there appeared a neat oval shaped hole cut into the stone flooring. The deep fissure was eye-shaped as José had reliably informed him, converging at two points, the first close to his left shoe and the other about four feet away.

As he knelt down to get a better look, a gentle breath of warm air brushed up against his face. Shining the torch down into the depths, the beam captured glimpses of complex shapes and patterns, covering the interior walls, an elaborate mural made up of tiny mosaic tiles that continued down into the well as far as the torchlight would penetrate. On the opposite wall, he noticed an inscription. He carefully manoeuvred round to the other side and, kneeling down again, leaned over the edge to examine it more closely.

He tilted his head to view the strange collection of words and symbols contained within the inscription, but the language was unfamiliar to him. Suddenly, there was a second, more powerful blast of hot air, accompanied by a faint smell of jasmine. A splintered memory skittered across his mind. Ella was in the bedroom. She was naked, standing in front of the dressing table mirror, brushing her hair with slow methodical movements. He approached her from behind. She leaned back and rested her head on his shoulder. He caressed and kissed the nape of her neck, while his hand brushed lightly across her breasts and slowly reached down to the soft warmth between her legs.

The fragrance lingered in his nostrils for a few seconds and then vanished. Staring down into the depths of the well, the black emptiness now seemed comforting and reassuringly simple. He swung his legs over the side and inched closer to the edge. One more inconsequential movement would be enough to send him tumbling into the void and the unbearable pain of his loss would cease. As he started to lean over, his body teetering on the brink, the silent roar inside his skull was suddenly shattered by a voice somewhere behind him.

"They think it might be the Metro."

Jacob jerked back with a start. A silhouetted figure was standing in the doorway. "Who's that?" he called

"It's Anna." The manager's daughter stepped tentatively into the room.

"Christ almighty, you gave me a fright." Jacob stood up and stepped back from the well.

"The warm air that comes up," she continued, "the line runs pretty close to here."

"What do you want?" he asked, impatiently.

"My father sent me down to check you were OK."

"I'm fine."

"You know you're not supposed to be on the other side of the barrier like that."

"I'm just having a look."

"It's dangerous," she said, imitating her father's voice.

I'm a geologist, I'm used to heights – and drops."

She moved towards him. "Do you want a cigarette?" She held out the packet.

"No, you're OK. Go and tell your father I'm fine."

She moved closer still and lit her cigarette, blowing the smoke into Jacob's face. "What do you think?"

"About what?

"The well."

"It's not what I expected. What does that inscription say, do you know?"

"I haven't a clue." She shrugged. "You can read about it over there." She pointed to a small plaque on the rear wall. As Jacob directed the torch at the wall, the beam illuminated the girl's face for a second.

"Turn that off," she said, shielding her eyes from the light.

He climbed back over the barrier and as she moved out of his way to let him past, he glanced at her again. Her face was slightly flushed and swollen, as though she'd been crying.

"I can't believe how hot it gets down here," she said, wiping her eyes with the back of her hand. She followed him over to the plaque.

"You know your friend, the Sevillaño?"

"He's not my friend."

"Your work colleague or whatever."

"What about him?"

"He made a move on me down here."

"What?"

"It was so disgusting. I mean, he's about as old as you. Some guys just feel the need to try it on, no matter how repulsive they

223

are."

"What do you mean, a move?"

"You know, he said a few things, with his big fat hands."

"Oh."

"He said I could be one of his subjects. Whatever that meant."

"Did he say anything about the English girl he was looking for?" Jacob interrupted her again.

"No. I think when he realised he couldn't have her, then I was his second course for the day if you know what I mean?"

"And did he say why he needed to see the well?"

"I just thought he wanted me down here so he could, you know." She smiled.

"But he was down here on his own, wasn't he? Your father said he let him in."

"That's what he thinks. If my father knew what he'd done, he'd have cut his throat." She looked directly at Jacob. "Men are all pricks, aren't they?" She spat out the words and then sucked hard on her cigarette, blowing a smoke ring that spiralled straight into Jacob's face.

"Pretty much." Jacob replied.

"Does that make you one, then?"

"I'm the only exception," Jacob said, grinning at her.

She moved in closer to him again.

"I didn't think old guys still thought about it that much?"

"How old is old, then?"

"Oh I don't know, just old, like you. Maybe, thirty-five or forty." She inched closer to him. "Do you think about it that much?"

"Look, Anna. I haven't got time for this."

"This what?"

"All this flirting."

"Don't flatter yourself!" She stepped back from him with an indignant swagger. "I'm only here because my father made me come down, otherwise I couldn't give a shit if you fell in to our shitty well and broke your fucking neck, OK?" She started to walk out but then stopped in the doorway. After a moment, he realised that she was crying and he went over to her.

"I'm sorry." He placed his hand on her shoulder to reassure her, but her skin felt strangely hard and leathery against his palm. He glanced over to look. The exposed area of skin above the strapline of her top was heavily scarred and malformed by what appeared to be a severe burn injury. It continued up her neck and the back of her head was completely bald with similar damage to her scalp.

She turned around.

"Is it because of this?" She held out her left hand. All that was left was a melted stump with one finger protruding from its centre.

"Of course not," Jacob said, trying not to look shocked.

"It's a bit of a passion killer," she said, covering her hand with her sleeve.

"Honestly, it's got nothing to do with that. I'm sorry if I upset you. I didn't mean to take out my own problems on you."

"He keeps me locked up like a bird in a cage," she said, wiping the tears from her face. "Sometimes I think I'm going to explode. I just want to get out and live, you know?"

"You mean your father?"

"I think he feels so guilty." She fumbled in her pocket for her cigarettes and grappling with the lid, she tried to pick one out.

"Here let me." Jacob took the pack from her shaking hand. "How did it happen?" he asked, helping her to light her cigarette.

"I was two and he came home drunk. They think he must have left something on the cooker." She puffed at her cigarette manically. "The doctor said that my cot saved me."

"Was anyone else hurt, your father or mother?"

"My father escaped unhurt, but my mother and my big sister Claudia died. She'd be twenty-three now."

"I'm sorry."

225

"How could that bastard survive unhurt?"

"I think your father probably just wants to protect you," Jacob said.

"He's suffocating me. Sometimes I wish I'd died in my cot and I could be with them." She began to cry again.

"Give me your hand," he said offering his. She looked at him for a moment and then held out her good hand.

"No, the other one."

"What?" she said, pulling back in surprise.

"Give me your hand," Jacob repeated.

She studied his expression for a moment, unsure of what to do, but then complied. And rolling back her sleeve, he gently took her disfigured hand in his.

"You know, I didn't even notice your burns before," he said quietly.

"Everyone notices."

"Seriously, you are a beautiful young woman, what else is there to see?"

"Creep!"

"I mean it."

"Who's going to want me? That Sevillaño weirdo, he didn't want to know. The bastard called it a defect."

"One day you're going to meet a guy who doesn't see any of that."

"Like you."

"You don't want someone like me. Sooner or later, I'd let you down." He looked directly at her. "We all have to live with scars, some we can see and some we can't . But believe me, the ugliest and most painful are the ones right here." He tapped the side of his head. "You have to do what you want, and not what your father hopes that you want."

"I just want to breathe in some of my own air, but he watches me day and night. He trusts no one. What hope do I have?" She dropped the end of her cigarette on the floor and stubbed it out with the heel of her shoe.

"He'll have to let you go eventually and if he doesn't, then hit him with a hammer while he's sleeping."

She giggled for a moment and then she leaned over and kissed him on the forehead.

"What was that for?"

"Thanks," she said, "you're a kind man."

"Being kind to strangers is easy," he said.

She looked at her watch. "I've got to go. My father will be back soon." She turned to leave. "I hope you find your wife and she can forgive you for whatever it is you've done." On her way out she stopped in the doorway and called back to him, "Why are you middle age men so obsessed with that fucking well?"

Jacob laughed but, before he could reply, she was gone. He listened to her heels clacking on the steps as she made her way back up to the lobby. He gathered up his things and went over to the plaque on the wall to read the inscription.

This beautiful example of ancient antiquity was discovered in 1972 by a local tradesman working on a burst water main in the cellar of the hotel. It is believed to date from approx. 300BC.

Following extensive restorative work, an elaborate tiled façade was uncovered. Scientific analysis has so far been unable to accurately measure the depth of the well, however it is believed to extend beyond 2 km, making it one of the deepest hand dug boreholes in the world.

Scanning down, he stopped at the last paragraph.

The eye-shaped design reflects the religious and spiritual beliefs of the period. Wells were often considered to have mystical regenerative properties and many believed that they offered a gateway to the divine sea and eternal life. This unique specimen would have formed the focal point of a temple or holy place, attracting pilgrims and followers from far and wide.

And at the bottom of the display, there was a short translation of the phrase within the mural that he failed to decipher. It read:

Through the traveller's eye, the soul may journey home.

On his way back out, he stopped and glanced back at the well, and as he turned to leave, he felt something shift under his shoe. He raised his left leg slightly and a tiny ripple appeared on the surface of the stone slab. It fluttered across the floor, gathering length and pace as it approached the well, gently rocking the barrier back and forth as it passed underneath. When it reached the opening it paused for a second, forming a small distended wave, that then gently rolled over the side and vanished into the darkness. He switched off the light and returned to the reception.

"Don't forget your bags," the manager said as Jacob walked past. The manager handed him his belongings and he continued to the entrance. "Can I have my key and my torch," the manager added briskly.

"I must have left them down there."

The manager muttered under his breath and went back into the office.

As Jacob left the hotel, he spotted Anna at an upstairs window. She was watching him, waiting for him to go. She raised her disfigured hand, smiled for a moment and then disappeared behind the curtain. He slipped his bag over his shoulder and set off back to the train station.

In the Garden of Earthly Delights

It began in the heel. Tendons in the ankle tightened, contracted and elevated the rear of his sole. At first he thought he must have twisted something on the long walk from the station to the museum, but there was no pain or swelling. Within minutes it had spread along the length of his left foot, his toes slowly curling upwards like new shoots of grass searching for the first rays of the sun. He extended his leg and stretched it, fearing the onslaught of cramp, but the muscles in the calf and thigh felt relaxed. He tried again. He raised his foot and placed it over the first step, but it steadfastly refused to make contact with the surface. Leaning further forward, he used the weight of his body to force his shoe downwards but the harder he pushed the greater the sole resisted. He leaned on the stone balustrade and looked up at the entrance. A large group of American tourists were filing in with a flustered looking attendant on the door anxiously trying to maintain order. Jacob counted the steps from the bottom to the top.

Thirty-nine, quite a climb with an errant foot, he thought. After the attendant had ushered in the last of the Americans, he noticed Jacob struggling at the bottom of the staircase.

"Está bien ahí, señor?"

"No, not really."

The attendant nodded and came down to help him. Jacob put his arm around the young man's shoulders and together they slowly made their way up. "39 up but 38 down," Jacob said when he reached the top.

The attendant looked at him bemused.

"39 pasos hacia arriba y 38 hacia abajo. ¿Cómo puede ser eso?"

The attendant ignored his question. "If you want more help, please tell me, OK?" he said in English.

Jacob shifted his weight onto the left leg and it almost buckled under him. The attendant caught his arm.

"Be careful, perhaps you should sit down for a while."

"No, I'll be fine." Jacob sensed that, given a moment's rest, he would be able to proceed. Holding onto the door frame, he pressed down on his left foot and tentatively slid forward, his sole skimming lightly across the surface of the floor. It was an easier manoeuvre than he had anticipated. He had been a keen ice skater as a child and this involved much the same technique. He let go of the frame and entered the museum. The girl behind the reception desk looked up and smiled.

"Bienvenido a El Prado, señor."

"Baroka Obscura?" he asked.

"Mil pesetas, por favor."

He fumbled in his coat pocket for change and, dropping a pile of debris on the desk, started to pick out a few coins.

"Another twenty pesetas," the girl said quietly.

He searched his trousers and the bottom of his bag but he was still short of the full amount. The girl handed him the ticket and pursed her lips as though to acknowledge their secret transaction.

"Thanks," he said, smiling at her.

"Hand in your bag over there," she said, pointing to the cloakroom desk at the back of the hall. Shuffling over, he removed his notebook, pencil and a reel of thread and handed the briefcase to the cloakroom attendant.

"El abrigo, señor."

Jacob removed his coat and the attendant hung it up on a rail behind him.

"Cierran a las 19:00. ¿Esta bien?" The attendant handed him

a ticket.

"Numero noventa y tres, para recolección," he added.

Jacob followed the crowds through the main hall, up the grand staircase and then towards the temporary exhibition room at the end of the corridor. About half way along he passed the entrance to the Velázquez gallery and as he walked by, someone ran out through the doorway and collided with him, making him lose his balance and fall sideways onto the wall opposite. As he stumbled back to his feet, a tour guide ran over to help him.

"Está bien?"

"I'll be all right. Just leave me alone."

The guide let go of his arm and returned to a group of onlookers standing in the doorway of the Velázquez room. Jacob glanced along the corridor, but the assailant had vanished into the approaching throng of tourists. He steadied himself and continued along the corridor towards the exhibition gallery.

A large CAC advertising banner was draped above the entrance, along with two exhibition posters propped up on mahogany lecterns equidistant on either side. Each poster displayed the slightly distorted detail of an eye. The pupils stared down the corridor at Jacob forming a disconcerting impression of a face gripped by terror.

Jacob approached one of the posters and examined it. The detail had been blown up to such an extent that it appeared heavily distorted. He leaned in closer to see if he could pick out anything familiar but that only made things worse. He gave up and approached the attendant standing in the door.

"Ticket, por favor." The attendant held out his hand in expectation.

Retrieving it from his shirt pocket, Jacob handed it to the man and entered the gallery.

The room was half empty, the walls displaying only a few paintings, most of them Jacob didn't recognise. There were the usual assortment of Baroque favourites, scenes of peasant domesticity, gods and goddesses, cherubs, half naked men and women staring confidently back into the world. Most of it seemed rather mediocre and predictable. He turned 360 degrees, scanning the room for The Chaliced Hand, but it wasn't there. He approached a rather bored looking attendant sitting by the door.

"Perdón señor, I'm looking for The Chaliced Hand by Manuel Piñero. I was told it would be here."

"What was the name again, sir?" the man said slowly, as though waking from a long restful sleep.

"Piñero. The Chaliced Hand."

"Let me check the catalogue." He reached under his seat and produced a large lever arch file.

"Piñero, you say?" He flicked through three or four pages and ran his finger down a long list of tiny hand written names and numbers.

"I can't see a Piñero. What is the name of the painting again?"

"The Chaliced Hand – or La Mano Chalise. Please, it is very important. I was told it would be here in this exhibition."

The attendant continued to flick backwards and forwards, but then stopped.

"Here he is. Number 23. Oh, that explains it?"

"What?" Jacob asked.

"It's downstairs."

"Where?"

"Through the doors." He pointed back into the room.

"Sorry?" Jacob looked again but still couldn't see any door.

"I'll show you." The attendant got up and Jacob followed him to a large oval pillar in the centre of the gallery.

"Go through here and Gallery B is at the bottom of the stairs." He pointed at the pillar.

"What?" Jacob repeated.

The attendant pressed the wall, and with a soft click, a narrow door appeared and swung open into the room. Jacob pulled it open further and peered into the interior of the pillar.

The attendant nodded and returned to his seat by the entrance. Jacob entered and descended a spiral staircase to the lower floor.

Gallery B was very different from the main exhibition upstairs. The lighting was subdued and there were glass cabinets packed into the limited floor space. Jacob peered into the first casement he came to. Inside there were a selection of artefacts and what looked like personal items displayed with numbers next to each: a lace handkerchief, a small decorative mirror, a single page of a letter and a collection of eye brooches. Jacob moved in closer to try and read the inscription at the top of the letter but all he could make out was one word, Quero.

Moving further into the gallery, he examined the contents in various other cabinets until he reached the centre of the room. Along with the personal mementoes, the room also contained mannequins dressed in 17th Century garments. To his left a headless figure was clothed in an intricately patterned gown with beautiful lace gloves and tiny black leather shoes. Over on the far right, another was wearing a courtier's outfit, complete with waistcoat, breeches, thigh length leather boots and sword. The walls were festooned with flags and aristocratic paraphernalia, but Jacob still couldn't see The Chaliced Hand, or any other paintings for that matter. He turned to go back upstairs, but then noticed a solitary painting on the wall to the left of the exit. In the gloom, it was difficult to distinguish much of the detail but as he approached it, Jacob soon realised that at last he had found what he had been looking for; the girl, the room, the light, lines, pigments and perspective. There was no question in his mind that this was the work of Piñero, but as Jacob scanned the composition, it was clear that something was radically different.

He inched closer, and as he had anticipated, the composition captured a moment some time before the event depicted in the Glasgow work. The girl was alone in the room, standing by the fireplace. In her left hand, she was holding an unopened letter with a deep crimson seal in its centre. Her expression was one of contemplative joy. The table and glass were absent from the scene, as were the dead pheasants. The fire was unlit but set for use. The room appeared to be more or less the same, but with one major difference. The layout was in reverse. The girl and the fireplace were now on the right hand side and a small window at the rear was on the left. It was as though the whole image had been flipped like a reflected image in a mirror. The girl's left arm was extended as though she was pointing at something beyond the frame, but then the image stopped abruptly. Jacob stepped back again. The painting was incomplete. It was as though the whole right hand section had been torn off. He read the notes on the wall.

La Mano Chastite (alt. La Mano Chalise) approx. 1656

Artist: Unknown (possibly Lesser Known Baroque artist Manuel Piñero)

Manuel Piñero born: unknown; died: unknown

During a period as protégé and friend of Velázquez, Piñero enjoyed some initial successes as a court artist, completing a number of commissions, but although he was a skilled craftsman, his work was forever overshadowed by the genius of his teacher. Soon, Piñero's compositions were dismissed as inferior pastiche. His relationship with Velázquez deteriorated and he became embroiled in a number of high profile scandals. It is believed that one night, in a fit of rage, Piñero attempted to destroy his entire collection of paintings. The remains of The Chaliced Hand was discovered in a basement room in Madrid in 1922. Following substantive restoration work, previously unseen details were discovered in the work, including the royal seal on the letter in the young girl's right hand, and a shadowy figure reflected in the mirror at the rear of the room. The letter may be from an unknown royal admirer from the court of King Philip the IV. The identity of the figure in the mirror remains a mystery. We can only speculate what the remainder of the scene may have looked like. The scorch marks on the edge of the painting were left intact by the restoration team to help the viewer imagine what the girl may be pointing at.

A noise made Jacob turn. An elderly man had entered the gallery and was shuffling from one display cabinet to the next. Jacob returned to the painting and leaned in to the composition to examine the mirror. There was an indistinct shape of a person reflected in the glass. The outline had been lightened slightly in places so as to separate the shape from the darkness around and behind it. No features were visible but the figure was either wearing a hooded cloak or had long hair. He opened his notebook and retrieved a postcard of the Glasgow painting. He held it up and moved back until the postcard appeared to be approximately the same size as the painting. Closing one eye, he shifted the card this way and that until he achieved optimum optical proximity. The juxtaposition confirmed that the room was a near-identical but reflected copy of The Loss of Innocence, but with one significant addition. In this painting, there was an extra lamp hook on the ceiling that was not present in The Loss of Innocence. The shape and decorative detail seemed familiar. He opened his notebook again and carefully flicked back through the damaged pages until he found some previous entries he'd made on Las Meninas. He scanned through the first, second and then third page of notes until he came to a quote he had scribbled at the bottom.

In the ceiling the two empty lamp hooks accentuate the sensation of austerity (from Miranda, J.G 1983 Las Meninas, El Otro Lado del Espejo).

He closed the book and removed his reel of thread from his pocket. He was about to take some measurements when the elderly man stepped in front of his path, blocking his access to the painting and obscuring his view. Jacob shifted to his right but the man followed a moment later, continuing to obscure most of the work. Distracted and flustered, Jacob rewound the

235

reel, closed his notebook and went back upstairs.

He stopped short of the entrance to the Velázquez room and peered round the corner into the gallery. Cautiously, he slid his left foot over the threshold and as it hovered just above the surface of the floorboards, he gripped the door frame and gently propelled the rest of his body into the room.

Las Meninas dominated the space around it in much the same way as a bully dominates the school playground. Velázquez's other masterworks displayed in the octagonal room seemed somehow diminished and beleaguered by its presence. Even at this relatively early hour, there were significant numbers of people milling around the painting. Some stood back, their mouths open, attempting to take in the scale and the unrelenting surprise of the work, while others could only deal with it in small doses, squinting at little areas of detail and shaking their heads in disbelief. Jacob moved further into the gallery. Avoiding eye contact with the painting, he focused on the shape and layout of the room, the distribution of light sources, and the interplay between the painting and the pattern on the gallery's wooden floor. He positioned himself carefully at a point he believed to be the exact centre of the space. It had taken a number of minutes and carefully paced calculations to choose the right spot. He moved a few inches to the left and then back again to the right, adjusting his position. When he was sure he'd found the reference point, he was ready to look.

Instantly, the painting appeared to swell out and surge towards him like an impenetrable wave of darkness. The canvas pressed down into his face, forcing his eyeballs to rotate inside their sockets. Thick, tar-like fluid forced its way into his nose and mouth, down his throat and into his lungs. He couldn't breathe. He began counting out his panic mantra in an attempt to offset the sensation of drowning.

"One – two – three – the air… four – five – six…"

But the sensorial assault persisted. He thought he was going to pass out and tried turning away, but his limbs refused to move. His lungs now felt as though they were about to burst through his rib cage. He began to lose consciousness and closed his eyes in preparation for the fall. But as he did so, normality returned. The weight of the invisible wave on his chest disappeared, the fluid receded and his airways cleared. He gulped in mouthfuls of oxygen until his heart rate slowed and he regained his senses. After a minute or so of controlled breathing, he felt he had recovered sufficiently to open his eyes again. This time, the painting remained where it should be, and he set to work.

He opened his notebook and across two blank pages drew out a large rectangular frame. This he then divided into seven sections that roughly corresponded to the key sections of the composition and numbered them in a clockwise rotation. First he considered Professor Bárbola's initial piece of evidence, that the dog was actually too large in relation to the figures behind it. The dog's main role within the composition was to draw the viewer's eye down to the bottom of the painting and then back up again to the man standing in the doorway. But it seemed to leap out of the painting when viewed in juxtaposition to the dwarf. However, it was in proportion to the mysterious figure behind the group of girls. The Professor appeared to be right, the illusion of perspective generated by the inclusion of the dog was wrong. It looked like it may have been added at a later date, but he needed to check the measurements. He pulled his reel of thread from his pocket and he was about to begin when a group of American tourists entered the gallery and approached the painting. They gathered around the canvas and their large collective body mass obscured his view.

"Not again, for fuck's sake," he muttered under his breath. He waited, staring at the floor while trying to maintain his concentration. After a few moments his left foot started rocking gently backwards and forwards on a cushion of air between the sole and the floor. The movement spread up his leg and soon his entire body was swaying in time with the rhythm of his breathing. As he rocked, his frame slid forwards and then backwards a few inches across the floor, pulled by gentle kinetic energy provided by the pendulum-like action. Finally, the noisy tour guide instructed them to follow him to the Goya and they all disappeared through the rear door. Jacob's body stopped rocking, he re-positioned himself and continued.

As he stared at the entirety of the composition, geometric lines began to appear, criss-crossing the canvas, linking the eyes to the easel and then down to the dog and back again to the shoulder of the artist. Familiar patterns began to emerge as he scanned the image. The use of line, light, pigment and representations of perspective all tallied with The Loss of Innocence in Glasgow. Piñero's creative presence within the composition was everywhere. He looked up at the two lamp holders on the ceiling. They provided key perspective reference points to emphasise the depth of the room. They drew the eye down towards the figure standing in the doorway, but there was also a line running down from the centre of the first lamp to the boy's foot in the foreground. The design of the holders was identical to the one depicted in The Chaliced Hand. Jacob's hand shook as he wrote the observation in his notebook.

He approached the painting and moved up to the rope barrier in front. In the bottom right hand corner, the boy was playfully resting his left foot on the dog's back. But on closer inspection he could see that the child's foot was not quite touching the surface of the dog and looked a little odd. He leaned over the barrier to try and get a closer look. The foot was clearly elevated and the relative angle indicated a completely different relationship with the subject beneath it. He unwound some thread and tried to reach out across the gap to calculate the distance from the child's knee to the end of his shoe. As he held up the thread, he could now see a linear relationship between the end of the boy's shoe and the dog's front paw resting on the floor, but he was still too far away to be sure. He climbed over the barrier and within seconds, two burly security guards appeared from nowhere. As they approached, one whistled and gestured for him to climb back over. Reluctantly, Jacob did as he was told. The guards approached.

"Lo siento," Jacob said.

One of the guards waved his finger in front of Jacob's face. "Se lo prohíbe."

"Lo siento, señor, I am short sighted and I needed a closer look. With your permission, could I look again, just for one minute?"

"No, está prohibido," the security guard repeated.

Jacob cursed and returned to the centre of the room, and was about to write down the observation when a flash of intense light forced his head upwards. A single ray of sunshine shot through the skylight window directly above him. The beam caught the top of his head, passing straight through the length of his body, and seemed to illuminate the floor beneath his left foot. He shifted sideways and the small, perfectly formed sphere of spectral light on the floor followed the movement of his sole. The glow began to pulsate in an erratic rhythm that matched his heartbeat. Jacob felt a warm rush of euphoric heat race from his legs and up into his chest. He could feel the light penetrate the arteries and blood vessels in his heart and lungs. Suddenly, his spine arched backwards as a burst of radiant energy stretched his body upwards towards the roof of the gallery, stretching bone and sinew to near breaking point. But then, as abruptly as it had appeared, the beam vanished and the euphoric heat flicked off like a switch.

Someone tapped him on the shoulder and he turned round. It was the elderly man from the gallery downstairs.

"It's real, isn't it?" the man said, pointing at the painting.

Jacob noticed a strong smell of urine that seemed to be emanating from the man's clothes. He was wearing a filthy beige flannel suit, his trousers held up with a knotted tie and his jacket smeared in yellowish stains. There was a small metallic badge attached to the lapel with the now familiar words

239

¡NUNCA MAS! displayed in bold crimson lettering across the centre.

"Do you know how he did it?" the old man continued.

"Did what, who?" Jacob's mind was still befuddled by what had just happened to him.

"How the artist managed to create something so... contemporary." The man ventured closer and Jacob pulled back slightly.

"He had a camera."

"Really?"

The man tapped the centre of his forehead. "Click Click."

Jacob tried to change the subject. "Where are you from?"

"I'm a traveller – I'm travelling and taking pictures – click click." He tapped his head again and sneered, exposing rotting yellow-stained teeth. "Are you taking measurements?" He pointed at Jacob's notebook.

Jacob backed away but the man followed.

"I tried that once – thought I could work out how he did it. But it's no good because it's all in here, click click, chakra." He thumped at his chest and then pointed back at the painting. "But he abused his gift. He wasted his talents on sorcery and jiggery pokery, – nasty businesses – of the mind."

"What do you mean?" Jacob was growing impatient.

"I'll show you." He went over to the painting, and, reaching into his jacket pocket, he removed what appeared to be a small compact mirror. And turning with his back to the edge of the canvas, he held the mirror up to his shoulder. "Just one moment, I need to be in just the right position. There, I have it now. Come, look."

Jacob turned to leave the gallery.

"Please," the man called to him. "You won't believe your eyes."

"Oh, what the hell?" Jacob muttered under his breath, and, positioning himself directly behind the old man, he leaned down to look into the mirror. The man's hands shook and the reflected image rattled around inside the frame of the compact.

"Can you see it yet?" the man asked.

"Your hand is shaking," Jacob replied impatiently.

"I'm sorry, I'm somewhat agitated."

Jacob shifted slightly to get a clearer view. The image wobbled around until finally, for a moment, the reflection settled in the frame. The shadowy male figure in the top right hand corner of the composition had vanished.

"What the fuck!" Jacob spun round to look up at the painting looming over him. The figure was back within the scene, but the extreme viewing angle distorted his features. He now looked familiar, as though Jacob had seen this character somewhere before. He returned to the man who was now facing him.

"How did you do that?" Jacob asked.

The man leaned in further towards him and thrust the mirror in his face.

"What do you see?"

Jacob pulled away from him and as he did so caught a glimpse of the reflected image in the mirror; a long pronounced nose, a grimacing mouth and bleached white penetrating eyes set against an impenetrable darkness behind.

"Click click," the man said.

Jacob retreated but the man pursued him.

"Click click." The man extended his left hand and repeatedly twisted his wrist as though he were flicking at the spool on a camera. Jacob turned and ran downstairs. But he could still hear the man's voice directly behind him.

"Click, click, chakra!"

When he reached the cloakroom desk, he fumbled frantically in his pockets for his ticket. "I can't find it," he said to the girl.

"What does your coat look like?" the girl asked politely.

"Long, black overcoat with a briefcase. Hurry!" he said, looking repeatedly over his shoulder. But the man was nowhere to be seen. When the girl returned with his things, he stumbled out of the museum and across the expansive courtyard. And as he fled through the gardens, two enormous eyes, staring out of a giant exhibition banner, followed him all the way down to the avenida and then out into the darkness of the Madrid night.

Fluid mechanics

"Excuse me, is this seat taken?"

Jacob looked up from his notepad. A young woman was standing by his table.

"No," he said, wiping mayonnaise from his mouth.

"Is it OK if I sit here? It's just that the café is so busy."

"No, no – I mean, yes, that's fine."

She sat down opposite him and picked up the menu. "Are you a regular here?" she asked, reading through the list of dishes.

"Yes, I suppose I am."

"Is there anything you'd recommend? I can't make up my mind."

"The mozzarella and ham ciabatta is pretty good. Actually, it's all very good."

"So do you come here every day, then?" she quizzed him again.

He closed his notepad and put his plate on top of it.

"Sorry I'm disturbing you. I'll shut up."

"No, not at all." He looked at her properly for the first time. She was soaked through. Her hair was tied back tight against her scalp making her features more pronounced. Some strands had escaped and dangled in front of her face, with droplets of water swinging precariously on the end. He thought she looked tired, bedraggled and a little lost within herself. He was instantly attracted to her. He picked up the conversation again.

"Yes, more or less. I work just round the corner."

"Where's that?"

"At the University. I'm a lecturer. Well I'm a postgraduate researcher, but I do some lecturing."

"What's your subject?"

"Earth Science."

She placed her hands face up on the table and extended her fingers. Jacob studied the movement for a second and took another bite of his roll.

"It helps me relax," she said, aware that he looked a little uncomfortable. "I've got a trapped nerve in my shoulder and when I get tense, it starts to twitch and irritate me."

"Oh." He picked at the remains of his salad.

She gently clenched her fists and relaxed them in a slow rhythmical motion. Jacob was beginning to find the repetitive movement a little erotic. He took a sip of coffee.

"What do you do?" he asked

"I'm a student."

"What subject?"

"Fluid mechanics. Don't ask me why. It was my parents idea of a good career move."

"Don't you like it then, the subject, I mean?"

"Oh dear, what's there to say about fluid mechanics? Let's just say it doesn't move me."

They both smiled. A waitress interrupted their conversation. "I'll have what he's having and a cappuccino," she said, pointing at Jacob's plate.

Jacob looked at his empty cup and then his watch.

"Sorry, am I holding you up?" she asked.

"No, I'm fine. I'll have another black coffee, please." The waitress repeated the order and returned to the counter.

"So what would you study if you had your way?" Jacob continued.

"Art."

"Really?"

"Oh yes. That's my real love, and music, too. You see that poster over there?"

"What, the John Coltrane?"

"You know John Coltrane?"

"Of course, who doesn't?"

"My parents, to name two. That's why I came in here. I saw the poster and thought, this looks like a good place to be."

"So you've never been in before?"

"No, I suppose I've been too busy with boring assignments and life crap. I live on the other side of the campus so I don't come over here that often."

"I take it your parents are not great music lovers then?"

"I'm at the end of a very long line of scientists. Appreciation of the arts in my house goes about as far as carols at Christmas." She leaned forward and rested her elbows on the table. "So how long have you been teaching at the University?"

"A couple of years. I'm working on my PhD and I'm hoping they'll give me a permanent job at the end of it. What about you?"

"Second year, undergrad. Two more years to go."

"You could always retrain and go to art college. Defy your parents."

"Nah, I think it's something you have to do your whole life. It would have to be a total commitment. I'd have to poison my parents and bury them in the back garden. They'd never forgive me."

"They would. Anyway, don't they want what's best for you?"

"You don't know my parents. It would seem like such an irresponsible and illogical step. I don't have a say in it. Anyway, I'm thinking of switching to Law."

"Why Law?"

"I thought I could specialise in science cases, make lots of money and keep my parents happy all at the same time." The waitress returned with the order. "Do you mind? I'm starving."

"No, you go ahead. You look like you need it."

She broke the sandwich into three or four pieces and started eating. Jacob sipped his coffee and studied her movements. She was a methodical and careful eater. After every third or fourth bite, she sipped her coffee and wiped the corners of her mouth with her forefinger. She looked up.

"Sorry, am I staring?" Jacob felt the blood rise in his face.

"Yes, you are and it is very disconcerting."

They smiled and he retrieved his notepad from under his plate and pretended to write some notes on the back page. After another few mouthfuls and sips of coffee, she looked up and tapped his notepad with her fork.

"Do you believe in fate?"

Surprised, Jacob sat back in his chair. "What?"

"Do you believe in fate?" She put the teaspoon down and clearing a space, laid her hand on the table, upturned with the fingers spread as wide as they could go. "Do you think all these lines and cracks really mean anything?"

"I haven't really thought about it."

"Life, love, heart, fate, health, are all measurable in some way, like these are?" She ran her finger along a line that extended from the base of her index finger to the edge of her wrist. "Come on, you're a scientist. You must have an opinion about it."

"That's a very odd question to ask a stranger."

"I'm a very odd person." She smiled.

"May I?" She nodded, and, leaning forward, he lifted her hand to examine the palm more closely.

"So are you into all this fortune telling stuff?" he asked.

"Is that a philosophical or a scientific question?"

"Which one is that?" He traced a line from right to left across the width of her palm.

She held his finger and redirected it gently downwards towards her wrist. "This is life. This is health. And here is love. That one is head, I think. And down here is…heart." His finger brushed against her ring.

"That's beautiful. Is it white gold?"

"I know what you're thinking," she said, studying his

246

expression.

"Do you?"

"I'm not."

"Not what?"

"You know, hitched."

"Oh."

"It was my grandmother's wedding ring." She turned it around with her thumb nail. "White gold and platinum. For some reason it only fits on that finger." She looked up. "And anyway, it feels kind of comfortable there. It helps ward off evil spirits."

"Like me you mean?"

"Exactly."

She took another bite from her sandwich. "You still haven't answered my question."

"What question was that?"

"You know."

"Well, I'm an Earth scientist, I suppose there is a certain amount of fate involved in the way the earth evolves and develops."

"What does an Earth scientist do exactly, apart from travel the world on all expenses paid field trips?"

"We study everything to do with the planet; rocks, climate and weather systems, landscapes and minerals. We look at how and why all of these elements change over time and how humans interact with and are responsible for influencing some of those changes. So we study the Earth to learn about the past and in many ways foresee what is to come, because all of these elements contain codes and data that can help us predict the kind of future to expect."

"Like global warming?"

"That's right."

"So in a way, the Earth is a bit like the lines on my hand."

"Yea, formed over millions of years." He smiled.

"You know what I mean."

"The Earth's surface and what goes on underneath is a living history book and at the same time, it's also a bit of a crystal ball."

"Does that mean you do believe in fate then?"

"Fate might be too emotive a term, how about predictable structures. I believe that the Earth and all of its elements, and living beings, including ourselves, operate and follow predictable and organised patterns of movement and change."

"You really think human beings do this?"

"Of course, but there are significant rogue forces."

"What are those?"

"Well, free will for one. Man's belief that he can control his own destiny. That he can somehow operate outside of elemental laws of physical and mathematical science, that in some way, we are superior and stronger than these forces. That's when we hit the skids with nature and get into all sorts of bother."

She took a sip of coffee and rested the bottom of the cup close to the edge of the table.

"I think you are wrong."

"What?"

"You're in scientific denial."

"What do you mean?"

"You talk about plans and organisation, but what if none of this is structured? What if we are all just particles of hydrocarbons floating around randomly bumping in to each other?"

"But we have proven evidence of structure. You must know this when you study fluid mechanics."

"Yes, but what if the evidence is simply our brains trying to make sense of a long complex series of arbitrary incidents." She began to tip the cup backwards and forwards with her forefinger.

"But that's just random theory. Hasn't it been disproved?"

"Yes, but only by those who desperately need to re-affirm some sort of order. Maybe the world would be just too frightening to live in if we all existed in perpetual chaos. It frightens me."

"It frightens me, too. You should see the random chaos in my flat. I suppose you could call that living proof."

She picked up her cup and dropped it down on the saucer with a clatter. "I've got to go."

"What?"

"I'm late."

"What for? Sorry, I don't know why I said that." Jacob stood up.

She opened her bag and searched inside until she found her purse. "Do you know how much?"

"Don't worry, I'll pay for it," he said, surprising himself with his offer.

"No please, how much is it?"

"I don't know. I tell you what, you can give me it back the next time."

"What next time?" She smiled nervously.

He held out his hand. "I'm Jacob, by the way."

She put her bag over her shoulder and removed a pen from a side pocket. "May I?" She gestured towards his cigarette packet on the table.

"Go ahead."

She picked it up and scribbled something on the inside of the lid.

"Call me, OK?" She handed him the pack and left the café.

He waited a moment until he was sure she had gone, and then opened the lid. Inside, she had written,

Ella – 0036 301106237

El Ángel Caído

The heat from the morning sun roused Jacob from a troubled sleep. He sat up and rubbed at his eyes until they began to adjust to the intensity of the light. His head throbbed with a dull thumping pain that pounded against the inside of his frontal lobe. He looked around.

The park was quiet. On the far side of the lake, one or two couples clung together as though nursing each other's hangovers. A solitary rollerblader practised twists and turns on the walkway, and down by the lakeside, a man and small boy were attempting to launch a toy yacht. The man knelt down next to the boy and dropped the boat into the lake. He pushed it gently and after a moment, a light breeze fluttered through the small white sail and the boat gently drifted away from the side. The boy clapped his hands and jumped up and down with excitement. Jacob watched the boat as it floated to the other side, its delicate movement failing to disturb the mirror-like surface of the water.

He removed his bag and coat and undid a few buttons on his shirt. The sky was a perfect blue and, despite the hour, the temperature was already above 80°. He stood up, stretched his legs and looked around for somewhere to buy a coffee. Further into the trees, he spotted a kiosk. He gathered up his belongings and went to investigate. It was only a small wooden shack but it seemed to sell everything you could possibly need to live permanently in the park: shavers, soap, toothpaste, fast food, cigarettes, booze and even clothes. The man behind the counter was in a state of semi-undress and his hair was dishevelled as though he'd just got up. Jacob managed to locate a stash of small change in the side pocket of his bag.

"Expreso," he said, depositing the coins on the counter.

The man puffed out his cheeks and reluctantly prepared Jacob's liquid breakfast.

"¿Azúcar y leche?" he asked, between yawns.

"Si."

As Jacob stirred at his drink, he glanced down at the newspapers on the rack below. The front page of El Mundo declared,

Asesinado Activista de Nunca Más

He looked at a second and third paper and they were all running the same headline. Picking one up, he skimmed through the article.

A body was found by a neighbour on the morning of 21 September... Police have confirmed that the corpse was that of Professor Bárbola, a prominent Nunca Más activist and outspoken opponent of the Government's involvement in the war... Police have revealed that a small knife-like object had been used to puncture the victim's neck and severe a main artery. It is believed that the victim bled to death."

"¿Va a comprar ese?" The man in the kiosk was glaring at him.

"No," Jacob responded abruptly and folding it in two replaced it on the rack. The man muttered something under his breath and disappeared into the back of the kiosk. Jacob grabbed the paper and made a quick exit through the trees and down to the lakeside. He put his coffee on a park bench and continued reading the article.

It is believed that Professor Bárbola had been a member of the Verum Dei Sect, a mysterious and notoriously secretive organisation that has been linked to occult practices, and a number of sources have claimed that his death may have been the result of sadistic and ritualistic activity.

He put the paper down on the table and emptied out the contents of his bag next to it, spreading out the scraps of notes and scribbled observations, postcards and street plans he had collected over the last few days. And then he began to place items in order, grouping related information together. Somewhere in the assorted mess of evidence there was an answer to all the chaos that was throwing him from one desperate situation to the next. His movements became frantic. Postcards and notes flew off the table as frustration and rage got the better of him. After a few moments, he slumped down on the bench, dropped his head into his hands and began to sob uncontrollably.

"How could she do this to me?" he repeated over and over. His left hand started to shake. Clenching his fist, he shook it out to try and stop the spasm, but within moments it had spread up through his arm. He folded it under his chest but that made his whole body judder up and down. He let out a loud roar.

"Where are you, Ella?" he screamed into the cloudless sky.

Something bounced off his head and he spun round. A small group of teenagers had gathered behind him.

"Hey borracho! ¿Quieres jugar un juego?" One of the boys flicked another pine cone at him and it hit him in on the cheek.

"Fuck off!" He stood up and gestured at them with clenched fists.

"Ooh, van Damme," said one of the boys.

Jacob gathered up his things from the table and stuffed them back into his bag. The boys continued to taunt him.

"Van Damme Bam Bam!" they jeered.

"I'll kick your fucking arses," Jacob retorted, and swung his bag wildly over his head. But suddenly the jeering stopped.

"¿Como hacer que?" one of the boys asked him, open mouthed, pointing at his feet. A second gang member was kneeling down behind Jacob, flicking a length of twig back and forth in the narrow gap between Jacob's espadrilles and the ground.

"I'm the fucking devil," Jacob hollered, lunging towards the group. He grabbed one of them by the throat and pushed him to the ground. The others ran off leaving their friend to fend for himself. The boy choked out an apology and held his arms up in submission. Dragging him by the collar of his jacket to the edge of the trees, Jacob roared abuse into his face, and then after a moment of intense silent intimidation, he let him go. As the boy scurried away, he stopped and shouted back, "El Ángel Caído!"

Jacob motioned towards him as though about to give chase, but the boy about-turned and disappeared into the woods.

He returned to the clearing, and using the bench for leverage, he tried to force both his feet back down into the dirt, but they stubbornly refused to co-operate. He relaxed the muscles in his legs and let go of the picnic table. Practising a few more steps, and then a lap or two around the bench, he felt confident enough to venture out of the park and back into the city. Collecting up his papers, he found a small passport-sized photograph of Ella tucked between two postcards. She was young, probably still in her twenties, sitting in a bar somewhere. She was holding up a glass and pulling a ridiculous face. She looked happy and alive. He ran his finger lightly over the surface and slipped the photo into the breast pocket of his shirt.

Glancing back at the lake, the man and boy had now gone, but they'd left behind their boat which bobbed up and down helplessly in the middle of the lake. The movement of its tiny hull generated shockwaves that rippled outwards, disturbing the surface tension until the reflected image of the park was

253

completely obliterated. When the first wave finally reached the far shore, Jacob closed his bag, put on his coat and headed slowly for the gate.

La Decoradora

It was after 4.00 when he finally located the forger's shop. It was tucked away at the end of a narrow lane in the Latina district of the city. The building looked tired and neglected, with gangland graffiti and faded posters covering the walls. A weather-worn hand-painted sign dangled precariously above the entrance to the shop, and on the other side of filthy windows, two small paintings were propped up on dust-covered easels, a Picasso and a rather diminutive-looking Rubens, with three voluptuous nymphs bathing by a stream. Jacob pressed his face to the glass and peered in, but the lights were out and he couldn't see beyond the grime on the glass. He tried the door but it was locked. Adjacent to the shop was a second door that appeared to be the entrance to the flats above. He pressed the service buzzer on an intercom system and, after waiting a moment or two, tried again. There was no response. In frustration he pressed all the buttons, running his finger up and down the numbers repeatedly until finally the tiny speaker cackled to life and a voice hissed through the static.

"Si?"

"Estoy buscando al Señor Almir, el proprietario de La Decoradora," Jacob said, leaning in closer to the intercom.

"Hola. ¿Estás allí?" he said, pressing his ear further into the box.

There was a sudden rattle followed by a loud wail of high-pitched static and then the speaker went dead. Jacob jabbed at the buttons again but when the voice didn't respond, he thumped the unit with the side of his fist. The casing cracked and a section of plastic dropped to the ground. As he bent down to retrieve it, the door swung open and an elderly man stepped out, almost knocking Jacob over.

"Lo siento," Jacob said, moving out of his way. The man was exceptionally tall and was wearing a knee-length Burberry coat with a black fedora pulled down over his eyes. Ignoring Jacob, he set off down the lane towards the avenida. Jacob followed him.

"Disculpe, estoy buscando al Señor Almir."

The man continued walking.

"El Marroquí." Jacob was now alongside him. The man stopped and turned.

"Who are you?"

"Mi nombre es Jacob Boyce. Tengo que hablar de un asunto urgente."

"Are you English?" the man asked.

"Yes."

"What business do you have with Señor Almir?"

"Do you know him?"

The man looked up, momentarily revealing the side of his face. But then he carried on.

"José sent me," Jacob shouted to him. The man stopped again and turned. "From Barcelona."

"Señor Miró?"

"Yes."

"Soy Almir. ¿Que quieres?"

"How do you do, señor." Jacob extended his hand, but Almir refused to shake it.

"José gave me your name and address. He said that you could help me."

"With what exactly?" he asked, switching from Castilian to English.

"I'm involved in some research and I need your advice."

"What research?"

"José said you were an expert in Baroque art."

"Flattery will not diminish the debt." Almir's English was infused with a refined French accent.

"Sorry?"

"Your friend still owes me two hundred thousand pesetas. Have you brought my money?"

"I'm afraid not."

Almir looked Jacob up and down. "I have an urgent appointment, excuse me." He started down the lane.

"He showed me the room." Jacob called.

"The room?" He squinted back at Jacob.

"The store room, in Barcelona."

Almir approached until he was directly in front of Jacob, his skeletal frame was towering over him like a contorted crane. Jacob could now see the whole of his face. His skin was dark and pulled tight across high, pronounced cheekbones. He looked gaunt and emaciated, and his eyes were bulging out of their sockets. Almir stood for a moment silently contemplating Jacob's appearance.

At first Jacob looked away, sliding his left foot backwards and forwards over the surface of the pavement, but then he joined in, matching Almir's gaze in what appeared to be an uncomfortable game of nerves.

Finally, Almir broke away. "Come with me." He turned back towards his shop and Jacob followed. "Are you Scottish?" he asked, as he unlocked the door.

"Yes, from Glasgow."

"You rattle your R's like a North African."

"That's because we are North African." Jacob's joke seemed to lighten the atmosphere slightly.

"Please excuse the colourful aroma," Almir said, as they stepped inside. "It's canvas glue. Traditional resins are made of horse fat. It's very effective but the smell can be quite rancourous."

Jacob glanced round the room. The interior appeared to be

some kind of gallery or exhibition space. But the walls were bare and the floor space was covered in empty picture frames stacked up in rows according to size and shape. In the far corner, five or six folded easels lay tangled together like knotted trees, and on a counter top at the rear of the room, there were rolls of canvases bundled together forming precarious pyramids of varying heights and widths. On his way through the door, Jacob tripped over a large tea chest.

"Be careful; I'm having a clear out," Almir said.

As he negotiated his way around the chest, Jacob glanced down into its contents. It was crammed full of broken frames, twisted hinges and gluey nails and screws. Amongst the debris, was a torn fragment of discarded canvas. He cocked his head to get a better look at the disembodied detail painted on its surface. It was a female hand. The palm was upturned with the second and third fingers tucked under and the first pointing out of the box directly at him.

"This way." Almir gestured, and they continued through the shop, down a narrow hallway to a small kitchen area at the rear of the building.

The room was fairly austere with few signs of domesticity. There was a small metal sink in the corner with a couple of plates resting on the rack, an ancient rusty cooker under the stairs and a yellowing 60's style refrigerator squeezed into an alcove.

"Coffee?" Almir asked, dropping his keys onto the worktop.

"Yes, that would be good, if you have time."

He removed his coat and hat, revealing a brilliant white head of hair that seemed to simultaneously illuminate the room and darken his skin tone. He was wearing a rib-hugging polo neck sweater that was pulled in at the waist by a wide, brass-studded belt. A gold link-chain necklace was wrapped tightly around his neck, emphasising his rather peculiar shape. His flamboyant appearance seemed completely at odds with his surroundings. On the floor by Jacob's feet there were piles of neatly-stacked newspapers and magazines, and on a small kitchen table a copy of El Pais lay open. Its headline, *Asesinado Activista de Nunca Más* glared up at him like a silent scream.

"Sit, please," Almir said.

Jacob removed his coat, and slumped down at the table. As he waited for the kettle to boil, he scanned through the article again.

"I hope you like it black and sugar free." He handed him a small white porcelain cup and saucer.

"That's perfect, thank you."

Something brushed against Jacob's leg. A large dog had appeared from nowhere and was sniffing around the bottom of his trouser leg.

"Don't worry about him, his size can be deceptive. He's a pussy cat." Almir spoke quietly to the animal and ran his hand along its back. The dog wagged its tail, dropped down at Jacob's feet and pushed its nose under his shoe. He slid his foot away and folded his legs under his chair.

"I met this guy," Jacob said, tapping the newspaper with his finger.

Almir looked up.

"A few days ago in Barça. José invited me to one of his lectures."

"You met him?"

"It was a CAC event. José introduced me. He had a few interesting things to say about Piñero."

"It's a real tragedy, for his family, I mean." Almir picked up the paper.

"Did you know him?" Jacob asked.

"I only knew of him. He was an academic. I tend to avoid those types as much as I can."

Jacob stifled a grin.

"Smoke?" Almir produced a pack of Gauloises from his shirt pocket.

Jacob removed a cigarette and steadied Almir's shaking hand

as he lit the end for him.

"Rheumatoid arthritis," Almir said, between puffs, "it causes the muscle to spasm." He stretched out his fingers to relax the tendons.

"It must make it difficult for you to work, to paint I mean."

"Cognac and Demorol. The combination seems to take the edge off the pain." Almir blew a long plume of smoke high into the air.

As Jacob sipped his coffee, he could feel Almir staring at him again.

"Is that a Velázquez?" Jacob asked, pointing over the forger's shoulder to a small framed picture on the rear wall. "His face looks familiar. It's one of his self-portraits, isn't it?"

"Painting the self is an interesting concept," Almir said, removing the picture from the wall and handing it to Jacob. "I often wonder how feasible it is to represent oneself in art when it's so difficult in life."

"It's amazing," Jacob said, holding it up to the light to get a better look at the detail. "It looks so old, all these cracks and blemishes across the surface."

"Looks can be deceiving; take a look at the signature."

He located a small dark scrawl in the bottom right hand corner of the painting, and turning it this way and that, he tried to decipher the writing. The overall shape vaguely resembled Velázquez's signature but he couldn't distinguish any individual letter.

"Please let me assist you." Almir took the painting and turning it upside down, handed it back to Jacob. As he examined the insignia in detail, a combination of letters began to materialise within the swirls and loops. Jacob began to spell them out, "F-A-C-S-"

"Facsimile," Almir interrupted, "a duplicate but not a fake."

"Very clever."

"I think the words you are looking for are 'legal technicality'."

Jacob handed back the frame and Almir returned it to the wall.

"There is a very important distinction to make when you judge any painting," Almir said, as he attempted to relocate the canvas on its hook. "It's whether it is a good fake or a bad fake, and that is a bad fake."

Almir sat down opposite Jacob and dropped his cup down on the table with a clatter. "So what is it you want of me? Please don't tell me you are an artist, or worse still, an art historian?"

"No, I am a Professor of Earth Science." Jacob felt too weary to lie.

"I certainly wasn't expecting that."

"Sorry, I'm not explaining myself very clearly. I've been looking at a number of links between art and the sciences, specifically the relationship between geological phenomena and optical disturbances found in paintings."

"Disturbances?"

"Seismic phenomena."

Almir shrugged.

"Earthquakes," Jacob said, sipping at his coffee again.

"So which paintings are you talking about?"

"One in particular, The Loss of Innocence by an artist called Manuel Piñero."

"And do you think Piñero painted it?"

"Yes. Don't you?"

"Do you know that he rolls the brush between his fingers to create minuscule, almost indistinguishable, loops and swirls within the consistency of the pigment?"

"What?"

"Tiny movements, like this." The forger demonstrated by gently rubbing his thumb and forefinger together. "You can't necessarily see it, but you can feel it."

"So The Loss of Innocence is his work?" Jacob repeated, impatiently.

"What makes you believe that it is his?"

261

"I thought it would be obvious to someone like you?"

"You mean a professional liar?"

Jacob didn't respond.

"Enlighten me," Almir urged.

"The evidence I have collected along with various calculations I've made."

"Calculations?"

"I've been looking at mathematical models of analysis, geometric relationships within the composition."

"And so sung the little clod of clay."

"What?"

"You have a scientific mind." Almir flicked at some ash that had dropped onto the sleeve of his sweater. "So you think that your configurations of numbers and formulae will lead you to an understanding of—"

"The truth."

Almir laughed again. "Now there's a contradiction in terms."

"What do you mean?"

"It's not very often one hears the words Piñero and the truth co-habiting the same conversation. The problem is that the truth of any painting is located in the eye and in the mind, and the tiny shifts in pressure exerted by the artist's wrist, through the fingers and the fibres of the brush and finally onto the canvas. It is a question of fallible human judgement, and nothing to do with measurable rationality. A painting is a manifestation of the soul, the machinations of the human condition, not the geometric theorising buried away in a text book."

"What about Celini?"

"You *have* been doing your homework, haven't you?" Almir rolled the glowing tip of his cigarette lightly along the rim of the ashtray. "Celini was a dangerous lunatic and probably that's what attracted Piñero to him, like a moth to a flame. They are like-minded in that respect."

"But Piñero was using Celini's mathematical models. What

about his formula, the missing calculations?" Jacob said, rubbing at his eyes.

"I must say, you have made a very strange choice of subject matter for your research. I'm not surprised you've been having problems. Piñero is the grand master of deceit and disorientation. Perhaps that's why he was so unpopular. People like certainty and Piñero's vision is one of," he paused for a moment to consider the correct expression, "psychic pandemonium."

Jacob could feel his chest tighten and his eyes start to roll back into their sockets.

"And there lies the crux of the matter," Almir continued. "Piñero is not interested in truth or enlightenment, or any other noble grandiose cause. His raison d'etre, like every other forger and con-artist, is the proliferation of confusion, chaos and fear."

"I wonder if I could…" Jacob shuffled uncomfortably in his chair but Almir carried on.

"The forger is not respected; he is despised because with a careful choice of pigments and a simple flick of the wrist he perpetuates the overwhelming terror of uncertainty whilst simultaneously affirming the fallacy of universal design."

"Could I trouble you for some water?" Jacob slumped forward, almost falling to the floor.

"Steady!" Almir caught his arm. "Are you OK?"

"I'll be all right in a minute." Jacob raised his hand to his face and breathed heavily into the palm. The dog jumped up and weaved around the two men excitedly.

"Sit down!" the forger bellowed, and the dog returned to its place beneath the table. He got up and hurriedly filled a glass with water.

"Drink," he said, and Jacob gulped at the cold liquid. Within a few seconds, his airway cleared and his breathing slowed down.

"Would you like something to eat? I think I have some bread."

"No, water is fine." Jacob drank the last of it and Almir replenished his glass.

After a few moments, when he was sure Jacob had recovered, Almir sat down again.

"I'm afraid, monsieur, you may have wandered into an intellectual quagmire."

"May I?" Jacob said, picking up the pack of Gauloises.

"Are you sure you should be having one of those?" Almir frowned.

"It'll help."

"Piñero is a sorcerer," the forger continued. "He is playing with your mind and it seems to be affecting your health. If you want my advice, I would give it up before—"

"I can't." Jacob placed his hand on the table and slowly clenched his fist.

"Is there something else?"

"What?" Jacob looked up.

"It may be none of my business but is there some other matter troubling you?"

Jacob shrugged his shoulders.

"Please, monsieur, I am a professional liar, remember?" And for the first time, the forger smiled.

"My wife," Jacob said, finally.

"You are married?" Almir asked in surprise." You don't look like a man who is married."

"She's disappeared."

"Here in Madrid?"

"When I came home for work, she wasn't there."

"Ah, in England? When did this happen?"

"A few days, maybe a week ago. I can't remember exactly."

"So why are you in Spain?

"I tracked her down. Her mother has a place just outside Barcelona. She went there at first, but I think she is now somewhere in Madrid."

"Well, at least you know she's OK, I mean if you have traced her here to Madrid."

"I can't be certain of that" Jacob pulled at the skin above his left eye.

"And she didn't tell you that she was going, or leave you a note?"

"When I got back to the flat she was gone."

"Perhaps she was called away. Did she have business dealings in Madrid?"

"She came here with someone."

"Who?"

"I'm not sure exactly, a Spanish man, a Sevillaño."

"And you know this man?"

"No," Jacob let out a prolonged sigh, "but I think she might have got herself involved in something."

"Like what?"

"Something to do with the painting."

"She was helping you with your research?"

"Quite the opposite, she despised what I was doing. She was pissed off with me for spending so much time on it. I knew I was neglecting her but I just carried on."

Almir took another long drag of his cigarette, and blew out the smoke noisily. "I hate to say it, monsieur, but it sounds to me like—" He stopped, perhaps to reconsider his choice of words. "It's none of my business, but do you think she may have been having an affair?"

"I wish it were that simple. I fear that my research has uncovered some kind of criminal conspiracy and my wife has got mixed up in it somehow."

"And on what evidence do you base this rather imaginative conclusion?"

"Someone tried to destroy my notes. They removed important calculations. I think they want to stop me."

"Who?"

"The man she was with, the Sevillaño. I think he may be holding her against her will."

Almir rubbed his forehead wearily. "Monsieur, this is all a little far-fetched, don't you think?"

"So why would anyone want to steal my notebook?"

"You need to give this up. There's no conspiracy, you're emotional about losing your wife." He put his hand on Jacob's arm. "Go home and wait for her to return. She'll come back if she wants to."

Jacob pulled his arm away and sat back in his chair. Almir studied his anguished expression for a moment and then stood up.

"Come with me," he said, retrieving his keys from the side.

"Where are you going?"

"I'll prove to you that you are misguided," he said, offering to help Jacob out of his chair.

"I'm fine now." Jacob held on to the table and slowly pulled himself out of his chair. The dog got up, stretched and bounded over, wagging its tail excitedly.

"This way."

Jacob followed the forger and his dog back through the gallery and out into the street. They stopped by the adjacent door. Almir tapped in a few numbers on the entry system and tried the handle but it was still locked.

"Fucking vandals." He cursed and tried the combination again.

Jacob stared at the broken panel as the light shuddered on and off, and this time the lock clicked and the door swung open. The dog squeezed past them and disappeared into the darkness.

"He's in a hurry," Jacob said.

"He knows where he's going."

Inside, it was warm and humid, and they continued to a small archway at the end of a long passageway.

"Mind your head," Almir said, tapping at the cornicing above the arch.

The dog rushed through and the two men descended a set of

steps into the basement. When they reached the bottom, the dog started whimpering and scratching at a heavily bolted steel door.

"Just a moment."

As Almir fumbled with his set of keys, trying one and then another, the dog grew more impatient and began running up and down, weaving between their legs. At last he found the correct key, unlocked a large padlock and raised the security bar. He gestured to Jacob.

"After you. Or should I say, after the dog."

Holding onto the door frame, Jacob peered into the darkness beyond.

"Please."

Jacob cautiously stepped inside. The room was gloomy and he could barely see in front of his face. He inched forward, peering into the blackness beyond his outstretched hand.

"Wait." Almir shuffled past him and disappeared into the void. There was a sudden flood of light as he threw open a set of wooden shutters at the far end of the room. Shielding his eyes, Jacob glanced round the room. To his right, there were racks of canvases and frames but this time significantly larger than the ones in the gallery; drawings, sketches and paintings from a whole range of periods; Da Vinci, Rubens, Vermeer, a Velázquez. And to his left, a half-finished Rembrandt next to a Pizarro, propped up with a couple of Monets and a vibrant Chagall. Almir was at the top of a small flight of steps on the far side of the room, his frame silhouetted by the warm glow of the late afternoon sunshine streaming through the open doorway behind.

"I thought you said you'd given it all up," Jacob said.

"These are all my favourite memories. I couldn't bring myself to destroy them. The others you can see that are incomplete are strictly for my own pleasure. You're the first to see them."

In the right hand corner, Jacob spotted an easel and the framed back of a large canvas propped up against it, and on the ceiling directly above him there were two familiar-looking lamp holders. In an instant, he realised that he was standing in Velázquez's studio, or at least, an impressive replica of it.

"Is it real?" Jacob asked, turning back to the forger.

"It's whatever you want it to be."

"Did you create it?"

"I find it an inspiring place to paint. I can come down here and pretend I am someone else."

"But it's so accurate."

"It didn't really require much effort. In many ways, it was as simple as reproducing the details in a photograph. Anyway, look, I have something to show you." The forger slid a few large empty frames out of the way until he reached a six by four canvas turned to the wall. "Give me a hand here."

Jacob helped him turn the heavy frame over and lower it down onto the floor. "La Mano Chastite," he said, smiling broadly at Jacob.

"It's complete." Jacob stared at the painting in amazement.

"Yes, of course."

In the damaged painting, the girl appeared to be pointing at something or someone beyond the composition. But in this version, she was caressing the long dark locks of a male courtier. He was on one knee, his head bowed as though in prayer.

"He's dead," Almir said.

"What?"

"Or as good as. She's just knifed him."

"What is this?" Jacob said, turning to Almir.

"La Mano Chastite."

"I don't understand, I saw The Chaliced Hand this morning in El Prado."

"You saw a damaged painting called La Mano Chastite."

"So what is this?"

"This is a later version."

"You mean, this is what it would have looked like?"

"This is what it does look like."

Jacob examined the painting again.

"Look how he leans forward." The forger circled a section with his finger. Most of the courtier's face was hidden, but a portion of his cheek and an area around the top of the jaw line was just visible. "You see it? It's so subtle and delicate. Unless you were looking for it, you would miss it completely."

"What?"

"A faint streak of blood just below the jaw."

"I still don't understand. Have you recreated this from your own research?"

"Look at her right hand," Almir said, ignoring him.

Jacob followed the line from the courtier's neck, across the girl's tunic and down the length of her right arm. In a clenched fist, she was clutching the letter opener and on the tip of the blade, there was a small pinkish stain.

"A very calculated and subtle assault, into the neck and with a twist of the wrist, like so…" He demonstrated the movement. "…the carotid artery is severed. In a matter of minutes, our poor besotted fool would have bled to death."

"This isn't right." Jacob leaned further over the canvas to examine it more closely. "It's a completely different painting. The position of the characters, the colours and pigments."

"This is what I wanted to show you. This is the reason why your research is pointless."

"What – because you've made up some kind of imagined version?"

"It's not imagined. It's right there in front of you."

"This is the original? Jacob looked back at Almir in disbelief. "What about the one in El Prado?"

"I was particularly pleased with the illusion of fire damage and ageing. Convincing, isn't it?"

"Yours?"

"Necessity dictates."

"I can't accept this. Why would you have the original?"

"La Mano Chastite belongs to a trilogy of paintings which

269

includes your painting in Scotland."

"Three? I thought there were only two."

"The paintings tell a story," Almir continued, "and in any story there is a sequence of chapters and events. But if one of those chapters doesn't fit the next, then the whole deception collapses like a pack of cards. And it'll be quite obvious to everyone that some or all of those paintings are not what they seem."

"I don't understand."

"People may not care about Piñero, but they care a great deal about Diego Velázquez, particularly here in his own beloved country."

"I still don't see what you're getting at."

"Isn't it obvious?"

"Enlighten me."

"Towards the end of the 1960s, in the dying days of the Franco regime, a stash of canvases along with documents and letters were discovered in the walled cavity of an old disused chapel in the Eastern district of the city. News of the find reached the media and rumours spread that the horde might be a collection of early works by Velázquez. But the recovered documents revealed an altogether more sordid story."

"Professor Bárbola claimed that Piñero and Velázquez were lovers."

Almir laughed. "The Professor did savour the sweet scent of a juicy scandal. No, this was something a great deal more dangerous. As Velázquez's pupil and assistant, Piñero's role was often nothing more than that of a domestic servant. He would be ordered to fill in and finish off commissions for Velázquez's impatient clients, but more often, he would have to perform mundane menial tasks and housekeeping duties for his teacher. But as time went on, his skills as a painter improved and developed. Inevitably, he became frustrated with his treatment and lack of recognition, so unbeknown to his master, Piñero rented a small studio on the other side of the city and began to work on his own original compositions."

"Yes, I know all of this, so what?" Jacob was growing increasingly impatient with Almir's long-winded explanation.

At first, they were mere second rate pastiches of Velázquez and other contemporary artists, but then something mysterious happened."

"What?"

"Almost overnight, his compositional abilities took a significant leap forward. It was as though he went through some kind of creative metamorphosis."

"Why would that happen?"

"I don't know, but it was as though he had struck a creative seam of gold and, at every opportunity, he would secret himself away to work in his studio."

"But if he was so brilliant, why is he neglected and mostly forgotten?" Jacob said, dismissively.

"That's down to his mentor and teacher. Velázquez began to suspect that Piñero was up to something. So one night he followed Piñero to his studio. He was so enraged by his pupil's disobedience and disloyalty that he confiscated all of his paintings and banished him from the court." Almir lit another cigarette and offered Jacob one. Blowing another thick cloud of smoke into the air, he continued. "But when Velázquez examined Piñero's efforts, he soon realised that his pupil was a great deal more gifted than he had previously presumed. His use of geometric configurations, pigment combinations and the intricacies of detail equalled, if not surpassed, even his own exceptional creative talents."

"Was he jealous, then?"

"Seriously threatened is probably a better way to describe it. Piñero's abilities had the potential not only to obliterate his reputation as Spain's foremost court painter, but also put a halt to his financially expansive and extravagant lifestyle."

"So what did he do with them?"

"The simplest and most sensible thing to do, of course,

would have been to destroy them. However, Velázquez was a complicated man, so in a moment of divine stupidity he decided to set about re-working and re-creating the compositions, but this time complete with flaws, inconsistencies and imperfections, in effect, turning Piñero's masterpieces into second-rate fakes."

"But why would he bother? Surely his position was secure and he had nothing to fear from a mere apprentice."

"Velázquez had many enemies, both within and outside the court. Jealous rivals, people he owed money to, there were all sorts who would seize upon any opportunity to bring him to his knees."

"But to go to such lengths – it doesn't make any sense."

"Pride and vanity combined with an out-of-control ego, a typical artist in other words."

"So he halted Piñero's reputation before it had begun."

"Exactly. And when the paintings were complete, Velázquez invited influential guests to his studio to scoff at and deride the adulterated work of his errant pupil. Then, in the final coup de grâce, he convinced the King that Piñero was attempting to swindle the court and that he should be arrested and tried for treason."

"But what about Las Meninas?"

"What about it?"

"Who painted it?"

"Velázquez, of course." Almir tapped the end of his cigarette into his palm and then sprinkled the ash onto the floor.

"But Bárbola said that it was Piñero's work."

"In a sense he was partially correct. When Velázquez ransacked Piñero's studio, he discovered a number of plans and sketches, embryonic templates of a painting that strongly resembled Las Meninas. As Velázquez pieced together the notes and details that Piñero had left behind, he soon realised that Piñero had conceived a work of art that was so radical—"

"He plundered Piñero's vision," Jacob interrupted.

"He completed it, yes. As Piñero's employer, he had every right to do this. But he turned the tables on Piñero's original insult by swapping places with him in the composition, painting himself centre stage as the noble artist and Piñero as the unknown and unimportant figure at the back of the room."

"But I still don't understand why you were asked to fake The Chaliced Hand, if Velázquez had already beaten you to it."

"Come on, monsieur, think about it. Velázquez faked another artist's work and then had him killed? Don't you think the art establishment would wish to conceal that sort of information? The authenticity of Velázquez's entire catalogue along with his character would be called into question."

"That's a bit of an over-reaction. Does anyone really care what went on in the art world three hundred years ago?"

"You underestimate the sense of fear that percolates through this country. Velázquez represents so much more than simply a great artist to the people of Spain. He is the perpetual beating heart of a historically-fractured country. An attack on Velázquez would be seen as a declaration of war on the sovereignty and fragile unity of the nation. The state had to act quickly to suppress the truth.

"So you were called in to fake a forgery and save Spain's bacon?"

"A little white lie to suppress a darker untruth. I was commissioned to create a painting that removed Velázquez from the equation, just enough to satisfy the experts. A story was concocted that they were Piñero's paintings, they were presented to the world press, everyone was happy, and Spain kept spinning on its dysfunctional axis."

"This is all wrong," Jacob said, stepping back from the painting on the floor.

"I'm afraid it is not. The painting you saw in El Prado this morning is mine."

"So what's with all the fire damage?"

"A foil to throw the so called 'experts' off the scent. We came up with the story that the paintings had been damaged in the great Palace fire of 1732, and that a servant or footman had recovered them from the debris and sold them onto an unscrupulous collector. All very plausible, isn't it?" Almir smiled.

"And I suppose you're going to tell me that the painting in Glasgow is one of yours as well?"

"I can't be sure as I am unfamiliar with that version. I would need to have a close look at it."

"How many versions are there?"

"I can't remember exactly. I was very prolific in those days."

"But I have categorical evidence." Jacob searched in his bag for his notebook.

"What I find," Almir said, ignoring Jacob's increasing state of agitation, "is that if you hang a forgery in a gallery or museum, and it is there long enough, and the people believe it is real, then, over time, it becomes real. Truth and reality are as malleable as the softest of clay."

"Wait a moment," Jacob repeated impatiently.

"The paintings you saw in the storeroom are not fakes," Almir persisted. "They are the originals. The forgeries can be found on the walls of some of the greatest museums and galleries around the world, including your beloved El Prado."

"I have data and measurements that prove you are wrong, look here." He thrust the notebook towards the forger, but he refused to take it.

"You can live in denial as long as you please, Monsieur Boyce, but the truth is that fakery and lies are at the heart of all things."

There was a dull thud from the other side of the nearest wall and the dog, who was stretched out on the floor by the easel, looked up and started wagging its tail.

"What was that?" Jacob asked, looking over his shoulder. "Is there someone down here?"

"It's probably my ancient plumbing. It does that from time to time."

Jacob went over to the wall and listened again. The dog got up and followed him, and as he pressed his ear to the exposed brickwork, the dog licked his hand and scratched at the floor with its paw.

"I can assure you there is no one else here," Almir said. "This is a very private and secure space."

"What's going on?" Jacob turned back to him.

"I'm unclear of your meaning."

"Something isn't right here. You told me you had arthritis and that you'd stopped painting."

"I have stopped. As I said, this room is for my eyes only."

"So why did you let me in?"

"I wanted to alert you to the fact."

"My pointless research, I know."

"I'm only trying to help you."

A glint of light caught Jacob's eye and he looked down at the canvas on the floor. It seemed to be coming from inside the girl's clenched fist. He knelt down and examined the detail. Between her third and fourth finger, he could just make out the reflective sheen of a blade. He followed the line from the girl's wrist, up her arm to a flower-adorned crown on her head. Just below the crown, buried within thick strands of hair, there was a small triangular patch of bare skin. He looked back at Almir who shifted uneasily from one foot to another.

"Where's my wife?" Jacob moved towards him.

"Please, calm down," Almir said, stepping back.

"What have you done with her?" He moved closer still.

"I don't know where she is. That is your problem, not mine."

"You're a fucking liar." He kicked the frame with his foot and there was a loud crack.

"Please don't do that."

He booted it again and a corner joint let out a loud crack.

"Stop!" Almir cried.

"Are you all in it together, is that it?"

"I really don't —" Almir began, but Jacob was already over

by the easel.

"So what's under here?" He tapped the top of the tarpaulin with his finger. "Is that another one of your 'versions'?"

"Now that's enough. I'd like you to leave now."

"Can I see it?" Jacob put his hand on the top of the frame.

"It's my own work. It's got nothing to do with you or any of this."

Jacob grabbed a corner of the fabric. But before he could remove it, Almir caught his arm.

"I'm afraid I can't allow that."

"Let go of me!" Jacob pushed him away and Almir staggered backwards, falling over his excited dog. On the way down he clipped his head on the corner of the easel. He lay there for a moment completely motionless as the dog licked frantically at his face. Jacob thought he may have seriously injured him, but then slowly he began to stir until finally, he sat up. As he rubbed at the back of his head, a V-shaped gash appeared on his cheek and tiny droplets of blood began dripping onto the front of his sweater. He got to his feet.

"I'd like you to leave now," he said, pressing his hand into the wound. Jacob remained motionless for a moment, unsure of what to do next.

"Go!" Almir bellowed at him.

Jacob stumbled towards the stairs at the rear of the studio and when he reached the top, he glanced back. Almir was leaning forward with his hands resting on his knees, while his dog weaved between his legs, lapping voraciously at the blood which now flowed copiously onto the floor. Jacob turned and fled through the doorway and out into the faltering sunlight of dusk.

Café Wha

He ran through an alleyway that led to a long tree-lined avenue, and continued on until he came to a square. On the far side, a waiter was setting up tables beneath a large plane tree. He crossed the plaça and collapsed into a chair. Rubbing his hands anxiously on the rough fabric of his trousers, he tried to focus on his breathing exercises, but his mind kept leaping wildly from one question to the next. He began to fear that he had deliberately pushed Almir over, that he was capable of causing physical harm, or worse. It seemed that the further Ella slipped from his grasp, the more erratic and extreme his behaviour was becoming. He closed his eyes to escape the sensation of free fall but all he could see was the dog, its tongue rolling and turning in and out of its mouth. He thought he was going to be sick, and holding his hands up to his face, he emptied his lungs of air. After a minute or so, he inhaled, filling his chest with fresh oxygen. And as he let out a long gasp, a waiter interrupted him.

"¿Dígame?"

Jacob dropped his hands onto his lap and looked up. "Caña," he said at once.

The waiter returned with a beer and a small bowl of nuts. Jacob gulped at the liquid and before the barman had a chance to go back inside, he ordered a second. On the table in front of him he noticed a small triangular card. On one side, there was an impression of a Jackson Pollock painting superimposed over the face of John Coltrane, and on the other side, were details of a gig.

277

Bombissimo
Café Wha
23 Septiembre

When the waiter returned, Jacob asked, "¿Dónde está Café Wha?"

"¿Este es el Café Wha, señor?" The waiter replied.

"I thought it was in Barcelona." Jacob turned the card over again to re-examine the front.

The waiter shrugged and turned to go back inside.

"¿Cual es el grupo de esta noche?" Jacob called after him.

"Ellos están en ahora – is now." he said, blowing out his cheeks like an over-inflated balloon.

Jacob downed his beer and followed the waiter into the bar.

"¿Dónde?" he said, and the waiter pointed to a set of double doors at the back of the room. As Jacob negotiated his way around the empty tables and chairs, the waiter called to him.

"Señor!"

Jacob turned.

"¡Su factura!" he said, waving a slip of paper in the air.

Jacob nodded and pointing at the doors with his thumb, carried on. Continuing down the corridor, he saw a young woman at the end sitting behind a small table.

"Bombissimo?" he asked, as he approached her.

"Es el free jazz," she said, as though to dissuade him. Her hair was dyed bright red and styled into short, jagged spikes, making it appear as though the top of her skull was on fire.

"Lo sé," Jacob replied.

"Have you a ticket?"

Jacob handed her the triangular card he'd picked up from the table.

"No," she said, shaking her head, " a ticket is one thousand pesetas."

"Soy amigo de Álvaro. Debo estar en la lista de invitados."

"There is no guest list," she said, switching to English.

278

"I'm his music teacher," Jacob lied.

She looked at him contemptuously.

"I was a bad teacher," he added.

She smiled momentarily but then the frown returned. "Hold out your hand," she said, and she punched the back with an ink stamp that read,

CAFÉ WHA
WOW!

She opened the door behind her and Jacob went through.

The venue was completely empty apart from a weary-looking barman who was pretending to be busy, and two women who seemed a little uncomfortable. Jacob approached the counter.

"Caña," he said.

The barman took his time pouring Jacob's beer, as though making the most of having something to do. He placed it carefully on a mat by Jacob's hand, aligning the base of the glass exactly within its border.

As he sipped his drink, he turned towards the two women, but they had moved into one of the booths along the side wall, and were now engaged in an animated conversation.

"Where's the band?" Jacob asked the barman.

The barman shrugged his shoulders and continued fidgeting with the till. Jacob searched the bar for the stage. In the centre of the room, the band had laid out their equipment, on what looked like an enclosed dance floor, with guitars, percussion and various strange-looking contraptions cluttering up the space. On either side of the set-up, there were two enormous sets of PA speaker cabinets. Jacob heard someone behind him call his name.

"Jacob, my shoeless Scottish crazy man – you made it."

Alvaro came bounding up and shook his hand vigorously. "Man, I can't believe it. Look at you. You're here. You've come all this way to see us."

"Well, I—" Jacob was about to correct him but Alvaro leapt in again.

"In a pair of…" On Seeing Jacob's footwear, he let out a loud guffaw. "Funky espadrilles – man, you've come up in the world."

"Mm."

"Seriously though, what's with the gear, man?" he said, pointing at Jacob's dishevelled appearance. "What the fuck have you been doing, you look like shit."

"I slept in Retiro last night."

"Shit, man. You crack me," Alvaro said, shaking his head in disbelief. "When you didn't show in Barça, I thought that was that."

"Sorry, I was kind of busy."

"With your harem of dead chicks?" Alvaro nudged Jacob's elbow, spilling his beer. "Sorry, man, let me get you another."

Jacob finished the remainder of his drink.

"So how come you're in Madrid?" Alvaro asked, handing him a pint sized glass.

"I could ask you the same question."

"Shit, man, we're on tour."

"What?"

"Hey, don't sound so surprised, man. Our manager got us some corporate gigs, playing the Café Wha franchise around Spain. Tomorrow night we're in Zaragoza." He leaned in towards Jacob. "Apparently there's some kind of tax avoidance deal going down."

"Well that's fortunate for you guys," Jacob said, sipping his beer.

"Sweet and low." Alvaro extended his palm to slap but Jacob didn't recognise the gesture and ignored him.

"I really didn't think I'd see you again,"Alvaro continued. "You must really dig this mad fucked up music we play, eh?" He slapped Jacob on the shoulder, almost knocking his beer out of his hand again.

"I only came in for some free beer, but you seem determined

to spill every drop of it."

"You waste me." Alvaro laughed, and this time Jacob anticipated the slap, stepping back from striking distance. "Are you ready for another, my friend? We have a retainer."

Alvaro went back to the bar and after a moment of heated negotiation, he returned with a couple of large whiskies.

"Glen Morangee – that's the bitch that killed the president!" He downed it in one. "Come on, Espadrillo, keep up. You can't possibly listen to this shit sober."

Jacob took a couple of sips and winced.

"Shame on your Celtic ass." Alvaro took the glass from him and finished it off.

"Fuck it hard," he squealed. "Another couple of those and then I'll be ready."

He took Jacob by the arm. "Hey, let me introduce you to my band." He led him to a booth behind the guitar stack. Three extremely hairy men and the flaming-haired woman from the front desk were slouched over their drinks. As Alvaro and Jacob approached, they broke off from what appeared to be a heated conversation and looked up in unison.

"Hey, you guys, bitchin' 'bout me again?"

They looked at each other nervously and shook their heads. But then the girl said, "Yeah, Al, how come, you always get to break things? I want to break things, too."

The others nodded in agreement.

"Oh, come on guys, not now. I want you to meet a new friend of mine."

"Is he a record company exec?" one of the band asked.

"Shit, man. He's no suit. Look at him. He's my good friend Jacob and he's come all the way from Glasgow to see us play," Alvaro said, hoping to impress his sullen band mates.

"Wow," said the girl, sarcastically. "I thought you said you were Alvaro's music teacher."

"Shiiiit!" Alvaro squealed. "You crack me, Jacob."

The girl pulled another face and returned to her beer.

"OK, tonight, you can break things, Isabella, but I'm still the leader, all right?" Alvaro said.

Isabella pouted for a moment and then reluctantly nodded in agreement.

"Jacob, you sit down and I will obtain more of the retainer and return with the reward," Alvaro said, bounding over to the bar.

Jacob squeezed into the booth next to the hairiest member of the band. "Don't you get tired of him?" he asked.

"Like we want to kill." The man shook his head.

"What do you play?"

"I'm in charge," the man replied, swigging on his beer.

"He's the percussionist," the girl said, slapping her band mate on the hand.

"That must be quite tricky," Jacob added.

"Why?" the percussionist said between mouthfuls.

"Well, you know, it's difficult to hear much of any kind of… rhythm."

The percussionist laughed and before he could respond, Alvaro returned with a tray packed with more drinks.

"Look what I have here," he said, placing it in front of the band. "Let's kill these suckers and set to it, whatya say?"

Jacob rubbed his forehead. He was beginning to feel the effects of the alcohol but it didn't seem to be helping.

"Are you expecting more people?" Jacob said, glancing round the empty bar again.

"Just you wait and see!" Alvaro said, downing another whisky. He checked his watch. "I'd give it another thirty seconds or so. Watch the door."

Everyone turned and studied the entrance. They waited in silence for the thirty seconds to pass.

"That's over two minutes, Alvaro," the girl said finally.

"Patience, people." Alvaro smiled and glanced nervously at his watch.

Jacob stood up. "I think I'd better…"

But before he could finish his sentence, the double doors swung open and a small group of people began streaming into the bar. Soon, more arrived, and within a few minutes, there were queues forming at the bar and people gathering round the stage area.

"I told you. Am I the King of all things?" Alvaro yelled, pummelling the air with his fist.

"How did you do that, Al?" the girl asked.

"Again," one of the band members added wearily.

"Charisma and shit hot free love appeal," Alvaro said, clutching his crotch.

The girl grimaced and picked up a drink from the tray. Alvaro clapped his hands and the band got up to start their set, but one member remained seated.

"Are you coming, Paco?" Alvaro asked.

"No, I'm gonna sit this one out."

"Shit, man, come on."

"Look, I don't dig the vibe tonight, Alvaro. You can play without me."

"Fuck it," Alvaro said, and followed his band mates up onto the stage.

Jacob slid along the seat so that he was opposite him. He looked older than the rest of the band and his long oily hair was beginning to thin and turn grey.

"You know how he does it, don't you?"

"What?" Jacob asked.

"All the groupies and our enthusiastic fan base, he blows our retainer and our fee on them. They're only here for the beer."

"Like me, you mean?" Jacob said smiling.

The man laughed and held out his hand. "Paco," he said and they shook hands.

"So what do you normally play when you are not pissed off with him?"

"Various things, nothing important. I'm the manager."

"You don't seem that keen."

"I hate this shit. If you saw me play, you'd think I loved it but I hate it. It's all an illusion. Most of the band hate it as well."

"So why do you carry on?"

"Alvaro is a hard man to say no to. He's also my cousin."

"So none of you like the music apart from Alvaro?"

"Jorge likes it."

"Who's he?"

"The bassist, but he's shit. Anyway, why are you really here tonight?"

With a scream of feedback and a bestial wail from Alvaro, the band erupted into an explosion of noise. Jacob grabbed his ears and Paco smiled.

"You see," he shouted over the row.

Each member seemed to be playing a completely different number with conflicting time signatures and keys. Alvaro leapt around bashing this and kicking that, and roared into the mic with such ferocity, the guitarist's beer glass bounced off the PA speaker and smashed onto the floor.

Jacob tried to shout over the sensory assault. "May I?" he gestured, towards the tray of drinks.

"Go ahead." Paco nodded.

They both sipped their beers and turned to watch the band. Alvaro was now behind a large rectangular box, clutching a claw hammer. Every few seconds he'd raise his arm and bring it down on the box, which produced an ear-piercing screech. Paco shook his head in dismay and turned back to Jacob.

"So how come you know my pain-in-the-ass cousin?" Paco hollered over the din.

"I met him in Barça, on the night bus."

"And you're still alive?"

"Just," Jacob said, adding, "I'm looking for someone."

"Who?"

"My wife."

"Your wife is here?" he said, looking round the bar.

"No, in Madrid."

"Is she trying to avoid you or something?" Paco smiled and took a swig of beer.

"Maybe," Jacob replied, and as he reached for his beer, he knocked it over.

"Hey, steady man." Paco leaned forward and caught the bottle before it rolled onto the floor. "Are you OK?"

"Sorry," Jacob said, wiping a large puddle of beer off the table onto the floor. "She left for Spain a few days ago and I haven't seen or heard from her since."

"Do you think she might be in trouble?"

"I just keep hoping that she's OK."

"Shit. So you think she's here in Madrid?"

"I've been following up a few leads, trying to retrace her footsteps. I was in an art shop, near here, at the end of the Avenida."

"Is your wife an artist?"

"It's one of those tourist shops that sell reproductions of famous paintings," Jacob said, ignoring Paco's question.

"Were they able to help you? I mean had she visited the shop or...?"

"I met the proprietor."

"What did he say?"

"He fucked with my head. I don't think he was honest with me."

"So you think he knew something about your wife?"

"He was hiding something."

"Where did you say this shop was?"

"At the end of the road, it's an old art forger's shop called La Decoradora."

"An art forger?"

"Yes."

"What's his name?"

"Almir."

"What?" Paco turned his head to hear.

"Al- mir," Jacob repeated.

285

"The Moroccan?" Paco's eyes widened.

"Have you heard of him?"

"Shit, everyone's heard of him. A few years ago, he was never off the news or out of the papers."

"I knew he was once famous, but I didn't realise," Jacob said.

"I thought he was dead," Paco said, flicking a strand of hair out of his eyes. "And your wife knows this guy?" he said, pulling a face.

Jacob shrugged his shoulders.

"I hope she doesn't; he's not a nice guy,"

"He's an old man," Jacob said, anxiously.

"Yeah, he is now, but creeps like him, they don't just leave shit like that alone."

"You mean art forgery?" Jacob asked.

"A lot more than that."

"Like what?" Jacob began to feel the panic rise in his chest again.

"As I said, back in the seventies, there were stories in the paper about some kidnappings in Madrid and—" He paused to take a sip of beer.

"What, for Christ sake?" Jacob shouted.

"Bodies began turning up – of women – pretty gruesome stuff. Turned out, maybe twelve in total were discovered."

The music suddenly stopped. Jacob glanced over at the band. They were still playing but the sound had disappeared.

Paco continued, "They never got the bastard that did it, but The Moroccan was taken in for questioning."

"He was a suspect?"

"They couldn't pin anything on him, so all charges were dropped."

"So what's the problem?" Jacob said, trying to desperately rationalise what he was hearing.

"The papers unearthed all sorts on the guy, stuff that went way back to the days of Franco. Turned out he was into weird shit, you know, the black arts." He looked up at Jacob, who had bowed his head and was grinding his left hand into the corner of the table.

"Sorry, man. I think I've said too much. Like you say, he's an old guy," Paco said, trying to reassure him, but Jacob jumped up and, grabbing his bag and coat, climbed out of the booth. He pushed through the drinkers towards the exit. As he stumbled past the stage, the cacophony of noise suddenly returned, exploding inside his skull.

Alvaro was at the front of the dance floor, holding a large Spanish flag aloft and howling over and over into the microphone, "¡Nunca Más!..¡Nunca Más!" One or two people in the audience cheered half-heartedly, while others looked on bemused. Fumbling in the pocket of his jeans, he produced a lighter and set the corner of the flag alight. The flames quickly spread and within a couple of seconds most of the fabric was ablaze. He wafted it about above his head for a moment or two, but when he couldn't hold it any longer, he dropped it onto the floor and leapt manically in and out of the burning embers. A large plume of smoke belched into the air, quickly filling the bar with acrid, choking fumes. Within moments, the fire alarm sounded and the sprinkler system burst into life. Pandemonium ensued. Drinkers ran for emergency exits while the band dropped their instruments and tried to protect the electrical equipment from the torrential downpour coming from the ceiling. The bar man leapt over the counter and grabbed Alvaro by the throat.

"Fucking idiot!" he shouted and knocked him to the ground.

Jacob frantically fought his way through the mob of panic-stricken patrons and stumbled out into the square. The scene outside was equally chaotic. A multitude of fire engines and other emergency service vehicles were arriving from every direction as fireman raced past the sodden evacuees. Tripping over hosepipes and equipment, he cut between two fire engines, and when he reached a clearing in the mayhem, he stopped. There was a girl on the furthest edge of the plaça. Her head was bowed and she was rocking gently backwards and forwards. Suddenly, she looked up. It was Jude. He called to her and waved his arms to attract her attention but his voice disappeared into the wail of a siren.

"Wait!" he shouted to her again, but she turned and walked off towards the avenida. He gave chase and when he reached the road, she was already about a hundred yards ahead of him.

"Jude, please," he said, his voice faltering.

She carried on, heading back towards the forger's studio. He followed again, but he sensed that his body was about to give up on him. He stumbled on, almost falling over the weight of his own momentum until he could see her by the studio door.

"Stop," he gasped, his voice barely escaping from his throat.

Her body seemed to push in towards the building and then disappear into the shadows. When he reached the door, she had vanished. He leaned forward and desperately gulped in mouthfuls of air until his lungs began to recover. He tried the handle, but pulled his hand back in pain. The metal was hot and the paint on the surface of the door appeared to be blistering and bubbling as though a fire was raging on the other side.

"Jude!" he screamed, kicking at the door wildly.

Then, stepping back, he put his shoulder to it but the lock refused to give. To his left, he spotted an electronic entry system, identical to the unit on the other side of the building. Placing his hand over the panel, he closed his eyes and tried to visualise Almir's fingers hovering over the digits and then selecting the sequence. He punched in '3209' but nothing happened. He tried a variation, '2930', but still the door remained locked.

"Fuck!" he screamed and closing his eyes, he tried again, '2309.' The panel light flickered, the door rattled on its hinges and then it gently swung open. Jacob ducked down, expecting flames to roar out through the gap. But there was only darkness on the other side. Approaching cautiously, he tapped at the handle with his forefinger but the surface was cold. He pushed the door with his fist and went inside.

The Other Side of the Mirror

When he reached the bottom of the steps, the door slammed shut behind him. He turned quickly and looked over his shoulder, but there was no one there. Moving cautiously into the room, a hiss of warm, humid air encircled him like a slow, seductive whisper. The lamp holders in the ceiling were alight and the tiny flames in each of the bowls produced a yellow flickering glow that sent shadows dancing around the room. The forger's canvases that had filled the floor space were all gone, and the back of the room was now illuminated by a log fire burning within a large marble fireplace. To the right of the fire was a small oval table, and in the far corner, a mahogany-panelled door was slightly ajar. The easel was now on the far right hand side of the room and the dust cover draped over it now appeared to be made of velvet.

As he moved towards it, the door in the corner creaked and began to swing open. The forger's dog sauntered in, wagging its tail. It approached Jacob, sniffed at the sleeve of his coat and licked the fingers of his left hand affectionately. Returning to the other side of the room, it lay down and dropped its chin onto the floor. Jacob turned back to the easel and pulled at the dust cover. It gently rolled off the top of the frame and fell to the floor.

At first he thought the canvas was bare, but when he looked more closely, he could just make out a multitude of faint grey lines and geometric shapes that criss-crossed and weaved across its surface. The area had been divided into seven sections and within each there were scribbled notes, numbers and calculations. The numbers seemed to be sequenced in a repeating pattern that descended from the top right corner.

012898579801948767.

He followed the pattern as it weaved across the surface like a thin rivulet of water until it finally disappeared into the heavily-gilded, ornate frame at the bottom. He stood back and refocused his eyes. Across the canvas, the faint outline of a room had been lightly sketched over the screeds of annotations, and in one of the sections, the string of numbers seemed to form the shape of a nose, lips and chin. He followed one of the construction lines from the face, down to the left hand corner of the frame until it reached a small crimson mark that sat proud of the surface. Jacob knelt down and touched it. The substance was warm and wet, and it stuck to the tip of his finger.

A ceiling lamp fizzled and the flame went out, plunging one side of the room into near darkness. The dog whimpered and began wagging its tail. Jacob stood up. A noxious, sickly-sweet stench filled the room accompanied by the sound of a deep, low-pitched hum. Jacob stepped out from behind the easel and peered into the gloom. A figure was moving behind the shadow of the open door.

"Almir?" Jacob whispered.

The figure moved again but didn't respond.

"Come on, I know you are there," Jacob repeated impatiently.

"Look again," a disembodied voice said.

"What?"

The figure seemed to shift inside itself and sway slightly from side to side.

"The composition."

"Who are you?"

"You know who I am," the voice replied, deep and soft with

an eloquent Castilian accent.

Jacob glanced back at the easel.

"Do you see now?" the figure asked.

Jacob scanned the image, tracing the lines backwards and forwards across the canvas. The shape of the room began to define itself, with objects and details aligning, calibrating and materialising out of the chaos of interconnecting scrawls and scribbled notes. In a moment, the scene was complete.

"The other side of the mirror," the figure said.

The lamp holder crackled and sparked back into life. The burst of light momentarily revealed the figure's gnarled and distorted features. Facial skin had fallen away from the bone and flapped loosely from beneath its jaw. There was a deep gash across its left cheek that oozed a thick, pale yellow fluid. Its mouth was ripped on one side and the gaping hole exposed blackened rotting teeth.

Jacob turned away in horror.

"The spoils of war," the creature said.

"What aberration are you?"

"I am the reflected glory of your true self."

"Where's my wife?"

"If she can give a soul to those who have lived without one, then she is here."

"What have you done to her?" .

"She is waiting to be given form and purpose."

"Where is she?" he repeated, his fury growing with every second.

"She is waiting."

"For what?"

"Without certainty, she is incomplete."

"You bastard!" Jacob moved towards the creature.

"Stand!" The command reverberated round the room and the dog growled in response. Jacob stopped.

"She wanted to come. There was no force. She was ready," the creature continued.

"Ella!" Jacob shouted into the darkness. "You fucking kidnapped her, you and your psychopathic sidekick."

"The Moroccan is very loyal, but sometimes his tongue can be a little ...loose."

"What do you expect from a sociopathic liar?"

"And so I had to tighten it," the creature said.

Something hard hit Jacob in the chest and fell at his feet. It was a long circular coil of torn, bloodied flesh. Jacob stumbled backwards, almost falling over the easel.

"You shouldn't have bothered," Jacob snarled. "I didn't believe a word of his lies."

"But you believed the girl," the creature retorted.

"So who is she then? One of your stooges, sent to distract me?" Jacob said, his mind reeling in confusion.

"Her movements are of your own volition." The creature began to shift towards him.

"I saw her. Is she here now?" Jacob said, peering into the darkness beyond.

"She is always here." The creature grinned and, raising a gnarled, twisted limb, pointed to a section of exposed bone on the side of its head.

"What abyss have you pushed me into?"

"You take from me and I take from you," the creature continued.

"So that's what this is about?" Jacob said, shaking his head. "I understand it now."

"You do?"

"I got too close to the truth, and you didn't like it."

"And what is the truth, Jacob?" the creature hissed.

"Velázquez didn't vandalise your paintings, he tried to improve them, to save you from humiliation and ridicule. But even a genius like Velázquez couldn't salvage them. There's no message or hidden meanings or any kind of fucking solution. Your obscurity betrays the fact that your work is second-rate and it always will be."

293

"But you overlook one important detail."

"That you are a murdering evil bastard?"

"$V=mP^3$."

"I take it that is another one of your foils?"

"You found it for me."

"What are you talking about?" Jacob shook his head. "It was your insane friend Celini that came up with that delusional nonsense."

"It was there all along, tucked within the cracks and fissures."

"Cheap fairground trickery is not going to rescue the mediocrity of the work," Jacob said.

"You have a very enquiring mind, Jacob." The intensity of the hum redoubled in volume, and the deep rhythmical throb began to resonate inside Jacob's skull. "An unusually enlarged frontal lobe," it continued. "The procedure was interesting, like plucking a delicate feather from a quail's wing." The creature leaned in towards Jacob, its blackened tongue flicking manically in and out of its festering orifice, and when it was within breathing distance of Jacob's face, it whispered, "Thank you."

"You bastard!" Jacob screamed and lunged at it, but it slipped effortlessly from his grasp. He thrashed into the void hysterically and the dog leaped on him snarling and snapping its teeth around his face. He grabbed the folds of fur and skin below its throat and twisted his fist until the dog started whimpering. It jumped off and retreated to the other side of the room. The figure was now standing by the easel.

"Where's my fucking wife?" Jacob raged.

"Fate instructs her movements."

"If you've harmed her, I'll—"

"Kill me?" the creature sneered, his words gurgling through some hideous fluid.

Jacob could feel his limbs tighten as though a mortar was about to detonate inside his skull.

"Just let her go," Jacob pleaded.

"There was no force or coercion. She wanted the movement

to cease and now design will provide."

"She would never betray me," Jacob said.

"But you betrayed her, Jacob, you betrayed us all."

"I'll fucking destroy you," Jacob roared.

"She waits on the other side, for the stillness to complete her."

Jacob glanced back at the female figure sketched out on the canvas. Although unfinished, most of the key facial features were present. Gazing at the shapes for a few moments, Ella's face began to emerge out of the cacophony of scribbled lines and numbers.

"Such a pale and delicate complexion, a perfect subject for the artist's palette," the creature said.

But before Jacob could retaliate, he felt a blow in the centre of his back, and he fell forward onto the floor. He tried to escape the assault but something was pinning him down. An unseen force wrenched his head up and backwards, stretching his neck until he could barely breathe. And as every particle of air was squeezed from his lungs, he felt an intense searing pain in his side.

"Her fate resides with you, Jacob," the creature hissed into his ear. "The glass will rest or the glass will fall. Will she kill or be killed?"

"No!" Jacob rasped. He felt something cold on his windpipe.

"Chaos or design, you must choose. This shall be your atonement."

In a final moment of desperation, Jacob forced his body to twist sideways, just enough to free an arm. He reached behind and pulled the creature from his back. But as he tried to crawl away, the aberration forced him down again. It flipped him over and perched on top of him, its weight squeezing the air out of his lungs. Leaning down into his face, a bubble of thick yellow fluid oozed from the hole in the side of its mouth and splattered onto Jacob's cheek. He tried to turn his head away, but the creature held him firm. The drone was now deafening and on either side of him, unidentifiable figures were moving in and out of the darkness. There appeared to be others in the room, gathering and encircling.

"The moment is all but upon us. The flawed and the false shall be purged, and the beauty of truth shall prevail." The creature held out its gnarled fleshless hand.

"Do you recognise this?" it hissed, dangling the ivory-handled letter opener above Jacob's head. Turning the tip of the blade towards Jacob's face, it grinned and said, "In vita nos peto tripudium verum."

Then in one swift movement, it thrust the pointed end into Jacob's left eye.

Jacob shrieked in horror as the blade penetrated deep into his skull, and with the flick of its wrist, the creature hooked the eyeball out of its socket and sliced through the optical cord. The hum ceased, the room faded to darkness, and Jacob passed out.

Painting by Numbers

He was climbing upwards towards a tiny pinhole of light, his finger's grappling with razor sharp rock as he searched desperately for a secure hand hold. And straining every sinew, he hauled his limbs higher. His foot slipped and fragments of brick tumbled into the void. He pushed on until finally, his hand reached the freezing stark white of daylight and with the remnants of strength he had left, he dropped over the side and onto the cold, wet earth.

Now he was running, half-blind and near-hysterical, stumbling over rubble and debris. The soles of his feet were soon lacerated to a bloody pulp, but the searing pain only served to intensify his will to continue. Onwards over decimated ground, he reached the perimeter fence and searching until he relocated the narrow tear in the steel wire, he squeezed through, scrambled up the bank and along the avenue of giant chestnut and sycamore trees. Pellets of rain pummelled into his face like tiny cannonballs, and as his ravaged feet slapped against the wet tarmac, he left a trail of crimson footprints in his wake.

He cut across the park and through the side gate into the grounds of the museum. When he reached the bottom of the steps, two uniformed attendants approached him from the top. They held up their arms defensively and seemed to shout at him, but the drone obliterated their cries. One lunged at him, and Jacob punched him hard in the gut. The attendant fell to the ground, bent double in agony, while the other retreated, screaming into his walkie-talkie. Jacob took the steps three at a time and, pushing through the double doors, vaulted over the turnstile and into the foyer. But before he could continue, he was knocked sideways and fell to the floor, smashing the side of his face on the marble tiles.

An attendant was quickly on top of him. Jacob thrashed his legs around wildly, but the attendant resisted, pushing his knees hard into Jacob's chest while pinning his arms to the floor.

"Steady there, Jacob," the attendant said, digging deeper into the soft of his shoulders.

Jacob stopped and looked up at him.

"Do you no' remember me?" the attendant said. "I'm Ian. We met in the café this morning. We had a wee chat about your paintings by numbers book."

Jacob smiled.

"There you go. Are we going to behave ourselves now?" the attendant said, freeing one of his arms.

Jacob nodded but then reached up with a free arm and grabbed a handful of the attendant's hair.

"OK, OK!" the attendant yelled, releasing the other arm. Jacob sat up and smacked him on the side of his head and he slumped forward as though rendered unconscious. By now, two more attendants had arrived to help their young colleague, but Jacob quickly jumped up and, swerving around them, bounded across the foyer and up the staircase towards the Baroque Room.

As he approached the painting, he could hear the frame rattling violently against the wall, and when he was within a few feet of it, the movement stopped and the canvas settled back onto its hinges. And lifting his head, his eyes finally met the full horror of the altered image before him. His wife's petrified face stared out at him as a hunched figure, kneeling by her feet, set fire to the hem of her dress. The figure turned suddenly to reveal its face. But instead of the creature, Jacob gasped in terror as he gazed at his own grotesque and brutally-disfigured features.

It smiled, and inside his head, he heard the creature's voice whisper, "The reflected glory of your true self."

298

As the flames leapt up Ella's gown, she turned, as though to plead with Jacob to stop. He snatched at the frame and as he tried desperately to prise the painting from the wall, he felt a blow to the back of his head.

"Drop it," a voice behind him hollered and Jacob turned.

A uniformed police officer was standing over him with his baton raised.

"I said, drop it," he repeated, striking him again.

But Jacob ignored the assault and yanked at the painting until the hooks began to give. As the policeman continued to bludgeon him, Jacob pulled harder and with the last of his strength the painting finally came away from the wall, showering him in dust and lumps of plaster.

The canvas toppled onto him, exploding in a fireball of white heat and light, and in an instant, his body was a blazing human torch. At first he flailed around in panic as the searing heat ravaged his skin, but then dropping to his knees, he stretched out his arms to welcome the flames and hasten a speedy end. And in the dying moment of his being, Ella finally emerged from the inferno and reached out for him. As their flaming limbs entwined, she caressed and kissed his burning flesh until they were at last as one.

The fire quickly spread from the gallery to every corner of the museum, obliterating everything in its unstoppable path. And soon, an incandescent firestorm raged through the night, like a majestic, flickering new sun high above the Glasgow city skyline.

At the end of days, particles of dust settle within the cracks and blemishes of the fractured landscape. As the flux of perpetual movement from the observer to observed accelerates its merciless decline, accumulations of molecule and atom stretch the wound until an irreversible tear rips across the distorted panoply. Corrosion proceeds at rampant pace. Pigment and lustre fade to a meaningless murky grey, while palate, plot and players surrender to the unrelenting chaos of terminal decay.

In time, there will be no more, but an empty and discarded frame, randomly stacked atop a ceremonial pyre, waiting with endurance and hope for the Earth to reclaim it as her long lost and once-abandoned child.

PART III

Stasis

Sylvia picked up the brush and began running it through her hair. She stared at her reflection in the mirror as she performed the ritual, and after seven strokes, she switched sides and closed her eyes. The movement made her feel sleepy. The repeated action often sent her into a trance, a dreamlike regressive state where she was seven years old again. Her mother was behind her, the palm of her hand pushing down into the top of her head as she brushed the back of her long, blonde hair.

Sometimes the sensation was so intense she could feel the heat of her mother's body pressing against her spine. But when she turned round to look for her, the spell would break and she would vanish. So she would carry on, one side then the other, back and forth, her mind falling deeper and deeper down a well full of disembodied memories. She pressed the brush harder into her scalp. Now she was standing behind her own daughter, re-enacting her mother's movements, the same codified behaviours passed from one generation to the next. Resting her hand on Ella's shoulder, she felt the warmth of her skin through the soft cotton nightdress. Ella turned, annoyed with her, as bristles scratched across a section of bare skin buried in the thickness of her hair. Ella spoke but she didn't make a sound. Reaching down, Sylvia touched the girl's scalp with her forefinger and traced the outline of a smooth triangle of pale pink flesh.

Suddenly, her brush caught on a matted tangle and opening her eyes, the dislocated memory contorted and melted into the back of the room. As she pulled at the obstruction again and forced the brush through, a single strand snapped out. It wavered in mid-air, brought back to life by a sudden rush of static energy, but then it recoiled and wrapped itself around the handle. She picked it off and flicked it onto the carpet. Placing the brush back down on the dresser, she manoeuvred her chair nearer to the mirror. Up close, the wrinkled skin under her eyes and around her neck seemed to press against the surface of the glass, bulging out towards her, like bloated grey elephant hide. She opened her mouth to check her teeth, and as she forced a smile, the upper denture slipped and fell onto the lower plate. She pushed it back into position and widened her mouth further to stretch the muscles and exercise the joints in her jaw. She held the exaggerated grin for a few seconds, then relaxed her face and exhaled. Scooping up a glob of moisturiser, she applied the thick lotion to her cheeks, and gently massaged it in, increasing the arc of her finger until the cream covered most of her face. She continued until it had been absorbed, then replaced the lid and climbed into bed.

Propping herself up on two large pillows and straightening the blankets around her legs, she closed her eyes and tried to prepare her mind for sleep. But tangled thoughts continued to twist and contort inside her. She was so tired. It had been four years but the pain was still there, trapped inside her chest like a shard of shrapnel. Everyone said it would fade, but a part of her didn't want it to. If the pain faded, so would her memories. It was her greatest fear, that she would forget her face. She had photographs, of course.

One of her favourites was still hanging on the wall by the bedroom door. But although her pictures and Ella's personal effects had helped her and comforted her through the worst of times, she had come to realise that she no longer needed to cling to material reminders of her daughter to remember her, and that her fear of forgetting was unfounded. Her move to Spain demonstrated a strength of character that she thought she would never reclaim and that the time had come to contemplate a future beyond the pain of the shattered past.

She rubbed her eyes, weary of the same internal dialogue night after night. She glanced at the bedside clock and checked that the alarm was set. Tomorrow was a big day. The last thing she needed was to sleep in and miss her plane. She checked the date and flight times on her ticket again.

23rd September:
Dep: Glasgow 09.50
Arr: Barcelona 12.25

If she could manage about four hours sleep, that would probably be enough to get her through the rigours of the move. Opening her book, she withdrew the bookmark and started to read, but the words didn't make any sense. She flicked back a couple of pages and tried to relocate her place. It wasn't a particularly difficult plot, but it was hard to concentrate her mind on something other than what was to come. She got out of bed and went over to the photo on the wall. Her daughter was still there, locked inside the frame, on top of the same intransigent mountain. She was holding her arms aloft, welcoming the world into her life with a wide euphoric grin, while rays of bright morning sunlight bathed her face in a glorious golden hue. Sylvia turned away and bit down hard on her bottom lip.

"No tears," she said. She removed the picture from its hook and placed it face down in the box by the bedroom door. Turning to go back to bed, she changed her mind and went downstairs to make a cup of tea.

Stepping over boxes and rolls of bubble wrap on the floor, she filled the kettle and sat down to wait for it to boil. As she stared at the little light flicker on and off, her mind began to race again. Holidaying in Spain was one thing, but actually living there? How would she cope? Her Spanish was so-so and the house was probably unfit for long term habitation. Señora Vigo would look after her, of course, and all the villagers knew her well, but she was still an outsider, even after all these years. The kettle roared for a second and the button clicked. Sipping her herbal tea, she tried to control the sensation of panic spreading like a fluttering fan across her chest.

But her attempted meditative moment was interrupted by a noise at the back door. She turned and the cat appeared, pushing its head through the cat flap and then squeezing in. It cautiously approached the metal pet carrier by its bowl and sniffed the side.

"That's right," Sylvia said. "You're off to your Aunt Sue's tomorrow, until we can work out what to do with you." The cat returned to the flap and Sylvia leaned over to lock it. "Not tonight, I'm afraid. We can't have you wandering off." The cat let out a long whining complaint and rubbed its side along Sylvia's leg. She stroked its back, running her hand slowly along the length of its spine. It began to purr and circled around her feet. Somehow Ella's cat had survived the fire and was recovered unharmed from the roof of a neighbouring tenement. The fire brigade said it was a miracle. So for four years, the cat had been a reluctant guest, often complaining and frequently absconding back to its old home on the other side of the city.

She got up and, turning boxes round to read the labels, she finally located a small box marked *Pet Stuff*. Removing a sachet of meat, she emptied the contents into its bowl. The cat skipped over, sniffed at the food a couple of times but then pulled back.

"Are you not hungry either?" she said, picking up the cat and sitting back down with it on her lap. It turned a few times and then slumped down, licking at its front paw nervously. As she gently stroked it again, it tilted its head upwards and closed its eyes. Slowly, tiny ripples of sleep began to roll in. She resisted for a moment, but the sensation was too seductive and she let herself go.

She could see him beyond the reception, his face ashen with fear.

When he saw her running towards him, he stood up, as though to leave or escape, but she grabbed him by the arm.

"Where is she?" Her voice shattering the corridor like a crystal glass on a hard concrete floor.

He said nothing, but she had to know.

"Where is my daughter?"

He looked through her with dead, lifeless eyes.

Turning, she ran back to the reception desk.

"Please," a pitiful excuse for a word, "help me, my daughter, there was a fire."

The cat jumped off her lap, waking her with a start. Rubbing the sleep from her eyes, she stood up and re-tied the cord on her dressing gown. She felt cold and alone. It was time to leave this place for good. As she switched off the kitchen light and started back up the stairs, she could hear the cat frantically scratching at the flap. There was no turning back, she thought. Her life and destiny was sealed in a dozen labelled boxes waiting to be collected and shipped out in the morning.

Returning to bed, she adjusted her pillows, straightened the sheets and sank down into the mattress wearily. She picked up her book and tried to re-focus on the jumble of words that scattered across the pages. Finally, she was able to make sense of it and as she turned the third or fourth page, she lost herself for a moment and time skipped forward. She peered at the clock again, 1.24am. She closed the book and lay still for a second. Outside, the wind blew gently against the window, rattling the frame and causing the curtains to sway. She smiled. She had promised herself for years that she would replace the old sash windows with some up to date double-glazing, but there was no need to worry now. She dropped a pillow onto the floor and lay back, pulling the blankets up around her chin. She closed her eyes and waited for sleep to return. But just as she started to drift off, the telephone rang.

Not again, she thought, looking over at the clock. It was 2.39. She turned onto her side and pressed her hand against her ear. Tonight, she didn't have to answer it. Tomorrow, she would be gone and it would all be over. Another four or five rings and that would be that, but it persisted.

Eight, twelve, nineteen, twenty.

She sat up and turned on the light.

Twenty-six, thirty, thirty-four.

She got out of bed, put on her dressing gown and went downstairs. Perhaps it wasn't him. Maybe it was something else, an emergency. She picked up the receiver.

"Hello?" No response. "Hello?" Again, silence.

"Look, I am so sick of this. Please!" she said. The line clicked and static fizzled in the earpiece. "I know it's you. Listen to me, it's over. It's finished, do you understand? You won't be able to call here any more." The earpiece crackled and then disconnected. She hung up and stared at the cord as it recoiled around her wrist. She returned to bed and tried to close her mind to unwanted thoughts.

She followed the nurse to a small softly lit room. When she saw the bible on the table, she knew. It was as though the air was suddenly sucked out of her lungs, a thin dry vapour trail hissing under the door. She grasped at her throat and tried to breathe but there was nothing there to inhale. The nurse caught her as she fell, and laying her out on the carpet, ran to get help. Her hands searched for something solid to hold on to but the surface of the floor was like water, and her body started to sink. The carpet folded over her and as the room disappeared, she felt herself vanish into the dark horror of what was still to come.

Something woke her up again. She held her breath and listened, but all she could hear was the blood roaring in her ears. She switched on the bedside light and rubbed at her eyes. The house was silent. Outside, the rain pattered lightly against the window. She switched off the light and as she lay down again, there was a loud thump coming from downstairs. She got out of bed and pressed her ear against the bedroom door. There was somebody moving around, now, she was sure. But what should she do? Confront the intruder, hide in the wardrobe, call the police? She put on her dressing gown and edged out the door.

The hallway was dark, but there was a light on in the kitchen. She peered over the banister but she couldn't see anything. She slowly made her way downstairs, carefully avoiding the loose floorboard on the third step. In the hall, she picked up a vase and inched towards the kitchen. Halfway there, she stopped.

What am I doing, she thought, but her curiosity overruled her fear and she carried on. When she reached the door, she tapped it lightly with her foot and it swung open. The kitchen was empty and all she could see were the cat's eyes blinking at her in a corner of the darkness. She stepped back into the hall and made her way towards the living room. The door was open and reaching around the frame for the light switch, she raised the vase to her shoulder.

He was slumped in a chair by the fireplace. For a second, she didn't recognise him. His face was almost completely concealed by a thick greying beard and long matted hair. His coat tails were draped over the side and there was a long tear or slash across the fabric, partially exposing the shredded innards of the lining. His feet were bare and blackened with dirt and grime and his left hand was gripping his knee, exposing raw bloodied knuckles, while the other lay upturned and open on top of his trouser leg. There was something in the palm. She moved a little closer. Now she could smell him, a rancid, festering stench of body waste and personal neglect. She covered her nose with the back of her hand.

"How did you get in?" she said.

He didn't move but continued to stare intensely at the fire

grate. She looked down at the object in his palm. It was a key. He clenched his fist.

"I'll call the police." she snapped at him. "I mean it. I've done it before and I'll do it again. You have no right just to barge in like this."

He opened his mouth as if to speak and a thin string of clear saliva dribbled out and dangled from his beard like a wet transparent pendulum.

"For God's sake, this has to stop, do you hear me?" she said. She edged towards him. "Did you hear me, Jacob?" she repeated.

His left foot stretched out towards the hearth until his toe touched the tiled rim.

"I'm leaving tomorrow, I'm going," she continued. "I've sold the house. I'm moving away. So you're going to have to give me that key. It doesn't belong to you and after tomorrow, it won't belong to me either." She manoeuvred herself to within touching distance. "Give it to me," she said, snatching at it, but he pulled his hand back into the folds of his filthy coat.

"Please Jacob, it's over," she pleaded with him.

His shoulders sank for a moment and his body began to rock gently back and forth. Then very slowly, he raised his head.

"Oh my God?" Sylvia exclaimed. As he looked up, the tangle of dreadlocks fell away from his face, revealing a blackened, empty eye socket. The severed remnants of the optical chord were still visible within the wound. "What have you done to yourself?" She knelt down to examine him more closely. "You have to go to a hospital," she said, "you need to see a doctor."

"No!" Jacob rasped.

"But you have to. Let me ring for an ambulance."

"No!"

She reached out and touched his forehead, but he pulled back from her.

"No doctor," he repeated.

"At least let me call the hostel. Someone there will know

what to do with you."

"No!"

She stood up and shook her head in anger.

"Kill yourself if you want to, but don't try and drag me down with you." She waited a moment for some kind of response. "I give up," she said finally and retreated to the kitchen to escape the escalating sensation of panic. Leaning on the sink, fragmented memories of Ella's shortened life cascaded through her mind; her difficult birth and her tiny body stretched out and wired up to the incubator, her first smile and her first words, then racing onwards to school days, excitedly running up and down the hallway clutching her exam results, to university and graduation, and then her wedding day, standing with Jacob on the steps of the registry office, her arm locked tightly around his as though to prevent him from floating away from her.

But then the image of Ella faded and it was only Jacob that was left, a desolate figure in the hospital car park. He turned to her and she slapped him hard across his face, his cigarette flying from his lips. And as he walked away, she remembered his swagger and the arrogant click of his shoes on the wet tarmac.

Wiping her eyes on the sleeve of her dressing gown, she glanced down at the cat that was curled up, fast asleep on top of a box. This must end now, she thought, and she returned to the living room.

"Why did you leave me there alone?" she said, standing over him.

"She was dead," he said, his words gurgling through his throat.

"But I had to formally identify her on my own. You were her husband!" She was no longer able to control the pitch in her voice.

"It wasn't her. She was gone."

"I needed you there. I had no one. Why did you make me see my wee girl like that?" She started to cry. "No!" she said, running her forefinger frantically under her eyes.

"I had to," he said.

"And you don't think that I wanted to run away and pretend it wasn't happening."

"You're running away now, aren't you?" he said.

"How dare you say that to me, you bastard," she snapped. She turned to face the fireplace.

"On the day she died," he persisted.

She spun round in fury. "What would you have me do, cut my wrists, mutilate myself like you? I chose to move tomorrow because I don't want to be afraid any more. I'm so tired of grieving for her." She let out a prolonged nervous sigh.

"I killed her." Jacob said.

"We've been through this so many times," she said, turning back to him. "It was an accident, house fires happen all the time. You are not to blame.

"I lit the fire. She didn't want me to, but I ignored her."

"It's just one of those things, a terrible twist of fate.

"I filled the grate with paper and kindle."

"Stop it, Jacob."

"My hands were covered in soot." He examined his palms in dismay.

"Please?" she begged him.

"We had a row. I walked out and left her there to die."

"Marriage is made for arguments. Bill and I argued constantly, it doesn't mean we didn't love each other, and it doesn't mean you killed her."

"I should have come back for her."

"You have to let this go."

"I can't." He looked up at her, and for a fleeting moment, she felt sorry for him. It was difficult to ignore the tight bonds of grief that continuously pulled their lives together.

His head slumped down into the collar of his coat. She kneeled down next to him. "Listen, Jacob. Ella isn't dead."

He looked up at her again.

"She's right here." And she thumped her chest with her fist.

"It's taken me a long time to realise it but she never went away." She reached for his hand. "You have to stop tormenting yourself and start looking and listening, and open your heart to her again. Think about how you were together when you first met. You were inseparable, and you still are." She leaned in closer. "I know you think that I never liked you, but you made Ella so happy, and I loved you for that."

He looked up.

"I mean it. She told me every day how much she loved you. So, what you have to do is get better." She gently prised his hand open and took the key from his palm. "And if you let her in, she'll help you put your life back together." She slipped the key into her dressing gown pocket and then asked tentatively, "Are you taking your medicine?"

He didn't respond.

"Jacob," she persisted.

"It makes me sick."

"Oh God." She sighed. "You have to. Does your doctor know that you've stopped?"

"I don't trust him."

"But that's what happens to you when you stop, you recognise that, don't you?"

He pulled his hand away and she stared at him for a moment, unsure of what to say or do next.

"Wait." she said finally, "I have something that is better than medicine." She went upstairs to the bedroom to retrieve the picture frame and a small box from under her bed.

"Here," she said, placing the photograph in his lap. He picked it up and squinting at the image, he ran his finger across the glass. "She was so beautiful, wasn't she? That is how you must remember her."

He offered it back.

"No, please, you take it. You need it more than me." She removed the packing tape from the shoe box and placed it on top of the frame. "These are some other odds and ends I

315

collected together. A few little things she'd left here over the years."

He opened the lid.

"Take what you want," she said.

Reaching inside, he removed one item after another: a small brass teddy bear, a Mackintosh style key ring and a few postcards from her travels around the world. Half way down, he found a bulging envelope and opened it up. It was full of different types of badges.

"Those were on that tatty old jacket and bag she used to wear when she was a student."

He emptied them out into the box, and rifling through the collection, he picked out a small triangular insignia with the words ¡NUNCA MAS! in bold crimson lettering across the front.

"I finally emptied the loft of all her old clothes and handed them in to OXFAM," she said. "It seemed so pointless keeping them up there. I thought they could make better use of them."

He dropped the badge back in the box and continued his search.

When he reached the bottom, he snagged his hand on something sharp. He fumbled around until he located a small object and carefully fished it out from under a pile of trinkets.

"That was recovered from the flat after the fire."

The box slid from Jacob's knees and the contents spilled out on to the floor. He slumped forward as though strings had been severed above his head and shoulders. Sylvia caught him before he toppled and pushed him back into his chair.

"What's the matter?" she said.

His left hand dropped onto his knee and he began opening and clenching his fist manically. The shakes spread from his arm down his side and into his legs, and his body started to rock backward and forwards.

"Jacob, stop it!" Sylvia cried.

He didn't answer her but the involuntary convulsions

intensified.

"I'll get you a drink, wait." In the kitchen, she searched for a bottle of brandy buried in one of the boxes and poured a large measure into a cup.

"Here," she said, thrusting the cup into his shaking hand, and she steadied it as he gulped at the alcohol. After a few more mouthfuls, the shakes began to subside and his breathing became more even. She sat back down opposite. "I'm so sorry. I didn't mean to upset you."

"Our first anniversary," he gasped, taking another gulp of brandy, "she said it would bring me good luck for my new job."

"It's yours?" she said surprised, "I'm so sorry, I didn't realise. I assumed it was Ella's. It was one of the few things that survived the fire." She leaned over and picked it up off the floor. "I'm still not sure what it is," she said turning it over in her hand. "Is it some sort of artist's tool?"

"A letter opener," he said.

"It's very unusual. It must be very old."

"I came home late that night," he said, ignoring her. "I'd been drinking and in no mood for another confrontation."

Sylvia put the letter opener down on the hearth.

"She was in the living room waiting for me. She started in at me right away, saying that I had abandoned her and betrayed our marriage. She was enraged. I'd never seen her so angry before. She went on and on until eventually I snapped."

"What did you do?"

"I don't know why she'd moved it from my desk, but I found the letter opener on the mantelpiece. I raged at her and told her our marriage was a joke, and in moment of sheer spitefulness, I threw it into the fire." He paused and took another sip of brandy. "But just for a second, I wanted to harm her with it, stop her voice roaring in my head."

"And did you?" Sylvia asked, beginning to fear the answer.

"It would have been so easy, a simple flick of the wrist, like this." He thrust out his hand towards her and she drew back in

317

fright.

"Did you hurt her with it?" she repeated.

"I hurt her every day for ten years, but not with fists or knives. The abuse was a lot more insidious than that. My weapon of choice was neglect and psychological torment. I was a callous and vindictive husband. I might as well have stuck the blade into her throat, I'd done a lot worse to her."

"But you didn't do it, Jacob," Sylvia said, with some relief. "You threw it in the fire."

"And then she burned to death."

"Threatening my daughter with a knife is a terrible thing to do, but you didn't kill her."

"But I left her there to die. I abandoned her when I should have saved her."

"The fire was caused by an electrical fault in the kitchen. It would have happened anyway, only you would have died with her."

"I wish for that every day."

"But you have to live. We both do. For her sake, for her memory, we have to carry on."

"I'm a monster," he said.

"If you continue to punish yourself like this, then you are betraying her life and there *will* be no forgiveness. What you did was a terrible thing. Maybe you were a bad husband, but now you have an opportunity to be good."

"It's too late."

"No, it's not, Jacob. The letter opener survived the fire for a reason. You found it because Ella wants you to. She's trying to tell you that she forgives you."

"What can I do?" he said.

"Forgive yourself and she'll come back to you." She knelt down again beside him. "Hope," she whispered, gripping his arm. "You move forward and I move forward inch by inch, one tiny brave step at a time. And we'll carry her with us, here in our hearts, OK?" He looked at her. "Hope and forgiveness that's all

318

we have now." She stood up. "Now, I've got a flight to catch and you've got your wife to find," she smiled and wiped the tears from her cheek. "Let's get you up," she said, helping him out of his chair. "Shall I make that call now, and get you to A & E?"

"I'll walk, it's not far," he said.

"Well at least let me find something for your feet. I think I might have a pair of John's shoes in a bag somewhere upstairs. They may not fit exactly, but they'll get you home. I'll be back in a moment, OK?" As she turned to go, he caught her arm.

"Thank you," he said.

She rummaged in boxes and bags, but all she could find were an ancient pair of moth eaten espadrilles, a tired remnant from one of their infrequent visits to their neglected Spanish retreat.

"I don't know if these are any use," she said, returning to the living room. But he wasn't there. She checked the hall again and the front room. In the kitchen, the back door was open. She stepped out and peered into the dark, but there was no sign of him. She shut and bolted the door, and went back to the living room to make sure that he hadn't returned there. The shoebox and picture frame were still lying on the floor, but the letter opener had gone. Gathering up Ella's trinkets, she put them back in the shoebox and returned with them to the kitchen. She glanced over to the cat basket but it was empty. It must have escaped into the night with Jacob. Opening the door again, she was about to call for it, but she changed her mind. If it wanted to stay, that's what it was going to do, and perhaps that's what Ella wanted, too.

Pouring herself a brandy, she slumped down at the kitchen table and took a large gulp. The sudden hit of alcohol scorched the back of her throat making her cough and splutter, but as the chemicals raced through her bloodstream, she began to feel a growing sense of euphoria. It was as though the burden of the world had been prised from her shoulders. For the last four years, he had made her life a living hell, but now there would be no more phone calls and no more visits, and hopefully he would find peace and some kind of reconciliation with his own demons, as she had.

Rubbing her eyes, she yawned and finished the last of her drink. As she set the mug back down on the table she noticed a small black notebook balanced on the furthest edge of the table. She leaned over and picked it up. The cover was heavily worn and covered in stains and unidentifiable solid matter. Holding it between her fingers, she carefully opened it up. The spine was damaged and most of the pages inside were either loose or hanging by gluey threads. She slowly flicked through the book, scanning each page, but it appeared to be completely empty. But on the last page, she spotted a tiny scrawl written in the margin at the bottom. She held the book up to decipher the inscription and screwed up her eyes to try and focus on each word, but it was just too small. Removing the page from the book, she pushed it into her pocket and got up to unlock the cat flap, just in case the cat decided to return before the morning. She re-packed the brandy bottle and washed her cup. And picking up the notebook again, she stared at it for a moment, unsure of what to do with it, but then she dropped it into an overfull bin bag of rubbish by the back door. She switched off the light and went back upstairs to bed.

Removing her dressing gown, she slipped under the duvet, but after a moment, she sat back up and searched the bedside drawer for her glasses. She retrieved the page from her pocket and peered at the writing under the light of the bedside lamp. Now she could just about read it.

In vita nos peto tripudium verum.

She stared at the phrase for a few moments, trying to locate fragmented memories of Latin from her schooldays, but she could make no sense of it. Putting it down on the table with her glasses, she switched off the light and glanced over at the clock,

4:40am, still enough time for a couple of hours sleep.

She closed her eyes and a gentle hum floated in through the gaps in the sash windows, penetrating her mind like a swarm of benevolent bees. And as she tumbled into a deep and restful sleep, she imagined a chorus of cats gathering together on rain-drenched tenement rooftops, their siren song reaching out across the city and soaring upwards into the brave first light of a new dawn.

Note

This story is a fabricated figment of the author's imagination.

Diego Velázquez did not have an assistant called Manuel Piñero. Celini's Law of Empirical Wisdom is an elaborate and fictional construct. V=mP3 is an invented formula.

As far as the author is aware, Piñero's paintings do not exist and never have.

Fantastic Books
Great Authors

Meet our authors and discover our exciting range:

- Gripping Thrillers
- Cosy Mysteries
- Romantic Chick-Lit
- Fascinating Historicals
- Exciting Fantasy
- Young Adult and Children's Adventures

Visit us at:
www.crookedcatbooks.com

Join us on facebook:
www.facebook.com/crookedcatpublishing

Printed in Great Britain
by Amazon.co.uk, Ltd.,
Marston Gate.